AN OLD SPY STORY

Terry Morgan

Printed in the United States of America

Library of Congress Control Number: 2020915873
ISBN: Softcover   978-1-64908-288-6
          eBook   978-1-64908-287-9

Republished by: PageTurner Press and Media LLC
Publication Date: 08/25/2020

To order copies of this book, contact:

PageTurner Press and Media
Phone: 1-888-447-9651
order@pageturner.us
www.pageturner.us

During a long and exotic career with his own export business, (("Ollie") Thomas was also carrying out parallel assignments in nd the Middle East loosely connected to British Intelligence. B using threats and blackmail, his controller, Major Alex Donal was forcing Ollie to help run his own secret money making sch that included financial fraud, arms shipments to the IRA th Gadaffi and Libya, money laundering and assassination.

Now aged eighty six, recently widowed and alone Ollie still stru with guilt and anger over his past and decides to make on attempt to track down and deal with Donaldson.

"....I loved this plot.....international trade, bribery, corruption an murky workings of British Intelligence. The depiction of the may and middle men ring so true, as do the dubious business practices. (descriptions of far flung cities and their low budget hotels....easy read

"..A wonderful and moving love story from an elderly man's perspecti beautifully woven into it and the ending is masterful..."

"...I enjoyed it, exciting, endlesly beguiling and fun...."

"...This is no ordinary spy story. If you only read the chapter on S you'll know why."

"....a masterful tale by someone who knows exactly what he is wri about...."

"...thoroughly enjoyable from start to finish. A remarkable book.....

Contents

PROLOGUE

Sixty years is a long time to look back and realise I should have been more cautious over my involvement with MI6, the government's secret service. But I was younger then and was only concerned with finding ways to build my new business. I had no idea that offering to do one simple job would be like stepping into quicksand.

Neither did I know that MI6 was already racked with scandals, defections and mistrust.

Books have been written about big name spies like Philby, Burgess and Maclean. The extent of that treachery has never been fully told so perhaps, by writing this, I am exposing yet more inconvenient truths that were silently redacted. Unlike Philby and co, though, I was a total unknown to those who drank tea and shuffled paper in the corridors of power. No-one knew what Major Alex Donaldson was up to whilst drawing his salary and building his pension. No-one knew that Donaldson spent much of his time in a dingy office on the second floor of a block in Regent Street and in a smoky pub called The Feathers in a side street of Victoria.

I never questioned it either because I had no idea how secret Government departments worked. My upbringing had ingrained in me a bizarre sense of respect for those I imagined had greater knowledge and authority. I merely thought this was the way things worked and did as I was told.

What I slowly learned was that Donaldson was only very loosely connected to British Intelligence and, as you will see, it took me a long time to understand what was going on and far too long to do something about it.

I've always said it's never too late to deal with outstanding matters, but things have never gone according to my plans. Until the last few days, that is.

My name is Oliver Thomas. I'm eighty-six years old but when I was pulled from the passport control line at Heathrow Airport and escorted to an office like a common criminal age didn't seem to matter.

I was not unduly concerned about being arrested until a dark silhouette stood over me with his back to the window. For reasons you will learn, I have a deep dislike of silhouettes. I was tired and had no wish to look as if I was about to cry, but my spectacles had fallen off and my eyes were sore. The glasses had disappeared beneath the table alongside my black bag and walking stick so how could I have possibly seen the policeman's face through a stream of tears?

I suppose that growing old means becoming clumsy. I needed the glasses for reading but I could have ditched the walking stick. For a week I'd managed perfectly well without it. Things still bent and did their job.

In fact, a few days ago, I'd even had to run and bend down all at the same time. It was the only way to retrieve the gun I'd dropped.

PART ONE: DETENTION

Loss of dignity: That's the problem for most eighty-six-year olds.

It's like a sad return to the time when you were carried everywhere, were fed on milk and wore diapers but I'm luckier than some. During the previous few days, I'd shown I was still capable of doing the sort of things I did fifty years ago. More importantly, I'd completed a job that had been outstanding for fifty years.

I wiped my eyes with a handkerchief and watched the silhouette drag up a chair and sit down opposite me. "Come on Mr Thomas," it said. "Why would someone of your age fly to Spain, smuggle a gun past all the airport checks and surveillance gear and threaten another old man in his nineties?"

Did he really want to know? If so, how long did he have?

I glanced at the untouched pot of tea and the two mugs that sat between us. My interrogator was getting impatient but I was in no hurry. Patience is a positive feature of old age. When you reach eighty-six you've come to accept that time is running out. You stop thinking about time. Time has passed and time will continue. So why rush the present? For me, right then, nothing seemed to matter anymore. The job was finished.

"Tea, Mr Thomas? Milk?"

I looked down to check for my stick and the glasses. The glasses were retrievable. They were lying next to my black bag so I picked them up. The stick was another matter.

"Thank you," I said watching the tea and then the milk being

2

poured into the two mugs and noting how pale and unappetising it looked. "Would you remind me of your name again?"

"Andy Wilson: Inspector Andy Wilson," he replied. It might have been the tenth time he'd told me but it was the Wilson part I kept mishearing. Wilton? Willman?

"Ah, yes, of course," I said. I couldn't help smiling. My hearing's OK but people always say their own names too quickly. Perhaps he thought I was stringing him along or taking him for a ride because he then tried his question again. "So, any chance of an explanation?"

I tried the tea. I was right. It was cold, weak and insipid.

"As we used to say in the RAF, a shit, shower and shave would be my preferred priority," I said, aware of combining politeness with perhaps some unnecessary frankness. "One of my colleagues used to add the word shag to that list but I don't feel like one at present."

He seemed slightly amused. "Really? But would you please answer my question?"

"It's a long story," I said. "It goes back sixty years so it'll take that long to tell."

"Then give me a summary."

"Your friend who marched me in here said I'd need to start from scratch."

"Clive's got more patience. Just give me a summary. The only thing I know so far is that your name is Oliver James Thomas and you're from Gloucester. We got that from your passport but perhaps you could start by explaining why you had such a problem with a ninety-year old gentleman living in quiet retirement in a nice villa in Malaga that you shot him."

I looked at him and let him continue.

"Is it any wonder that the Spanish police have asked us to detain you, Mr Thomas? When a British national goes to Spain, uses a smuggled hand gun on another British national and then runs away or, as in your case, walks away using a walking stick, it poses the question of why.

"And while we're at it, what are you doing with five thousand Euros in a brown envelope? Is it unspent, holiday money?"

I've never done holidays. Holidays are a generational thing as if long weeks off work are an entitlement, but he wasn't to know that. "Did your Spanish friends confirm the name of this so-called gentleman?" I asked.

"Mr Alex Donaldson," he replied, "Which I'm sure you know anyway. So, I ask again. What's going on?"

I took a deep breath. "My wife, Sarah, died," I said, which must have sounded irrelevant to him. It wasn't to me. "And so, did Beatie," I added thinking that would confuse him into thinking this was a case of geriatric infidelity or promiscuity that had got out of hand and I felt sorry for him. He wasn't to know. "So is the bastard dead?" I asked.

Andy Wilson picked up his own cup, drained the contents and shrugged.

"Oh well," I said. "The bastard was far from well when I last saw him. He seemed about to suffer a heart attack as well. Perhaps I did him a favour."

Andy Wilson watched me and I suspect he was thinking I couldn't care less, that I was sitting back, relaxing after a job well done. In a way, that was true.

"I'd be happy to explain," I said. "But I trust you were taught the art of patience during your police training. As it all started more than sixty years ago, I need to start from the beginning. That could take a while."

"Go ahead," Andy Wilson said, "Make yourself comfortable."

Home comforts are not something that have ever bothered me but there was something else I desperately needed. "First of all, I'd be grateful for a toilet to avoid disgracing myself," I said.

Perhaps he'd been thinking whilst I used the toilet because when I finished he suggested moving to another room. "It's a spare office with softer chairs. Here's your stick and your bag. That suit you?"

I tried to sound appreciative. "Thank you," I said. "If we don't finish by midnight, I am sure I can find a room somewhere and we can continue tomorrow. I don't have any other pressing engagements right now and, frankly, the thought of returning home to the empty house in Gloucester and running the gauntlet of my nosy neighbour Fred Carrington is quite depressing."

The new office was much nicer. It had bookshelves, filing cabinets, a coffee table and, in the corner, a potted plant – a sad-looking Malaysian miniature coconut. I pointed to it. "I feel sorry for it," I said. "Trees like that should be left where they were born. I hope it isn't one confiscated by customs."

"You know something about customs regulations, Mr Thomas?" he asked.

"I ran an export and import company for most of my life," I said. "I know most of the dodges."

"You certainly know how to carry a gun onto a plane undetected, Mr Thomas. How many other little tricks are you up to?"

We were interrupted. A phone rang and he answered it. I thought it might be news from Malaga but no.

"Well, you won't be going far, Mr Thomas," he said. "We have another little problem. The long-term car park office reports that your car, an old Jaguar that you parked there some days ago, has no tax and no insurance."

"Yes," I admitted. "Things were rather hectic when I left home. I hadn't driven it for a while. But what about Malaga? Is the bastard dead?"

"He is in intensive care. Though I understand the Spanish police are also now taking an interest in some other matters."

"Good," I said. "Better late than never."

"So, tell me about your business, Mr Thomas. Are you still running it? I imagined you were retired. Is this some sort of business feud or just an argument over girlfriends?"

"It's far more complicated than that, Inspector. Do you want me to start from the beginning or not?"

Andy Wilson shrugged so I took that as a go-ahead.

"I started the business after the war," I began. "Sarah and I had just got married and moved to live in Croydon which was near enough to London, far enough into the country and yet near to the airport. Sarah called the house 'Brick View' and I knew she didn't like it but it was an era of austerity, ration books, waste not, want not and beggars can't be choosers.

"You wouldn't understand, Inspector, as you're far too young. But it was a good time for those with ambition and energy and I had ideas to start my own business. Exporting was what I had in mind.

"Ever since I was a boy and read about Captain Cook and stared at the illustrations I had always wanted to travel to more exotic places. I then progressed to books on Africa, Persia and India from the library. After the war, I decided I wanted to visit some of those places. That's how Thomas Import Export Limited was born. My son was born soon after."

I was just getting going when Andy Wilson interrupted. "Let's cut out the family history shall we, Mr Thomas? Are you still in business or not?"

"Yes," I said, disappointed by the interruption. "I suppose you could say I am – or, at least, I was. I've stopped doing tax returns but I suppose you could say my long-term business plan was not complete."

I saw him look at his watch and knew he'd quickly lose patience but I'd anticipated this. Talking was never going to be enough. I'd already written it all down but there was no harm in setting the scene.

"In the beginning I had big plans for Thomas Import Export," I said. "If you had asked me sixty years ago, how I imagined it might have grown I would probably have described a multi-national trading company with offices in New York, Paris, Hong Kong and Buenos Aires.

"But looking at me now, Inspector, in my old jumper, jacket and stained trousers how do I look? Do I look like a successful businessman who worked his socks off and risked his neck for fifty years? Do I resemble some of your flash, modern jet setters with their credit cards, laptops and exaggerated stories about top level meetings with bankers in Sheraton Hotels in places like Singapore and Los Angeles? Or do I look like one of the few who ventured abroad before the days of telexes, internet and international telephones and were to be found waiting around at squalid airports carrying tattered cases of samples and staying at doss houses in places like downtown Lagos?

"How, Inspector, do I compare with your vision of Mister Alexander Donaldson, as you are apparently required to address him, who is living, as you so politely put it, in quiet retirement in a nice villa in Spain?

"That bastard ruined my life, Inspector. And that of many others. I disliked him from the first time I met him but the feeling got worse the older I got and the more I realized what he was really up to. But since Sarah died and I found myself with the time and enough energy left I felt it was time to act.

"It all started in a pub, Inspector. Having been in the Royal Air Force, a few army and RAF chums used to meet up in the Feathers in Mayfair.

"Do you know the Feathers?" I asked him It was unlikely but I was trying to engage him in the story. "Is it still there?" I added. "Is it now covered in hanging baskets of geraniums and petunias and other tinsel? Does it now offer gastro food and serve organic quiche salads for lunch? If so, it has changed a bit since I frequented the dive in the fifties.

"But relationships between old chums often soured as we recognized our differences outside our uniforms. One sour relationship has taken me far longer to deal with than it should.

"The old man in his nineties, as you so decently refer to him, is a bastard of the first order, Inspector." I paused. "Have you ever met an old-fashioned money launderer, Inspector? Do you know any ninety-year-old gun running arms dealers or drug dealers? Tell me, how many of your friends are associates of Sicilian or Russian Mafia and hide out in places like Malta?

"Are you familiar with the big money that can be made by being the instigator of military coups or other subversive plots in places like Algeria, Sierra Leone or Chad? And do you know any nice people who ran the Provisional IRA?

"In your career, Inspector, have you ever found it necessary to arrest a really nasty but clever piece of shit that operates internationally and is still going strong and unidentified like some New York Godfather? Perhaps you have so perhaps you know the sort. Perhaps, with luck, your Spanish friends are going to find one who's been hiding in their midst for too long. Yet it's me who is under detention and I find that strange. But then, that's been the story of my life. Shall I go on, Inspector?"

What Andy Wilson was now thinking about me I had no idea. Perhaps he thought I, too, was an ex gangster, arms dealer, drugs dealer or money launderer. Whatever he thought, I didn't really care. It was all written down, cross-checked and referenced.

He looked at his watch again. "It's getting late," he said. "We need to decide what to do here but we're still waiting on information from the Spanish police."

"So, I'm not being charged?" I asked.

"You're being detained pending further enquiries."

"So, where am I to be detained?"

"Somewhere nearby. A hotel. Your car has been impounded and your passport is with us here."

He looked down at my black bag lying on the floor. "You're not carrying very much, Mr Thomas. When we checked inside it was just a bundle of old clothes, some keys and your brown envelope of euros. Is that it?"

I looked at it, too. I'm very fond of that bag.

"Italian leather," I said. "Made to order forty years ago by a craftsman in Naples. But you missed something Inspector. As did most customs and immigration officials for all the years. I used it to conceal things like my other passports. I held several at various times. On this occasion, it contains something else."

I bent down, ran my hand between the double lining and pulled out a copy of my handiwork of the past few months – a pile of paper held together with a bulldog clip.

"For you," I said handing it over like an overdue Christmas gift. "It's as good a police statement as you'll find anywhere. I wrote it just in case I didn't get back but there's a carbon copy, with my lawyer along with some other papers. I hope you enjoy it."

Andy Wilson took it and raised his eyebrows. Perhaps he'd never had a detainee arrive with a pre-prepared statement before. I watched him flip through the hundred odd pages. I admit it didn't have the sleek look of modern documents because I'd used an old typewriter which required a whole day of practice to remember how to use it. But it was all there.

PART TWO: STATEMENT

THE BEGINNING

Starting from my birth, eighty-six years ago, will be a pointless exercise and so I will begin with a time when, too often, I frequented the Feathers public house in Mayfair.

But, let me make it clear, I do not associate the Feathers with cosy, after works drinks with colleagues but with an ex British Army Major called Alex Donaldson.

Donaldson was a man I was, for many years, content to believe was dead.

But, sixty years later, I can still see Donaldson in his crumpled white shirt sat alongside his crony sidekick Jack Woodward on those red leather stools at the bar. I can still smell the stale Bass beer and see the Red Triangles on the soggy beer mats even now. I can still smell Donaldson's stinking Craven A cigarettes and see him deliberately puffing the smoke down the dark and cavernous cleavage of Betty the barmaid. Sophistication was never Donaldson's style.

The Feathers was always filled with an acrid blue haze, sticky with heat from a coal fire in a black grate with matching brass scuttle, poker, dirty brush and small shovel. I can still feel the sticky warmth on my face as I sat there trying to be part of this ugly scene whilst all the time thinking I would be far better off at home with Sarah sat by our own fireside.

I can still see Betty, as she then was, standing behind her bar, tolerating Donaldson's grotesque rudeness whilst cleaning her squeaking beer glasses with a cloth and winking at customers whenever their eyes rose from her cleavage.

I have had far too many dreams about this place because I was there far too often in the past. But instead of diminishing over time, the dreams have increased. Perhaps it is because, unlike many of the others who visited the Feathers, I never went there to be sociable but with what I now see as a misplaced sense of patriotism and duty to King and Country left over from the war.

Those meetings were usually arranged by a phone call to my Croydon office from Jack Woodward. Beatie, my office manager, typist and telephonist would take the call before handing the phone to me to decide. And it bothers me now how easy it had been for me to be persuaded to meet. But I was younger then and the young are much greater opportunity seekers.

Sitting on one of the red bar stools, Jack Woodward would gorge on little dishes of shrimps or cockles and when I came in, both of them, Jack and Donaldson, would already be there, hunched over their drinks as though they had been there for hours discussing what to say to me or how best to persuade me to do the next job. I would fight my way towards them through the crowd of smoking beer drinkers and Jack might get up but Donaldson wouldn't.

But it was my fault.

In the early days, I was far too easy going and had no idea what I was letting myself in for. Jack, being the politer one would shake my hand and, invariably, his face would betray something as if they had been discussing me for hours. Donaldson would continue facing the bar and Betty until I sat down on the next stool. Then he might turn and nod at me. No smile, no words, just a nod. Donaldson always wore the same grey gabardine mackintosh over his suit and tie and only after he nodded might he decide to follow Jack and shake my hand. Perhaps he knew it but I was always reluctant to touch Donaldson because I knew my hands would smell of stale cigarettes for hours as a result of that fleeting but disgusting contact.

Jack would order the drinks and perhaps more cockles and was always the one to pay Betty.

"Two and six, please, luv. Ta, luv," in her broad east London accent. Then Betty would slide over a tiny white dish that always held three small, sharp wooden sticks and the cockles that glistened with vinegar.

Before and since my dear wife, Sarah, died I have dreamed about the Feathers too often. Mostly they are colourful nightmares with accompanying stereophonic sound effects and smells included and I often wake up in a sweat because the nightmares spiralled out of control onto other things. The nightmares are almost always linked to Donaldson.

When I awake in the middle of the night or the very early morning with my lap soaked in whisky from the glass that had fallen from my hand I often wonder if I am actually suffering from some sort of new and unnamed form of senile dementia.

I fear I may have a new type of Alzheimer's disease distinguished by a vivid imagination and an uncanny ability to dredge up memories that are best forgotten. But I often amuse myself by thinking it should, perhaps, be called Thomas's Disease after its first recorded victim. I have even dreamed of seeing a definition of it in medical textbooks or copies of the British Medical Journal.

"Thomas's Disease: A condition of the mind characterized by symptoms that include an uncontrollable desire to analyse the past through dreams so that the sufferer finds it easy to pinpoint his past mistakes and weaknesses and finally decides to wake up and do something about them."

It is, I acknowledge, a long-winded definition but I feel it is accurate. But I often wondered if, perhaps, I was no longer remembering facts but embellishing things to make them more interesting. Perhaps, I just have an overactive brain that is long past its sell by date.

But I also have a theory that Alzheimer's disease is not really a disease but a useful and highly evolved mechanism for protecting the old and decrepit from realizing their predicament. I have often thought how much nicer that would be because Thomas's Disease is far worse. It is a punishing and painful disease that is all too apparent to its victims.

What is certain is that the nightmares I experienced up until the moment I decided to do something about their cause had been a mixture of historic fact and vivid imagination. But couple that with a mind-blowing ability to suddenly realize what had been going on beneath my nose and behind my back for fifty years and perhaps you will begin to understand why I needed to deal with it.

Writing this is part of that process.

I still can't accurately pinpoint exactly when it all started or when I suddenly saw the light. It was like the slow arrival of dawn when you can't sleep. You lie there waiting until you can stand it no longer and finally get up, go to the window and draw the curtains. But, in my case, I didn't see the rising sun. I saw that a dark and rainy day had already begun, that the time was far later than I had thought and I wished I had got up much earlier. For me, late dawning has happened too often and there is only so much cloud and rain a man can stand.

The final awakening began when Sarah became ill although even then it was not so much a sudden switching on of the light but gradual, like a dimmer switch being turned.

I had been feeling lonely which didn't help. I was certainly bored.

Sarah was sick and a nurse had been calling daily. She had become bedridden, as they once called it, and spent her days upstairs.

I, on the other hand, spent my days and often my nights, downstairs sitting in the chair by Sarah's favourite log effect gas fire but with trips up and down the stairs with cups of tea for Sarah followed by other daytime trips to the Co-Op supermarket for the newspaper and a few more bottles of Bell's whisky for myself.

I know I had been sitting around far too much but what else is an old man expected to do? But, to keep my brain occupied, I had also, mistakenly, started rummaging through an old box of papers and other things that had been gathering dust for twenty-five years in a cupboard upstairs.

Oh dear, what a mistake that was.

But then there were the nightmares, the main features of Thomas's Disease. I would wake up in the early hours or the late hours or even the daytime hours feeling uncomfortable, hot and sweaty and with an all too familiar taste of stale whisky in the back of my throat and an intense heat in my stomach like a gastric version of heartburn.

But what really used to wake me up was the uncontrollable and frantic tossing and sweating in the chair by Sarah's gas fire as I dreamed. I would hear voices. Jack Woodward's voice – he of the Feathers public house in Mayfair – was one.

And Jack might not even have been talking in English. It had been a habit sixty years ago, for ex forces chaps to speak "in tongues" as we humorously called it. Arabic was one such language. Speaking in an accent supposedly to resemble that of President Nasser of Egypt was Jack's little habit. Mixed up with conversations that included "bints" and "kazis", it had all become rather predictable but in one of my whisky fuelled dreams I clearly saw him.

"Sabbah el kheir, kaif hallak?" Jack was saying, his voice seemingly coming directly from the empty whisky glass I was holding to my ear like a phone.

"Good day" and "how are you" are easy enough Arabic words, but, having spent a while in Cairo, Jack was almost fluent and so his Nasser accent was quite realistic. My Arabic isn't bad though. It was picked up from many visits I made to North Africa and the Middle East and I can easily distinguish between Jordanian, Lebanese, Syrian or Egyptian accents. I had a smattering of other languages too or, at least, enough to direct various nationalities of taxi drivers to wherever I was heading.

I had even picked up some occasionally useful Russian words during a few lessons run by a Polish immigrant working out of a room in an office block off Whitehall. That was also sixty years ago but I still harbour memories of a dark room with dusty bookshelves, hard chairs, a stained wooden table and a single, dim light bulb that hung from the ceiling. It had felt like the Eastern Bloc in miniature.

But Jack, who also had the remnants of an English public-school accent to go with his Arabic, had not risen very far after the war. He became Donaldson's errand boy. He was the one who would phone me with a job to do and, stupidly as I now see it, I would agree.

Donaldson and Jack had been old but distant acquaintances at the time. We'd met, by sheer coincidence, at another pub in Victoria and it had all started as a few odd jobs that relied on a few years of RAF experience.

But, before I knew it, I was up to my neck in things. Not that I didn't find some of it exciting at the time. After all, I was young, enthusiastic, and motivated by the need to find opportunities and ideas for my new business. So, any chance to go abroad to mix with unusual characters of different nationalities looked like pure fun with the added potential of earning a shilling or two.

Actually, I was a natural and very good at it.

"Come over, this afternoon, Ollie. We want you to meet someone," Jack might say. And I might reply, "But I've got a Letter of Credit that I need to lodge before the bank shuts," which was often true as I was usually surrounded by paper and often due to fly off somewhere like Beirut the next day.

But so, began long years of evening meetings in the Feathers with two men, one of whom, Jack, was just tolerable, the other, Donaldson, a serious but sinister man who in the early days I never fully understood and later grew to hate.

And, from my small office in Croydon, Beatie, my newly found office assistant, would have been fussing around in her usual way but listening all the while. Beatie rapidly became indispensable to me but there was more to Beatie than I first realized.

But that's how it was in the beginning.

It was a creeping process made easy by my new business – a small venture that taxed the mind but offered endless opportunities for foreign travel whilst enabling me to mix legitimacy with the sort of antics that Donaldson and his crony Jack tempted me to pursue.

I didn't mind. No job was ever the same and, inevitably, I would meet someone who became a new customer or might lead to one.

But the assignments, as Donaldson always described them, gradually got more frequent. Business wasn't easy and I wasn't making much money after paying my overheads and Beatie's salary and I soon realized the assignments were impinging on my business.

Meanwhile, at home, Sarah was busy looking after our young son, Robert. There was not much saving going on. What little was coming in, was going straight out.

But Beatie would take the calls and I would find myself catching the five thirty train and then a taxi to the Feathers. And all at my expense and when it would have been far better and sensible to go home to be with Sarah and Robert and eat cottage pie and apple crumble.

And so, of course, Sarah got used to the loneliness.

She accepted it as part of my business but, looking back, I regret it so much now that it brings a lump to my throat just to write this. I should have understood things better so many years ago.

Suffering from Thomas's Disease, you see, has caused me to reflect on past errors of judgment. In the weeks and months up until the day Sarah died, I often woke up to find myself sobbing like a child.

And why, since Sarah died, do I still sit with lumps in my throat and tears in my eyes?

Because, in the weeks before Sarah passed away, whilst she was lying, gravely sick upstairs in bed, I was downstairs, drunk as a skunk and perhaps speaking to a voice from maybe sixty years ago, coming out of an empty whisky glass clamped to my right ear.

In fact, I have been known to be so far gone that the whisky glass would transform itself into my old black office telephone receiver with its twisted cable that I would waste hours trying to unravel, until Beatie came to my aid. "Tut, tut," Beatie would say, "leave it to me."

And I would say to her something like, "Here, you sort the blasted wire, Beat. I've got to run. See what you can do to finish these quotes off."

And I would push a pile of papers and price lists towards her as Beatie said, "Are you sure, Mr Thomas?"

And then I'd be gone like some stupid boy summoned by the headmaster.

But I was also driven by a sense of duty and patriotism. The assignments were for the good of the country, or so I believed. And if they could also be used to enhance my business, why not?

But my motivations were gradually driven by an added element of fear. And this was nothing to do with early onset Thomas's Disease.

This was a genuine fear for myself and my family and fear of other repercussions for failing to co-operate. Looking back, I can see that Beatie was also worried but, at the time, I was too blind to see it and so Beatie also forms a key part of this tale.

I sometimes still dream about Beatie, but please don't misunderstand me. Dreams about Beatie are never erotic. She was my age but always at least fifteen years behind the fashions of the day and I usually see her dressed in a pink twin set with her Imperial typewriter noticeably hesitating in its clatter as she listened to me on the phone. She would then glance furtively toward me over her horn-rimmed glasses, before looking quickly back to her work. Then the machine would ping back into action again as she hit the return.

But Thomas's Disease has enabled me to remember the look on Beatie's face whenever Jack Woodward phoned my office to invite me to another meeting.

Beatie's expression was particularly exaggerated on the rarer occasions that Donaldson rang.

I would put the big black phone with its tangled cable back on the receiver and glance at Beatie who quickly looked away. "How's it all coming along, Beat?" I would ask with diplomacy and just a little humour, in order to quell Beatie's far too easy embarrassment at being caught watching and listening. In fact, I see now that she treated all phone calls from Jack and Donaldson as if she was nervous. She seemed to dislike the intrusions as if she was an unwilling witness to an extramarital affair and would cough, unnecessarily, nervously and say something like, "Nearly finished, Mr Thomas. But should we copy the text in the credit exactly? You see they have typed dollar wrong. They have put doller – with an 'e'."

"Oh dear. Yes. Better had, Beat. I'll speak to the bank when I present the documents. We don't want to have to request an amendment at this stage. We should have noticed it before."

"Sorry, Mr Thomas."

I had appointed poor old Beatie because she seemed to be a lonely spinster but she was very good at her job. She came with a very good set of references although I have to admit that one of them was from Donaldson. Lonely Beatie was, in fact, indispensable but I now know she also lived in some sort of fear.

So, the few jobs I found myself doing for King and Country or, afterwards, for Queen and Country gradually became more and more frequent to the detriment of my business.

And the plans for them were nearly always laid while drinking pints of draft Bass bitter and slurping bowls of cockles at the Feathers.

I can see that bastard now. For some years, Donaldson had a thick moustache on his upper lip. One day it disappeared without warning although we never discussed such personal things. But it was then that I grew to notice and hate the white spittle that would appear on his lips when he got angry. And Donaldson could get very angry.

I can still see his eyes. They were furtive and he would look out of their corners so that he didn't have to move his thick neck. He would never read a newspaper but use it as a screen for his face while he watched others. In the Feathers his eyes usually looked down into his beer or down the front of Betty's blouse whilst congratulating me on my latest assignment.

I can still hear his voice. It would be accompanied by a spray of saliva especially towards closing time. The words themselves were predictable and invariably interspersed with public school, army-trained "old chap" and "dear boy". And there was a remnant of a Scottish accent that also became more pronounced at closing time. But, as always, I never questioned it at the time.

"Brilliant job, Ollie, old chap. Brilliant. Best man we've got for that type of job. Tripoli and Benghazi, huh? Not much in the way of beer there these days I understand. Tough assignment, dear boy, brilliantly executed."

And Donaldson would then swig the last of his beer and move on to a further examination of Betty's cleavage.

Sometimes we would move away from the bar stools and find a quieter corner, but the jobs were always explained as being for the good of the country with the full backing of the few in Government circles that needed to know. And they were always sold to me as small tasks that I could easily fit around my legitimate business whether it was Libya or any other part of the Middle East, West Africa or wherever else I went.

Donaldson himself had never travelled far although he clearly had overseas connections. I was soon, for example, to discover his links in Jordan.

I knew he'd been to Cairo once because that's where he probably met Jack but he was mostly office based. Where he lived, though, I had no idea. We never discussed private matters. It was the same with Jack, whose private life was also a mystery that I had no reason to ask about though I find I question it now.

In those days, not so long ago, a man's private life was best kept a secret, but if Donaldson knew something then blackmail was a useful tool for keeping people tied down.

And Donaldson and, by default, Jack, were connected in some way to British Intelligence hence the constant tapping of forefingers on noses. "Need to know basis, old chap, don't worry. All in hand."

COCKROACHES

By the late sixties, Thomas Import Export Ltd already held a number of agencies that often required me to get to know the holders of purse strings in the Libyan hierarchy. But then, in the name of freedom, socialism and unity, Colonel Muammar Gadaffi ousted the King and relabelled the country the Libyan Arab Republic. That whole area of North Africa featured rather highly in my life around that time, although it was, by no means, the only part of the world.

By the early seventies, politics had changed radically but I was still able to travel there although some of my old friends had already disappeared. Neither was I still earning much money for the business due to the distractions.

But on one occasion I decided to convince the Libyan People's Public Health Authority to buy bulk insecticides for their heavy cockroach infestations.

In reality though, driven by my sense of adventure, I was also fulfilling my part-time, unpaid job for Queen and Country by trying to make friends with Gadaffi's cronies and making the acquaintances of some of his less prominent enemies to add them to a growing list of possible informers.

I was not being forced to do it and even Donaldson knew very little about what I did and how I did it. But Donaldson soon realized that the little fish he had hooked some years earlier was quite adept at this sort of work and proving to be rather well connected.

I enjoyed the intrigue and the risk but it all got out of hand and I became very vulnerable. But as a result, I was making friends of people I actually mistrusted and shaking hands with those whose palms were already well greased.

Mohammed Saleh was one such.

We would meet regularly in quiet spots behind walls near the port in Tripoli or next to the National Pharmaceutical Company and Ministry of Health. Saleh was often impossible to see at first glance as his grubby beige suit blended with the dust and sand. He had also camouflaged himself rather well within Gadaffi's circles and had become a very useful contact. Saleh was very reliable and always turned up on time.

My mistake was in mentioning him to Donaldson.

Saleh behaved as though the only way to squeeze a small commission out of a visiting Englishman was to look identical by donning similar dust-stained attire. He wore a respectable small moustache like a dark brown, dishevelled, Arabic version of David Niven and was always keen to escape from the watching eyes and the whispering voices of Tripoli, for a bottle or two of Black Label, even if it meant crossing the water to Valletta.

He visited London occasionally and he and I often ate at Tiddy Doll's in Mayfair, around the corner from the Feathers.

I rarely took Sarah with me to meet my many foreign contacts but on one occasion she did join me because Saleh seemed to doubt my description of myself as a happily married man. But Saleh, feeling free of his Libyan shackles misbehaved himself and seduced the red haired, Irish waitress from Cork.

Sarah was impressed, not by the food, but at how easy it had been for the Libyan – fresh off the Libyan Arab Airlines flight – to carry out his seduction.

"Good gracious, dear. Is that how all those Arab friends of yours behave? Who'd have thought it?"

But Sarah, bless her, never knew about the meeting the next morning between Saleh and myself in Regent Street at which Saleh received some expenses in cash from Jack and then the fare for a taxi ride to Credit Suisse.

All Saleh had done for this was to provide a list of possible dissidents and their addresses which I had then passed to Donaldson in all innocence, expecting them to be handed on to the Secret Intelligence Services or some other Government body.

At the time, you see, I didn't really care who received the intelligence because I was convinced it was going somewhere official and so being put to good use.

But Saleh's bedding of the Irish waitress was perhaps the most innocuous part of Libyan-Irish relationships that I was later involved with.

I used to stay at the Libya Palace Hotel in Tripoli and often thought that if there was ever a need for an example of a den of spies, mistrust and suspicion all of it under the watchful eye of secret police then this was it. The Libya Palace, though, was convenient in that it was just around the corner from Abdul Wahid's office. Abdul had been my more official agent and his concrete block office was in a dingy, rubble-laden side street where the fat, brown American cockroaches scurried, too slowly, out of the way and were crunched underfoot on the pavement at night. This was the excellent legitimate market that I had spotted in my usual entrepreneurial fashion.

Abdul Wahid's office featured highly in some of my whisky-fuelled nightmares when Sarah had been sick and the dreams often started with a smell like dust in my nostrils. You see, Thomas's Disease often provides an olfactory dimension to nightmares and this one was like a dream within a dream, a sleep within a sleep. I was well aware of the perversity and would watch myself clamber off the bed clad only in my underpants. And, where was I? After a moment's searching within the mists of my dream, behold, I would find I was in the Libya Palace Hotel in a room along a dark corridor with a threadbare carpet where I could hear the ceiling fan squeaking, slowly, round and round. But everywhere was that smell of dust. It would be caked inside my nostrils and the skin of my face would feel dirty and stretched taught. The room was dark except for a small crack of light between the closed window shutters and in my dream, I would shuffle across the dusty floor in bare feet feeling the grit between my toes. Then I would lean over to open the shutters with their flaking, light blue paint.

I am fairly convinced that this really did happen to me once, many years ago, but, for some reason of nocturnal fantasy, the dream found me using my walking stick. And when I opened the shutters the vivid scene that met my eyes was not one that was common to Gloucester where I now live. For all I was able to see was a swirling grey dust, with paper and litter flying left to right. Piles of fine, grey sand had squeezed through to form small dunes accumulating on the peeling, wooden ledge between the shutters and the closed window and I used my finger to write something in the dust.

In this recurring dream, I wrote "SARAH".

I feel sure I had also written "SARAH" fifty years ago, but it was so long ago that I can no longer be totally certain. But the dream was enough. Writing "SARAH" in Saharan dust seems fitting enough.

But, outside, the neighbouring buildings were just dark grey outlines and the morning sun was just visible as a faint, red, disk like a Japanese flag, low above the flat roofs, disappearing and reappearing as the flying dust passed before it in thick clouds. The sand storm was like a hot, violent, London smog of stinging particles of sand.

But I usually awoke from these dreams to find myself sitting by Sarah's log effect gas fire in the sitting room in Gloucester with an empty whisky glass falling from my hand and with such a dryness in my throat and nose that I would find himself blowing my nose into the whisky glass to clear it.

And, whilst it might have been the heat from the gas fire on my face, I still felt it as though I was standing facing the hot wind coming straight up from Kufra.

But, because I was half awake and probably also half drunk, the dry heat would suddenly change to a humid, coal smoke heat and I would find myself back in the bar at the Feathers again with Alex Donaldson and Jack Woodward with Donaldson making all sorts of suggestions about how else they might be able to use Mohammed Saleh and other contacts I had made over the years.

And through the dreams and nightmares I can now also remember what I said to Donaldson after Saleh had returned to Libya after that night at Tiddy Doll's.

24

"But my business is suffering because of all this nonsense."

"Rubbish!" said Donaldson. "You're the one talking nonsense old chap. In your prime. My goodness. Best man we've got for those sorts of jobs. Mixing it with your business.

What more could you want, dear fellow? Good expenses.

Fifteen quid a day subsistence paid in cash and no asking for vouchers. On top of what you make on the business. Flights sometimes paid for or arranged."

"I've had enough," I said.

"Nonsense, old chap. You need a break. Take a few days off. Go away with that young family of yours. The seaside – Brighton, Bournemouth, Blackpool. There's an idea. Get a bit of clear English air in your lungs, dear fellow, instead of all that hot bloody sand."

But then my own voice had risen in anger at Donaldson's insensitivity.

"But by boy's at school. And, anyway, it's the middle of winter."

"Ah, yes. Never mind old chap – go another time."

"But I'm nearly forty," I had said, "I need to concentrate on the business."

"Forty is not old, dear fellow. Heavens above. I'm just as old. Feel like twenty. Just looking at Betty over there gives me evil ideas."

You see, I was already starting to regret my involvement and feeling that I had been sucked into something outside of my control.

Already, the early excitement had run thin and I knew I needed my business to start to earn some real money for my growing family, not waste time on errands for other people that only offered nominal expenses in return. I wanted to pull back because I felt I had already given up too many of my rights by allowing myself to be sucked in on a wave of lingering adolescence.

But I didn't pull out, partly because I really did believe I was doing something for the good of the country.

Later I didn't pull out for fear of the effects on me and my family.

But I was also from a generation where it was not right for the adult male to be seen to be in any doubt at any times. At all times, there must be certainty and boldness.

"Go on, you can do it, you stupid fool. Stop whining. What are you – man or mouse?"

It was the very essence of manliness. Never mind if you were shot out of the sky last night. I felt it was my duty to get back into the cockpit and to stop whinging.

THE ALGERIAN PARROT

Yousef was my agent in Algeria.

Whenever I visited, Yousef would sit in a squeaking, swivelling chair high up behind his large desk looking down on visitors. There might be half a dozen of us sitting or standing around trying to catch his attention as he held overlapping discussions with everyone and flapped at buzzing flies from the abattoir next door. As the only foreigner, I would be granted pride of place in a sagging chair looking up at him whilst I struggled to sell him tractor parts or cans of insecticide in poor Arabic and French. I was an old hand at Arabic ways and well used to this form of selling but add in the regular interruptions from Yousef's parrot and you will see why I am cynical about the skill sets of current sales and marketing consultants.

You see, Yousef kept an old, green and red parrot called Pierre in a bottomless cage on the coffee table that all of Yousef's visitors shared to place their cups. The table, itself, was inlaid with fine, polished marquetry and Pierre would sit there and listen all day long to Youssef's business deals and the traffic noise that wafted in through the open window along with the meat flies from the butcher's shop on the street below.

Youssef employed an elderly and crippled assistant, Mohammad, who would be summoned to bring pots of thick, sweet Arabic coffee or mint tea at frequent intervals. But the parrot's call was louder and clearer than Youssef's and he spoke far better Arabic.

"Mohammad, Mohammad. Gahwa, Gahwa," he would call.

The parrot would call every few minutes and Mohammed would appear, breathless from waiting downstairs, unsure if he was

27

being summoned by Youssef or by Pierre. But, anxious as ever to please, Mohammad would bring the same dirty, damp cloth with him and, whether the summons was from bird or man, use the opportunity to lift the cage and wipe the table top clean of fresh parrot droppings. Pierre always made sure there was something fresh to clear and patiently watched the messy proceedings from his perch with his head on one side, white eyelids blinking in astonishment at the stupidity of man, before breaking into his repertoire of car and motor bike sounds from the street below.

"Beep, beep. Vroom, vroom. Bzzzzzzzzz."

But I am writing this, not so much for entertainment, but in order to put Algeria into context and to point out that I told Sarah about the parrot more than once to cheer her up. It didn't work the last time because she fell asleep. Sarah was sleeping a lot towards the end. But, in the past, when I told her she would always say, "Well I never," and then smile.

But describing what I did in Algeria and other places like Syria and Jordan gives you an idea of what I had become involved in.

My problem was that I mostly did as I was told, especially by those who were older or more experienced or for whom I felt I should show respect. Donaldson held a higher rank than me, you see. Rank doesn't make a better, or more decent, person but that is how it started. I still behaved like the good little boy I had been when grandma asked me to fetch something from the grocer. I was far too willing to do jobs for others with less likeable traits and my respect was often misplaced. I really should have learned a lot more from the things my mother said.

"Mrs Ricketts tells me you took three bottles of milk at school today, Oliver. That's very naughty, you know."

"Sorry, Mummy, but Ronald told me to."

"But you should know better than to listen to that nasty boy Ronald, Oliver."

"But he said his sister was sick and needed building up."

"You really believe that silly story, Oliver?

28

"Well . . .!"

You see, I found it hard to rid myself of this over willing habit when I grew up and joined the RAF. I would nod politely to Donaldson telling me that I was the best person for a job. In fact, I asked far too few questions.

Back in 1956 when I was still fairly new to Donaldson's games my business with Youssef in Algiers was just starting. But it was also a time of troubles in and around the Mediterranean from Cyprus to Algeria and Morocco. In Algeria there was guerilla warfare with Arab nationalists and, on one trip, little did I know that the French Premier Guy Mollet was also in town.

But Donaldson clearly did.

This time the Feathers pub was where I took delivery of a small package to take to Algiers. Donaldson had also scribbled an address on a scrap of paper in his usual untidy scrawl.

"Easy job, old chap. Just drop it off at the address here. After midnight, would be best. Someone will take it off your hands. Everything done and dusted. No questions asked."

"What is it?" I asked, looking at a light, cylindrical object wrapped in brown paper.

"Just rolls of film, apparently, old chap. Nothing important so I'm told. Need to know basis. Safe as houses but just don't lose it, old chap or we'll all be in the shit."

"Why?" I asked.

"Wouldn't know, old chap. It's on a need to know basis. Top brass. Mum's the word and all that. Don't worry. It's for our fresh young Queen and the good of her loyal citizens, bless her cotton socks and sparkling crown."

I let those derogatory words pass, bit my tongue and said, "The address. It's a house?"

"A villa, apparently," said Donaldson as though this meant it was superior.

"Who does it belong to?"

"Fuck sake, man. Why do you need to know that? Just hand the bloody thing over at the bloody door and fuck off back to your hotel or wherever you are staying." A blob of white spit appeared on Donaldson's lower lip and another blob landed on the table top next to my beer. Donaldson was getting mad.

"Just wondered," I said, "is the drop to be made to a Frenchman or an Algerian? Just so I don't give it to the wrong man."

"For your information, it'll be an Arab, a bloody Algerian," Donaldson said and swigged his beer. Jack looked embarrassed.

"Thanks," I said, reluctantly. But then I decided to ask for a bit more.

"Big villa?"

"Bloody hell, man. Why the questions? Fucking big villa I expect. It belongs to the French Government – the bloody Governor General, himself."

"Oh, I see. So, will the Governor be there?"

"How the fuck should I know. He never answers the bloody door anyway, whether it's morning, noon or night so after midnight you'll get welcomed by his fucking night servant I expect. Just hand it over, old chap. Then you just fucking disappear."

That was it.

Three days later I was in Algiers and after my meeting with Youssef and landing a small order for fan belts and spark plugs I returned to my hotel. Then, come midnight, and this is where I realize I may be

opening a can of worms that the current Foreign Office and the French equivalent may like to know about, I crept out again to find a taxi.

It was a very dark night, warm but cloudy and the streets were empty and silent but an old Peugeot taxi was parked outside and I got in, gave the driver the address on Donaldson's scrap of paper and we drove off. All the while, I could sense the taxi driver's wariness of me.

All I was carrying was the small parcel of what I thought was film. The object wasn't heavy and, in order to get through customs, I had concealed it in a piece of copper tube that I had labelled as a commercial sample for Youssef. It was my usual practice.

So, on my way to the Governor's place and in the darkness of the back seat of a taxi with the package now out of its copper tube, I could feel that the glue holding the brown paper covering had worked loose and in the fleeting light from passing street lamps, I caught a glimpse of a small, round, black object like a miniature fire extinguisher with a length of red wire attached to it. This clearly was not photographic film and I began to feel uneasy. But because I really did not want to know what it was and being still sat in the darkness I tried to cover up the gap with the rustling noise obviously upsetting the taxi driver even more. But then the package completely ripped and as the black object rolled onto the seat and then onto the floor by my feet, the taxi stopped at what looked like our destination – a manned gatepost leading to a row of private villas. The suspicious taxi driver, hearing the thing fall, turned around. With the troubles in Algiers at the time I think he thought I was carrying a small bomb. He was not far wrong.

He switched on the dim interior light of the ancient Peugeot taxi.

"Qu'est-ce que c'est, Monsieur? Qu'est-ce qui a fait ce bruit?"

My French is not so good but I knew he was asking me what I was carrying and why it had made a noise. Although I couldn't see his eyes, I could sense he was very nervous.

"C'est un extincteur," I said, hoping I had used the right French-Algerian word for a fire extinguisher though in fact I had no idea what it was. I was groping under his seat where the thing had rolled and I knew he was thinking about jumping out of his cab.

I also said something about it being "tres petit" but by then the night-time gate keeper appeared at the window of the taxi. They exchanged a few words in Arabic, the driver flicking his thumb backwards in my direction and the gatekeeper peered in at me in the darkness. But we were allowed through and a minute later the taxi stopped at the gate to a big villa. I was expecting the driver to wait for me but he was clearly too nervous and asked for his fare. Not sure how I would get back but not wanting to cause any more fuss I paid him anyway and he reversed and disappeared back to the gatehouse in a cloud of exhaust smoke leaving me holding the object barely concealed in its brown packaging.

I pulled a brass handle on the gate and heard a bell ring somewhere in the darkness. A dog barked and a light came on and I could then see a courtyard and someone carrying a torch came out from behind a black Citroen car. He came up to the gate and shone the light into my face through the metal bars. "Je m'appelle Thomas," I said trying some French rather than Arabic. I could just make out the dark face of a younger man, shorter than myself, wearing a long white shirt which reflected the light from his torch.

"Monsieur Thomas? Mr Oliver?" "Oui," I said.

"You have something?" The young man clearly spoke English and I was grateful because I needed to use a word that I couldn't recall the French or Arabic word for. 'Leaking' is not a word that often needs to be translated.

"Yes," I said, "but there is a problem. I think it's leaking."

Indeed, it was, for as I held it, my hands felt as though they were holding a large, dripping pebble with a strand of thin seaweed hanging from it – a cylindrical, pebble, smooth and shiny, but still wrapped in the remnants of its packaging.

The boy, for he was hardly more than a teenager, opened the squeaky gate but, instead of coming in, I knelt down and placed the object in the dust on the ground. The boy shone his torch onto it and also knelt down. We both looked at it. I carefully removed the last of the packaging and without speaking we both stared at it. I smelt my hands. They smelled of a mixture of petrol or acetone. I wiped them on my trousers and then bent down to look at the object. It was, indeed like a black, miniature fire extinguisher without its handle but with a red wire instead of a nozzle and a wet-looking screw top.

"It's OK," the young man said, confidently, and he picked it up and shone his torch on it. I joined him, towering above him by more than a foot.

"I see before. No problem. We fix. Explosive mixture different this time that all. No worry. Not explode. No battery.

We fix. Fucking French."

Thinking he meant to abuse the manufacturer I said, "No, it's English".

The boy grinned up at me, a good-looking lad of about seventeen with black, shiny eyes and a moustache sprouting above his upper lip.

"Fucking French mean dead French."

"What is it?" I asked this clearly far more experienced youth.

"Fucking parcel bomb for fucking French Governor. You not know? We must kill."

"Ah," I said, "I thought this was the Governor's villa." "Oui, c'est ca. A demain. Insh'allah. Fucking French Governor. We sort, no problem. Merci, Monsieur."

"Ah, "I said, still sniffing my hands. "So, I can go now?"

"Oui, d'accord. Merci."

"But I have no taxi."

"OK, I take you in Governor's car. He not here. With girlfriend."

"Is that the Governor's car?" I asked, pointing at the black Citroen.

"Oui, c'est ca. I get key."

"What about the bomb?"

"No problem, I leave by tree. Aziz fix later. Wait."

An hour later, I was back in my hotel having been on a wild drive with many wrong turnings in a car stolen from the French Governor General and driven by a multilingual Algerian teenager who didn't stop talking about a local hero called Ben Bella and the Melbourne Olympic games.

The Governor survived because I read about him in a paper a few weeks later.

They eventually won their independence but, oh yes, Algeria was in a frightful mess at the time with Moslem fanatics and killings and the French doing some very unseemly things which never really came to light. But if anyone who reads this wants to know more, please ask.

And who, from the safe haven of a dingy Regent Street office was in a position to pick up threads of official intelligence and seize an opportunity to try to make some money out of this by using an innocent English courier who wrongly thought he was actually doing something approved by the British Government? Why, Donaldson of course and it was not the first or only time.

But it was only just dawning on me that Donaldson had some methods and motives that, to me, didn't seem to match what the British Government might normally endorse. I should have pulled out there and then and put up with the flak from Donaldson.

But I didn't, and then it became impossible.

But why, you might ask, was I so naïve at the time? I have been asking myself that for years and even more so during the last year. But the only answer is that, at the time, I never really believed that someone in a highly placed, salaried and pensionable civil servant position could live with so few principles without any sense of duty and pride in their country. I assumed that that was the way it worked. But it became clearer and clearer that Donaldson was looking on every conceivable opportunity that came in his direction as a way to make money for himself.

But I made and lost several friends along the way as a result of what I did and it hurts me now if they thought it was me who failed them.

One had been a naïve, well meaning, but misused Moroccan student to whom I subsequently discovered I had been giving deliberately false information to pass on to another contact in Casablanca. Looking back I now know it was me who was the naïve one. I passed the student's own information back to someone from the French Embassy, all with some form of connivance with Donaldson. It really was all very complicated and I had not fully understood what I was doing.

The problem was that, to some extent, I enjoyed the secrecy and the risk and preferred not to know too much. I still enjoy my memories about my ride in the Governor's Citroen.

But everything increasingly impinged on my legitimate business.

And I was, by that time, developing a very clear sense of what was really wrong with the world and that I may not really be helping anyone other than Donaldson. It certainly wasn't helping my business.

But, mixed up as it was with my business, the so-called assignments seemed to blend in well and some jobs were little more than delivering notes, reports, rolls of film or cash inside brown envelopes or rolls of newspaper. To me, it was antiquated, old style intelligence gathering and delivering.

I left Algeria on one occasion just before an earthquake hit killing hundreds of people. Sarah heard about the tragedy but it was a week before I managed to get a telephone call through to Beatie from Amman to say where I was. Those, you see, were the days of poor or non-existent international phone connections and of cables, before the telex and long before the facsimile machine and e-mail. Sarah had been so cross with me when I returned home. I remember her crying.

But whatever I was doing and wherever I was, she was never far from my mind.

I would haggle in dusty, back street souks to buy a few small silver trinkets and charms for Sarah's bracelet that still lies in a drawer with other jewellery. Over the years, it became heavy with tiny pieces I bought whenever I was away and had the time to wander, like a tourist, through narrow streets.

There were tiny coffee-pots from Syria, crosses and stars from Israel, an antelope from Kenya, cow bells from Switzerland and Austria, a bunch of tiny keys, a tiny Voortrecker wagon from South Africa and a scarab beetle inlaid with malachite from Cairo. But on that memorable occasion in Amman after the earthquake I found a tiny, nativity scene, in silver, complete with Mary, Joseph, a crib with an overlarge baby and three sheep.

"Well I never! Silver Christmas carols." That was how Sarah had described them.

MONKEY PUZZLE

I **start this page after two days of sitting and drinking** but I have not slept. It is a struggle to clear my mind sufficiently to write and I still have a long way to go.

Sleep, I believe, is a pastime of the young and of those whose energy is consumed by physical and mental endeavour. Insomnia, on the other hand, is an affliction of the old and those whose energy remains untapped. These latter souls – and I am one – will sit, think and drink, and with lights still blazing deep into the night, spend useless hours wandering in circles around the house. I have become such a depressed wanderer.

It is hard for me to admit this but, in my effort to explain things, I will swallow what remains of my pride.

You see, over the last few months and years, I have spent hours peering through the curtains of the upstairs windows like a nosy old woman. I am well aware of the pathetic creature I have become. The only thing left of my manly persona is the whisky bottle I am usually to be found clutching in my hand.

This peering from the bedroom window first began when Sarah became ill and was confined to bed. I have spent hours watching Sarah asleep in the bed. There is little that is more depressing than watching someone with their eyes shut, unaware of your presence and who seems to have entered a sort of time warp where nothing is happening. It is an interesting scientific fact that contemplating a universe where there is absolutely nothing goes nowhere. But Sarah barely moved once she fell asleep.

Towards the end, she barely moved during the day either but, at night, she was particularly still. Towards the end her breathing also became irregular and noisy. But I would perch on the edge of the bed near the pillow looking down at her although if I had had a drink or two, I tried not to get too close in case she smelt it. Sarah's nose, you see, was one part of her body that still worked. But if I was sober, I would often stroke her forehead or her hair and talk to her even though she was asleep.

Then I might go to the window.

I would part the curtains, wipe the condensation from the glass and peer out into the darkness. Last autumn, just before Sarah died, I was watching as a mixture of wet snow and rain fell onto the road below. Large, wet, snowflakes floated through the bare cherry tree on the overgrown lawn. First, they seemed to fall downwards then, as the swirling wind caught them, they were swept upwards again, disappearing back into the darkness. The long grass of the lawn looked orange in the street light but everything was still too wet for snow to settle. A car drove slowly past, its headlights picking out rain mixed with snowflakes and reflecting off the wet road. And, in the distance over the rooftops opposite, stood the cathedral, already floodlit for the season, its spire outlined in a dimmer, foggy light. A Christmas tree lit with tiny red, blue and yellow fairy lights stood in the window of the house opposite.

The Carringtons at number 26, now named Grey Walls, always wanted to be the first to show how Christian and festive they were and it was only November.

I once told Sarah, "The Carringtons would put up a Christmas tree at Easter, if competition really hotted up."

I had not spoken to Fred Carrington for weeks. Mrs Carrington had been in hospital and I only knew that because Fred told me. We sometimes met in the local shop where I would spot him scanning the racks of the wine and spirits shelves with a guilty expression on his face. The poor man would be furtively glancing around as though he feared Mrs C might be lurking, somewhere in the vicinity. But standing there, watching what little life there was unfold from behind the curtain, I wondered who, if Mrs C was still in hospital, had put up that tree. I was immediately disgusted at my interest in such petty issues but such, you see, is the intellectual height of insomniacs who ponder on such trifling matters and so fail to tire their brains.

Fred, I decided, didn't seem the sort to have done it himself as the competitive streak undoubtedly came from Mrs C. Perhaps his wife, whatever her other name was, was better now. Perhaps Fred had been forced to fix the tree in place in a bucket, wrapped it in coloured crepe paper and Mrs C had done the more interesting part of decorating it.

The house to the right of the Carringtons, number 28, now called The Laurels, was always in darkness. As I write this, I can see it through the curtains but I have no idea who lives there. It was once rented out to a family who shouted a lot and appeared to own at least six cars which they parked on the pavement between the garbage bins.

The house to the left was number 24 but I can't tell you its name if, indeed, it has been given one. But it, too, is in complete darkness. Such is the mysterious lifelessness that depicts certain streets like this.

I often look at the monkey-puzzle tree that stands stark against the gap between numbers 24 and 26. It is clearly visible in the street light against the orange hue from the low clouds that seem to constantly hover over the city and I often ponder about monkey-puzzle trees and about those who thought they were useful adornments for urban, English gardens.

They are, as trees, so brutal, stark and unbending and I have never seen it move, even during a gale. This is a particularly dirty tree that looks depressed but does not know how to die. It is a tree that appears lonely, homesick and out of place in England – a tree that should probably have stayed at home in South America. But it had not been given a choice. It, or its parents, had been brought to England, shipped here like an unwilling immigrant by someone with distorted ideas of interest and beauty with ideas to exhibit it in grand, English country gardens. It had done its best. In fact, it had made the most of its new home. This was, in fact, a particularly courageous specimen that might, if it could speak, admit that true happiness had eluded it since it came to Gloucester. If it could speak it might also tell you that it possessed undying patience and tolerance in abundance but that now it only half-believed the stories it had been told of high, snow-topped mountains in its birthplace of Chile and Argentina. It may have heard from other, older monkey-puzzle trees about soaring condors and of how its cousins provided nesting sites amongst their spiky armoury for far more exotic birds than the local sparrows that it was familiar with. It knows nothing of the stark terrain to which it is so much better suited and I am sure it dislikes providing shelter for the ugly, rusting shed and it tries its best to ignore the concrete post and the street light that shines at night.

In fact, I think it hates its safe, suburban life. I think it would have preferred the risk and adventure of coping with wild gales and other forces of nature. Its life is too mundane, you see.

Standing there, peeping from behind the curtain, I always feel sorry for that tree. Perhaps it also saw the eyes, peering like a ghost from behind the curtains of the upstairs window opposite and sympathized. That tree and I were like friends who had never spoken.

The view from the bedroom window is not one I would have chosen, but it is, I suppose, better than the view in Croydon, where the far horizon could be measured in yards. But a detached gable-fronted house in Gloucester had been the only sort affordable when I finally sat down to count the savings. It had been close to essential amenities, as Sarah used to call the shops and post office. But it had also been close to Robert, my son, and his family, which was the real reason for Sarah – that is before Robert decided with just a hint of guilt, to pack up and move to America within weeks of our arrival. The post office, too, has of course, now moved away.

But for Sarah, she was returning to somewhere closer to her Gloucestershire roots, and the house had given her a sense of comfort, which I saw no reason to undermine.

Personally, I would have found it far more exciting to live in a mountain hut in Chile next to a Monkey Puzzle tree or in Cape Town, Cyprus, South East Asia or any of the sixty odd other countries I have visited over the years. You see, I still prefer to feel hot sun on my face, not cold, wet, sleet. And I still need space and fresh air to breathe. But I owed it to Sarah to do what she wanted, not what I wanted. It was her turn, so to speak, to decide what we should do. She said she felt safer there and I now know why.

So, instead of buying a much larger villa with several acres of land in Cape Town we used all my remaining resources to buy a gable-fronted house in a side street of Gloucester.

Even Cheltenham would have been better and I tried hard to persuade Sarah of that. Cheltenham still has a certain ring of sophistication and affluence. It possesses an air of grandeur left by generations of retired military who have travelled the world, seen a lot, done their bit for King or Queen and Country and finally come home to roost in manageable apartments in Georgian streets. Cheltenham gathers secret intelligence by clever electronic surveillance of distant lands.

Cheltenham also calls itself the gateway to the Cotswolds. Certainly, it feels closer to the higher hills and the watery, more southerly valleys of Stroud and Painswick, of Cider with Rosie villages and stony cottages. Cheltenham is spring and summer – a town of glorious flowers in sunny parks. Gloucester, on the other hand, is like autumn and winter – a city of wet sleet, of oily water slopping about in old, disused docks, of dull brick terraced houses and industry.

But back in November, as I was peering from behind the curtain, I remember Sarah moaning in her sleep. I turned to check her as she moved just a little and settled once more. Her hair lay across her forehead, her face just a little orange in the reflected light from the street lamp. I watched her mouth move and heard her mumble something. It was the familiar sound of Sarah sleeping that I had listened to for nearly sixty years and I listened to her for a while longer.

That night, it was the only sound in the world. Sometimes, I decided, I had not heard her because, wrongly, I believed that what she was saying was not important. I had listened but had not heard. Sometimes I did not hear because I did not understand. Sometimes I did not hear because my mind was distracted and too far away. And once, but only once, I did not want to hear because we had argued. I looked away, back towards the window. I looked away because Sarah had known about Kings Cross. And Kings Cross was where Donaldson had started to turn the screw.

HANKY-PANKY

"The address is on there."

Jack was pointing to the usual, scribbled message on the back of an old, brown envelope. "Pick it up before you get the train. It's just a package I understand. D wants it taken up."

D was Jack's occasional name for Donaldson.

"So, what has she got?" I asked Jack.

Jack shrugged. "Search me. Works for the Israelis but going back to Tel Aviv tomorrow I gather."

"M?"

It was another ridiculous initial because we loved codes. M was Mossad. Jack had known what I meant but he shrugged again, said nothing and looked away. Later I took the underground to Kings Cross Station. It was a late evening in July and still light and I was getting out of a taxi and looking around at street numbers, finding 46, and ringing the bell next to the name that said Weizmann. A woman in her mid-twenties came to the door and let me in. I followed close behind her as we walked, round and round, up three flights of dark stairs and entered an airless flat that smelled as though it may, until recently, have remained unoccupied for months.

I remember that room so clearly. It had one high window open to the deep blue sky from the heat of the summer evening. But the bed looked slept in and the gas stove held a kettle that was steaming. A small suitcase lay on the floor, clothes tumbling from it. And a brown briefcase lay on the bedside table beside the only electric light that was switched on.

She had introduced herself as Leila and asked me if I would like coffee. Then she had filled the kettle from a single, cold water tap over the white, porcelain sink. I had sat on the only space available, the bed, and waited while she talked and washed two cups.

"We have to wait for Simon to arrive. We don't have everything yet."

She spoke in a husky Arab-Israeli accent tinged with American and pronounced Simon first in the Arabic way – Semaan and also in the more familiar Simon.

"Simon should be here very soon."

I asked her a few questions but knew it was unwise to pry too much because I was merely doing favours – my innocent courier role as usual.

"I go home tomorrow," she said, "El Al. You fly El Al before?"

We talked similar generalities and she came to sit beside me. It was high summer, as I said – a hot July evening. The warm, eastern Mediterranean sun was shining from her dark brown eyes and I knew she was wearing nothing underneath her open necked shirt. Her smooth, brown, bare legs were parted at the hem of her short skirt. I remember her sighing and constantly looking at her watch as she continued with small talk.

"If he is not coming by ten o'clock, then maybe he is not coming until morning."

Her manner of speech and accent was very appealing so I used the time to practice my few words of Hebrew with a few remembered words and sentences. She seemed to like it and laughed and joked in Arabic. "My Arabic is now better than my Hebrew."

And then we both told jokes about Arabs and Israelis, then a few more, but less political. Her Arabic was, indeed, good and I had started to wonder about her precise nationality but was too cautious to ask outright because I was only there as a trusted aid for Donaldson. She laughed again and seemed to like touching my leg with her own, just like Gladys Hargreaves used to do when I was eleven at school.

But time passed and Simon had still not arrived by ten.

After another mug of Leila's delicious coffee, though, I remember nothing except feeling unusually relaxed and tired and lying backwards on the bed with my head on the pillow. I must have passed out and it was many hours later that the sound of people talking woke me. It was six in the morning and a man, presumably Simon, had arrived with an envelope and had let himself in with a key.

But I found, on waking from a sleep that was far, far deeper than normal, that I was missing my trousers and shirt. I was partly covered by a bed sheet but mostly I was covered by Leila's arms, legs and long, jet-black hair. I also had a severe and throbbing headache.

But Simon had seemed surprisingly unconcerned and went about the task of making coffee for himself while Leila dressed beneath the sheet and I recovered my clothes that I could not recall having removed, from the floor.

Then, later that evening, after a long and tedious train journey to Edinburgh with my headache only receding slowly, I arrived at Donaldson's office in Morningside. I gave him the sealed, brown envelope and he asked me how I had got on with Leila. Then he winked at me.

I remember Donaldson's winks. They were always made with a sideways nod of his head and a smug grin. Donaldson never smiled much but, when he did, he exposed a row of big, yellow teeth.

"Jolly energetic bit of totty, don't you think, old chap?"

I hated the suggestive nature of Donaldson's words and I told him I did not know what he was talking about. But the worst bit was to come. Donaldson went on.

"Sarah rang the hotel in George Street because you failed to ring her last night. Tut tut, old chap."

I looked at Donaldson, puzzled. "Sarah?" I asked. "But Sarah has no idea I'm in Edinburgh, least of all where I might be staying."

Donaldson looked unconcerned. "Ah, yes, sorry, old man. Jack would have told Beatie to phone your wife to ring the hotel in Edinburgh, as it was urgent."

I looked at him, my heart now starting to beat in my chest. "But I'm telling you my wife didn't know I was going to Edinburgh. Neither did Beatie. And what, on earth, could have been so urgent?"

Donaldson then turned his back on me. "Well, I don't know, I'm sure, but everyone seems to know something now, old chap." He slapped me on the shoulder and looked at me as if he was about to reveal more. He did.

He opened the envelope I had brought with me but had not opened because it was not mine to open – naïve devotion to Queen and Country you see. Then he sat, inspecting the contents while I worried what I would say to Sarah when I got home.

And so, it was, two days later, that Sarah and I started to argue about who, what, why, when and where. As usual I made a complete mess of explanations, as the only person in the world that I could never deceive with words was Sarah. I may not have always told her everything but what I did say was always the truth.

But my real anger lay with Donaldson who knew full well that I never talked to Sarah about my other life.

But Donaldson had got what he wanted. He held up something that he pulled from the envelope, placed it on the table and read from the scrap of notepaper that was inside.

"Ah. Yes. You see. Just as I thought, Leila liked you – a lot. She says here that you didn't tell her your name but she asks me to tell you she would love to see you again next time she's in London. She likes the photos you took of each other. She says to tell you she'll keep them as a memento – until the next time."

It was the only time I had argued with Sarah but it was not the first or the last time with Donaldson. It was the first and only time I met Leila. But Donaldson would often find time to mention her and the photographs and I knew full well that he was the one keeping them as a memento.

"Seen Leila lately, Ollie? Good job Sarah doesn't know about you, you rascal. But she'll soon see the photos if you ever step out of line. Mind you, I wouldn't mind a bit of Leila myself sometime. What?"

The visions in the darkened bedroom window disappeared and were replaced again with the pale reflection of my own face and at the equally pale form of Sarah still sleeping in the bed behind me.

So, I wandered downstairs again, filled my glass once more and sat staring into the log effect gas fire wondering if those photos still existed somewhere. Perhaps they were filed in a box in some dusty cellar somewhere and had been turned up by a couple of cleaners or low-grade civil servants tasked with reducing the volume of paperwork still in storage.

"Seen this one, Bert? Quaint bit of hanky-panky and other goings-on in the corridors of power. Must have been a few years ago though, Bert. See? The girl's mini skirt is half way up her arse – and look, no bloody knickers. Dirty old man whoever he is. Lucky sod! Ha ha!"

But Donaldson had started to turn the screw.

REYNOLDS

Donaldson then gave the screw another turn.

I had been to Algeria again on business but then flew to Amman in Jordan because Donaldson had apparently set me up with an appointment with the Ministry of Defense.

In Amman in the evening I would often visit the souk to look for a small gift for Sarah. When I returned to my hotel that night a bearded Arab in smart white dress was sitting waiting for me and running a string of brown coloured beads between his fingers just as I was fingering my new found present for Sarah in my pocket.

He stood. "Salaam Alekum," he said with his hand outstretched. There was the briefest of pauses. "Mr Thomas?"

Now, this was surprising because my passport for immigration and visa purposes when I arrived in Amman had been a special one, prepared and given to me by Donaldson in London. It was all done in readiness for the meeting he'd arranged with the Jordanian Armed Forces the next day.

This new passport was in the name of David William Reynolds and I had not shaved whilst in Algeria and Egypt so as to better match the photograph.

My Oliver Thomas passport lay secure behind the lining of my black case. At the time I held three passports in the name of Thomas although I normally only carried one. The others would have been at home or lodged with Embassies awaiting visas for future trips. On this occasion, the lining had been the hiding place for the Reynolds passport until just before my plane landed in Amman. Then, just before touching down, I had hidden the Thomas one, recovered the Reynolds one and passed through immigration as David Reynolds.

Faced, then, with a visitor in the hotel lobby addressing me as Oliver Thomas, I was, at first, unsure how to respond. I decided on caution. "Alekum essalaam. And you are?" I asked.

"Derhally, sir. Fouad Derhally. Major Donaldson informed us you were staying here," he said.

"Major Donaldson?"

"I think you know him, sir."

I maintained my caution. "I do?" I said.

"Yes sir. Mr David Reynolds also confirmed you were staying here."

This was odd, because I was, ostensibly, David Reynolds.

"Mr Reynolds?" I asked.

"Yes, sir. He is coming from England," the man said in his Arabic way.

This was true, but it was still very odd.

"And where is Mr Reynolds at present?" I asked the man.

"He is coming from the British Embassy, I believe, sir."

"Is he? And how do you know Mr Reynolds?"

"He is arriving yesterday, sir. He was fly to Amman from Algeria."

Even now, years later, I remember exactly how the man spoke. But it was me who, as Oliver Thomas, had flown from Algeria, just the day before. The confusion combined with the heat of a late afternoon in the middle of July in Amman brought on a sticky sweat. But what happened afterwards has been a recurring nightmare that produces regular sweats even in December in England.

I walked with the Arab to the corner of the hotel lobby and we sat, briefly, by a potted palm and ordered coffee. We talked pleasantries until it arrived in a pot and was served by a bearded man in white robes and a red sash into tiny cups on a brass tray. Little was

47

said and the coffee ritual only served to extend the time I spent with the man. But eventually he said: "So, sir. There is an appointment for you, as arranged. You will meet General Najib Jamal tomorrow. At eight in the morning, sir."

The man spoke to me over sips of the coffee but never looked directly at me. I know his eyes were black and that one manicured finger bore a fine gold ring with a blue stone. But there was no eye contact. Then, with an over vigorous shaking of hands, he left.

It was ten hours later that the man called again and escorted me to a black, official looking car parked outside. Sometime later, we arrived at the gate of what I took to be a military headquarters with guards and guns outside. We were ushered through and then I was asked to get out. The black car drove off leaving me standing in the heat of the hot morning sun, but I was immediately met by another man in army uniform and taken across a compound, past flat roofed buildings and through a door into a surprisingly plush office.

I can recall everything about that room.

The General, or whoever he was, because he had discarded the jacket part of his uniform and so the badges and ribbons were not apparent, was seated at an elaborate desk with a gilt framed picture of a young King Hussein behind. He was flanked by three younger, military men, who wore khaki uniforms and off set berets. And there was a fourth man in a crumpled, dark, grey suit and tie, looking not unlike myself but with a better developed beard, who looked distinctly English and also distinctly nervous.

The view of that office is imprinted on my mind.

Perhaps it has been embellished by time, but despite the briefest of minutes I spent there it is still very clear. There were other ornate frames bearing inscriptions – passages from the Koran drawn in gold and red and conveying messages probably of peace and praise and loyalty to Allah. But the room itself did not convey a message of peace, goodwill and loyalty.

"Mr Thomas. Please come with me."

I can hear the order even now. There were no pleasantries, hand-shakes or invitations to sit, because the General was already standing. I was taken through to another room. The others followed, including the Englishman who appeared reluctant but said nothing. Then came the invitation to sit. An outstretched hand pointed. The seat was hard, with no arms and I sat with my hot, sticky hands clasped in my lap. The General, if that is what he was, talked whilst the others stood around him in their smart uniforms and shiny boots.

The Englishman, for that is what he proved to be, was standing beside one of the soldiers furthest from the main group. It was then that I saw the handcuffs and heard the words that I still remember to this day.

"This is Mr Reynolds, Mr Thomas. Mr David Reynolds. Mr Reynolds has made a few mistakes. He talked too much to the Israelis, Mr Thomas. Far too much. About what is not important. What is important is that from today we would like you to become Mr Reynolds. It will be very useful for everyone. You can also be Mr Thomas. But for certain tasks related to the ongoing situation in the Middle East, of which you are well aware, it has been decided that it will make things, what shall we say, easier – no convenient – no, efficient yes, that is it, efficient. It will be more efficient and convenient if you are able, occasionally, to take over from Mr Reynolds, for the goodness of international relations – officially.

"What is more, Mr Thomas, our mutual friend Major Donaldson approves of this bold plan. That is also what we say – official. Ha."

The General finished by laughing a little as though embarrassed. I, myself, stood up, objected and asked for a better explanation. But the General just raised his hand. No more explanation was forthcoming. But the menace came all too quickly.

"Your wife – Mrs Sarah, isn't it, Mr Thomas – and your son. Robert, isn't it Mr Thomas? They must not know. Do you understand? No one must know. No one knows about this most important decision even now, except our mutual friend Major Donaldson. Major Donaldson knows. Major Donaldson knows everything, you see. Major Donaldson is a good friend to us. He has arranged everything. Even our young King does not know, Mr Thomas. "Some things are best dealt with in – how shall we say – in strictest confidence. It is best for everyone. Even your Queen and your own Prime Minister – no one knows. No one then has to deny knowledge about your legitimate business activities and you can run your other very useful assignments as Mr Reynolds whenever it is appropriate. It is safer for you. That's it – safer and better. It will be easier for you also. And it will be very useful for relations, you understand. You see how it is?"

I had not understood at all, but I had, suddenly, become David Reynolds and was about to become further enmeshed in a sticky web of intrigue that lasted years and where struggle meant even more entanglement. I had been caught like a fly in a spider's web although it felt more like barbed wire.

But things had then happened very suddenly.

The General nodded to the soldier who was fastened by handcuffs on his left hand to the silent Englishman. The man undid the bottom button of his khaki jacket with his free, right hand and a shiny black pistol was taken from a leather holster inside.

The real and mysterious Mr Reynolds who had, so far, said nothing, froze. He stared with wide eyes at me, his fellow Englishman and apparent replacement and the blood visibly drained from his face. But still he said nothing. The gun was raised to the side of the head of the real Reynolds. The poor man closed his eyes and seemed to clench his teeth. Then there was a bright flash and a loud bang as the man's head twisted violently over his neck. A red hole appeared above the ear and the body slumped to the ground with one arm still upright, attached to the uniformed assassin. Blood gushed from the hole onto the floor.

I admit I was in too much of a state of shock to say or do much after that, and what happened in the minutes after-wards is unclear.

I remember Reynolds' body being dragged away by the handcuff that held him to his killer and being pulled through a doorway to a darker room with what looked like a plain concrete floor. I saw the soldier who had shot him release the handcuff from his own wrist and the body of Reynolds slump to the floor. I remember the line of fresh blood that ran from just a few feet from me across the floor to the other room. I also remember the General taking me by the arm and me pushing him away. But what I said or shouted I cannot recall.

I then remember both my arms being held by the other soldiers as I tried to fight myself free, but it was pointless because my legs and body felt weak from what I had just seen.

But, as I was marched back out into the sunshine, I remember the General talking non-stop in short, incomplete sentences as though it was just a routine morning's work.

"Such a pity," he repeated probably ten times and there were other words that I think he spoke. "But that is the way of life."

"We must all obey our orders."

"At last, we now have a very fine replacement. This is good.

It is best for everyone. We must carry on this good work."

"This will be better now, you will see. Insh'allah. Things are clearer now."

"Major Donaldson, he will be pleased with this. I shall report immediately."

With that, and with me still in a state of shock but not wanting to instigate a fight when I knew I was totally outnumbered, I was bundled into the same black car I had arrived in and, in a daze, I was dropped off at my hotel.

I felt completely numb.

I went to my room, still in a state of shock and there I removed my glasses, washed my face and stood before the mirror looking at my new appearance. The fact was that, even to myself, I didn't look like Ollie Thomas anymore. I suppose it was the light beard and my hair which was plastered down with a parting on the wrong side. Then I went to lie on the bed, took out my Oliver Thomas passport and laid it next to the Reynolds one.

I picked up the phone to call the British Embassy, thinking they might help but then stopped myself because I was already afraid of what I had got involved in.

Then, in my mind, I went over and over the words spoken to me earlier.

"This is Mr Reynolds, Mr Thomas. Mr David Reynolds. Mr Reynolds has made a few mistakes. He talked too much . . . It will be very useful for everyone if you are able, occasionally, to take over from Mr Reynolds, for the goodness of international relations . . . What is more, Mr Thomas, our mutual friend Major Donaldson approves of this bold plan."

And then the threats: "Your wife – Mrs Sarah, isn't it, Mr Thomas – and your son. He is called Robert, isn't it Mr Thomas? They must not know. Do you understand? No one must know."

I remember thinking about Sarah back at home and looking over at my white shirts hanging in the wardrobe and remembering that Sarah had carefully washed and ironed them before I left home and I remember tears coming to my eyes.

What the hell had I become involved with?

I thought about phoning home but then thought better of it because of the threats.

"No one knows about this most important decision except our friend Major Donaldson . . . Major Donaldson is a good friend to us . . . He has arranged everything . . . Even our young King does not know, Mr Thomas . . . Some things are best dealt with in strictest confidence . . . Even your, Queen and your Prime Minister . . . No one knows . . . No one then has to deny knowledge . . . You can run your other assignments as Mr Reynolds whenever it is appropriate . . . It is safer and better . . . It will be easier for you also . . . It will be very useful for relations. You see how it is?"

Oh yes, I was really starting to see how it was and what I was involved in.

I stayed in that hotel room for more than a day before finally venturing out and going to the airport to catch my scheduled flight home. And all the time I thought I was being followed. On arrival at Heathrow, I still felt too upset and afraid to go home immediately so I stopped off at my Croydon office and fell onto my familiar seat behind my desk.

It was past five so Beatie had already left.

I had never ever phoned Donaldson in the past but I had a London phone number in my book that Jack had once given me "for emergencies" although I had no idea where this phone was. I dialed the number. But it rang and rang and I gave up.

I gave it ten minutes and tried again until someone eventually answered it. To this day, I do not know who it was, but it sounded like a young boy of around twelve years old. I asked to speak to Major Donaldson but there was a silence from the other end and whoever answered, hung up.

So, I tried Jack's number, again one that he had told me I could use in an absolute emergency and to my amazement, Jack answered. I remember blurting out to him what had happened as he listened mainly in silence broken by platitudes like "I see", "I really don't know," "that's really surprising" and "that must have been such a shock".

I then started to blow my top at Jack.

"Surprising? A bloody shock? That's a fucking understatement. What, the hell, is going on here?"

Jack fumbled with words in his usual pathetic style.

"Yes, it can be a very messy business at times," was about the only sentiment I could extract from him.

"Messy? So, what the fuck's Donaldson playing at? Where the hell is the fucking bastard, I want to know?"

"I understand he's in Scotland on business. He is expected back in a few days."

"On bloody business?" I shrieked, "I thought this was the bloody Foreign Office or civil service! Manned twenty-four hours, seven days a week, Christmas and New Year and never closed. I, myself, have even been phoned on a Christmas Eve.

And I was in bloody Teheran! But when it's me who needs something, they've bloody well gone out."

"Yes, what I mean is he is on Government business in Edinburgh as I understand."

It was useless. Jack's uncertainty about the whereabouts of Donaldson was clear. I went home.

That night was the first time I mentioned to Sarah about moving the business abroad and starting again. I couldn't bring myself to tell her why but I didn't get a chance anyway.

"But I was about to break the good news to you, dear.

Robert and Anne are getting married soon."

"Are they?" I said, shocked by more fresh news. "No-one told me."

"No dear, you've been away a lot. But we can't possibly just pack up and move. Not now and, anyway, we'd need to talk about it a lot more."

And that was it for three days until I eventually got Jack to fix it for me to meet Donaldson at the Regent Street office. Beatie clearly knew something had happened but, as usual, after just one question to ask if I was not feeling well, she was all for trying to focus on the business.

"Mr Farouk telephoned from Paris, Mr Thomas. He was anxious to meet you. I told him you were away so he said he'd phone again when he's next over."

"We've had the results of the Tunisian tender we quoted for. We didn't win it, I'm afraid."

"The Letter of Credit came in from Kenya, Mr Thomas, but the expiry date is so short I don't think there's any time left. Shall we ask for an extension?"

"Many of the bottles of hospital disinfectant we shipped to Syria were broken on arrival and the customer rejected it. There is a dispute now on whose insurance it is covered by. What do you think, Mr Thomas?"

Clearly there was not much good news, but frankly I couldn't have cared a toss about the business at the time. I was far too worried about how to deal with my other problems and my mind was on what to do about Donaldson.

Naturally Jack was also present when we met in Regent Street. Jack was the most unlikely person to intervene if it came to a physical fight but Donaldson knew that Jack's presence meant he could control things to his own advantage. I was in a rage even before I got to his office.

"What the fuck is this, Major? What the hell is going on? Is this the way the Government treats its agents? Who sanctioned it? You? Who the hell was this poor guy Reynolds whom I'm supposed to impersonate? Is this just one big game? Does her Majesty's Government endorse assassination in the name of security and intelligence? And what are these threats to my family? I assume you know about this?"

I went on and on as Donaldson sat there behind his desk, picking his yellow teeth with the corner of an empty packet of Craven A and scratching his head as though I was boring him.

Jack watched, standing in the corner by the door.

Even then I was behaving as though I still believed Donaldson was perhaps just another pawn in some sort of high-level game played out by politicians and senior Civil Servants and that this was just the smelly downwind side of anything to do with International Intelligence. I still believed that he had his own bosses lurking somewhere in Whitehall.

"You knew about this before I went to Amman, didn't you, you bastard? What more do they want from me? And what if I don't go along with it? What will happen then? What are you going to do, Major? Shoot me? Shoot my family? Go to fucking hell!"

Donaldson still sat there.

"You can all go to fucking hell! I'm finished," I repeated and turned to go to the door.

But there was a scraping sound behind me as Donaldson pushed his chair back.

I heard a hissing sound and saw Jack visibly jump from where he was standing.

"If you walk your fucking stupid arse out of here I warn you, Ollie Thomas, you're bloody finished."

I turned.

Donaldson was standing now, his hands resting on the bare desk, his face having turned puce. A strand of greying hair had fallen across his forehead and a blob of white spit shone on his fat lower lip.

"You're in this shit up to your fucking neck," he scowled.

"Sit down!"

"Fuck you," I said and turned and put my hand on the door knob. It didn't turn. I rattled it. I shook it. It was locked.

"Sit the fuck down!" Donaldson roared and sat down himself but his face was still bright red.

Jack cowered close to me and I looked at him. He seemed to nod at me.

"Sit down," Donaldson ordered again.

I still stood.

I looked at Jack again. His hand was now out towards me, palm down, as though trying to make me relax.

"As I said, you're in some bloody big shit, Ollie," Donaldson said, slightly more quietly, "But stop a minute and think, you stupid bastard. Yes, I knew something about Amman. After all, we fixed your nice new passport. Fact is Reynolds made some mistakes. He went native so to speak. But we still trust you, Ollie. Otherwise you might well have met the same fate by now. Someone else might be carrying an Ollie Thomas passport today."

He stopped, perhaps waiting for that sinister message to sink in. "Trust me?" I shouted. "Since when has trust had any place in all this fucking crap?"

"We've trusted you for several years, Ollie. You're a good agent. Useful. Valuable. Very clever in your own way. Your big advantage is your business, Ollie. Reynolds was an employee. On the books, so to speak. You're more of a freelance. Not so easy to spot. Look on it as an opportunity. Carry on. Don't be so bloody nervous. If it all turns out you never know what other opportunities might crop up."

I stared at him, hardly believing what I was hearing.

I heard Jack coming across as though he, himself, was already more relaxed. It was as though Donaldson had just convinced him by such a brilliant acting performance that he was certain that I would also be totally convinced and that all my concerns would be completely deflated.

"Opportunities," I heard Jack say quietly and he nodded pathetically.

Donaldson glanced at him out of the corner of his eye.

I will remember this single word from Jack Woodward for the rest of my life, not for the support or encouragement he was offering but as an example of the sort of person Jack was. He was an office boy and a yes man who ran errands and who behaved, as I have often imagined him to be, like some sort of creep.

I suspect he was in the quick sands as well but he was such a creep that he could live with it.

But echoes from the pistol that shot Reynolds have ricocheted around my own skull for years and I have lived with the implications of that shooting ever since, as you will see.

I can barely remember what happened immediately after that argument with Donaldson but, suffice it to say, I knew I had become totally enmeshed. To struggle at that stage was pointless and to explain to Sarah was impossible. I had to face this alone. But I left determined that one day, somehow, I would get my revenge.

JACK WOODWARD

The drinking sessions leading to my nightmares usually start in a fairly civilised manner. Sometimes I start off thinking about people from the past while drinking a cup of tea and munching on a plate of toast and Marmite. But then I progress to the whisky as I've given a lot of thought of late to Jack Woodward.

The last time I saw him was twenty-five years ago, in London at the Cumberland Hotel on Marble Arch. Somehow, he had found out about our newly acquired Gloucester address and I received a letter with a phone number and a note suggesting a meeting. I wasn't at all keen on the idea and even considered writing "moved away" on the envelope and sticking it back in the post but I mentioned to Sarah that an old friend wanted to meet up and she suggested I go.

"It's nice to meet old friends, dear. You mustn't lose touch." I didn't mention it was Jack or explain our connection. I think if she had known more, she may not have been so encouraging. But, anyway, I took the train up and we met.

It hadn't been so long since we last met but he looked so much older and arrived propped up on a stick. I remember him waving it. He was also nervously rubbing his chin as usual – a man who had spent his entire career under the control of others and completely out of his depth. He also smelt, strangely, of cigarettes but never seemed to smoke.

Perhaps he lived with a smoker. I sometimes wondered about that but I never knew anything about Jack's private life.

Had Donaldson been there it would have been pints of beer, but when Jack was alone it was gins and tonic as though he had a different side that he didn't like showing to Donaldson.

There had also been crowds of people in the hotel with some sort of conference going and it was clearly an unsuitable meeting place, but Jack and I found a corner. Looking back, I remember that last meeting because of what Jack seemed to be trying to ask me amidst the surrounding chaos of babbling conversation, chinking glasses, lemon slices and cherries on sticks. But it was ideal territory for Jack who preferred the anonymity that crowds provided.

Jack was probably nervous about meeting me. After all, he had witnessed some pretty fierce arguments between Donaldson and me that had almost ended in murder. So, I suppose, with the crowds around him, he felt safer if I should suddenly turn on him for being party to everything Donaldson had done.

But I think Jack was just as much in the shit as me and so I behaved impeccably.

We reminisced a little although it was too noisy for anything detailed.

We reminisced about Cairo because Jack liked Egypt and the sights, sounds and smells of Egypt are still as clear in my own mind as they were fifty years ago, when I first visited.

I was then in my thirties, lean, tanned and healthy, energetic and needing the excitement. It was a place, not of cars as now, but of thin, brown, underfed horses pulling carts with colourful harnesses and of camels tethered in rows. I can still see the tall palms on their slender trunks and feel the hot sun from the endless, cloudless, blue sky. I would walk down dark, shadowy alleyways with shady traders selling everything from frightened, bleating sheep and goats to gold, perfume and unseen women and watch value being meticulously added to raw Egyptian cotton by men sitting, turning the handles of black and gold Singer sewing machines and making anything to measure. I can still see the busy River Nile with snowy white sails drifting at less than walking pace in the windless heat. The dusty, flat roofed buildings, the colour of the encroaching desert as though they were deliberately camouflaged. From the air, they were often just that – blocks of stones, the same colour as the Pyramids but with dubious, military functions.

It had been Jack who had first asked me if I was interested in supplementing what little income I was then drawing from Thomas

Import Export Ltd. Looking back, I realise it was Donaldson who had made Jack put the proposal and they knew all along what bait they needed to catch their fish.

Being fresh out of the air force and with the war still on everyone's minds, doing something more for King or Queen and Country was the only reason I needed at the time.

Later on, of course, I thought of myself as a fish caught on a line. I was like a small fish in a big pond tempted by a thin worm called patriotism and held in place by a sharp but invisible hook called industrial espionage or plain, old fashioned spying. It was naïve and stupid but utterly typical of me at that time.

I admit to still being an unusual mixture of a reliable, faithful little puppy and a Rottweiler with a mean streak. I also know I'm also a bit of a conniving bastard myself especially if I detect the slightest reason to be a bit impatient of others as you will discover. I suppose the older I got the bigger the conniving swine I became but it was the company I was keeping, you see.

Jack and I continued during lunch in the grill but with silences that grew longer and longer. Jack did enquire about Sarah, if I recall, but, in the way of things, I would not have gone overboard with descriptions of our domestic life.

"Well, thank you", that would have been my response, because she was – at that time.

Jack had never met Sarah so to him she was just a name. But then he said something else. "So, you're not moving abroad then, Ollie?" It was unusual and far too personal for Jack.

"No," I replied. "Sarah prefers England."

Sarah didn't even have a passport whilst I once ran with four different ones at the same time. Sarah and I did get as far as the Isle of Wight ferry once but she hated the thought of flying anywhere.

"She gave no other reason, Ollie?" Jack was pressing me.

"She just feels safer in England I think."

"Did she say that?" Jack persisted. "I can understand the need for feeling safe. The tentacles of the past can sometimes reach a long way, Ollie."

As usual I failed to pick up the signs. Looking back and watching the nightmares from behind closed eyes, I now read far more into Jack's comments. He was prying. He was checking. He was trying to find out if I had plans to move away or disappear. So, had he been sent to the Cumberland Hotel? Did his invitation to meet come from the kind heart of a past work colleague or was he there because he was a trained poodle and a yes man who was still being hung on a string?

Twenty-five years is what I needed to realize what was going on under my nose.

In my ignorance of what was motivating Jack, I laughed because I did not understand why he was asking. "Ah well. You know women, Jack. They like their home comforts."

But did Jack know women? Probably not. I assumed he was single because he never mentioned anything about a family. In those days one was left to think that someone like that might have other tendencies but if so, it was not a subject for polite conversation. Looking back, I wonder if Jack was being blackmailed because of illegal practices. It seems highly likely.

But Jack then summed up our brief conversation about family matters. "Knows where she's better off then, Ollie." Perhaps Jack had got the answer he wanted by saying it himself.

Then it was back to current affairs. Margaret Thatcher had just come to power and was talking to Mikhail Gorbachev. But Donaldson was never mentioned. Not even by reference to D.

THE VOICE INSIDE

I **only have a few friends who are still alive** but one of them lives somewhere in my sub conscience.

Perhaps I've become a sort of psychopath with a dual personality and it's just another symptom of Thomas's Disease. Whether it is a different person or just a carbon copy of me I am not sure but sometimes I talk to him as a separate entity. At other times I consult him as if he is my doctor or psychiatrist.

I admit to spending an inordinate amount of time considering my physical and mental health, although I suppose that's natural for someone of my age who wonders whether he'll wake up next morning. Perhaps this explains the short naps of the elderly in that they wake up regularly in order to check that they are still alive.

The phenomenon of the other personality is especially noticeable when I doze off after if I've had a drop too much. Whatever the cause, the conversations with him are highly stimulating and I feel I need to explain in order for you to understand my mental state and my reasons for writing this.

Spending far too much time sitting in the chair by Sarah's log effect gas fire with a glass of Bell's, or even a bottle, in my hand is not a good start. But after a glass, or two, I often find myself talking aloud.

I often talk about Sarah, although if she had been sat opposite me instead of upstairs, she would have been shocked at my dishevelled appearance with the wet stains of whisky around my crotch. But the drinking is really a distraction.

If I am giving an impression of a long-term drunken layabout or an uncaring husband who beats his wife, then the truth is quite the opposite. In the same way that I tolerated Donaldson for so long, I also went along with Sarah's wishes even though they have often led to me sometimes feeling depressed and unfulfilled in my retirement.

Sarah seemed content with the quiet backwater life in Gloucester. I didn't want to retire to there. My plan was to move somewhere interesting like South Africa or South-East Asia, but Sarah told me so in no uncertain terms that she saw no need to move. She cried about it once when I pushed the subject too far.

"Please, dear. Stop it. I don't want to go anywhere. Robert and Anne can come without any problems. It's fine here. I like it. I feel safe here. We're both safe here. Please don't keep on."

Perhaps Jack had known Sarah better than me when he said: "She knew where she was better off then, Ollie."

In my efforts, not to worry Sarah with my own problems, I failed to realize that she had worries of her own and that they were mostly caused by me and what I was doing. Hindsight is a terrible thing and can be a trigger for all sorts of nightmares.

Sarah liked our domestic life the way it was.

In days gone by she would sit at home, reading, sewing, listening to the radio or watching television whilst waiting for me to return from my travels. She grew accustomed to it I suppose and felt comfortable and at ease with the familiarity. She carried none of life's baggage that had weighed me down with all its hypocrisy, stress and worry. She liked a simple life and sought no great adventures. I was the opposite. I found suburban England monotonous and grey. I still do. Even high summer here cannot be guaranteed to produce reliable sun. And even when it shines it seems to cast dark shadows on brick and concrete.

What fun is there in that? There is no colour here. It is so bland and so depressing.

Summers here are far too short. How much more pleasant and enjoyable it would have been to spend nine months in sunshine and return here for the summer. Despite Sarah's problems with

Croydon, I felt we'd moved from Brick View, Croydon to Brick View, Gloucester. She didn't like that joke.

Croydon, in the early days had already become a multi-coloured, multicultural society and Gloucester is catching up. Parts of Gloucester have become like the back streets of Karachi, Dacca or Trinidad with local stores selling halal meat, frozen Bangladeshi fish, Pakistani vegetables and herbs and shelves stacked high with tins of bamboo shoots, tamarind, green leaves preserved in brine and half fermented gourami fish. It has, in some respects, become a more varied and interesting place to live, but it is the drab English way of life that I dislike and the backward steps the country seems to be making in so many other respects.

I am a very long way from being what is, these days, called racist, though. Some of my best friends have been Arabs, Africans and others from widely different cultures and I miss them. I miss them badly. How much better to sit drinking Metaxa after dinner with my old friend Alex in Athens or sharing a bottle of icy arak with Farouk in Baalbeck or sharing just a bottle of Black Label with George in Ghana.

These days, I think I prefer the flair, the imagination and the dynamism of those our politicians have decided, in their bizarre attempts to instil tolerance, we call minorities. Politicians only breed intolerance with their stuffy attempts to address the matter. Every official form I see these days seems to require me to identify my colour or my racial origins. Of what good is that? Surely, it's racist just to ask the question. When the census forms come around, I usually put Bedouin in the "other" box under ethnic origin but nobody notices.

I decided, long ago, that it was the natives of Britain who have changed over the last fifty years. Other than a brief phase in the sixties, where now is the flair and style? Where is the imagination? Where is the energy? Where is the sensible but radical thought and determination to change the world for the better?

I am probably just a cynical old man but the young seem to have been de-politicized by excess and too much wealth. They have become less inspired and less adventurous because they have too much.

They go on so-called gap years to Bangkok or Bali after three years learning golf management or public administration at University. They go with their credit cards, mobile phones and health insurance, with their hair styled and gelled, their teeth looking like rows of piano keys and dressed like film stars. And they send email messages to Mum and Dad back home, who like to show they fret about them even though they are probably in the midst of a messy divorce anyway. And even when they have an adventure, such as getting lost for a couple of days in some tame woods, somewhere, the world's press or TV seem to descend on the area in droves to report it.

That is not adventure. To die in some remote spot with your body discovered a century later is the way to leave your mark because it leaves behind a mystery.

But neither is there a patriotic determination to strive because it is removed from their sense of purpose by excessive wealth and social security. Society has changed. It has been replaced by one in which entitlements supersede responsibilities. It has been replaced by a society that lives risk-free knowing it can depend on a safety net of social security.

This is the type of thing that goes on in my mind even during rational, sober moments. But during the more intoxicated times I can wake up thrashing around in the chair by Sarah's gas fire to find myself groaning aloud in anger and frustration about the way of the world or its injustices. I have become a cynical, depressed, old man who gets just as mad about my own past life as I do about the current lives of others but I didn't used to be like that.

It is not a sign of good, mental health. So, is it another characteristic of Thomas's Disease or of old age in general?

The psychiatrist living in my head tells me I need to do something before it's all too late. He asks me if I care if I die in the process. And I say no because frankly I couldn't care less.

But after all this dreaming, drinking, dozing and mental l turmoil, I wake up. But then I feel uncomfortable, sweaty, angry and frustrated and I stink of stale whisky.

65

So, I often have a quick glance around the untidy clutter of the sitting room where I half expect to see three bloody porcelain flying ducks on the wall and have another swig, perhaps direct from the bottle.

I then might relieve myself with a blast of wind direct from my arse and carry on where I'd just left off. But then the nightmares about Donaldson start all over again.

But there are still one or two things I like. Things I can only do when sober. One of them is my car.

I have owned several in my time and they always provided a small means of escape from the depressing feeling of being housebound whenever I returned from overseas. My itchy feet are legendary.

Even Sarah enjoyed drives into the countryside and odd weekends away when I first retired and we moved to suburban, bloody Gloucester. But it was only ever temporary, short-lived relief. She would complain about the price of petrol and I would go into the garage and talk to the car and say things like, "Oh well, old girl, perhaps we'll go out next week."

But I used to think of those occasional country drives with Sarah like a vase of fresh flowers. You arrange them so prettily in a vase and enjoy them briefly but they die so quickly. And what is left? The empty vase again. I thought, too, that in later years when age caught up with both of us that even the car would have to be garaged for good or, worse, sold. I'm glad it wasn't sold for when the feeling takes me or I feel particularly morose, I have been known to take the car out.

The Jaguar is getting on a bit now – twenty-five years old, in fact, but I still tinker with it, as Sarah used to say. The phone rang once whilst I was in the garage and I heard her say: "He's tinkering with that infernal car of his again."

But I check it, charge the battery up, switch it on, rev it up and give it a polish. The smell of leather seems to have disappeared over time but perhaps that's my sense of smell. It's still in good nick. One hundred and sixty thousand miles on the clock and it purrs like a kitten with its V6 engine.

I check the oil and often sit in it, even when I myself am also well oiled. One night recently I was so pissed that, even though it was three in the morning, I sat in it and looked at myself in the mirror. I turned the ignition key and, of course, it fired immediately and ticked away like a Singer sewing machine. Then I opened the garage door, reversed it out and walked around it and looked at it in the street light. A few nights later, I drove off in it and, before I knew it, I was in Stroud. I drove out on the Painswick Road as I hadn't been there for months. It was eerily quiet, but a lovely clear night with a bright moon. I stopped and went to look over a gate into a field and watched a fox in the moonlight. I was tempted to drive out towards Cirencester and on and on and on. But I suddenly thought about Sarah and drove home. But Sarah had barely moved since I left her.

I slept like a log that night. It was extremely therapeutic.

But, more often than not, because I didn't like leaving Sarah, I would sit there getting pissed and listening to the only sound I could detect – the blood flowing through my fucking ears.

Blood running through your ears seems to hiss like a river in a meadow. You can hear it bubbling over the pebbles and rocks, like the babbling brooks of old poetry, though, I used to think that maybe the description was better suited to the babbling I did with myself.

I am a babbling Thomas – a quite distinct species to the other type, the doubting Thomas.

Some days I spend hours listening to my ears. Sometimes I moved or fidgeted a little to create another sound but mostly it is because the confounded chair has become so uncomfortable.

Time passes, minute by minute and I seem to descend into a state in which it is hard to imagine another world outside the sitting room window. And all that for a man who travelled the world for fifty years and wished he still did.

Instead I would spend hours trying to imagine those outside in the darkness who were perhaps far less fortunate even than myself. I would imagine the homeless, the sick, those working to keep the wheels of industry turning and those who keep the gas flowing in the pipe that leads to Sarah's log effect gas fire.

I envied them because they were still contributing something and I wasn't.

But after Sarah died, I decided there was still time left for me to do something.

There was a big piece of unfinished business to deal with.

ASSIGNMENTS

"**M**oatassim will meet you at the airport in Luxor. Leave the package with him and make your own way back to Cairo. Moatassim's one of our best chaps – Sudanese fellow."

Those were the sort of instructions I continued to be given in the Feathers.

Most of the time, everything went as smooth as silk although my dislike for and suspicions about Donaldson grew more and more intense. But I was too busy to sit and decide what to do about it.

That first meeting with Moatassim was the start of a good friendship and we met several times over a period of two or three years with talks about starting a joint business venture some time. But it never happened. Moatassim was a bright and intelligent Sudanese Moslem with deep tribal scars on his cheeks, but with a strange and touching desire to be British, white and Christian and play cricket for England.

"I like to be the stump; Mr Oliver and I can make very good leg spinning."

I remember Moatassim's smiling face even now but like other similar friends, Moatassim just disappeared – suddenly. Perhaps he went back to Khartoum. Perhaps he went to Saudi Arabia. Perhaps, more likely, he fell foul of others less enchanted with Western customs.

But during the years after I had acquired the additional identity of David Reynolds, I rapidly learned that my particular style and approach seemed to offer all sorts of opportunities. I was actually very good at it and admit that it was all quite interesting although sometimes a little risky. But I often sought out situations well before they were likely to find me. I become very adept at it.

You see, I was still an entrepreneur at heart and quick to see an opportunity. The problem was the better I got at it the more the assignments I was given. At one point they were coming so thick and fast that they were dominating my life to the detriment of my business. As soon as I arrived back from one overseas trip, Jack would be on the phone with another request for a meeting at the Feathers.

By then, Beatie had become very familiar with Jack's calls although she still showed signs of nerves on the odd occasion that Donaldson himself phoned.

"Mr Woodward for you, Mr Thomas."

"Thank you, Beatie," I would say.

And Jack, never long in getting to the point he had phoned for, would say things like: "Fancy a look at some good quality figs in Algeria, Oliver? Catch up with your friend with the parrot?"

Or it might be: "How about trying to sell a few of your tractor spares in Nigeria, Ollie? We've got a good contact with a local chief, and anyway, the Department wants someone to pop up to Kano and then down to Port Harcourt on an assignment. Bit of local trouble with the natives I hear."

Or: "We've had a notice about a commercial opportunity for lorry tyres in Damascus, Ollie. Any interest? For the army, I gather. Might be a few other bits and pieces of interest and a few leads – commercial and otherwise, if you get my gist, once you get there. Build on your connections. What do you think?"

Or: "There's some medical equipment needed in Baghdad, Ollie. X-ray equipment and the like, but with a few alternative openings for a vivid imagination like yours. You should get out there. Pick up the tender documents. Meet your old friend the General while you're there, Ollie."

Some of the earlier calls offered genuine business opportunities but the longer it went on the more concerned I became for the effect on my business. And Donaldson would always remind me about the photographs he held or what had happened to Reynolds.

"Best to fly out before Friday, Ollie. Assad needs everything in Beirut by Friday midday prayers latest otherwise we're all in the shit again – you especially. No need to go into the city of course."

It was the Lebanese civil war and few people were mad enough to go anywhere near the country. But I did. There was still business to be found and I was a businessman with things to sell. If Beirut was off limits, I could always get a taxi from Amman up to the border and doing things from Cyprus was another option.

That was my life at that time. Does it sound like fun to you?

"Keep your fucking head down, Ollie. Ha, ha. But don't even think about changing sides and working for the competition. The consequences can be very, very, nasty for you, your family....... Don't get caught out, Ollie? Ha, ha."

I was always Ollie this and Ollie that when Donaldson wanted something for himself. Most people called me Oliver. Or Mr Thomas. Or David Reynolds.

Sarah called me Oliver, but only when she was serious.

She called me "my husband" if she was talking about me to friends. She would call me "Sir", when she was mocking my seriousness. She would call me "sweetheart" sometimes when she felt like it and "Mr Thomas" when she was joking. But it was "dear" most of the time.

"Go down, now, dear. I'm all right. No need to fret yourself. It's not too bad, today."

I loved her calling me "dear". When addressed by others as "dear", the word seems to acquire a different meaning. It seems flippant, derisory and sometimes insulting. I feel as though the word has been stolen from the only person who knows what it means and, so, is the only person who is allowed to use it.

I usually call her "my love", because that is what she was.

I called Donaldson a bastard because that's what he was and it was a fair and accurate description of him. He would laugh. Later, I started calling him a crook but, by then, we had stopped laughing altogether.

Jack called me Ollie because Donaldson did and because Jack was a company man who obeyed orders and kowtowed to the corporate view. Except, of course, it wasn't a corporation but linked to British Intelligence. Donaldson was the crook who ran the Mafia side of MI6. That much I slowly grew to realize although it took me far too long to fathom it all out and by then, I'd become so firmly entangled in it, it was difficult to cut free.

That's when I became a conniving bastard. It was a sort of means to an end.

OPERATION CHRYSALIS

"**N**ever mention retirement to your wife unless you've got enough money to live on."

Those were my wise words to someone in a bar somewhere, forty years ago. But it wasn't just the money and it wasn't just Donaldson. Other people also had long arms.

When Gadaffi came to power and was at the peak of his international infamy. I was known in many Libyan circles as David Reynolds. I would fly out of the UK as Reynolds and enter Libya, Egypt, Jordan, Syria, Iraq or Iran as Reynolds.

And on my return home I would still be Reynolds, a businessman according to my passport and business card and operating, for the purposes of security from a Post Office Box number in Victoria, close to the station. It was something I had not got around to mentioning to either Sarah or Beatie. I suppose this is a good example of duplicity but I was merely trying to make the most of a difficult situation. I didn't want to be beaten.

But I would be Oliver Thomas if I went to Israel, parts of Western Europe or Africa.

Thomas Import Export Ltd was the business I ran from the Croydon office, a legitimate business with interests in thirty odd countries – more if I had had the time. The turnover was never as much as I wanted or, indeed planned, but this was mostly due to the fact that I really wasn't able to devote enough time to it.

Thomas Import Export was always on the lookout for opportunities, whatever they were.

I would even deal in certain types of military hardware if an opportunity arose which was why I kept the POB address in Victoria. But don't misunderstand me. This was very small-scale arms trading, things that came my way and oiled the wheels of relationship building. And, anyway, the main business needed the revenue.

For whatever reason – duplicity or connivance or the desire to provide my wife and family with what I felt they deserved - my life had become a bucket of worms and I now want to explain my connections with Malta and Libya as an example of how a bucket of worms became a snake pit and how I began to gather evidence against Donaldson.

I was becoming frightened for myself and my family. Jobs for Donaldson were increasing. The starting point for the Malta and Libya episode was, as usual, a phone call from Jack to the office where Beatie took the call.

"Mr Woodward called, a while ago, Mr Thomas. Would you meet him tonight, at the usual place?"

That meeting, as always in the Feathers, led to me flying out to Athens as David Reynolds to pick up a package at a café in Piraeus to take to Cairo. It was easy, routine work and a few days later I was in Dokki where I met up with a man from the American Embassy. Despite his obvious Middle Eastern appearance, the man appeared to be an American national and I guessed he worked for American Intelligence.

But, with no questions asked, I handed over the package as instructed at the hotel bar and, job done, flew first to Benghazi being closest and then on to Tripoli on some Thomas Import Export business.

But it was something the American and I had chatted about – plane hijackings and terrorism – that I was to be reminded of over the next few days.

This was also the time of fighting and bombings in Northern Ireland and the time when Gadaffi and Sadat were busy talking big ideas designed to put the fear into the West and create Arab unity where none existed.

I met Gadaffi twice.

It was always very brief and unplanned and he would have known me as David Reynolds. Looking back, I think Gadaffi had been briefed that I was some sort of agent for an anti-British, anti-American establishment. I was, of course, the complete opposite but on both occasions, the Colonel had wandered into the tent where I was meeting some of his entourage. We hardly spoke more than five words and I did not need an interpreter.

You may wonder how I was able to get so close, but I kept trade secrets up my sleeve. I knew where someone might go to buy a few North Korean torpedoes or a few tons of German fertilizer or even French antibiotics.

I had honed a habit of dropping words and phrases into conversations like scattering wild seeds in a garden. I'd forget about it for a while but be astonished to find when I returned, weeks or months later, that a few seedlings had sprung up and someone was wanting advice on how to make them produce a few flowers and seeds of their own.

I was, I discovered, running a rather specialized, free consultancy. I never bought and sold anything obnoxious myself, of course, but I sufficiently well-connected I could have if I wished. This intelligence was worth a huge fortune if I had been willing to sell it and as I write this, I am puzzled by my own behaviour. It is the subject of much of my nocturnal self-psychoanalysis.

Should I be condemned for failing to exploit the value of what I knew for my own and my family's benefit? Is it a punishable offence to admit to and write about it now? Or does the fact that I'm even mentioning it suggest that I'm really a soft bellied businessman with a social conscience?

I dreamed once that I was selling butchers' knives to a parish priest but the priest suddenly transformed himself into a wide-eyed fellow with red horns, a khaki uniform and rows of medals. Does that show that I was born with a certain morality that meant I'd never be truly successful in business?

My mother saw the dilemma when I was nine but her advice probably killed off any chance, I had to make big money. "Don't listen to that nasty boy, Oliver."

At arm's length, this particular nasty boy in his uniform and row of medals seemed totally mad but strangely likeable. Gadaffi mostly lived in a large Bedouin tent similar to what you imagine King Arthur might have lived in with his Knights during country pursuits around Wessex.

Not only was the man himself often to be seen bedecked with exotic caps, multi-coloured ribbons and golden buttons but the tent itself was hung with trinkets and laid out with plush carpets and cushions that covered the packed sand floor.

On the first occasion, I met him he gave me just the quickest eye to eye contact before grunting and disappearing once more as though he knew there was an Englishman in the tent and wanted to have a quick peek. As he wandered in pushing the tent entrance to one side everyone, myself included, got up from our cross-legged positions on the carpet and bowed our heads.

The second time, six months later, after word had gone around that I was back, he did more than grunt. In he came and, as before, we all stood up and went silent. It was probably a sign of fear.

Then he raised his hand and wandered over towards me and I briefly thought my time was up.

If you've ever seen a recent photograph, you will know that he has a frightening smile that produces a deep crack in his face like an over-baked double split loaf. This feature was apparent even when he was much younger.

I nodded, tried to smile and held out my hand in my British way. But he did not take it. Instead, he stopped just beyond hand shaking distance and stared at me for a few seconds, his facial cracks disappearing somewhere in an instant. Then he spoke.

Strangely, as I thought then, he asked me, in Arabic of course, if I liked Irish people.

Quick as a flash I said, "Yes, but I trust Moslems more than Catholics, Sir."

It was utter bullshit as I have no preference, either way, and it was a very brief response spoken in my very best basic, slow Arabic.

But I had made a point and Gadaffi smiled again amongst his craggy features. He did not look at me again, or reply, but just nodded and sauntered out of the tent leaving me with Mohammed Saleh and the others.

We remained standing after he had left and they muttered things amongst themselves. Then they all came over to shake my hand once more and to pat their chests with their hands. I knew I had done rather well. My trust ratings rose.

But that is how I excelled. I excelled at bullshitting. Colonel Muammar Gadaffi would have been a useful case study for psychiatric analysis of the sort I practice on myself when under the influence of Mr Bell although I doubt whether he'd be such a compliant patient as I am with myself. Neither would Gadaffi have appreciated the consultant's final diagnosis so I would advise any psychiatrist not to hang around to wait for his fee.

But Gadaffi's Irish question had intrigued me and when I later left to return to Benghazi I thought deep and hard about it. At that time, Gadaffi was trying to cobble together some sort of union with Syria and his much bigger neighbour to the east. It was uncertain how genuinely interested Sadat really was. Most likely, he regarded Gadaffi as a nut case but that is only my own opinion.

The next day I met up with a man called Farid, with whom I had become very friendly over the months. We met in the foyer at the Omar Khayam Hotel in Benghazi, drank some bitter sodas and agreed to talk more over lunch.

Now, in those days, lunch or dinner at the Omar Khayam, invariably started with sheep's brains and I have dreamed about Omar Khayam lunches many times over the years.

I once suggested to Sarah's doctor that he try eating sheep's brains. I told him I thought it was his duty to eat them as part of his right of passage into the medical profession and that he might have found it educational to dissect them on his plate or put them under a microscope to check for scrapie before devouring them.

Sometimes, when brains were in short supply, the Omar Khayam would serve sheep's eyes but I much preferred brains, especially if I was hungry as there is so much more goodness in them – not much taste but far more nutritional value.

I have wondered if the onset of Thomas's Disease can be traced back to the past consumption of Libyan sheep brains, although my diet was so varied at times that the disease could probably be linked to many other meals. After all, I have eaten sheep's brains in Iran as well, but food hygiene in Tehran was not as good as in Benghazi. In Tehran I had to call the waiter over to point out that a cockroach had got its feet stuck in my brain although it had clearly managed to wriggle free having left one of its legs behind. But I digress.

As Farid and I ate I was wondering how to use him. Perhaps you can add exploitative to the growing list of my faults but my main reason for meeting him was his closeness to Gadaffi. In reality, of course, Farid hated Gadaffi as much as I hated Donaldson but that was what made him so useful.

Farid told me he had been asked to do a job that looked as though it might be linked to activity of the sordid type that Gadaffi specialized in but I didn't delve because I don't think Farid knew what it was either. But, as the job required him to make a quick trip to Malta, we arranged to meet there in a few days for another chat.

After lunch I took the last flight of the day to Tripoli, stayed overnight in the Libya Palace Hotel and, next morning, I was in Malta.

Now, bear in mind, no-one back home, least of all Donaldson, Beatie or Sarah knew where I was and I didn't bother trying to telephone anyone as it was nigh on impossible getting phone calls out. What to say was often a dilemma. Should I have said that I had just met Colonel Gadaffi and was now enjoying a few days in the Maltese sun? Should I explain my meeting in Cairo with someone from the CIA?

If I'd phoned Sarah to tell her where I was it would have meant nothing at all to her and all I might have got in return would be a lengthy description of the poor quality of Brussels sprouts to be found in the Co-op.

So, I spent two day walking the dusty streets of Valletta and drinking coffee and whisky in bars. But I wasn't bored as I will explain.

Britain and Malta were not on good terms at the time and much of it was related to Gadaffi's influence just a stone's throw away across the water. Newspaper headlines were full of it and, one morning, as I waited for Farid to turn up I bought an English language newspaper to catch up on developments and, always liking to soak up the local atmosphere, I sauntered into a cafe along the promenade in Sliema and sat outside in the sun reading my paper.

Malta was one of those places I had always wanted to take Sarah.

It would have been ideal spot to set up shop and build my North African business. It's a sunny paradise although you can almost throw a pebble from the beach on one side of the island to a beach on the opposite side. The Maltese are good people and remind me of Greeks for some reason, though it's probably the way the old men gather to sip their coffee and chat. So, there I was, soaking up the warm morning sun among a group of such elderly Maltese men seated at adjacent tables.

But behind them were three others with Northern Irish accents. Their words, although quietly spoken, wafted over to me in the still air and above the sound of chinking cups and saucers, seagulls and the rustling sound of my newspaper. It was as though the soft Belfast tones were amplified by the morning air and a surrounding, stone wall. The group was huddled together, their cigarette smoke floating towards me. The accents were heavy but, hiding behind my newspaper, I found no difficulty in picking up odd words.

And it was the name Cahill that made me look up from my newspaper and glance innocently towards the Mediterranean.

I ordered another coffee using just three simple words of Maltese so that the Irishmen were not distracted by an English accent.

And, before I knew it, I was on the spot ready to pursue yet another job for Queen and Country, which, to my continued personal regret would prove once more to Donaldson the unique talents of the little fish he had netted so many years before.

By then Donaldson was already building his own business and, with my naivety running high, I fell – hook, line and sinker.

"Right place at the right time, dear fellow! Don't know how you do it, old man." That's how that the bastard had put it. But what should I have done? Shrugged and walked away?

Perhaps I should have left my newspaper lying on the table, walked all the way back to Valetta and got the next flight home. But it was not my style to stifle inquisitiveness and what I did next only went to further substantiate the snippets of information that Farid brought with him later and add to all the other bits of tittle tattle that had come my way.

I stayed there, sitting in the morning sun, later sliding my chair back a little into the shade partly because it was getting hotter by the minute and partly because I needed to retain my anonymity. I even picked up the Maltese language paper lying on the table next to me to appear to be enthralled by Dom Mintoff's latest protestations. Regular doses of hot sun had given me a permanent tan anyway and by then, being fifty-something and, with two days of stubble on my face, I probably looked surprisingly similar to other Maltese.

After two more coffees and boredom with a newspaper I could not read, I was pleased to hear one of the Irishmen call for the bill. The other two got up and passed within a couple of yards of me. On the bare, right arm of one of them was a blue tattoo.

The third man joined his friends to lean on a stone wall looking out to sea before they all lit more cigarettes and strolled away.

I followed them to a small hotel in Valetta, not far from my own. Then, because I was still waiting for Farid and had nothing better to do, I watched the reflection of their hotel doorway in a shop window. A blue and grey Vauxhall Victor taxi then drew up outside the hotel and disgorged two other men.

Now, to someone who had visited the Libyan Arab Republic too often and had, in fact, only just arrived from there, it was obvious to me they were Libyans. What's more, I recognised one of them by the limp in his right leg. His name was Ben Youssef.

There was little more I could do so I went back to my own hotel to check if Farid had left any messages.

He hadn't, but next morning he phoned to say he'd just arrived and was in a coffee shop close to the Grand Harbour looking over towards Fort St Angelo.

Farid had brought information.

He described how he'd been in a meeting, two days before, with some of Gadaffi's closest contacts in a farmhouse on the outskirts of Tripoli and had heard about a vague plan to blow up American and British planes on the ground at airports in Europe. He had heard about an audacious plot to hijack a plane just after take-off at Heathrow and crash it into the Houses of Parliament or Buckingham Palace and plans to ship guns, rocket-launchers and ammunition to Ireland to add to the chaos, death and disruption of anything to do with the British. Gadaffi liked that sort of thing.

These plans, Farid told me, were well advanced and as they were drinking illicit Scotch whisky and getting more and more loose-tongued, one of the more fanatical members had described rumours coming out of Beirut for bombings, hijackings and suicidal plane crashes.

Gadaffi had particularly liked the idea to steal crop-spraying planes in USA to drop anthrax spores or chemicals on residential areas and government complexes.

I asked Farid how he was able to be part of the group and still get away to Malta.

"Because I have jobs to do," he said. "Today I have to drop papers off to a shipping company. "

I asked what the papers were about. He didn't know. They were sealed.

I asked why the Colonel wanted my views on the Irish recently.

"Ah, he is very keen to help the Irish," Farid said, "I think the papers I am carrying are connected to this."

"So, you are passing these papers to a local shipping company?"

"Yes."

It was clear that something was going on and it was logical to link it to what I'd heard and seen the day before. "You want to help, Farid?" I asked.

"What do you want?"

"Information about guns, rocket-launchers and ammunition going to Ireland."

That hot, still and cloudless Maltese morning is still so clear in my mind but I ended up risking my life for something that, even now, has never been adequately reported.

"Maybe, he said. "But it's risky."

I immediately recognized his problem. Money.

"Let me speak to someone," I said. "We can probably do a deal."

Farid agreed.

Farid's advantage was being a member of a large Libyan family of some influence. He was able to pick up valuable intelligence. What's more, Farid held some IOUs from certain people within Gadaffi's regime that were worth calling in. And Farid wanted to get out of Libya.

He wanted to buy overseas property. Like other Libyans, he'd been finding it more and more difficult to leave the country but short visits to Italy, France and Switzerland had left a taste for, perhaps, a villa on Lake Geneva, a small place on Majorca or even an apartment off the Champs Elysees. Farid, what's more, had a few girlfriends dotted around who were proving expensive. Farid's personal requirement was for cash in a big way and he was well placed to offer services to British or American Intelligence if they could be persuaded his information was worth paying for.

Farid typified the sort of person I often discovered and befriended during my travels. This was what made me so useful to Donaldson.

I thought about the problem for a while and decided, for lack of any better solutions to phone Jack Woodward. Phoning Donaldson's number and expecting a direct reply was pointless but with some well-chosen words in Jack's ear, Donaldson would quickly appear on the end of a phone like a genie from a lamp.

I went across the road to a phone box with a big pile of coins, phoned Jack, got through unexpectedly quickly, span him a quick yarn and told him to contact Donaldson urgently and that I'd phone back in twenty minutes. It worked like clockwork. Twenty minutes later I was speaking to Donaldson on a crackling phone line and, as expected, he jumped at the idea.

I think Donaldson had access to some kind of officially sanctioned Government slush fund somewhere that he could dip into occasionally. Raiding the fund for straightforward intelligence gathering was unlikely to get him too excited but if there was something commercial in it, his eyes lit up.

Farid was still sat waiting in the coffee bar across the road from the phone box.

I replaced the receiver, backed out of the phone box, walked over to the coffee bar and sat down.

"It's agreed," I said. "What you get will depend on the quality of your information. If they can intercept an arms shipment, you'll get twenty percent of its estimated value paid direct into the Jersey account I set up for you. If you can get names of Irish people involved, you'll get a thousand pounds per name. But don't just invent Irish-sounding names, Farid, OK?"

A wide grin spread across Farid's unshaven, brown face. Thoughts of villas, swimming pools, apartments and strings of easy European girlfriends were going through Farid's mind at that time.

But I'd made another mistake. I'd involved Donaldson again.

I can see it now but I should have spoken directly to someone in the Government or in Northern Ireland because, looking back, the bastard had clearly only seen it as yet another self-serving commercial opportunity. But it was urgent.

Sitting with Farid, several ideas of how to do it had passed through my mind but none could be dealt with urgently and from a coffee shop in Valletta. I thought about speaking to someone in a more clear-cut part of Government like the Home Office but I had no wish to break my cover as I wasn't sure of the implications.

I thought about phoning my local Member of Parliament from Valetta, explaining where I was and what I was doing but the idea was laughable.

I had read that the man had proved totally inept at resolving minor issues within the Croydon Social Services Department. So, the chances of getting him to deal satisfactorily with a case of international terrorism by phone from Malta were remote. And I would have had the same problem with him as I had with Sarah in not knowing where to start to explain. I certainly had no desire to inform him that one of his constituents was working undercover for a mysterious part of the Government's Overseas Intelligence Services.

So, I did the simplest thing and involved Donaldson thinking that if I could see this thing through I might, one day, use it to expose Donaldson. As you will see it wasn't such a bad idea after all. It just took time.

Farid and I parted.

He went back to Libya to see what he could find out and I flew home with plans to return as urgently as possible.

By lunchtime next day I was in the Regent Street office with Donaldson and Jack.

Operation Chrysalis was the ridiculous code name Donaldson invented when I explained more. The fact that I instigated it and ran it single handily had no bearing on Donaldson's penchant for codes. Perhaps, though, he needed it to sound dramatic to squeeze cash from his slush fund.

"We'll code it 'Chrysalis', old chap. Moths crawl out of chrysalises like flutter byes don't they, old man?"

The reasoning behind Donaldson's code was that one of the Irishmen I had come across had a nickname, 'Moth'. His surname was O'Halloran and police records showed he had a poorly drawn tattoo, supposedly of a Death's-head hawk moth on his forearm. I was eventually able to confirm this as I soon got far too close to the man.

FARID

Sarah, bless her, never understood all of my coming and going and had long given up asking. Neither, or so I thought, did Beatie understand.

My traveling, around this time, had little to do with my business, which was what I was paying Beatie to run in my absence. My own income was suffering and I found it hard to explain to Beatie. I often ran out of good excuses. She would seem agitated if I said I was going abroad again before I'd even had time to ask her for a report on the past few weeks.

"But Mr Correia is coming from Lisbon, Mr Thomas and bringing with him the sales people from his Angolan office."

"Yes, I know, Beatie, but they'll just have to wait till I get back. It'll only mean them delaying things by a day or two."

"But, Mr Thomas . . ."

"Never mind, Beat. Don't fret. They need us more than we need them. They'll wait, you see."

That was the sort of thing I used to say. It was poor management because I needed them far more than they needed me. But my flippancy came from someone who, out of necessity, was wearing two identities and was self-trained in the art of diversion. My superficial confidence concealed deep worry. If I ever stopped to think for too long panic would set in as I imagined Sarah sitting alone at home while Robert was at school and with doors and windows that were far from secure. And then Jack would call and off I'd go again.

It was a time of living nightmares not the whisky-fuelled nightmares of the present.

I may no longer have been quite the same person I had once been but what was driving me was still the same. Once I had the scent of something in my nostrils, whether it was a chance to clinch a deal or work undercover in the false belief it was for Her Majesty the Queen there was be no stopping me.

It was 1971 when I met Farid in that coffee shop and agreed his commission.

It was a time of riots in Ulster, IRA threats to bomb the mainland and I had become involved in it as a shadowy businessman carrying a case with a concealed lining and several passports.

I returned to Malta.

We sat in the same pavement coffee shop with its umbrellas sheltering us from the July sun. I wore my horn-rimmed glasses with their plain lenses, my hair parted on the right and an unshaven face. I was David Reynolds, because that is who Farid thought I was. Farid was speaking in his soft accent.

"Yes, I know Abu Hassan. We have met many times. He has told me many things. Our big leader is very keen to give help but he will expect many favours in return I think."

"Who is he helping?"

"Your Irish friends."

"And what sort of help is he offering?"

"Arms and ammunition, of course. By boat."

"A boat coming from where?" I asked.

"Benghazi."

"And going where?"

"Somewhere in Ireland."

"And it involves Malta?"

"For sure. Malta is very convenient for them. And I am hoping it is a big boat David, because of my commission."

"So, when and who is involved?"

"They are already here, for sure."

"Here? In Malta? Now?" I was shocked at the timing.

"Of course. They are very efficient. You need to be ready."

Was I ready? And why was I involved? Sometimes things didn't happen at all. Sometimes they happened so quickly there was no time to think.

"One man – I think his name is O'Halloran – he is arriving from Rome," Farid said. "He will meet with others. I don't know who but they are probably Irish. Then they all meet one called Ali Ahmed, also Ben Youssef, the man with one short leg, you know."

I knew Ben Youssef.

"Is O'Halloran an Irish name, David?"

"Yes, so that's one thousand pounds already. Well done!"

After that we probably joked about the size of the shipment. It would have been bizarre humour, the sort that discussion about plans to impose death and destruction on others always seemed to encourage.

I knew just by reading newspapers that the British government was concerned about sponsored terrorism and that Libya was a prime suspect. There was internment in Northern Ireland. Hundreds of IRA supporters were being rounded up and the British military involvement in the province was at a high level. Fear of terrorist activity abounded and innocent lives were already being lost.

Farid and I said goodbye shortly after that.

He probably went back to his small hotel in Sliema to await developments and, probably, to see a girl and drink some whisky. I went to the airport to check on flights from Rome.

Waiting and watching people coming and going at airports was something I was well used to doing. I still have one of my old briefcases, a hard, steel one that doubled as a seat when waiting at airports like Luqa where seats were in short supply.

This faithful companion became very battered over the years but it always provided a very comfortable seat and always contained some torn-out pages from the ABC Flight Timetable so that I always knew how to change an itinerary from the back of a taxi. People use mobile phones these days, but my system was just as efficient. I also kept a mental version of parts of the timetable in my head and at Luqa I sat on my briefcase and worked out all possible routes from Rome.

These were days of crackly arrivals and departures announcements but Malta was already a popular holiday destination and, being July, I found myself mingling with families as they arrived in large groups.

It was getting late, around ten in the evening and the latest crowd was already dispersing when I saw a dark, tousle haired man wearing a short sleeved white shirt and carrying a small, black bag and jacket. He was looking about him as if expecting someone to meet him. He reached into the pocket of the jacket he was carrying, pulled out a pack of cigarettes and a lighter and I followed at a distance as he walked out into the night and stood beneath a streetlight near the taxi rank. He lit a cigarette.

And there it was – in the overhead light and the brief flicker from his lighter – I saw a tattoo on his bare right arm. Standing, as I was, twenty-five yards away in the dark shadow by the closed newspaper kiosk I was unable to see the detail but it was, undeniably, one of the men I had seen during my first encounter at the café.

The airport, both inside and outside, became unnaturally quiet as everyone departed but I still stood, unmoving, in the shadow and watched as he waved away taxis who approached him as though he was waiting for his own transport. I watched him pace up and down until a two-tone grey Austin Cambridge car pulled up.

The front passenger door was opened from the inside. O'Halloran, for that is who he turned out to be, picked up his bag, opened the rear door, slung the bag on the back seat and climbed into the front beside the driver. For a moment, nothing happened as though they were sat inside greeting one another. Then the car pulled away.

From my shadowy retreat I walked to the queue of waiting taxis, got into the first one and asked the driver to follow the Austin Cambridge.

We followed it into Valletta, past quiet squares, along Republic Street and into some side streets where it suddenly turned into a smaller side street with high balconied houses and closed-up shops and then into what looked like a cul de sac. I touched my driver on the shoulder.

"OK, go past. Drop me by the street light," I said as the other car turned into the cul de sac and stopped by a sign that simply said "Hotel". It pulled half onto the pavement between two other parked cars, its headlights went out and doors opened on both sides.

I paid my driver and turned to watch the two men from the Austin Cambridge disappear up some steps and through a doorway to the small, cheap hotel.

Still carrying my briefcase and newspaper, I wandered up the road to the hotel sign, passed it and glanced inside. It was dimly lit but the two men were leaning on a reception desk checking in so I crossed the road and stood in the shadows wondering what to do next as the two men left the desk and went up a flight of stairs. It was eleven thirty and very quiet except for voices coming through the shuttered windows of a ground floor apartment behind me.

I decided not to hang around but walked back to my own hotel just a block away. But, by seven the next morning, I was back. Sense of duty, you see.

At five minutes past seven I was leaning on the stone wall of an apartment block opposite the other hotel as black shadows cast by the rising sun, grew shorter and darker and as people passed by on their way to work. Some boys came to kick a football and a woman came to clean the hotel steps with a bucket of soapy water and a mop and at seven fifty a short, overweight man appeared and chatted to the woman as she leaned on her mop. At seven fifty-five both went back inside.

That I can recall such tiny detail from so long ago is, I think, another symptom of Thomas's Disease. On the other hand, how Sarah seemed unable to recollect even recent events was a constant puzzle to me. So please, have pity on a man afflicted with such a memory and I ask to be excused for the detail that follows, but perhaps all near death experiences are indelibly imprinted on the mind.

At eight o'clock, three men emerged from the hotel.

One was O'Halloran. The second was one of the other Irishmen I had seen in the coffee shop. The third was Ben Youssef, the Libyan with the limp. They stood on the pavement in the full glare of the morning sun, smoking and apparently waiting. Then, whoever it was they had been waiting for, emerged from the hotel entrance. It was another European, a man I had not seen before so I sauntered a short distance down a shadowy alleyway to be out of sight.

When I sauntered back again, one of the men was stamping out a cigarette on the pavement and unlocking the driver's door of the Austin Cambridge. Thinking I might lose contact with them, I walked briskly to the end of the cul de sac to where it joined the main road and, as luck would have it, found a taxi that had just dropped off another passenger. I told the driver to wait.

Minutes later, the Austin Cambridge appeared, turned into the road and stopped almost alongside my taxi. The four occupants were deep in conversation, their arms hanging through the open car windows. Blue cigarette smoke wafted so close I could smell it.

"Where do you want to go sir?" My driver was getting impatient.

"Follow that one," I said and, with that, we drove a short distance into the centre of Valletta and Republic Street where it parked outside a stone office block. I paid my taxi and watched all four men go up some steps and disappear through an open black door so I wandered past to see what was written on the brass plate outside. It was a company name written in English, Italian and Arabic: "Sicilian and Mediterranean Shipping Company Ltd".

Because of my devotion to Queen and Country, I had barely eaten since breakfast the day before but now found myself in a busy street full of coffee shops, restaurants and cafes with the smell of coffee and warm, fresh bread all around. But duty still took precedence and so I stayed at my post, watching the street.

It was then that an idea struck me.

One block further down was a shop offering motor bikes for hire. So, with one eye still on the black door opposite I hired a moped, signed a form, came out and sat astride it, wondering whether I now had time to quench my desperate thirst. Such, though, is the life of an unpaid undercover agent that just as I'd decided to snatch a quick bite to eat, the four emerged yet again, got into the parked car and drove off.

I followed on the moped whilst trying to work out how to drive the wretched machine and find my balance. Ten minutes later, we were back at their hotel. They parked the car once more and went inside. I watched them go up the stairs and propped my moped against the kerb.

By then, I knew exactly what I was going to do. I walked straight into the hotel behind them.

At the entrance, I fumbled with my keys and nothing in particular in my jacket pocket to waste time as I heard them talking somewhere on the wrought iron stairs. Then I heard a door shut and things went quiet. So, I strolled inside, across the black and white Italian tiles to the reception desk and hit the brass bell.

A short, fat, balding man in a black waistcoat, the one I had watched earlier sitting on the steps, emerged. I asked him for a room and checked in as David Reynolds because that was the passport I was carrying. He took my passport from me, as was the habit at the time, promising to return it later that day. The practice always concerned me but I was well used to it.

The name of the hotel, too, became apparent once I got inside. "Hotel Belmont" it said in more wrought iron across the reception desk – not that I have ever seen any beautiful mountains in Malta.

I was handed a key to Room 3 on the first floor and made my own way to a small room, clean and sparsely furnished but perfectly adequate. The washing facilities, though, were of the shared variety. They were outside on the landing and in the usual Italian style of large taps, rust pocked bath, chipped black and white tiles and big, ornate mirrors. The toilet, too, was just an updated version of Thomas Crapper's original design with water that gushed like a waterfall once a chain that looked as though it could have held the Titanic to the dock, was pulled. Everything was for the use of all residents on the first floor and I did wonder who I might be sharing it with but I wasn't planning to spend much time there.

I spent the first few minutes listening to the sound of feet walking about directly above me. Then, because it was hot and the single ceiling fan did not seem to work, I went downstairs, out into the street, bought a bottle of water and a newspaper and returned to sit on a chair near the reception desk. As I sat there, the black telephone on the reception desk rang and the fat manager appeared from the room behind, took the call, first in Maltese and then in Arabic, as he seemed to realize the nationality of the speaker.

I heard him say the name McDonnell, quite clearly.

Then, as he ran a thick finger down the page of his registration book, I heard the name O'Halloran. It was pronounced less well than an Irishman might have, but it was enough. He put the heavy black receiver on the desk and, with a groan of someone who hated climbing stairs, struggled up the steps, holding on to the iron railings to the second floor. I heard an echoing knock on a door on the floor above mine, followed by voices and then he made his ponderous way down again followed by another who seemed even slower. By the time they arrived in the foyer, I was standing on the stone step outside with my back to the inside. I knew the effect it would have from inside, a black silhouette against the bright sunlight outside, but I was listening hard.

The man who had followed the manager down was the Libyan, Ben Youssef with the limp, which explained the slow walk down stairs. I heard him pick up the phone.

My Arabic, as I have said, is not fluent but it is good enough to follow the gist of conversations. It was obvious that the caller was doing the talking. Ben Youssef replied occasionally in monosyllabic grunts. "Ayawuh – Ayawuh – Bookra – Shookrun."

Youssef, I decided, was receiving instructions and he repeated "bookra" (tomorrow) several more times. Then Youssef, himself, started talking, a few longer sentences liberally scattered with names and words I could follow:

"Ayawah, insha'ala. Talatta, O'Halloran, McDonnell, Callaghan. Hotel Belmont. Sicilian Mediterranean Shipping Company."

Then I had heard a new name, Guido Perillo.

The Italian name Perillo had been on a separate brass plate alongside the shipping company's office. Guido Perillo was registered as a lawyer but Perillo was a family name I knew well.

Having friends in Naples whom I visited from time to time, meant that I knew that Perillos were everywhere, driving tipper trucks, running back street car repair outfits, providing scaffolding for construction jobs, acting as travel agents. You name it, the Perillos ran it. Perillos were prominent by their numbers and the one I knew was up to no good on a hillside leading up to Mount Vesuvius.

That the fat manager of the Hotel Belmont was also Italian or, more specifically, Sicilian had already struck me. Over the years, you see, I have developed a fine ear for recognizing nationalities. I could pinpoint accents even if I did not properly understand the language. Arab nationalities are easy. Libyans, Egyptians, Syrians, Jordanians, they all have different accents. But I could also separate Milanese, Roman, Neapolitan or Sicilian Italian.

I also had a nose for smelling trouble and I knew that I had checked into a Maltese Mafia stronghold. The Hotel Belmont seemed to have the additional merits of welcoming Irish and Libyan terrorists.

Meanwhile, I was still standing on the stone steps, facing the street, my ears straining to pick up words of the telephone conversation going on behind me. It finally ended in a ring as the receiver was replaced. It was enough. I walked away, down the steps and out into the hot sun to think yet again.

But this particular job was only just beginning.

REFLECTIONS

That was the way it was for me at that time, in the late sixties and all through the seventies. I can relate a dozen similar stories if you can be bothered to read a second edition of this record but this story must suffice for now.

But, do you now see how one experience would lead to another? One event would merge with another and somewhere down the line, weeks, months or years later, things would always link up.

This was the lonely lifestyle of business travel before the internet, before mobile phones and before everyone and his dog, decided it was their right to travel by air. I was an expert. I was experienced. Few could have combined running a business with undercover work more suited to professionally trained intelligence officers. Even fewer could have coped with the additional pressure I was under from that bastard Donaldson with his never-ending threats to me and my family. But there was still this dwindling thread of patriotism running through me. I still hoped that at least some of what I was doing might be for the good of the country of my birth.

Patriotism was what was driving me as I walked away from the Hotel Belmont but actually doing something is impossible without experience and a certain set of skills.

I had most of the essential ones in abundance. My problem was that whilst I had an ear for unspoken messages and a nose for smelling trouble, I would miss the sign that told me I was being set up.

It was about to happen in Malta.

It happened again some years later in Ghana as you will see.

As I left the Belmont deciding what to do next, I was also pondering on my life and especially on Sarah, sitting at home, waiting for me to return.

I knew that what I had decided to do was risky and I knew I'd never explain it to her when I returned home. Why?

Because I would often arrive home culture shocked by the familiarity of home surroundings and with no desire to start explaining everything to Sarah the moment I walked through the door.

My mind would be buzzing with things that had just happened, things that were still going on and things that I needed to attend to as soon as I got away again. That is not the way a good husband should behave.

Even after perhaps a week when, once more, I was acclimatizing to domestic matters, something else would intervene and the chance to sit and explain would be lost forever.

Recently, in a fit of disturbed sleep, I dreamed of a time when I watched money being thrown from an upstairs room of a hotel in Kano. US Dollars came floating down like confetti. But this was not a dream. I had been in the back seat of an old Peugeot car and was looking up through the side window. I could hear gunfire all around me. Confusion reigned as people ran and shouted, some gathering notes in armfuls, others running away. Red dust swirled, smoke spread and a fire raged.

Should I also write about this? But it is beyond any short and simple explanation. This statement has barely started and is already too long.

Probably I should explain in order to explain myself. It was, after all, mixed up with that bastard, Donaldson.

If I did tell you, perhaps it would explain money laundering, Donaldson style, laundering that, on that occasion, had gone badly wrong because someone panicked and emptied several suitcases out of the window so they could deny possession. But Donaldson, as he always did, had engineered a situation that enabled him to be far removed from this fiasco and was able to relax in his Regent Street office and laugh in his usual grotesque manner at my explanation of what I had seen. After I left, I imagine he picked up his phone, swore at someone at the New Nigeria Bank and threatened to come around and remove their testicles unless they sorted it.

Then there was Beirut, of course, but we will return to Lebanon later because it features in a later episode. But, in passing, let me just ask if you have ever sat in the front passenger seat of a car and ducked your head in the nick of time before a bullet embedded itself with a crack of glass and a thud into your headrest? Then, with your head buried between your knees, have you then had to put up with the sound of bullets bouncing off the car door and the screeching of tyres, as you sped off through rubble-laden streets in a cloud of concrete dust?

Perhaps you have but have you ever tried describing it to your wife when you're back home, are still hearing loud noises in your head and she's asking if you'd like more custard with your apple crumble?

So, does this short reflection help to explain the direction we are taking in this statement?

A MUGGING

Let me return to the streets of Valletta and a description of me as I walked away from the Hotel Belmont.

By the time I'd reached the end of the street, I knew exactly what I wanted to do. I also knew it would be very risky.

I'd given the bastard a few threads of the story to find cash to pay Farid but he knew none of the details. Only I knew what was really going on and I had no need of advice. There was no-one to give it anyway.

I stayed away from the Hotel Belmont until mid-afternoon by sitting in a bar, watching others, thinking, and replacing my depleted calories with bread, goat's cheese and tomatoes. Then I returned to the hotel, retrieved my Reynolds passport from the sleeping fat manager and went to my room where I lay on the bed with the shuttered window wide open listening to the sounds from the street below.

The hotel was very quiet.

There were no sounds of feet upstairs and I knew the fat manager downstairs was on his siesta. So, I crept downstairs to the marble-floored reception area in my socks and stood for a while to check if anyone else was around. The manager was asleep, his head in his arms on the table inside the office behind the reception desk. A fan was blowing the man's few, dark, straggly hairs and a couple of big black flies buzzed around a plate bearing the remains of his lunch.

All the keys to the nine guestrooms, except my own, were hanging on hooks behind the desk. It was the only evidence I needed that the room above mine was currently empty. I thought about taking the keys there and then but thought better of it and crept upstairs to the second floor to stand outside the room above mine to check. It was quiet. I turned the brass door knob but it was, as expected, locked.

I checked the lock. It was an old one, strong and unlikely to break without a lot of noise and force, so I crept downstairs again and took the key to Room 6.

(I was wearing socks, which were, according to Sarah, a Christmas present from my sister Meg in Walton-on-Thames. I had been away that Christmas having got delayed in Karachi so had failed to receive them in person but I later thanked Meg and told her they'd come in useful when creeping between hotel rooms in Malta. Meg and Sarah were shocked but I forget my explanation)

I opened the door and went in, shut the door behind me and looked around. It was identical to my own room except there were piles of dirty clothes on the floor and smelt strongly of cigarettes. A crumpled pillow lay on the floor in one corner and a prayer mat and towel in another. And, underneath the bed, was a brown bag that had been pushed almost out of sight.

I heard a noise in the street below, checked but saw nothing, pulled the bag out, opened it and looked inside.

There was a bundle of yellow cloth at the bottom and I touched it. It was hard and I lifted it out, unfolded it and stared at the pistol that lay in my hands.

I have never liked guns. I hate that heavy, metallic feel and the dreadful feeling of pain and death they convey. I sniffed it, folded it back into its cloth and put it back.

There were papers with notes that I quickly glanced at. There was a notebook that I flipped through. There was a letter written in Arabic and a small, pocket-sized address book with names and addresses in Belfast, Londonderry, Dublin, Liverpool and London. And there was a sheet of folded paper like a shopping list, hand-written in English.

It was the type of list I might give to Beatie for her to type up an invoice but I'd never given her one like that before. This was the sort of thing someone running a sophisticated and large-scale civil war might need to buy.

So, what did I do?

I stuffed everything except the pistol into my pocket and crept out. I locked the door behind me and went downstairs to my room on the first floor. Then, after just a quick look at my spoils, I decided to check out of the Hotel Belmont. I wrapped everything I'd found in my newspaper because I had no personal belongings with me and my Samsonite was at the other hotel. I went downstairs, still in my socks.

The manager was still asleep.

I hung up my own key and that of Room 6, left some cash as payment for the few hours I spent there, put my shoes on and rode away on the moped which was still parked outside.

Then, because I was not sure what to do next, I took a ride along the coast road to think. I rode to a point where I could see the island of Gozo and sat there in the shade of some rocks until the sun sank like a red ball in the sky.

My decision was to find Farid and then to leave Malta as soon as possible. I had no wish to sit around, knowing three IRA gunmen and their Libyan and possibly Mafia backers were looking for one David Reynolds who had occupied a room at the Hotel Belmont for a few hours, had rummaged through their belongings and run off with a shopping list of armaments.

I found Farid in his usual coffee bar.

It was my nature not to talk, at least immediately, about what I now knew. Experience had proved it was far better to keep things up a sleeve to pull out when necessary, rather than come out with it immediately even if one's own mind was bubbling with things to say. But Farid had had his own pieces of information obtained by means, which he, too, did not seem to want to talk about.

"Trust me, David," he said. "I spoke to someone today. A boat left Benghazi."

"Already?" I said, shocked by the news.

"Yes. It was all planned some time ago, before we got to know," Farid said.

"When did it go?"

"Two days ago."

"Where is the boat going?" I asked.

"Palermo, I think," Farid said. "After that – who knows –can you guess, my friend?"

I remember Farid shrugging.

"Is it the boat we knew about?" I asked him.

"I believe so," Farid replied.

"And the name of the vessel?"

"Licata."

The name had slotted in place like a piece of jigsaw. Licata was a small town on the southern coast of Sicily and it all tied in with the Sicilian shipping agent in Valletta.

"But, David . . ." Farid went on, "I think it will change its name soon – maybe somewhere off Malta. They will change the shipping documents. They will paint a new name on the boat. They will change everything. They have played that trick before."

"Do you know the new name?" I asked.

Farid didn't know.

There was not much more that Farid could offer. The rest of the information including the shopping list was wrapped inside my newspaper on the back of the moped. It looked now as if they'd already done their shopping.

I left Farid for what turned out to be the very last time shortly after that.

I rode to the airport to confirm a flight out for the following morning. At eight o'clock I dropped the motorcycle back at the rental shop opposite the Sicilian and Mediterranean Shipping Company, found a café and relaxed for an hour or so. Then I started to walk the half-mile back to my original hotel.

My problems were only about to start.

In Valletta it was nearly midnight. The streets were quiet and it was cooler with a fresh breeze coming in off the sea. It was as I was walking into the side street, a hundred yards or so before my hotel came into view, that I saw someone standing in the shadow of a shop front. My adrenaline level was already high and my reflex reaction was to slip into the shadow of another shop doorway and stand there. I was less than a hundred yards away from the other shadowy character and only carrying a rolled-up newspaper containing stolen property so I stayed there sweating, thinking and with my heart pounding.

My first thought was that I was over reacting and imagining things. My second, more realistic, that I had been seen, that someone knew what I had done and had found out where I was staying. I had also checked in at the hotel as Reynolds.

At the time, I could not explain it but later I could.

I had checked in at the Belmont as Reynolds. My Oliver Thomas passport, though, was in its usual place in the lining of my black bag and I'd booked my flight home as Thomas. It was vital I retrieved it.

So, I stood there for ten minutes, occasionally peering around the shop wall into the street. Whoever it was had not moved. Now and again, I could see the red tip of a glowing cigarette and a plume of smoke blowing from the doorway in the breeze. Then I thought I saw the tips of two glowing cigarettes and decided that the smoke drifting out of the shop entrance looked like it was made by more than one cigarette. What looked like two pairs of feet moved on the pavement and the more I looked, the more I was convinced it was two people, not one. And the more I thought about it, the more nervous I became.

The problem was that the street was another cul de sac. There was no other way in or out of the hotel and, even if there was a back way in, it was unlikely to be open at this time of night.

I decided to take a chance and walk boldly towards the hotel but I still had the bundle of newspaper under my arm and the contents were going to be a give-away if I got into a tangle. Looking around my dark doorway I saw a possible solution – I suppose it was luck, but it had happened to me once before.

In Algeria once, armed with a roll of newspaper containing more than simple newsprint I had been faced with a similar situation of not wanting to be found with anything on my person. I remembered what I had done then and, looking around the shop doorway, the same solution seemed a distinct possibility.

In Algeria, the streets were often littered with the detritus of human life. The only problem in leaving a bundle of old newspaper held down by a piece of stony rubble alongside a rubbish-strewn public highway was to remember which stone hid the bits you wanted to recover later,

The streets of Valletta were far cleaner and swept more regularly but a bundle of old newspaper was, I thought, still not a bad place to hide stolen goods, if only temporarily. I looked around my hiding place in the shop doorway and, as luck would have it, above the door was a ledge. Above the ledge was a wooden sign showing the shop owner's name that was falling away from the stonework, leaving a small gap and I found I could just reach it by standing on the stone sill of the side window. That's where I stuffed the newspaper, spreading it flat so that most of it slid behind the sign. Hiding the newspaper was only the first problem. I now had to return to the hotel stay alive to recover the newspaper.

I couldn't wait all night so I decided to walk briskly towards the hotel as though I had just returned from a happy evening spent in a bar.

Perhaps the decision was wrong but what other options were there? As I got close enough to smell the cigarette smoke, two men sprang out and bundled me roughly back into the doorway. With a pair of big rough hands around my neck I was pushed backwards so hard that my head hit the stone wall with a thud.

Stars flew around my head and in front of my eyes and I had to gasp for air through the small gap left in my throat. The throttling hands then forced my chin back and a knee kicked me violently in the stomach.

It all happened very quickly.

For a second no-one spoke. I couldn't have spoken anyway but when I heard the voice, I knew that although this was Malta, far from home, I was involved with a couple of thugs who were probably quite used to night-time forays in the back streets of Belfast.

"Who the fuck you think you are, huh? We don't like no messin' 'round. Got it? Who the fuck, are you, huh? Bastard. Where the fuck is the stuff?"

The words were hissed rather than spoken and a smell of beer, cigarettes and bad breath wafted over me. Then I felt something sticking in my ribs. Perhaps it was the gun that had been in the yellow cloth but I never saw it. I just felt it.

It was forced between my ribs so hard that the pain was almost worse than that from my throat and my head. Through the red mist and stars, I then saw a face streaked with greasy, strands of black hair just inches from my nose. Then the other face came into blurred view, the one I had already seen at the airport. O'Halloran's hair looked better groomed, thick and wavy but, as I tried to focus, a muscular arm came up and a heavy fist landed on my cheek. Just before it hit, I saw the tattoo. To me it looked like a skull and cross bones as the brains inside my own skull rattled and the cheek bone felt as though it had cracked.

That mugging seemed to go on for hours. The pain in my head and cheekbone was the worst although both my arms were up behind my back and felt as though they might also crack at the shoulder blade at any second.

I heard O'Halloran say something amongst the noise in my head. "OK. Shut the fuck up. Lost your fucking voice, have ye?"

Even in the middle of the assault, the words struck me as typically Irish and under different circumstances I might have laughed and told an Irish joke. But this was no time for humour.

"OK, Sean, that's enough," O'Halloran, said, seeming to show some pity, but his face was only an inch from mine and the spit from his mouth and the stale tobacco breath was taking over as punishment. He moved to three inches away and, with Sean still holding my two arms up behind my neck and his knee in my back, O'Halloran hissed more oaths through his yellow teeth.

Hissing loudly was probably wiser than shouting because the shop owner and his neighbours in the apartments above were probably fast asleep. I suppose I could have screamed but, despite the circumstances, it seemed unmanly. If I was going to die, I wanted to be found with a mouthful of blood and broken teeth not with my mouth open screaming as if I'd been raped.

Screaming was impossible anyway because my teeth were pressed on the stone wall and I could feel the skin of my scalp starting to tear as the hair was dragged out in tufts.

"Like he says, you bastard. Who, the fuck, are you? Fucking English! MI fucking 6 is it?"

He clearly didn't understand that MI6, British Intelligence, used unpaid volunteers, but the words were hissed into my face as a statement not a question and proved they knew at least something about me as I still hadn't spoken a word.

"OK, Sean, let the fucker speak. Where's the stuff you bastard?"

I felt my jacket pockets being checked and my wallet pulled out. The Reynolds passport came with it. There was little else. There wasn't much in my wallet either, as I never carried much change and my traveller's cheques, business cards and other bits of paper were at the hotel.

"Let's see that. That's him. Just as I thought. Mister fucking David William Reynolds. Fucking company director. What sort of fucking company director comes raiding fucking hotel rooms? Speak you bastard. What's up? Where's the fucking stuff you filched?"

The language was not good and Sarah would have been shocked to know I mixed with such people but the grip on my throat lightened just enough even though the back of my head and ribs felt badly bruised.

"I don't know what you're talking about," I think I managed to say.

"The fucking papers – you stupid fucking sod. Where . . . are . . . they?"

The last three words were spoken slowly as though O'Halloran thought he was talking to an imbecile.

"I'm sorry I don't know what you're talking about," I mumbled as saliva and probably blood ran down my chin.

The grip on my throat lightened a little more. So, did the pain in my ribs, but only because the gun was now pointing directly at my forehead.

"OK, you fucker. Stop messin' We know you were at a hotel earlier. Some fucker broke into our room. It was you. Comprennez? Got it now?"

And so, it went on for several minutes more. I denied everything. I tried to grab my wallet and passport back, thinking this was the most likely response of someone who was the subject of a common assault rather than someone who really had stolen their personal property.

But miracles do happen and I was saved by another stroke of luck.

Having now slumped to the ground with two faces inches from mine, a gun at my head and my wallet and passport already inside the unyielding hands of the greasy one I had heard a car coming. The two Irishmen heard it as well. The greasy one stuck the hand that was not holding my passport firmly over my mouth and nose and pushed my head hard against the ground.

"Shut up, you fucker. No fucking move, do you understand?"

The taxi stopped, out of sight, up the road somewhere probably near the first shop doorway and my hidden newspaper. I could hear other male voices, some laughter and the taxi engine and above the din in my ears a dog barked somewhere. Then there was the sound of footsteps, of people walking towards the shop doorway where I was lying with two Irishmen sat on top of me. I heard the taxi as it did a U-turn in the road and subconsciously wished I was not staying in a cheap hotel in a cul de sac. O'Halloran then hissed through his teeth, directly into my face.

"OK, bastard. Get up. Walk. No fucking tricks OK? This'll be right behind you."

Again, I felt the gun, this time in my ribs as O'Halloran pointed up the road towards where the footsteps were approaching but away from the sanctuary of my hotel. His friend Sean managed to get one last punch into my right kidney, but I was grateful for the chance to stand up.

"Quick, now, you stupid sod. Walk. Just watch your fucking steps."

I remember emerging, staggering slightly, from the shop front to see two men walking towards us. They both wore white shirts and dark ties undone at the collar and both carried their jackets and brief cases in their hands – foreign businessmen returning from a late-night meeting somewhere. They looked like Laurel and Hardy but they were talking, laughing and having fun and, suddenly, I wanted to live again.

The Irishmen followed me out, closely, the gun still digging into my back.

Even now, I remember the next few seconds so vividly. The two businessmen looked towards me and stepped off the pavement to give us room to pass and I took the only chance I had. I broke free and ran behind them. To shoot at that point would have been pointless. It would not have brought back their precious possessions and might well have killed one or both of those innocent chaps.

They clearly thought better of shooting. But they weren't going to give up. They pushed away the two men and tried to grab me again but I ran, I sprinted across the road, dodged behind another parked car and kept running, keeping my head down before re-crossing the road and sprinting for my hotel thinking that at any second a bullet would embed itself in my back.

And, as I ran into the open hotel door, I remember glancing back where the two men in white shirts and ties were standing looking up the road watching the two Irishmen walking the other way. One of the white shirts picked up his briefcase, which he'd dropped and then they continued walking towards the hotel, still looking behind them.

The hotel night porter came over to me. I was panting, bleeding and dirty, sitting in a chair, holding the back of my head, my nose, my chin and my ribs when the two businessmen walked in. "You OK, señor?" one of them asked me. "You have problem with zees men, yes?"

"Yes."

"You wanna polizi come, señor, yes?"

They were slightly drunk Spaniards.

I told them I'd be OK.

"I shink very homosexual, señor? I shink you lucky we come den, I shink."

This was, perhaps, the most amusing part but at the time I did not feel like laughing. I thanked them and the porter, went to my room and bathed my wounds. At five thirty I checked out of the hotel. I recovered my newspaper together with its contents from the shop doorway, hailed an early morning taxi and went to the airport. I wasn't going to wait for my reserved flight to London so I took the first available plane out in the name of Thomas. A short while later I was in Nice in the south of France.

AFTERMATH

Imust have looked a shocking sight for the Air France staff both at check in and on the aircraft. I hid the agony of the bruised ribs and explained it was a motorcycle accident which brought sympathy but I couldn't hide the badly cut lip and two swollen black eyes.

It was when I was safely onboard that I started to ask myself how the two Irishmen knew about me and where I was staying. I was sure someone somewhere had tipped them off.

I didn't go home immediately but slept in the office. Next morning, I called Donaldson. "Bad luck, old man. Never mind old chap, still in one piece." That was the extent of Donaldson's concern.

"So, we're passing all this on?" I asked him, in my purest innocence whilst still wincing from the pain in my ribs.

"Leave it with us now, old chap. You've done your bit. Go home and nurse that black eye."

I never did find out what Donaldson did with the information. As for me, I had read through the notebook and other notes I'd found in the Hotel Belmont on the plane to Nice and on the connecting flight to Heathrow. I memorized names and addresses and can still remember some. The information was quite clear and was invaluable.

There were names – Arab, English, Irish and Italian.

There were phone numbers and addresses of people in Dublin, Belfast, Tripoli, Naples and even New York. There was a note of the name of the boat name Licata and, beside it, probably its changed name: MS Bally.

There was a pencilled diagram of a section of the northern Irish coastline and the name Donegal. It all seemed perfectly clear to me. The boat that had left Benghazi, sailed to Palermo, changed its name somewhere off Malta and then offloaded most of its cargo in a small bay near Donegal.

I was not inexperienced in matters of moving things around by boat but no one asked me and as far as I know the boat was never tracked and never stopped.

Investigations should have started. I should have been interrogated. Searches and arrests should gave followed and charges brought with at least some sort of mention in the press. But there was nothing. Even now, questions should be asked and one reason for writing this statement, however belated it is, is to request a proper investigation.

My mistake was in involving Donaldson by speaking directly to someone in the British Government or in Northern Ireland but, as I explained, there wasn't time.

But, looking back, I can see it now. Donaldson was already on his way to becoming a serious crook.

"Operation Chrysalis" as Donaldson himself called it for the few weeks that he maintained any interest was eventually forgotten although I would deliberately mention it whenever another code was invented for a job.

I mentioned it to Jack once. but Jack didn't like what I said. It embarrassed him. "That bastard is obsessed with codes," I said. "Are you sure he isn't sexually aroused by odes and initials?"

Jack was embarrassed by that. Any mention of the word sex and he'd flush like a teenage girl.

But I, having already, risked my life. did some more investigations of my own. If I could do it then why not British Intelligence? I worked out exactly where that boat would offload and I recovered shipping documents through contacts I had at Lloyds. That shipment had arrived in Donegal in early autumn. Some of its huge cargo of arms had probably been hidden temporarily in farm buildings near Donegal, buildings that were never searched. Instead, most or all of it, was on the streets and in the hands of the Provisional IRA by early 1972. Of that I am sure.

But I had done my bit for Queen and Country.

And what happened to Farid and his promised commission?

Farid was a good man, living under very difficult circumstances. His heart was in the right place and he was a very good friend to me. But he never got to buy his fancy apartment in Majorca because six months later his body was washed up on a beach near Leptis Magna with a bullet hole in his head and a rope tied and wrapped around his body and neck.

No one who didn't have other good, Libyan friends would ever have known about this murder. But I know about it. So, who blew the whistle on Farid? There was only one man who knew – Donaldson.

And what was my reward?

There are two things that I remember.

First of all, I got a replacement David Reynolds passport, even though I could well have managed without it. "Don't worry, old chap, we'll report it as lost. Not go into the sordid details of who rifled your pockets. Forget it old chap. All in a day's work, eh? Ha ha."

My second reward came some months later. I was reminded of this just today when picking through old newspaper cuttings from around 1972.

February 22nd 1972 was the day the IRA bombed the 16th Parachute Brigade headquarters in Aldershot at lunchtime.

March 21st 1972 was the day that six died and one hundred and forty-six were injured whilst out shopping in Belfast. And there were others – similar reports of atrocities committed around that time. These cuttings, torn from newspapers just a few months after my trip to Malta were held together with rusty paper clips and had lain unread for forty years in a box upstairs in the spare bedroom.

And there was another cutting from March 3rd 1973.

I had been innocently walking from somewhere to Victoria Station with my mind probably on things I'd been reading about the war in Vietnam or the referendum on British rule in Ulster when I happened to pass the Agriculture Ministry in Whitehall.

I had already heard police sirens but it was nothing unusual at the time and I carried on my way to catch the train back home to Croydon. It was just after I'd passed the Ministry building when I heard a scream and, almost simultaneously, a huge explosion. I found myself knocked to the ground by some sort of invisible force from behind. I must have been miles away in my thoughts but all sense of where I was or what had happened left me.

Everything then went silent but my stomach was hurting.

I opened my eyes and knew they were still working as I was staring at the pavement with dust and bits of glass and metal falling all around me. The pain in my stomach was because I was lying on top of my briefcase with the arm and my hand that had been holding it trapped beneath. And I knew my nose was still working because I could smell burning as a thick cloud of black smoke swept past me. Everything was silent because my ears no longer worked but I knew what it was – a bomb.

I struggled to my feet, checked for signs of blood and decided I was still in one piece. I rubbed my ears because I still couldn't hear and turned around to a scene of devastation.

Smoke and flames were rising from what was once a car, debris was lying everywhere and so were people. Men who, a few seconds earlier, had been wearing pin striped suits were now sat or lying in what looked like dirty rags not five yards from me. A woman was lying with blood trickling from her head. Another man was crawling toward her. Further away and closer to the burning car, bodies lay, some moving, some still, some with smoking clothes. Smouldering debris was everywhere and a black shoe was lying almost next to me and next to the shoe a piece of red tissue which looked as though it might once have been a hand.

I remember going to the stone wall of the building and leaning on it with my briefcase at my feet whilst I rubbed dust from my eyes and sound back into my ears.

Other people came running out of the Ministry office door, a porter in his uniform standing with his hands on his forehead staring at the scene in disbelief and I did likewise as I stood alone trying to recover my senses.

That newspaper cutting showed that one person was killed and about 250 injured in London that day after car bombs outside the Ministry building and the Old Bailey.

I was, I suppose, fortunate but in no fit state to help anyone. I declined hospital treatment and my hearing slowly returned so I dusted myself down and carried on towards Victoria Station.

Police, ambulance and fire engine sirens were now everywhere and, due to police advice and rumours of other bombs, train timetables were disrupted so I found myself with about half a dozen other shell-shocked individuals in a pub near Victoria Station where we sat around exchanging stories about near death experiences.

But during the inevitable silences between forcibly assembled groups of strangers who'd survived only by pure luck I sat with my ears still echoing and my gritty eyes staring into a glass of Bell's whisky and thinking about a boat load of weapons and reminding myself that only Donaldson knew where I was staying in Valletta on the night of that mugging.

Donaldson may not have actually planted the bomb that had nearly killed me but he was involved. Reasons for everything that ever went wrong pointed to Donaldson.

So, my second reward for uncovering an IRA gun running scheme with Gadaffi was to find myself very nearly a victim. I had feared that those Irish muggers in Malta might still be after my scalp but I suspect Donaldson would have put them off that. At the time I was far more valuable alive than dead.

But that was my life during the sixties and seventies.

The Malta story will suffice for now because to relate others about Nigeria, Ghana, Serra Leone, Lebanon, Jordan, Iraq or Syria will require a second edition or an extension to this statement to equal War and Peace.

But sometimes I got so mad with things that I had a desire to close the legitimate Import Export business altogether and see if, by concentrating on my other life, I could do as well, or better, by taking bribes or dubious commissions. I could probably have become an international version of Farid. But look what happened to him.

In times of anger I'd think to myself, to hell with it all.

To hell with it if I was caught and slammed up in some rat-infested jail in Karachi or Khartoum with the other local riff raff and got fed bread and water. Perhaps I'd be there until some British newspaper got wind of it and managed to take a photo of this thin, bearded old chap wearing a loin cloth who spoke English as if he had once lived in Croydon but who had forgotten who he was. But so be it.

Fuck the lot of it, I thought.

If you can't beat the bastards, then become one yourself and join in the fun.

And hearing Jack's words ringing in my ears like some creepy, hand wringing character from a Charles Dickens novel didn't help. "Opportunities, Ollie, opportunities."

Yes, I really did stop caring for brief moments – until I thought about my Sarah of course.

Sarah was like a rock on which I stood to scan the wider, brighter horizon.

Fortunately, things always looked better from that higher position and so I never did join the bastards but I was very close sometimes. But for an organized chap like me, my emotions were all over the place.

For instance, it wasn't so easy making phone calls from places like Maiduguri or Ouagadougou thirty or forty years ago.

I would telephone Beatie occasionally if I had an hour to spare to sit in my hotel room dialling and redialling. By the time my middle finger was red, sore and blistered I might get through. By then I'd have forgotten what I wanted and the shock of speaking to someone with an English accent didn't help. I'd often start off talking to her in pidgin.

And then Beatie would try to engage me in trivial conversation, about who had written, or who was in town, or who wanted to meet me. All this, too, on a poor, crackling line that was likely to break at any second and when all I really wanted Beatie to do was to convey a simple message to Sarah.

Phoning Sarah would always bring me down to earth and I'd long to rush home to be with her.

"I'll be back tomorrow, my love," I'd say.

"That would be nice dear. We'll wait for you. Robert is doing his homework but I'll make us an apple pie. Doris gave me some lovely Bramley's yesterday."

GUILT

I started by writing a statement but perhaps it is also a confession.

I have had some restless nights recently and now there is something I need to get off my chest.

After I'd finished writing the statement about the IRA, Malta and Donaldson last Tuesday afternoon I finished off my stock of Bell's whisky. So, I took a stroll to the off license to replenish it because my mood is a little sombre.

Last night, for instance, as I was nursing a bottle and staring into Sarah's log effect gas fire, I heard buzzing like a swarm of bees in my ears.

I know the whisky was to blame but tropical rain was thundering on to a tin roof almost deafening the real thunder from the skies above.

In my mind, you see, I was sitting on a hard, concrete floor, dizzy, just as then, as a clear liquid of almost neat alcohol made from palm fruit was being handed around in a dirty, chipped cup.

For geographical references, this was me having a nightmare about or dreaming about or just thinking about – I can't remember which – sunny Nigeria. This will certainly explain the weather, the building and the company I was sharing.

The sun doesn't always shine in Lagos and, on this occasion, the heavy rain had started while I was at an open-air night club – the Pink Coconut.

The band was still playing somewhere outside, protected from the downpour by some sort of corrugated shelter. Even though I was staring at the log effect fire, I could hear it. The sound of drums and a saxophone was pounding in my chest and a strong smell like stale sweat filled my nostrils.

I was in a very mixed gathering – a noisy one, and mine was one of only two white faces.

There was an intermittent light of sorts – not firelight, but flashes of blue from the lightning outside.

Sat there, as I was, in Gloucester, forty years later and with a fuddled brain, I struggled to remember and imagine how it was. Then, as it all became clearer and I remembered, I desperately struggled to forget. This is a classic symptom of Thomas's Disease but, by then, it is always too late.

Besides the flashes of lightning was the yellow flicker from a dim bulb that dangled in the corner. Two wooden chairs stood either side of a table the only furniture in the room. Suddenly it was all starting to come back and I remember fidgeting in my chair by gas fire in Gloucester because the concrete floor in Lagos was so hard and uncomfortable.

There was a bluish haze that came from half a dozen glowing tips of strange smelling, hand rolled cigarettes. There was a hissing and splashing like a waterfall as water poured in sparkling torrents from the tin roof, past the window into a deep, muddy flood that was streaming in through the open door. Mice the size of small rats had scampered for cover when I had staggered in with the others to escape the deluge and my shirt was clinging to me like warm sweat.

Once inside, and with my eyes barely focusing, I watched an army of nocturnal ants moving across the floor near the wall, up the table leg to a plate of chicken bones – the remains of someone's dinner. A small lizard was benefitting as well by picking the ants off with its darting tongue as they passed by.

The occupants of the two chairs were already dozing with their heads lying in folded arms on the table. One arm moved, struck an empty beer bottle and it started to roll. It rolled in a semicircle and fell with a thud onto the floor but did not break. Instead it came to rest with a clinking sound against the table leg.

The only other white man present lay, apparently asleep, with his mouth ajar. His head lay partly on the bare, dark brown knees of one of the girls whilst she curled her fingers in his long and greasy hair and leaned back on the wall. Next to her was another man whom she was looking at, rapidly, up and down, up and down, with wide, inviting black eyes and she smacked him provocatively with her spare hand. She was shouting and laughing. The laughter was loud and coarse to encourage him and he then responded by sticking his hand into the depths of her lap.

"Aye, keep them hand away, man. You be get too much drunk, man, ha ha."

The men, too, were punching each other in drunken gusto – the same gusto that was bound to lead to a fight later if something was said the wrong way or a woman showed a preference. Meanwhile, the short, fat, handmade cigarettes glowed, the smoke billowed around and my wet shirt still clung to my back and front.

My eyes fell on the other white man. Frank Marshall was English. This was confirmed by his grey socks, sandals and his pale but grubby safari suit. Like me, but far more so, Frank had succumbed to the beer of earlier so he was now missing out on the local liquor. And around Frank, on the floor, sat or lay perhaps a dozen others, mostly men, some in sweaty, open necked shirts or with unnecessary ties that had become twisted or untied. They were dark figures who mostly ignored me because I had already achieved my objective of being accepted into their dubious company – and, anyway, they were now too drunk to care.

The "being accepted" part of relationship building had taken me the best part of two days. I knew some of their names, like Yemi, Onje, Augustus and Bola and I had their business cards tucked away somewhere.

They shouted in a mixture of English and Yoruba, but the conversation, if that is what it was, had strayed a long way from sober ideas to divert government funds into overseas bank accounts into drunken jokes about the merits of several wives. Someone had shouted at me across the floor for my views. But they had been much too far gone to hear my quieter, muttered answer that one was already more than I could possibly hope to manage.

Except for one person, that was.

She was sitting in the corner. She was sober so she was smiling politely and not laughing but clearly trying to avoid my eye.

Her long, dark brown legs were together, outstretched on the floor and wrapped in a tight and colourful dress that I had watched her hold up out of the muddy water when we ran in from the rain. The hidden legs pointed in my direction, but the bare toes flickered up and down, up and down, like the long eyelashes that circled her eyes. She looked just a little out of place. Perhaps it was shyness.

I watched her through the smoke.

Her black eyes, surrounded by that brilliant whiteness, caught the light, shone and sparkled and, now and again, they clearly glanced in my direction. They were alert, thinking eyes, intelligent with a touch of sympathy in them. They seemed filled with worry about where she had suddenly found herself and I knew she sensed my own discomfort. Her look invited me to make a decision. The black skin of her face glowed with a satin smoothness, because she was sweating less than the others were. Her lips were pink and her long, bare, arms stretched from strapless shoulders to lie between those straight legs that pointed in my direction and she sat, upright, not leaning on the man next to her, not slapping or punching or laughing or shouting.

And I had already seen her long black fingers, with the wide gold rings, that waved away the cigarette that was offered. Her hair was a miracle of artistry, full of miniature plaits interspersed with rows of tiny, multi-coloured beads that sparkled like her eyes. She listened and watched and now and again I saw her glance at a gold watch on her dark wrist and then at me.

Shrieks of high-pitched laughter were coming from the other corner where two men in the crumpled remains of business suits lay with two younger, black women, one in a short, tight, floral dress.

One girl looked as though she had already started to discard some clothing but it was so dark and the girl so black that I could not see for certain. But I knew the one who was still dressed. She had earlier introduced herself as Mary. She had sat on my lap at the Pink Coconut and had got as far as sticking a hot, pink tongue into my ear. She was already high on something but whether it was alcohol or some other concoction I did not know.

But after the searching tongue had failed to impress, she had pressed thick lips to my cheek, breathed beer and spicy joloff rice over me and hissed noisily into my ear about sharing the air conditioning back at my hotel. I didn't like to tell her that the power had failed earlier and there was no air conditioning but, all the time, she was running her fingers up and down my inner thigh. I had excused myself at that point by going to relieve myself in the bushes.

Oh yes, such were the excitements on offer during visits to Lagos in the seventies.

But as I sat there in the chair in Gloucester remembering Mary's tongue and still smelling the chilli and fish that escaped alongside it, I felt something heavy in my bladder as though the need to relieve myself in the bushes was now a necessary reality.

The half-asleep status had become a quarter-asleep status, as my extended bladder seemed fit to burst. Had it been three, four, five or six large glasses of whisky?

Perhaps I had had no glass at all and was just taking it direct from the bottle but I really had lost count. For years, I had been getting up at least once per night, sometimes twice.

So, I moved to try to ease the weight on my weakening sphincter as my mind still flitted between past and present and my hand that held the whisky flitted between my lap and my mouth. Someone, somewhere, was telling me that I was sitting by the fire in Gloucester and not in Lagos and that there were no bushes and that a proper bathroom with a flush system and Sarah's pink towels were available if I needed them. But it all became just a rumour that died as the more exotic reality of dreaming took over once more. So, I gave up worrying about my bladder for a while, took another mouthful of Bell's and returned to the past in Lagos.

Such are the symptoms of a really bad bout of Thomas's Disease. Inside my head, everything was dark with just small patches of oscillating light reflecting off moving, black bodies, pink eyes and crumpled white shirts. My own closed eyes could no longer penetrate the gloom.

So, in my mind I took the cup that was being passed around. I licked my lips, swallowed and passed the cup to the next man, who laughed and punched my arm. "Hey, that good stuff man, eh? You like Nigerian wine eh? Better than that French shit, eh? Ha ha ha. You wanna puff as well?"

But my lips were dry despite the drinking and so I glanced once more into the corner of the room where the black girl with beads in her hair sat with her legs outstretched and now, just slightly, apart. The girl again looked first at me and then at her watch.

You see? Dare I continue to type this and so record it for posterity?

But nearly ninety years old, with an overfull bladder pressing on an enlarged prostate gland and still I sensed the erotic heat of equatorial Africa in my groin.

But it was one of the other girls who had then crawled across towards me dragging her short floral skirt across the wet floor with her buttocks raised. She had raised her head to smile a drunken smile and pulled herself onto my lap where she pressed her half-exposed breasts against my chest and took my hand and pushed it into the wetness between her legs. I knew what she expected me to do but I was now being watched by the other girl in the corner and, instead, I politely pushed her away, excused myself and went outside for a piss in the rain.

And when I turned around, I saw the sober girl from the corner standing at the door behind me, waiting.

Forty years have passed and yet I still think about Angie.

About Angie with the shining, black hair, the multi-coloured beads and the long, long legs that later wrapped so willingly around mine.

About Angie with the round and beautiful face, pink lips, white teeth and the radiant and beautiful smile that I remember as though it was yesterday.

Angie was different from the rest and showed me the throbbing passion that was at the heart of everything that is good about Africa. With Angie I spent a long, long night in an air-conditioned room and found the help I needed to see through one problem but found, yet again, how easy it was to forget the most important person in my life.

I can still see Angie lying asleep on my crumpled bed at the Airport Hotel in Ikeja and still see her glorious African smile that filled two, dark nights with sun.

Angie was all about laughing and talking and caressing and touching for hours and wanting to continue forever. Angie was the one, whose naked body I washed in the brown drips of Lagos water that we squeezed from the tap while trying to understand each other's culture and knowing all along that there was so little difference between us.

And when she fell asleep, I played with the tiny, multi-coloured beads and the finely plaited strands of black hair that hung across my own shoulders. As she slept, I stroked her dark brown face, looked into her black eyes and I kissed her. I touched and watched the movement of her pink lips and looked down her silky body to her hips and on towards her long legs, watching her firm breasts gently rise and fall as she lay beside me.

I lay there for hours, my mind troubled with what I should do about my wife, my family, my business and my other life. This was the defining moment when I felt I had to decide, one way or another.

I was not just at a simple crossroad, though.

I felt I had arrived at a complicated junction without a map but with signposts pointing in all sorts of different directions. Some pointed to places I knew I didn't want to go, others to places that sounded good but I knew were cul de sacs. Others pointed to unknown places that sounded satisfactory but were shown as via this and past that and by way of somewhere else. And I couldn't turn around and go back to where I had begun because the route was far too long and tortuous and I might lose myself again.

The nice places to go meant giving up everything and starting again but still meant someone looking over my shoulder for the rest of my life in case I spoke out of turn or went to the authorities. And I still had not earned anything like enough to take an early retirement.

I battled with the dilemma of whether to fly home or just fly away, trying to explain the guilt that was wracking my very soul yet building on the guilt just by lying there.

I thought about completely disappearing, losing myself and adopting a new identity. But then, in my mind, I would see Sarah standing by the door still waiting for me to return home for years and years to come and I knew I could not live with that.

And so, those few short days turned into a long, long battle with myself that began on the flight home with me imagining Sarah sat waiting at home. Guilt wracked my very soul.

I knew if I phoned her from the airport on arrival to say I'd be home in thirty minutes, that she'd be standing waiting on the pavement outside the front door when I turned the corner of the street.

And before I was even fifty yards from the house, I knew she would be walking or even running towards me. What does this tell you not just about my own feelings but Sarah's?

I am eighty-six years old but I have only just matured enough not to feel too stupid to write things like this. I have previously shied away from expressing unmanly feelings and still dislike writing words like the ones that are now starting to spill from my fingertips. But as I might be dead when someone gets to read it, I suppose it won't matter.

Despite what I had just done, I still loved Sarah you see. I loved her deeply.

I didn't tell her, of course, but she was the one I would need when everything around me had returned to sanity and who I would need when I was too old to care anymore. And I was more than prepared to do my bit if she deteriorated before me. So, at that complicated junction in my life, did I eventually decide which road to take?

Yes. I took the road to what sounded like a big, fine place of light and sanity where the signpost read: "Domesti City via the little village of Patience-while-I-sort-things-out."

And so, as I always did, I phoned her on arrival at the airport. And, of course, just as I expected, thirty minutes later Sarah was standing there when I turned the corner and my guilt tripled in strength as I watched her run towards me to grab my hand and pull me towards the house.

But I couldn't make love to her that night even though I know she wanted me to. I couldn't for too long and I know that Sarah knew something had happened.

I remember her asking me more questions about that trip than usual. I hoped that perhaps she thought I was just distracted by my work. I know, however, that I became a different person for a long while afterwards as I tried to fathom out what to do. We had already arrived at the village of Patience-while-I-sort- things-out, you see.

But, as usual, she said nothing. It was as if she was waiting for me to have a mental breakdown and come clean on everything. But I am too stubborn for that. Or perhaps I just have a masochistic streak which makes me plough on despite everything.

For months, she watched me, she looked at me and tried talking to me about nothing. But she never asked me outright.

Perhaps I should have admitted everything including my other double life for Donaldson & Co. Perhaps an argument would have cleared the air. But my mind was unsure about too many things.

When at home I would sit there thinking, pretending to read the paper but becoming more and more angry about Donaldson and his increasing threats. By then I hated the man and was plotting things of my own.

But I could never have told Sarah that what I was thinking might, if it went wrong, be putting her own safety in jeopardy. It would have been like an admittance of failure of my career and business and I wasn't ready to give that up just yet.

During those weeks and months, I thought that perhaps she had found out about Angie. Perhaps I'd talked in my sleep. More likely, though, was that one of those intoxicated Nigerians in that rain lashed building in Lagos had been a lackey of Donaldson and he had said something.

But what did Sarah do?

Nothing, except continue to wash my sweat ridden shirts and dust covered trousers and iron my suit when I came home and continue to ask me whether I fancied roast beef on Sunday because I'd missed the last three weekends.

Why?

Well I suppose it was for the same reason that I would also run towards her when I came around the corner and saw her waiting for me.

You see, since Sarah died, I now know that, all along, she knew far more than I ever thought.

So, does this show the way that Sarah and I knew what was best for each other? I think that is the case.

Sometimes, silence is like gold. Perhaps silence is also like diamond, because it would have been that sort of wedding anniversary for us next year.

These recent nightmares are caused by realizing that the one woman I knew I should not have deceived and with whom I should, undoubtedly, have shared my feelings more openly was probably far more intuitive than me. I now think she actually understood everything and she especially understood the acute depths of loneliness that can afflict a man who travelled alone and whose commitment to his job had meant he had become trapped and caught up in the same knots he was trying to unravel. But, most importantly, I think she knew I loved her and would always be with her right to the end. And so, I was. For that I am very happy.

But my eyes are hurting and this typewriter ribbon has run dry.

Written above in the last few inches of fading ink is my description of a personal guilt. What follows below, written in the darker, fresher black of a new ribbon, is another sort of guilt. What follows is my admittance to being an innocent accomplice to murder.

You see, it was Donaldson's style to create situations where people who had become a nuisance would be dealt with in such a way that they were forced to become compliant. He was adept at this sort of thing as, having already become a victim, I knew all too well. Compromising photographs and being forced to use a false identity were examples of what kept me on message. But Donaldson's inventiveness had no boundaries.

I handled this next assignment in a completely detached and unemotional manner as if it was just another routine business transaction. I knew I wouldn't get paid but the reward was in knowing that it would postpone any immediate impact on Sarah and my family. Mostly, though, I took part because, at the time, I saw no viable alternative.

For this assignment I was a subcontractor who subcontracted it out to another. Donaldson, of course, was the one who had subcontracted it to me but I still don't know if someone had subcontracted it to him or how far up the chain it went. But this is how things happened. Fortunately, sometimes, those that find a corpse lying at the foot of the mountain can point to vultures living amongst the clouds at the top.

Nevertheless, I still have a guilty conscience and so it forms an essential part of my statement. But, frankly, whatever happens, I don't really care anymore.

For even now, when I turn the corner at the end of the road, I may be carrying some clinking bottles of Bell's whisky, but the only thing I still look out for is Sarah running towards me.

A SUB CONTRACT

It was Nigeria again and once again I was to meet Frank Marshall.

On this occasion, though, another Englishman was also arriving in Lagos. He was not booked to stay at the seedy Airport Hotel where I normally stayed and neither had he flown Economy.

This man was well connected in British Government circles and so had flown First Class and, on the invitation of a Nigerian Government Minister, was booked to stay at an official residence in the better end of Lagos and anyone with a nose for an opportunity to cash in was sniffing around as the opportunities provided by the arrival of this particular representative of the British government were endless. Donaldson, of course, was quick off his mark.

It had started, as always, with a phone call and I had been summoned to meet Donaldson and Jack in the Regent Street office.

"Mum's the word, old chap," he'd said at the start. "So, don't ask. Understand? We're all in this shit and what you don't know can't come and bite you in the arse later. Got it?"

"But it would be nice to know a bit more," I said. "I mean......"

Jack remained his usual serious, passive self but Donaldson raised his hand to stop me.

"He's a bloody homo, old chap. A fucking pansy. Got it? I know you like Israeli and African women but don't tell me you're in to queers as well, old chap. Frank will fill you in once you get to Lagos. Fill you in! Sorry about the choice of words but you have to laugh to keep sane. Not only is he a queer but a peer. So, what we have here is a queer peer, old chap."

I was, facing the familiar silhouette of Donaldson as he stood, his hands fiddling with something in his trouser pockets, before the open window of the Regent Street office. It was summertime and, outside, there was the sound of car and taxi horns and a traffic jam.

"He's a bit la de dah!" That was Donaldson's next description. "He goes for the chaps, not the bints like your friend, Mohammed what's it in Tripoli you once told me about. The one with the funny handshake you met in the park one Friday afternoon after prayers. Got it now, dear fellow?"

"And he's a frequent visitor to Africa?" I asked.

"Where there's a big willy there's always a little filly."

Jack shuffled in the corner, now deeply embarrassed.

"Better be careful, old chap. No direct eye contact, alright? Greedy little sod, from what I know. Gets off with anyone who looks him in the eye. Nice touch in cravats, too. Might take it off in Africa, I suppose, if he gets too hot under the collar. What say you?"

"Good lord!" I said.

"Yes, that's it. He's a Lord. House of Lords and all that. Got an inkling now who the blazes we're talking about?"

A few minutes later and it soon became clear that, in Donaldson's devious mind, Frank Marshall was the ideal person to be involved here and I was being asked to subcontract out a certain job.

"That's it, old chap. Just fix the meeting with Frank. Nothing more than that. No need to know the sordid, bloody details."

As usual, it was not enough for me. I needed far more and, under the circumstances, it seemed reasonable. "What's he done for Christ's sake?"

"No need to know, dear fellow. Just do your job. Check him out, just for the record so to speak. Ask the questions. Make sure you swat up on your artillery and pharmaceuticals. Impress him – though not too much, if you get my gist.

"You know, old chap, you've done this sort of thing before. But think Africa. Think jungle. Think the dire consequences of widespread mud hut terrorism. Think sweat and grime. Think Mau Mau. Think about the famine and mass starvation that might follow an unauthorised coup. Just think you're doing your Queen and Country proud, old chap."

"But the man's well known – famous in fact." I said with my usual utter naivety.

"Infamous old chap. Think infamous."

"But what's he done?" I repeated, knowing all too well what my persistence would do.

Donaldson finally lost his patience and I heard him say, "Ffffff," beneath his breath as he turned away.

The humour was gone, replaced with his usual bristling anger and impatience. The rustling sound from inside his pockets increased but then stopped altogether and the hand emerged. He turned back, pointing to his nose and the voice became more intense. "Frank will get the job done, not you. You just line it all up, understood?"

"Exactly what job? What does Frank have to do? Does Frank know more than me?" I asked.

Donaldson's impatience went up another grade. He stepped forward and leaned on the desk, his face just a foot away, spittle on his fat lips, his voice a hiss.

How I hated that bastard's face. Even after all these years. I remember his red face and his lips glistening with spit.

"Frank knows where he is best off. He just does his job. You could learn a thing or two from Frank. There's serious money at stake here........."

He stopped as if realising he'd just made a mistake. "......Not to say lives of course."

I stood my ground, facing him, nose to nose and pushed him further, picking up on his mistake of mentioning money. "Money? What money? Does Frank get any for whatever it is he'll do? Do I get any? Anyway, Frank is a friend of mine. He's no friend of yours."

Jack coughed and moved closer to the door but Donaldson stood up and walked around behind me and then back to the window. His black silhouette stood there for a moment and then he exploded.

It was as if something had finally burst inside the man. As if this particular case was giving him all sorts of private headaches. He tried his usual tack of suggesting it was orders from above.

"For fuck's sake, man. If there was an option, we'd take it. The man's a security risk. The FBI, SASF, the French, they're all starting to take notes. He's a fucking liability. He's an international embarrassment. He's been messing around in his dandy fashion with everyone from Gadaffi to Lumumba and from Ian Smith and Jomo Kenyatta to Nkomo.

"He's a bloody fool but too close to you-know-who to get officially chopped. What's more, we know he's started taking money in the form of commissions. He seems to think it's a perk. And he's so bloody naïve he's started spouting on about it rather too openly and doesn't understand that if he's not careful he'll get it in the neck from someone sooner or later anyway."

Donaldson went quieter for a second, breathing deeply, as though trying to summon some patience from somewhere and perhaps also thinking he'd said far too much already. With his back to me he stared down into the traffic jam below.

My own mind was still full of questions and what Donaldson had already said still wasn't enough for me. The word assassination had not been used but it was perfectly clear to me that I was being asked to take a part in some sort of plot worthy of Guy Fawkes. What exactly was Frank being asked to do?

Did governments really keep departments to do jobs like this? Did actions like this involve other countries? America? France? Were things like this done with their tacit approval or was this a purely British problem? Why not just sack the man, I thought, or was a simple sacking impossible due to knock on effects elsewhere? I had no idea. After all, I was only a simple, small businessman.

Then, of course, I remembered I had already witnessed one assassination.

I was there when David Reynolds was removed for reasons I didn't understand. Unlike this new target, Reynolds was virtually anonymous but, by imitating him, I had become deeply involved in his death. Was Donaldson ordering me to help in another disappearance?

I looked behind me at Jack but he merely glanced away and grabbed the door handle as if he'd need to escape. Then Donaldson turned to face me and I heard my own dreadful thoughts spoken aloud.

"I heard you've already done it once, old chap. So, you're bloody used to it."

"What the hell are you talking about?" I asked.

"I heard you were the only one there when that poor chap Reynolds got it in the neck. Remember? God knows what went on there. But I heard you had him shot and then stole his passport." He then turned away again.

Behind me, Jack did something more with the door handle and exited. The door clicked shut and I was alone with Donaldson.

"You fucking bastard," I said and I leaned over his desk, knocking his phone and went for him but he seemed to anticipate it and moved just out of my reach. I was already half way across the desk and about to jump onto it as the phone fell with its bell ringing to the floor. Donaldson took another stride back to the window, turned to face me, put his hand into his jacket pocket. It came out holding a handgun.

He pointed it straight at my head.

"Calm it, Ollie. Believe me I won't hesitate to use this fucking thing and David Reynolds will die for the second time."

I stopped half on and half off of the desk, but there was only one thing on my mind.

Sarah.

What the hell had I got involved with?

I retreated from the desk staring at the gun and Donaldson's red face. A big lump of white spit had settled on his lower lip. My whole body was trembling with anger and fear.

And it was as though Donaldson was reading my thoughts yet again.

"And if Reynolds gets shot, no one will know about it, Ollie, because he's already dead and doesn't really exist. As for fucking Ollie Thomas, it'll be assumed he's just flown off somewhere to fuck his African bitch and hide."

Neither Thomas's Disease nor my most vivid of nightmares allow me to remember what I did or said after that. I think I felt just as I do now – a total numbness.

Sarah was the most important thing to me and the only way was to continue until I could, one day, find a way out.

But I still remember Donaldson's final words: "So, better sooner than later, old chap. You're going there anyway on your own bloody business, aren't you? There's nothing to it. All you have to do is to introduce the pansy to Frank. Now fuck off. Get out of here."

Donaldson knew I had no reason to go to Nigeria for my own business. Not just at that moment in time.

I left to find Jack standing nervously at the top of the stairs. Behind the closed door, I heard Donaldson laughing.

I went home in a deep sweat to break the news to Sarah that I was going to Nigeria for a week or so looking for a few new agents.

Instead, I found myself up to my neck in a sordid plot, which I did not understand. But, as usual, once involved, however marginally, there was always a risk of implications if things went wrong. It became another case that Donaldson would remind me of regularly over the coming years. There is no doubt about it. I had become his shield. He was putting me between himself and any future implications.

The man's normal demeanour was one of a scowling, bitter but uncompromising man and rare attempts at laughter which normally only accompanied a lecherous leer towards a woman's breast followed by a coarse joke which only he would laugh at. He rarely, if ever, laughed normally. The laugh from behind that closed door was one I will never forget. It was as though he had cracked a joke. But Donaldson's jokes were not meant to be funny but to intimidate.

To this day, I remember Donaldson's laugh as like a ravenous hyena or one on heat calling for a mate. I once saw this in a David Attenborough film but far more often I saw it in nightmares. In those nightmares, it was a flea-bitten animal with yellowing teeth, a sloping back and Donaldson's face. It would stand, head lowered, sniffing around a carcass that was my own body left half eaten by African lions.

In my sleep, I would cover my ears and try to deafen the noise of Donaldson's laugh.

But Donaldson's allusion to African women had also got me worried as, until then, I thought this particular experience was a secret only between Angie and me. Sarah and I had, gradually, worked around my quiet, guilty patch and things were back to normal. But it was at that point that I decided Sarah knew something about Angie.

Somehow, Donaldson had fed a snippet of something into a chain of Chinese whispers. There really was no end to the bastard's list of ways to ruin others by scattering distrust.

I really have no wish even to recall Angie nowadays but she still comes back as though, forty years later, her own life, unlike my own, has stood still.

But Thomas's Disease means that my dreams know no boundaries and, as I have explained before, I am regularly haunted by ghosts, people long since thought to be dead, known to be dead or at least irrelevant. They seem to return as though deliberately trying to remind me of the parts of my past that I have no wish to recall.

In my mind, Angie still looks and sounds the same. She still has the same, husky, deep voice that reminds me pathetically of holiday brochures, of hot, white, sand and coconut palms that lean towards a flat blue sea. These days, I have to force myself to realize that even Angie would be in her seventies by now. Perhaps she is dead.

Perhaps, she has young grandchildren who go to school in Lagos in navy blue shorts and white shirts carrying old-fashioned, brown leather satchels over their shoulders. Grandchildren who laugh and play and run and kick empty coconuts or Coca Cola cans with bare feet and who smile wide smiles at the world through perfect white teeth that they have inherited from their sensuous grandma.

Perhaps they still laugh because, like all children, they had not yet learned what life holds in store.

And, after my brief involvement, I also dream that perhaps they aren't even black.

Perhaps they are only light brown or even piebald. Perhaps their grandma, Angie, has already died, of old age. Perhaps she died with secrets intact or died whilst being tortured to release her secrets.

Most likely, dreams tell me, Donaldson knew far more than me. Perhaps Donaldson even knew about illegitimate children and where they were.

So, do you now see the nightmare scenario that can arise through being a sufferer of acute Thomas's Disease and having too much time for thinking and dreaming and drinking?

But there is so little time left. I am an old man and I'm writing this just in case something happens to me.

Fortunately, I have already got a good way through this statement but it is far from complete. There is far more to tell and explain and my fingers and hand are hurting although my typing speed has vastly improved.

Not only that but I've got a headache and my chest is hurting.

MEDICAL REPORT

It was heartburn, I think.

It says nothing on the pack of Rennies about stomach acid being caused by whisky. My head still hurts a little but the brain inside is brilliantly clear. In fact, my brain is far clearer now than before the drink. My brain is as good now as it was sixty years ago and other parts of me that you might imagine are completely defunct also work. Just dreaming about Angie proves that point.

It's when I stand before a full-length mirror, that I see the problem.

For that is when I see a naked old man with poor muscle tone and a smooth, white stomach that restricts the vision of what hangs beneath. There are wrinkles in places where wrinkles should never be. My joints look misshapen and many of them crack and squeak like un-oiled hinges. Hands and wrists that were once permanently tanned and liberally scattered with dark and manly hair are now bare, blue veined and blotched with melanin. My nails are brittle, broken and yellow and athlete's foot is rife. I have knees that sometimes give out under strain and hurt for an hour or more if I kneel to mop the floor. I have a backbone that sometimes feels as if it might snap and I have such poor hearing in one ear, that my neck seems permanently bent on the downwind side.

After I've finished this section, I'm going to the opticians for new glasses. But I have no faith in their abilities to improve sight. It is their pseudo clinical attitudes and fancy instruments that suggest highly honed medical skills but which are just a clever prop for sharp commercial practices.

"Would you like to try these on, Mr Thomas?"

"How much are they?"

"Two hundred pounds but you get your usual over pensioner's discount."

"No thanks. I only want to see through them, not look like Elton John. I'll leave it for now, thanks."

My hair used to be thick and black and held in place by Brylcream and combed into neat partings either on the right or left side depending whether I was Ollie Thomas or Reynolds. Now there isn't much left to cut but I dislike visiting barbers who scratch across the thin skin of my skull with sharp combs. I used to get my hair cut in Cairo but now cut it myself although my fingers have lost much of their precision, especially when they're cold.

I recently tried to pick up a coin that I dropped on the floor in the off license but felt like an elderly Calcutta beggar, desperately gathering scattered coins. And all the time my eyes, far from concentrating on the location of the coin, were trying to see how many people were watching.

The worse thing is if my neighbour, Fred Carrington, sees me because he smirks.

My eyes run, constantly. Saline flows down my cheeks if I venture out in the cold wind and is guaranteed to find the only unblocked duct in my body. It runs into my nose forcing me to stop to wipe both red eyes and nose like a sobbing boy. And I often drop my stick at the same time. I know the blasted thing is going to slide off my arm before it slides. So then comes the dilemma of whether to concentrate on the mucus or the stick.

When I eventually get to meet my maker, I hope it's not a cold day and the Lord greets me with tears and a running nose. But let me introduce you to Frank, Olga and another Lord.

FRANK & OLGA

I **blame myself for telling Donaldson about my friend Frank
Marshall in Nigeria.**

Frank was already caught up in quicksand before I knew him but
as soon as Donaldson heard about him, the quicksand became like
deep shit.

In some respects, Frank was well suited to Donaldson's style
in that he certainly didn't run his business on a strong set of ethical
principles even though he was supposed to be in pharmaceuticals.

Frank managed a run-down business from an asbestos-roofed
building in Ikeja employing a small team of ladies in faded, green
overalls who poured thick red cough mixture from big drums
into small bottles, stuck labels on the bottles and put the bottles
into boxes. Frank also made money from deals he negotiated for
international pharmaceutical companies.

Frank was a commission agent of the old school. He was the
underpaid, dishevelled, sweaty, expatriate side of overpaid pin-
striped, eau de Cologne corporate life.

He was there for those who sat in plush, oak-panelled
boardrooms with Chinese carpets in Basle, Paris and London.

He was there for those who could then claim legitimately that
he was solely responsible for the manner in which the orders they
accepted were obtained. Bribery, you see, is subcontracted out even
more often than murder.

In short, Frank ensured that many of the pharmaceuticals
selected for importation by the Ministry of Health into Nigeria were

not for the well-being of the nation's poor and sick but for the well-being of the officials who ran the Health Ministry and the directors and shareholders of corporate Switzerland and America. But to stay on the right side of what little law was upheld, he was a mere manager of the business.

Frank was a fixer.

The company chairman, to whom he owed so little, was an ex Minister who had once been in charge of the Nigerian Ministry of Health. It was the ex-Minister who did the travelling to London, Basle and New York, wearing his Saville Row suits, staying at the Nigerian Embassy and lunching with the manager of the New Nigeria Bank in Cannon Street.

Meanwhile, poor Frank stayed entirely in Lagos with occasional trips to exotic spots like Kano, Port Harcourt and Ibadan. He had ventured as far as Ouagadougou once and had been to Accra several times.

So, Frank's international business career had not materialized in quite the way he had foreseen when he had first arrived in Lagos with his bag of samples as an immature young export salesman. But, his appointed role as occasional escort or agent for people he thought represented Her Majesty's Government had given him a sense of importance, however false and however short lived.

Frank's English wife had taken one look at Lagos and left him many years before to return to Maidstone. So, Frank lived with a very dark woman who wore a very recognizable and ornate headscarf like a turban. She spoke an extremely rare, native dialect, a little French and even less English. But it didn't seem to bother either of them as they communicated mostly through grunts and sign language. Sex is, after all, a fairly similar exercise wherever you go.

She had come from a place we once called Upper Volta and Frank had imported her into Nigeria in exchange for a few crates of cough mixture when he went on a visit to Ouagadougou.

Frank called her Olga as if she was a blonde Russian but this was far from the case. I suspect that Olga was actually the closest Frank could manipulate his tongue to say her real name, which stretched to many long syllables and included strange clicking noises unknown to anyone outside Olga's village.

Olga acted as wife and maid and they lived an exotic tropical existence in a fortified concrete villa with a corrugated roof and surrounded by rolls of barbed wire, several grubby Alsatian dogs and an ageing Nigerian ex policeman with a pistol tucked in his belt.

Frank spent the mornings in his factory overseeing quality control and production schedules. He then lunched at the Red Lantern Chinese Restaurant, where he had developed a remarkable resistance to no end of gastric complaints and then spent his evenings at a notorious den of sophistication in Ikeja where he concluded his business deals if he could stay awake long enough.

And just to remind you or to connect things up, it was at one of these high society gatherings at the Pink Coconut, where I met Angie.

On that trip, my first sight of Frank was as he pushed his way through the crowds of jostling, sweating, humanity. As always, he was wearing his stained safari suit, sandals and grey socks. He was shouting, cursing and waving a rolled newspaper but his arrival had been very timely because the hot and stressed Immigration Officer sat at his high desk in his unnecessarily thick uniform and rows of medals, had been questioning everyone's right to enter Nigeria.

And until Frank arrived it looked as though there might be difficulties with my right to enter the country. My vaccination certificate for Yellow Fever was not in order and this was vital for compliance with the sophisticated bureaucracy of Nigerian Health and Immigration Policy. But Frank's newspaper had done the trick, containing as it did several crumpled Naira notes tucked inside. I remember him tapping the Immigration Officer on the shoulder.

"Here, General, whatever you bloody title is, catch up with the news. Have a looksy at the sports page. Lagos Loonies beat the Kano Crappers. It's all there. It'll make your eyes smart."

Frank often spoke so fast that it did not matter what he said or to whom he said it or whether or not English was their first language. And I have never seen Frank in anything except the same, grubby, beige safari suit. He had long hair in an untidy Beatle style that seemed totally out of place in Nigeria. He had a red, sweaty, sun burned face and, on that occasion, a burning cigarette was cleverly tucked between the same fingers that held the newspaper. His blue eyes had taken on a permanent sparkle from too many evenings in rooms filled with ganja smoke or other narcotics.

But, payment received, my passport was duly stamped. It was shoved towards the edge of the desk for me to collect and Frank's General disappeared behind his high desk to conceal the newspaper and its contents beneath his chair. Frank had grinned, grabbed my bags and shouted at me to follow.

"Come on. Don't lose me, for Christ's sake. Let's get out of this fucking hell hole."

Despite his recent appointment of working for the Crown via Donaldson, Frank was not known for his sophisticated use of Queen's English. Frank's company car, too, was also less than sophisticated. It was a rusting Peugeot with sagging seats, the body parts held together by layers of dried, red mud.

Frank only had two real friends.

One was Olga and the other was sat waiting in the car with the engine running.

Frank's driver, Smart, was a young, athletic Nigerian who, if opportunities for fulfilment had been available, looked as if he should have tried professional boxing or athletics. Smart was not smart but he was very reliable. He would do anything Frank asked and would drive for hours without a break, even sitting in the car in the hot sun whilst Frank refreshed himself in the shade of banana trees at roadside beer houses.

"So! Ollie!" Frank shouted above the general melee. "Got a cable to say you'd be coming."

We clambered into the car and Smart drove off into the traffic.

"Where are you staying, Ollie?"

"Airport Hotel."

"Luxury. Must be on good expenses."

The Airport Hotel had never struck me as luxurious but I let it pass. Fried eggs were the only breakfast at the Airport Hotel. Sometimes they were the only lunch and the only dinner. It was never boiled eggs and never poached eggs. It was only ever fried eggs. I had queried it one morning. "Sorry sah. No water." It was the obvious explanation and I should have known, after all I'd cleaned my teeth in beer earlier.

"How are you doing, Ollie? Business good?"

"Yes. Can't grumble. Dodging and diving, bit of this and a bit of that, you know."

I would often speak like that to start with although it depended on the person I was with. Frank was a suitable person for this particular style and I needed to create the early impression that, today, I was not in the business of bothering about too much legitimacy. Frank needed to know that anything would interest me if I had a chance to make a quick buck. And if this meant a bit of under the counter stuff to get around stuffy government regulations that got in the way of healthy international trade, frankly I couldn't have cared a fig.

This was often true I have to admit. It was a vital necessity to keep my agenda flexible in case something cropped up. But behind whatever façade I created and whatever impression you might get I was, in fact, a complete professional in international trading and export. There weren't many like me then and probably even less nowadays.

"Pharmaceuticals interest you this time?" Frank was doing his own prying into my motives for being there.

"Always," I said.

"To ship home or ship elsewhere?"

The number of pharmaceutical wholesalers in England who would have risked their reputation bringing in medicines that had passed through Frank's factory was going to be limited. But Frank was prying and the questions were already sufficient proof that he was going on what Jack must have told him because Jack and I had discussed pharmaceuticals as a ploy before I left. It was unlikely however that Frank knew anything about Donaldson – yet. Such was the manner in which the man operated.

I was dropped at the Airport Hotel and I thanked Frank for meeting me, told him I had another meeting early the following morning in Lagos and suggested we meet for lunch. With that, Frank's red mud plastered Peugeot drove off in a cloud of blue smoke with Smart at the wheel.

I had fried eggs, rice and beer for my dinner that night. But next morning, after an uncomfortable night spent scratching in a bug infested bed that smelled of stale sweat, I took a taxi to a much plusher residence in downtown Lagos for my meeting with the spoilt English heir to half of the Scottish Highlands. My job was to use bullshit to introduce him to Frank Marshall.

This distinguished fellow held an Oxford degree in Ancient Greek but his business training had probably been limited to reading "Teach Yourself International Trade". It didn't matter. Unlike most of us, the man's upbringing meant he was automatically destined for the House of Lords and a type of diplomatic immunity wherever he went or whatever he did. He had risen through family connections to a role as a sort of government advisor on African affairs although, at the time, Africa was not regarded as a Foreign Office or a Defence Ministry priority. His only knowledge of Africa appeared to have been as a boy of six living with his parents for a year in Nairobi.

Not content with the thought of one day inheriting a Scottish Castle, the odd commission paid into a Swiss account was starting to take on the innocent legitimacy of normal, day to day expenses to top up his income and he was becoming a liability for diplomatic progress on many fronts. He had started out as a spoiled child. Now, on the frail excuse that Her Majesty's diplomats, unlike small businessmen, needed refreshing after seven-day stints visiting the Third World, he was being spoiled by attending too many cocktail parties, staying at too many hotels on Park Lane and eating at too many places like the Ritz at the expense of others. He was in fact thought to be becoming, or already was, a risk to national security.

Having been mistakenly employed by the Foreign Office and the Ministry of Defence he was known to have acquired information that was strictly confidential and, also since the age of six, he had been well known for being unable to keep secrets for very long.

He would go to Nairobi, Khartoum and Cairo and then back to London for his refreshment and then find an excuse to go to places like Addis Ababa, staying, of course, at The Hilton Hotel. It is strange I had never met him before, but his itinerary and mine had never coincided and, anyway, his choice of hotel would not have been the same as mine.

On arriving at his temporary Lagos residence, I was sure I could smell smoked bacon and toast being cooked. It turned out to be a small, private hotel or guest house built in the colonial style and so a full English breakfast would have been quite normal.

Surrounded by a high, concrete wall with metal spikes along the top, it hid amongst a small clump of high coconut palms. But the garden was a sea of red mud because it was morning and dark, thunderclouds had only just finished depositing an inch of rain in the space of half an hour.

When I arrived, the hotel's gardener was sweeping flood water full of floating debris, but his toils were in vain. A foot of water had already breached the front steps and a gritty, red stream was running into the open plan reception area where someone else was sweeping it out of a rear door.

But I knew what to do. I took my shoes off, folded my trousers to my knees and put my briefcase on my head as a shelter from the water still dripping off the palm trees. Suitably attired, I waded towards the building and up to the long wooden reception desk. Above me was a high ceiling with a huge, creaking, wooden fan that slowly turned, hitting the top branches of a tamed coconut palm growing from a clay pot. The muddy, red water ran across the scratched marble floor between low wicker chairs placed against dull, unpolished wooden coffee tables showing round stains of tea and coffee spilt from cups.

It was steamy and hot but, despite the conditions, a waiter hovered with a tray and an off-white cloth draped across his arm ready to serve coffee to a few white guests sat in mud stained suits. A white woman in a light chiffon dress and a wide brimmed hat sat with her long legs crossed, nearest to the clay pot and with a cigarette in a long holder held between her thumb and first finger. Her feet, fortunately, were on a dry part of the floor, proof that the floor itself was uneven.

I had met her once before at the Embassy, the wife of a diplomat but I couldn't remember exactly who she was. She was not the Ambassador's wife, I felt sure, but she was the sort of longer-term resident to be expected in a place like this. The equally unsuitably dressed receptionist, sweating in his black suit and bow tie seemed to be expecting me.

"Yessah. Mr Thomas, is it? You are expected. The Lord is waiting for you sah."

I have never forgotten that greeting. Ever since then I have wanted my entry into heaven, whenever it came, to be announced like that. The pity is that I never told anyone, not even Sarah.

The Lord was not slow in appearing but I have always hoped that the real Lord, if we met, would avoid the visual image that this one created.

Donaldson's latest assignment minced towards me with his hand outstretched like a peacock on a catwalk and I could not help wondering how someone who apparently spent so much time travelling in Africa and the Middle East could look so anaemic and pristine. He wore pure white slacks and shirt, shiny brown shoes with a matching belt and a white hat, slightly less frilly than that of the diplomat's wife sitting in the other corner. But his main adornment was, as Donaldson predicted, a cravat. This was a long, wide, multi-coloured specimen made of the finest silk, which he swished like the tail of a pedigree filly in season.

"Ah, Mr Thomas? Good morning. I'm so pleased to make your acquaintance. Glad you could make it. Sorry about the weather here. Damned messy at times. But been here before, I expect, have you? If so, you'll be quite used to it. Damned perspiration. Seems destined to leak from every conceivable orifice, don't you think?"

As advised by Donaldson I tried hard to avoid eye contact but became immediately uncomfortable about the way my knee was being touched. We sat in the opposite corner to the diplomat's wife who kept flapping at flies with a handkerchief, which she held in the hand that was not holding the cigarette and we began with a general discussion about my business. I quickly, deliberately and sneakily dropped in a suggestion of some interest in military supplies to North Africa.

But with no prompting he said: "Yes. I have to say that my confidential discussions in Tripoli suggest that arms get in through Chad anyway. So, whatever we can do to ensure we supply direct will limit their clandestine operations. Keep some control. Don't you agree?"

What, on earth, was this man talking about, I thought. We had only just met yet he was taking no precautions. He could not possibly have known who I was or how a small import-export business based in Croydon might possibly fit around official Foreign Office or Ministry of Defence policy. And, at the time, I was probably more of an expert on Libya than anyone in the British Government. I certainly knew all about Chad.

Then he said: "Cup of tea? I'm sure we can order some."

He waved at the waiter holding the grubby towel and ordered tea before moving rapidly on. "So, Mr Thomas. May I call you Oliver? Tell me just a little about the other opportunities I hear you've been lining up, besides the military ones, all of which might benefit from my input and a little official backing and encouragement from Her Majesty's Government. We so need to keep all our options open, but at all times we wear our desire to help British trade openly on our sleeves."

I wondered what to say at that point but was well used to handling inquiries about my business, even when they were often at odds with the other jobs I performed for Donaldson.

What I found myself saying was a figment of my imagination but one founded in such confidence that if challenged to give more detail would not have required me to dig too deeply to appear utterly convincing. It was an acquired skill that had required some good practice. I also knew that Frank would back me up.

"I have some pharmaceutical interests here as well," I said. "A small, local operation – an agency, distributorship and some small-scale local manufacture. It is a joint project with Pennex

Pharmaceuticals. Their headquarters are based in Kent. Do you know them?"

"Oh Kent, the Garden of England. How lovely," he pronounced with great delight.

"Yes, well," I said, moving my leg again, "We need a few high-level government contacts to help win a few contracts. Ghana, Sierra Leone, Liberia – that sort of area. Your name cropped up."

"As it would, Oliver."

With that he gave a toothy smile, I got my knee patted and the cravat swung wildly. But the response was obviously positive and I was encouraged to continue despite the hand now resting more firmly on my knee.

"Well. I wonder," I said, "would you care to meet the local manager of the plant tomorrow morning? Say ten o'clock? He's a British chap – name of Frank Marshall."

"Of course, I'd be delighted. Here?"

"Well, I thought you might like to meet him at the factory."

"What a splendid idea. Ah, here's the tea."

And that was all I did face to face with the Lord. I left shortly afterwards to meet Frank for lunch.

ASSASSINATION

The incentive for Frank was that he had been promised a commission and other benefits and someone had to make this offer whilst trying to explain the whys and wherefores in more detail. That job was, of course, mine.

As the subcontractor living half way down the mountain I was to subcontract the job down to Frank who lived on the edge of the jungle. My job was to persuade Frank to subcontract it to someone else living right in the middle of the jungle. That person was Smart. But do you now see how easy it is for those at the very top to deny ultimate responsibility for their instructions? They sit in offices far removed from the factory floor and only venture out to point towards jobs that need to be done.

Sometimes they even get others to do the pointing and nothing is ever in writing of course. After that, they retreat to their offices once again.

It was obvious that Frank had already heard something before we met for lunch at the Red Lantern.

I guessed he may have met someone on the commercial staff at the British Embassy - the same man who, apparently, would call at Frank's factory from time to time with other requests.

I learned all this at the Red Lantern by plying Frank this time with gin and tonic. The gin and tonics were poured in and Frank's heart poured out. He got more and more drunk and then more and more emotional. "You're a good mate, Ollie. You see . . . well, fuck . . ."

Frank had been almost in tears and the embarrassment had been such that I had spent most of the time in the Red Lantern studying the food-stained red flock wallpaper, which is why I remember it.

Frank's south London accent, that he had almost forgotten in favour of Lagos speak, improved all the time, as the gin took effect. Quite why I had plied him with so much drink I don't know, but I had an uncanny urge to find out how Donaldson worked on others and Frank proved to be an excellent case study.

Frank was more used to beer, the local concoctions, and other forms of exotic stimulation, the sort that was inhaled, rather than drunk. His Beatles hair cut was lying down across his sweating forehead, his eyes were red, his tongue was loose and his soul was being hung out to dry. But fortunately, in this state, his speech was slower and much easier to follow.

"See, Ollie, this time the bastard came with an official, bleeding letter from the Embassy stating that all British subsidiaries operating in Nigeria should adopt a code of practice when dealing with the Nigerian Government. Code of bleeding practice! I ask you, mate, what a load of shit!

"Anyway, we are not a subsidiary anymore. Wholly owned Nigerian buying raw materials from the stupid fuckers back home. So much for their commercial savvy, eh? But it was as though the commercial attaché himself was as clean as a whistle and all the rest of us were on the take or bribing officials left right and centre just for the bloody hell of it.

"We all know what they get up to at the Embassy. They can be as corrupt as any in the ranks of pen-pushing bleeders in the Nigerian Ministry of Health for example. If they can make some dash without too much fuss they will. But I was one of the few fucking local Brits they knew who was dealing directly with the local assholes. The rest, particularly those silly sods with their fucking suits and polished shoes passing through on short trips, all go through the Embassy and always seem to know who to see. They seem to know before they even catch the bloody B Cal flight out. They are promised action but that money may need to be placed in certain accounts.

"They aren't disappointed either. Fuck no. The money disappears from where it is put and they get the contract – a thousand times the size of the dash. It's the same with all types of business here – telecommunications, roads, civil engineering, water, electricity, medical equipment. You know, Ollie, mate. All those public services, utilities and things that'll still never fucking work properly even after the next fifty years."

How right Frank was. He was telling me nothing I didn't know but I listened nevertheless. Despite his condition, Frank had vision and was still being realistic. Everyone knew it. Millions of pounds of good Nigerian money, money that would be publicly announced as destined for improvements to the country's infrastructure. Money that would never flow down to the pockets of the millions who really needed it but end up in the pockets of Nigeria's elite, the military, or in the pockets of international businesses who would never complete their sides of the bargain. Money that would end up in the private bank accounts of diplomats, politicians and other middlemen, men who, if the folks back home ever knew about their extra-curricular activities, would and should have lost their jobs and the hefty pensions that always came later.

That was the sort of money that seeped through cracks in the system and lined the pockets of people such as Donaldson. And if I had wanted to, I could have lined my own pockets. If I had I would certainly not be sitting here in Gloucester typing away on this old machine.

"So how does your own Chairman fit into the scheme of things?" I asked Frank.

I was already pretty sure that this was Frank's weak spot and I had not yet got to the point of giving Frank the envelope that contained a passport and air ticket from Lagos to London.

Frank sat back in his Red Lantern chair, his eyes flashing beneath the greasy strands of hair as Mr Ho the proprietor fussed around his best customer, clearing the dregs of tinned chicken and sweet corn soup and handing it to his apprentice, a serious Nigerian boy aged about ten who scurried off towards the kitchen dropping spoons and forks all the way.

Frank leaned forward again and downed the last of the gin, the thick slice of orange and a small lump of ice sliding out, down his chin and on to the tablecloth. "His fucking Excellency, you mean?"

He laughed a drunken, bleary-eyed laugh and then beckoned with his forefinger to come closer. "Shhh – not so bloody loud, Ollie. Got me by the short and curlys, ain't he? Know what I bloody mean, mate?"

We stared at one another for a moment. Frank's eyes were moving from focussed, to wandering, to half shut.

"Go on," I said, to encourage him.

Frank looked inside his empty gin glass. "Get us another, Ollie. It's good to chat. I only get to talk to Olga when she's finished fucking me and we never go into much detail as I'm always too knackered."

I suppose that showed a degree of sensitivity and intelligence remaining inside Frank and I suddenly felt sorry for the man. He couldn't have been more than thirty-five. Yet here he was living with an African woman he couldn't talk to and caught up in some sort of quagmire, unsure what to do and merely succumbing to the inevitable. I knew the feeling and perhaps I'd been lucky. But for the grace of better fortune perhaps it might have been me sitting there dribbling onto the table with Mr Ho's special chow mein noodles dangling from my mouth.

Frank continued with the verbal diarrhoea, probably a precursor to the gastric version that was to come later.

"You mean His Excellency, Doctor fucking Abu Fayinke, one time head of the Ministry of Health, now Chief Executive, puke, puke, of Pennex (Nigeria) Ltd and still the unofficial controller of all the sodding freaks and pen pushers who claim to be working for the good of the nation's health? Also, brother to this chief and that chief, friend to every politician in Lagos, Ibadan, Port Harcourt and Kano? Also, the best mate to all the chiefs in Sokoto and Rivers State, first cousin to General whatsit and every other big tit in the army? Mr Fucking High 'n Mighty? Wined and dined by six of the world's most unethical pharmaceutical companies and on the best of dishonourable terms with all those who run the Nigerian Central Bank. I shouldn't be saying it like that but you've got to live here to fucking know, mate." He stopped and then added: "You mean that Chairman?"

"That sounds like him," I said.

Frank looked at the gin and noodle splattered red paper covering the table.

"You know what else, mate? Even the bloody ex policeman who sits guarding my fucking house allegedly to protect me from every cat burglar and murderer this side of Maiduguri is really there to stop me escaping at dead of night. You think he's more likely to shoot raiders or shoot me?"

Frank then started tugging on a corner of the red paper like a sulking boy. He tore a piece off, twisted it expertly between his thumb and first finger to form a small, rigid cone, stuck the sharp end up his nose and used it to soak the mucus that was running from each nostril.

Meanwhile, Mr Ho brought the next gin, left it by Frank's elbow and left.

Frank said nothing for a while as he waited for the nose plug to work. Eventually, he extricated the sodden twist of paper, tossed it on the table, grabbed the fresh glass and all but downed it in one.

"Can't you just pack up and go?" I asked him, whilst looking at the wet plug which had landed near my plate.

"Got me by the short and curlys," Frank repeated.

"How?" I asked.

"Not enough money that's how. You need money to fix things around here. I got as far as checking in at the bloody airport once until someone suddenly decided my passport wasn't in order. Got into a right fight. Fucking bastards said I didn't have the right stamp in some place on page thirty-six, no bloody signature on this and that, no bleeding cross on a T somewhere . . ."

"The Embassy – couldn't they help? It's their duty to help a British citizen." I asked although I already knew the answer.

"Don't make me laugh, Ollie – conniving bleeding swine, they are. Seem to think I don't play by the local rules so leave me to my own bloody ends. Wash their hands so to speak. I got arrested once for peeing against a wall and was carted off by my shirt collar with a bamboo stick the size of a bloody tree trunk stuck down by belt.

"God forbid. They all do it. You see notices on all the fucking walls. 'No Urinating Here' but everyone, including the fucking women, deliberately piss on the notices themselves. Or go shit behind them. But me, oh no! White you see. Got dragged off around the corner, paid my fine from my wallet and walked away. I told the Embassy. They laughed. Shouldn't piss on walls they said. Fucking useless bastards."

Frank paused briefly but soon restarted. "I found out the bloody Immigration Officer was in the pocket of his Excellency as well. Also, he pays me in Naira. What's the fucking use of that? I came here with nothing. The wife's got the house in Maidstone and a new bloke. And . . ." He tailed off, tearing off another piece of red paper.

"And?" I prompted him.

"Then there are all the others. Those you met the night we went to the Pink Coconut."

"Augustus and Co?"

"That's them. Oh, great friends. Any or all of them could get me arrested at a moment's notice if they wanted. The only one that's OK is a girl called Angie. But one is a senior police officer. Know that? I know you thought he's in Defence but, well, he is sometimes but it's more like a protection racket.

"That's the way it is. Bloody confusing. They carry all sorts of fictitious business cards. Another one is a lawyer. Know that as well? Another is a brother to Major Big Tit. And one is the fucking manager of the bank where my money goes. They watch me like hawks between using me to act as the authentic, white face that goes with some of their money laundering activities. Scary, innit?"

"And what about Pennex back in England?" I enquired with great seriousness.

"I'm nothing to do with them now. It's sold, I think. Here, we're wholly owned Nigerian Company but I didn't know it was happening till it happened. His Excellency's bright idea."

"So, what do your pals, whom I met that time at the Pink Coconut, think I'm here for?"

"You think they really care? As long as there might be some swag at the end of it or they think you might be looking to swing a thing or two. I'm the honourable white face again you see. They smell a nice, big lump of dash somewhere. I'm the buffer between white hypocrisy and black corruption."

We both sat back, probably looking and feeling exhausted and for a brief moment, Frank looked a little more sober. I chose that moment. "So, what do you think I'm here for now?" I said because we had still not yet discussed the other business.

Frank looked bemused. "Christ knows," he said. "I just got a message you were coming. No one spoke you understand. Someone left a letter from the Embassy with one of the girls at the factory marked Private and Confidential. It just told me to meet you. Name, flight number, that sort of thing. I assumed it was the fellow from the Embassy from Florence's description and I smelt another chance to get me out of this fucking hole. But it was signed by a guy called Jack Woodward. I knew the name Woodward," Frank continued.

"My dishonourable Chairman has a habit of name dropping sometimes. He likes to make out he is connected at high level in UK and even mentioned MI6 once. Fucking crap. But the note said 'we' God knows who 'we' were – understood my predicament and would try to find a way out in return for a few favours. The message said to call someone at the Embassy but it wasn't an Embassy number, I know that.

"I called anyway but it took a whole bloody day to get through. I spoke to the chap who answered the phone. He sounded foreign – not sure where from – not English – Arab possibly – there's a few Lebanese here. I asked him what was meant by favours. Course, he didn't know. He knew nothing and, of course, there was no one there to ask. They think I'm mad. So, in the end, I just turned up to meet you."

Frank leaned forward holding his head as though to stop it spinning around.

"That's about it," he concluded forlornly.

"Well let me explain," I said.

I described my meeting with the Lord and that he would be visiting Frank's plant at ten the next morning. But then I came to the tricky bit.

"Can you arrange a further visit to your other factory, Frank?"

"What other factory?" Frank asked.

"The one you plan to build to allow for your expansion plans. The one you'd like to build amongst the lush green forest up near Ibadan. Ask Smart to take him there. You don't need to go. Just say you've got another site manager up there. Smart has friends near Abeokuta, doesn't he?"

There was no need for me to say anything more. Frank clearly understood what was needed and he fell silent for a while. As I waited for him to think, I beckoned Mr Ho to bring us coffee.

The chipped cups and saucers arrived and for a while we sipped the coffee in yet more silence although I could sense Frank was tempted to drink his direct from the saucer which was already half full anyway. Finally, he said, "Mmmm."

Taking this as an agreement, I said, "So, do you want to know the pay-off?"

"That would be very nice." Frank said without looking up from his saucer, which had parted company from the cup and now sat on the edge of the table ready to fall off. Suddenly he sounded extremely polite but perhaps he was at the end of his tether. He looked up and tried grinning, although the result was not a pleasant sight.

"Want to know what I've got in my case if you agree?"

"That would be very nice," Frank repeated.

I bent down to my briefcase and, at last, produced the brown envelope. "Jack Woodward gave me this for you. In my opinion, you'll need to get an urgent haircut and a new suit or something to look like the photo or you might get recognized by your Immigration friends. In here is a British passport with correct stamps and everything else you'll need, or so I'm led to understand, and an air ticket issued in the name on the passport. It's all in order. You just turn up at the scheduled hour. Fly out of Kano so you don't meet your Immigration

Officer friend. Call Jack on arrival in London and he'll sort you out with some more money as well."

"OK," said Frank. "So, all it means is that Lord Fancy Pants needs to get permanently lost, is that it? But I don't do anything and you don't do anything."

Frank had said it aloud. It didn't sound nice like that but we were both pretty much in the same sort of shit. "That sums it up,"

I shrugged, but with a nasty picture of Donaldson in my mind because 'permanently lost' was one of Donaldson's favourite expressions. It was used to describe the fate of anything that was no longer required, from a piece of paper to a human being and I remember how he had put it to me as he stood, silhouetted against the window. "Just think of it as another German or a bloody Jap old chap. The enemy, you know. You probably shot down one or two of the bastards in your time. Never thought of it twice afterwards, did you? Did your job for Mr Churchill and hey presto, back in the cockpit, and on to the next job. And, on this occasion, you don't even have to pull a trigger."

It was to be Frank who had to organize the details. But even Frank was to be removed from the actual task. On refection it seemed to me that Frank was aware a job like that might come his way. Perhaps Jack had already pre-warned him of a need to pay for his release from his prison. Perhaps Frank had already done something similar so was used to it. It was, after all, Frank who'd fixed my visit to Amman where I witnessed the assassination of Reynolds.

Our final minutes in the Red Lantern were spent in agreeing that Smart might be just the man to carry out the deed.

In fact, Smart turned out to have all the attributes for the job.

From what I heard later, once the Lord had been introduced to Smart who had been fitted out with a new pair of tight, white slacks, red socks and a royal blue, open necked silk shirt the battle was half won. Smart looked really smart for the first time in his life. Even Frank had made an effort and worn a cleaner safari suit.

The following day the Lord went to inspect a non-existent pharmaceutical factory and was never seen again, having displayed none of the skills required for a miraculous resurrection of the sort the other Lord specialized in.

There were some-short term diplomatic difficulties between Nigeria and London when it appeared that the Nigerian authorities were not exactly falling over themselves to find out what had happened to the son of a diplomat and ex politician. Perhaps it was an unfortunate bush incident, after all several known criminals and bandits operated in the area. It was also perhaps a fortunate coincidence that two French businessmen disappeared a few weeks previously. One had been found naked and murdered on a patch of wasteland near the airport. The other had disappeared without trace.

And Donaldson had found a way of ensuring that a few well-placed suggestions as to what the man, with his particular habits, may have been up to, soon laid the story to rest. One Sunday newspaper had a field day on speculation and even the extended family of the Lord in Scotland shut up for the embarrassment that might have occurred.

But guilt over my own contribution has never been laid to rest because Frank . . . well. Poor Frank. To this day, I am not certain what happened. Frank never made it to Gatwick airport. Something went drastically wrong because he was picked up at Kano airport with his false passport and ticket and he, too, disappeared. And the next time I went to Lagos, Pennex (Nigeria) Ltd wasn't there.

When I crept around one night to look it was just an empty, boarded up factory surrounded by barbed wire. Someone had even stolen the asbestos roof. Frank's concrete house had also been treated in the same way. Frank had been obliterated and so had Olga.

When asked, Embassy staff just shrugged and said they had assumed he had returned to England. Jack also shrugged and said he was mystified and that Frank's unclaimed expenses were still showing in the accounts.

The man was always called "The Lord". There was never a name or an official title. At times the poor man was mentioned in the same way as one might recall a sick dog that had had to be put down. At other times, though, Donaldson would infer that high-level investigations were still going on, that scapegoats were being sought and that arrests might be on the cards. And at those times he would look at me as though I was the sacrificial lamb, tethered and ready to be offered up if there was ever a necessity to save the skin of himself or others. "I heard they're still looking into the Lord's disappearance, Ollie. Weren't you the last person to see him?"

My discussion with Frank at the Red Lantern had continued well beyond the handing over of that brown envelope and, as usual, one thing led to another. In this case, Frank taught me things about money laundering Nigerian style and I was soon able to put Frank's information to good use.

My friend on that occasion was a Nigerian called William Akinbiyi.

GATHERING EVIDENCE

"**W**ill o' the lisp, more like, ha!"

Donaldson once tried to make a joke about my good friend William Akinbiyi. I didn't like Donaldson insulting my friends.

William had a pronounced lisp, which Donaldson found amusing. We were in his Regent Street office. "So, that's your black friend, Will, is it? I liked his mithing ethith and his yeth, thir, no thir, free bag fool, thir."

"William's an honest man, unlike some I could name," I said.

Donaldson had already drunk beer and several glasses of wine and was in a bad mood. He turned to face me with spit on his lower lip. "And what the bloody hell are you implying?" he shouted.

I didn't reply but continued to sit in the chair on the other side of his desk and stared at the floor between my legs. I was silent but only because my own anger was welling up inside. The bastard moved from the window, grasped the back of his chair, sat down and swung round to face me. His face was flushed. Silence always made him madder.

"For fuck sake. The whole bloody place is awash with corruption," he said. "Top to bloody bottom. The only way to get to the bottom of it is to chance your arm a bit."

We'd been discussing corruption involving charity donations but it was one of those occasions when Donaldson would imply that we, being the innocent party on the side of law and order and bound by officialdom, could only beat them by joining them.

I saw through it of course. Donaldson didn't want to beat them at their game or chance his arm. Donaldson wanted a slice of the cake.

Still sitting staring at the carpet and unable to look Donaldson in the face I asked him another question that had been troubling me since he'd demanded I introduce him to William.

"But what the hell has this got to do with Her Majesty's Government?" I said. "It's the problem of the Nigerian government not ours."

This was just the sort of question Donaldson disliked. There was a moment's silence before he exploded again. "Christ's sake, man. How many times have I got to say it? Instructions are instructions, understood? Just get out there and get to the bottom of it."

"What bloody instructions?" I asked, "Whose instructions? You think I don't know what you get up to Major?"

I was pushing it, still not wanting to directly accuse him of manipulating things for his own financial gain because I didn't yet have the evidence. But he knew what I was getting at.

"Instructions are to be obeyed, otherwise shit hits the fan," he replied, still trying to play the innocent one.

I tried to stay calm, but failed. I was already mad about things he'd said during lunch with William. He wanted me to go to Nigeria.

"No," I said. "I've already told you. I've got visitors coming over in the next couple of weeks – my Angolan agent is coming, then I've got a Tunisian chap. I dislike letting people down and . . ."

I wasn't allowed to finish, because Donaldson's chair creaked as he suddenly leapt up and leaned over the desk towards me. One of his hands clamped on to some paper, crumpling it still further. The other slid across the polished surface knocking the black telephone, which gave a sharp ring of discomfort at being hit.

Jack, who had been cowering near the door as usual, jumped.

"Go now." Donaldson shouted. "Not next month, not next week, A-S-A-P, got it? This is fucking urgent. Cancel the bloody Angolan. Postpone the fucking Tunisian. Leave the bloody country on the next available bloody flight. This is the best chance we've had for months. It cannot be delayed, do you understand? It is imperative we nip it in the bud."

A few more, well-worn phrases poured out along with the spittle but it was the intense anger and desperation that unnerved me. It was as though Donaldson's personal livelihood depended on it and as though he himself was under enormous pressure to act. As usual, though, he finished with a threat. The Frank job had only just passed and memories of the threats he'd made with the gun pointing at me were still very fresh.

He swung his chair around to face the window again, took a deep breath and spoke in short sentences in a surprisingly quiet voice as if forcing himself to control his impatience and anger. "You know, Ollie, old chap, once you're embroiled it's difficult to pull out without all sorts of complications setting in. Government doesn't like it. Always looking for a scapegoat to save face. I've seen it before. They watch you like a hawk. Got to stay one step ahead. Wait for them to lose their jobs. Blasted civil servants always linger though. Asking questions, tipping off Ministers. Don't know what it's like at the sharp end. Comfy offices, good pensions. Bloody paper shufflers."

I wasn't clear what he was trying to say as I already thought he was one of those paper shufflers with a good pension, albeit enhanced by income from illegal extra-curricular activities. He swung back again and leaned back.

"You're a man who likes a bit of spice in his life, Ollie. Never seen you as a bloody paper shuffling civil servant. Like the cut and thrust. Bit of a loner. Not one to sit behind a desk all day. Like me in a way. Need the excitement. But once you're in it, you're in it. No way back. Need to make a living. Save for the future. Got a wife and family to think about, but ideal chap for these sorts of jobs. But there's a lot at stake here old man. We are – all of us – up to our necks in shit. Marked men, one way or another. Step out of line and your fucking throat's cut. We're all pushed and leaned on from somewhere. I'm leaned on. You're leaned on. But the pushing and leaning has to stop somewhere, Ollie."

Donaldson paused for effect. "But you, old chap, are bottom of the scrum, so to speak. Who, the fuck, do you lean on?"

I was still staring at the floor. But I was seeing Donaldson, yet again, for the man he was. I looked up to see him staring, unblinking. Jack was coughing nervously in the corner.

I shouted back at him.

"You know who I lean on, you bastard – my wife. But I don't lean on her in the way you lean on me. I rely on her for a touch of sanity. There's a clear difference – not that you'd understand. She is the one bit of common sense left around here. Perhaps if you were sufficiently human to have someone yourself, you'd start to understand, you bastard."

Donaldson's face reddened and his lower lip trembled as if a nerve had been touched. He then took another deep breath. "Then you know what to do, old chap. Go out there for her fucking sake."

He stood up and went to the window to stare down into the street below.

"And what if I don't go?" I said.

"Then she'd soon get to know about the shit you're involved in, old chap. What's more, she'd get to learn a hell of a lot more if you failed to make it back in one piece."

He stopped, apparently waiting for things to sink in but I was already hardened to this sort of comment. We'd been here many times before so I just sat there thinking. I knew Donaldson was only driven by personal gain but it was taking me far too long to piece together the evidence. Even with it I'd still not know what to do. I glanced over at Jack who had been watching the scene. But he averted his eyes.

Jack never had the look or manner of a sophisticated crook. He was a lackey, up to his eyeballs in the shit as well. And did he really understand or have the balls to realize what Donaldson was up to? I still wasn't sure so I stared at him until he turned away.

As far as I knew, Jack never ever went to the Whitehall office which Donaldson would sometimes mention. Instead, he seemed to operate loosely through Regent Street without an office, desk or even a chair to sit on. He would stand there as though he had just wandered in and was about to wander out again.

But I, at least, was starting to see things in a different and perhaps more accurate light. It was as though the shadows that the new light cast threw a clearer picture on the truth. Jack reminded me of a show I once watched in Singapore where stiff, unmoving, Chinese puppets made from flat, lifeless cardboard held on sticks were, once reflected from behind, brought to life as moving beings with changing shapes and characters. If you had the patience to follow it and could tolerate the tinkling music coming from a cheap, wooden xylophone a story slowly unfolded.

I thought about the many assignments I had been given by both Jack and Donaldson over the years. Some could be considered legitimate in that they may, I suppose, have been of use to British Intelligence. Perhaps these had been requested and sanctioned from higher up. Perhaps.

Others, however, were more akin to commercial investigations like industrial espionage of more use to bigger businesses or other organizations that could use what I found out or even sell it on. But approved by Government? It was unlikely. Donaldson tried to make these latter assignments smell a little better by a touch of perfume from a bottle marked "best interests". This fresh proposal that Donaldson was so worked up about clearly fell into the latter category but he was so visibly stressed that it looked personal.

That's why I was pushing him. I was trying to make him feel so uncomfortable that he cracked and shed some light on his motives. But Donaldson was made of granite as hard as that used to construct his office in that tenement block in Edinburgh. It seemed to me that Donaldson was somehow behind this unfolding Nigerian drama that was to involve William Akinbiyi, just as he had been behind the Frank affair and the Libyan-Irish affair.

A silence descended but I could hear Donaldson breathing heavily. I stared at the quivering Jack Woodward and shook my head at him trying to provoke him into doing or saying something. "So, what do you think, Jack?" I said and added, after a calculated pause, "Old boy, dear fellow."

Donaldson shot me a look and said nothing but he turned to Jack with a look that was enough to turn a bottle of milk sour. Jack was expected to say something. Jack was there to back up Donaldson, say the right thing, lock the office door whenever necessary, smooth things out, calm things down and gently persuade me to go along with things. He was there to say yes, yes and yes again.

To my great surprise, Jack coughed and opened his mouth. "It needs someone with commercial contacts, Ollie. Not the usual government or diplomatic ones. There's a lot of it going on." He coughed again and looked at Donaldson who was still staring at him with an expression that suggested that this was a fair start but not enough.

I could see what Donaldson was thinking. Keep going, you stupid bastard. Give him more. And if you don't help me out here, God help you as well.

Jack clearly saw a problem so he tried again, stroking his chin. "Yes," he said, "A lot going on."

It was laughable. God knows what Donaldson thought. What Jack meant, of course, was that there was a lot of bribery and corruption going on but no one needed a small-time office manager and yes man to tell us that.

But Jack was, you see, doing his imitation of a Charles Dickens character. In my mind, I often compared him to Uriah Heap, a character you may recall that was noted for cloying humility, obsequiousness, and insincerity. Jack was similar although instead of making reference to his "umbleness" like Uriah Heap, Jack would refer to everyone's sense of "duty".

Uriah Heap wrung his hands but Jack's particularly nauseous side was a sort of sickening fawning accompanied by the stroking of his smooth chin. He clearly never grew out of this mannerism as he demonstrated when we met at the Cumberland many years later and he asked about Sarah. But he was right about a lot of things going on in Nigeria. These sorts of things had been going on for centuries and, as far as I know, still do.

But Donaldson had clearly had enough. He pointed a finger directly at Jack, the first time I'd seen this. "You fucking sort this out. If it's not sorted in ten minutes all fucking hell . . ."

He went out, slamming the door but didn't go far. In the brief silence that followed and while Jack and I looked at one another, I heard a match being struck outside the door. Donaldson was having a smoke but he was unusually stressed.

I waited. I planned to say nothing. This time it was Jack's turn. He moved a few paces and came roughly where I could see him out of the corner of my eye but then reverted to his Uriah Heap character. This time it was the fawning version. "You're the best, Ollie – the one D trusts. How's the Nigerian business? Going well I hope."

I couldn't see him but he was probably wringing his scrawny pale hands but I felt sorry for him though I don't know why.

"I haven't been back recently," I said. "What happened to Frank rather put me off."

"Ah, but there's commission in this one, I believe."

I turned to face him and found he was not wringing his hands but looking at me as if I always went weak at the knees at the thought of money. "And why would Nigeria want hardware?" I said.

He though I meant military hardware but I knew full well this was highly unlikely. I was, you see, trying to help him out of his predicament and find out what this was really all about.

"It's not that," he replied. "I think it's to do with aid money. It sounds complicated to me but D knows much more."

"Aid money?"

"I think so. It's been happening a lot lately. Money for agricultural projects, schools and that sort of thing. It goes astray. It finds its way into the Central Bank and then it.......it disappears." As he spoke, he ran both hands across his chin, cheeks and forehead as though just the mention of criminality gave him a hot flush. But then he held them up like a magician who had just made a white rabbit disappear. "Just like that!" He paused. "D knows a lot more."

Of course, D knew more. D was probably the instigator and the mastermind. D ran a whole division of the Mafia.

I decided to apply another test on this pathetic man. "And how will D work out my commission if ever we found a way to stop it. Ten percent of a million pounds' aid package seems interesting. But ten percent of a stolen Sunday morning church collection doesn't sound like much."

There was a pause. Jack was never that quick when it came to math. "Yes, well. I see. I hadn't thought about that. You would need to speak to D."

Jack could never have been a businessman but he was good at ensuring the availability of cups of tea. Jack was like Mohammed who cleared the parrot's droppings. He was good at conveying bad news such as the death of a forgotten acquaintance. And sometimes, under pressure or through utter naivety, he would make the mistake of offering a clearer picture of what was really going on.

"I'm not sure D wants it stopped," he said. "I think it needs to be redirected."

Ah! I thought. Now we're getting somewhere. I could see it now. This was not a plan to track money and make sure it didn't get into wrong hands. This was an attempt to track money and then move it directly into private pockets, probably Donaldson's.

"I see," I said thoughtfully.

But it was as if Jack was so dim that he couldn't see what was going on under his own nose, though, perhaps, he was temporarily overcome by the power of sitting in Donaldson's chair because he had moved around to face me on the other side of Donaldson's desk and even sat down.

Donaldson could still be heard outside but Jack had given me more reasons for suspicion and I was now intrigued. "OK," I said. "I need to understand more."

Jack went to the door and Donaldson returned still puffing on his cigarette.

Slowly I started to understand what was going on. It seemed that around two million dollars was lying in a Swiss bank account, destined to fund the purchase of medical equipment for small, rural health clinics in Nigeria. Of course, I smelled a rat. I knew I was being used but I also decided it might help prove my case against the man and if I could find a way to screw things up for him good and proper then I needed to seize it.

I agreed to help saying I needed a lot more information and left.

I devised a plan and contacted William to say I was flying to Nigeria and wanted to see him. I booked a ticket and then met up with Donaldson and Jack the day before I was due to fly to check if everything was still in place. Jack handed me a small buff folder. "The bank details are in the file, Ollie."

"Thanks. So, my suggested plan of action is still on?"

"Yes," said Donaldson.

"Nothing changed?"

"No," said Donaldson.

"And I receive one per cent?"

"Yes," said Donaldson and then added, "And I met someone from the Nigerian High Commission. I told him you'd be helping out."

I was shocked to think he'd involved others. "You did what?" I shouted.

"Trust him."

Donaldson rarely used the word trust. Trust wasn't something he understood and he always found it difficult to say the word. He rolled the "r" like a Scotsman and missed the last "t", so that it sounded more like the word truss. Trussed up was probably what he meant anyway.

"What chap from the High Commission?"

Donaldson tapped his nose, "Need to know basis old chap. No need to worry, it's all sorted. Relax."

I then saw something in his eye that meant he was now far less stressed. Donaldson had fixed something but I didn't yet know what.

I flew to Nigeria to meet William.

WILLIAM

That time on my arrival in Lagos, there was no Frank to meet me and take me to the Airport Hotel so I made my own way there.

Somehow, I doubt if it has changed much during the last forty years but I ate a dinner of fried eggs and rice and then, as night descended, walked the short distance up the red and dusty road to the club, the sound of drums and saxophones increasing as I got closer.

Mixed with the sticky, humid, air, was the usual Lagos smell of dust, beer and stale sweat and for a short while I forgot about Donaldson and why I was there.

The Pink Coconut club was largely a tin shack open to the air and mostly for the slightly better off locals. But as the only white face there I found myself, as usual, surrounded by ten or more girls standing, waiting and chattering outside the entrance waiting to be taken in. Then I ran the gauntlet of the men in charge and was asked to pay ten times the normal entrance fee.

But one of the most persistent girls held onto me with her sticky hands and escorted me inside, where we found a wobbling, metal table and hard metal chair in the dark shadows, somewhere under the corrugated canopy. She ordered me a beer and for half an hour I sat there, sipping cool beer, soaking up the atmosphere and listening to the loud and throbbing music that blended jazz and blues with a unique West African sound.

That night I had not had to wait long before William turned up.

It was past eleven and I was on my third beer but I heard his unmistakable voice as he approached through the shadows behind.

It was a voice that broke through the music. "Yeth. You mutht have theen him. You thaw him path thith way?"

I glanced around and the girl sat by me, helping me drink my beer also looked behind. "Ah. Yeth man. No worry. I thee him, now."

William's gleaming white teeth were the first sight to emerge from the darkness. "Hey, Mr Thomath – Ollie, my man," he said pushing his way through from twenty yards away, "Glad to thee you. Making yourthelf at home, I thee."

Then the tall figure of William appeared, holding out his big hot hands.

William's greetings were always the same. One large, sweaty hand would grasp mine. The other would be slapped hard around my shoulders. He scraped up a chair in the dry dust opposite and sat down. "Hey, haff girlfriend already. Very nithe."

The girl laughed and got up. "You wanna beer?" she asked William.

"Tuthka."

William slapped her as she squeezed by and the hand stayed there briefly, a finger easing its way under her bottom. She shrieked, wriggled and moved away to get his bottle of Kenyan Tusker. "So. Lagoth again, Ollie, my man?"

"Nice to be back William," I replied.

William Akinbiyi was one of my many business contacts in West Africa. He was an importer of farm tractors and other agricultural equipment having taken over the business from his father who had died in a farming accident while William was studying at University in England. We first made contact when I was looking for distributors for tractor spares. I met him at the back of a concrete-block house in Ibadan. "Yeth. I can thell one hundred a year with all thpare parth. We thervith tractors all over Nigeria from Lagoth to Kano, from Maiduguri to Calabar. No problem."

Confidence oozed along with the sweat from William and he had used his English University education to impress all those with lesser qualifications. These included a wide spectrum of local chiefs and politicians from crooked Christians in the south to money grabbing Moslems in the north. As such William was well placed to know a thing or two about how to manipulate the wretched system that had evolved. But he had his honourable side.

Despite his size, his speech defect and his occasionally coarse behaviour he was likeable. The hard, extrovert layer was a form of protection because, beneath that outer crust was a softer layer. He believed in fairness, respect for others and that you took as much as you could but only by hard work or by being better than the others. But it was the more visible, coarser streak that gave him an edge of respect from those in the more dubious quarters. They did not possess the sensitivity to recognize his deeper, nicer side. They thought that he was, like them, mean and selfish in all his dealings. They thought, too, that his respect for others was limited, like theirs, to those who could be snuggled up to, for material gain.

That next hour with William was spent in drinking and listening to music but the next morning, after my breakfast of more fried eggs, he came to the hotel and we sat in the shade of wooden scaffolding to discuss how to deal with the latest assignment set by Donaldson.

I told him exactly what Donaldson had told me – that large sums of money collected by charitable donations was going astray rather too often than made sense and that we were going to try to put a spanner in the works if possible. I didn't tell William that I rarely believed a word Donaldson said because that meant telling him about my experiences of the last twenty years.

But for William poor people who gave to charity had no right to see their hard-earned cash being siphoned off into the pockets of the rich and those with know-how and influence. So, it was not difficult to persuade William to ask a few questions and dig around a bit in banks and other places.

We brainstormed some likely characters and William came up with one very likely candidate. It proved to be spot on and what's more William knew where he lived and had a way to contact him.

I left him to do some more digging and I went off to see another of my business contacts to see if I could get an order to cover the cost of my trip. Two days later, we had devised a rough plan and were off on our mission.

We took a mid-morning internal Nigerian airways flight and by afternoon were bouncing along a red, dirt track in a hired car with the sun flickering between rows of banana trees on either side.

The car was swerving to avoid potholes filled with red, muddy water and William was driving with his sunglasses on, his seat on the farthest adjustment backwards and with one hand on the steering wheel and the other lying across the back of my seat behind my neck.

"Long way but muth get there before dak, Ollie, my man. Not eathy to fine thith plathe."

Throughout the ride, we went over the plan as best we could although we knew we had to be prepared to change things to suit the rules of their game. I told William that Donaldson had said he was the bee's knees.

"Bee'th knee'th, Ollie? What the fuck is that? I ain't no little bumble bee. I'm a wothp with a thting and yellow and black thtwipes. Ha ha."

Eventually, William stopped the Peugeot that was, by then, covered in red dust from roof to doorsills and we walked towards a big, concrete house along a muddy track somewhere in Calabar.

"Thith ith the plathe, man."

Later, in the same house, I sat around a table with William and another Nigerian man in cumbersome ethnic dress of white and gold. A short, fat lady, presumably a wife, in a long colorful dress served up a meal of spicy fish soup and mashed yams as a bottle of Black and White whisky circulated.

Much later, William and I groped our way back down the dark track to the car and headed off, slightly the worse for wear, to find somewhere to stay for the night. On the way, we chatted again.

"You thee, Ollie. There ith a lot of money going athtray. Millions."

It was true and a simple plan for transferring the two million US dollars destined for health clinics across the whole of Nigeria had been made very clear over the fish soup and pounded yams. William's digging and intuition had proved invaluable.

Our host for dinner had, only a year or so before, been the Minister charged with delivering the state's health care.

But the one-time Doctor and student from a British medical school who had risen to such heights had, suddenly, found he was missing a friend or two and was out of a job again. Having reached the heights, the only way now was in a downward direction and so he was looking for some income. He already had one or two accomplices but what he really needed was a legitimate company to bounce the deal off and move the funds somewhere.

That the one-time Minister seemed to trust William and me to help was, undoubtedly, down to Donaldson having said something to the Nigerian High Commission because the subject cropped up as we were emptying the bottle of whisky. "So, we are in good company, Mr Thomas. The wheels are well oiled so to speak."

And then he'd gone on a long and tortuous explanation of why the medical equipment wasn't really needed anymore now and that there was a far better use that could be made of the money if it was transferred elsewhere for other projects.

It was all the usual hypocritical nonsense and I think I probably dozed off or focused on removing hundreds of needle-like fish bones from the soup. I remember our host describing how he had recently joined other high-powered dignitaries in visits to local hospitals and schools, all desperate for funds and, for good measure, speeches had been given about the evil ways of international big businesses that drained the country's limited resources on needless infrastructure projects that always failed to deliver. And the press who followed in droves had been encouraged to take many photos of poverty and terrible living conditions.

Mostly they were being courted for votes, of course. I woke up as we arrived at the crunch point.

"We'll soon find a far better use for the funds," he was saying. "But it's the bureaucracy you understand. It takes so long to get the funding in place and then we have to line up all the medical equipment. By then the need has gone."

"So is the equipment already ready and waiting to be shipped," I asked noticing that William still had his eyes shut.

"Of course," he said as though I should have known. "And, of course, it is already paid for. We just need to find a way to release the allocated funds to use for other humanitarian projects. This is where you come in."

He passed the bottle and, once again, I filled my glass. I hit William with the bottle to wake him up but his head stayed, resting on his chest.

"Yes," our host went on, oblivious. "Your company will receive a number of Letters of Credit to cover the shipment. The total amount will be around two million dollars. The equipment is already paid for and waiting to be shipped. So, you don't have to buy it. Buying it would be a real complication and we would not want to put you to so much inconvenience. Then you will receive the shipping documents. You present them to the bank as usual and, under the terms of the credit, the funds will be paid into the Swiss Bank

That was why I was wide awake to hear his final words. "And that's it. Simple! No problem!"

I jumped. "I would prefer the money being paid direct to Thomas Import Export so we can deduct our charges first," I said. "Then we'll transfer the balance."

"Oh no, there has to be some trust here. But your percentage will be transferred immediately."

I was expecting it. It was the first sign that the plan I'd put to Donaldson had been changed.

"OK," I thought to myself. "I wasn't expecting to make much although one percent for my troubles might have been nice."

The question now was whether the rest of the plan would unravel.

The plan had been that I would hang onto the whole two million dollars while the scam was reported to the Government and the charity concerned. The authorities were then supposed to pounce. It was a lovely idea. So innocent. And Donaldson's job, as a servant of the Crown working for British Intelligence, the Fraud

Squad, Interpol or anyone else that might be interested, was to arrange the pounce.

William had missed all of this but finally woke up with a grunt. We left soon after that and groped our way in the dark through the bushes to find the car. Once in the driving seat, William fully woke up. He was still speaking as he drove around town looking for somewhere to stay.

"Nithe man, Oliver. Good food. Very fat you thee. Big money. Big idea. Well connected with all them high-grade politician around Calabar. He was Minithter of Health one time in the patht. Knowth all them big chief in Lagos too. Have big farm ath well. Told you already about that. Many people taking big dash to keep quiet. Travel a lot ath well. London, Thwittherland, U Eth A. Well known by High Commithun in London. Belong executive club with British Caledonian and Thwith Air. Friend of Thentral bank and ethpethially New Nigeria Bank. Talk to all them foreign politician too. Yeth, he very fat man. "

William suddenly braked and the car skidded to a stop and I thought he had spotted a place for us to stay but, instead, he looked straight at me and added: "He altho fucking big bathtard Ollie."

His final, conclusion made us laugh. "What to do then, William?"

"Good quethtion."

I didn't have the heart to tell him, that my worst fears were coming true. "I think we'll keep to plan A, William. What do you think?"

"Yeth, Ollie. Plan A is the bee'th kneeth."

Two days later I was home.

Three weeks later I arrived at the office to find Beatie with what looked like a smile on her face. A Beatie smile was a very rare sight. "Oh, Mr Thomas. Such good news. I've just opened the post. We've got six letters of credit for the medical equipment contract you mentioned. All confirmed. I can hardly believe it!"

Beatie must have seen the look on my face which was hardly one of ecstasy. I felt so sorry for her but couldn't possibly explain. "Ah! Good, "I said, trying to look pleased. "Let's see."

"Here, Mr Thomas. Look! The big one is for nearly half a million dollars, the smallest for two hundred thousand. I totted it up and it's one million, nine hundred and fifty thousand dollars. What do you think, Mr Thomas?"

"Mm," I said, "That was quick. Surprising really."

Beatie was almost beside herself with joy. "That's because you went out there, Mr Thomas. I knew you'd win a big one sometime."

"Good old William," I said. "He's done us proud."

"But the expiry date is so short, Mr Thomas. Look. It all needs to be shipped within eight weeks. How on earth will we organize it in time? And how are we going to buy the goods to start with? But I expect you have already thought about that, Mr Thomas."

Beatie was actually very good. She was far better than Jack and commercial realities never passed her by. Normally, such an order would have required me to buy the goods in advance which meant cash. But, for an order of this size, a bank loan would have been the usual route and a charge on our house would have been the security. There would have been other ways but if I didn't get paid for whatever reason, the upshot would be unthinkable.

I have experience of exactly that scenario as you will soon learn.

But this was no ordinary deal. The medical equipment was apparently, as our friend in Calabar had confirmed, already paid for and ready to be shipped. Beatie knew nothing of course.

"Special arrangement, Beat," I replied. "The goods are all ready to go and suppliers will get paid when we do. All we've got to do is process the paperwork. Margins aren't too good, but we'll make a little. Christmas bonus, Beatie."

"Oh, Mr Thomas, that would be nice."

With that I put her mind at ease and she set about her typing once more.

But let me explain now that the most commonly sought skill for fraud, especially international fraud, is to know how to get paid for supplying absolutely nothing. Empty containers are a good one or containers filled with crates of stones to give weight. An Iranian dealer I once knew was highly skilled in this type of business. All he needed was an accomplice or two living near his foreign suppliers.

The accomplice would arrange for right footed army boots to be shipped through one port and left footed boots through another port on the other side of the country. Naturally he refused to accept delivery on the basis of incomplete shipments or wrong contents and so didn't pay his supplier. The shippers then auctioned off the containers as useless waste and, of course, the same chap bid the highest? He then spent a week sitting in the dust of his warehouse in Tehran, carefully matching up the boots again and, hey presto, found himself in possession of two container loads of perfect pairs of army boots that were worth a small fortune.

In my case, all I had to do was wait whilst someone, somewhere, organized the shipment of eighteen containers of medical equipment. Then wait for the shipping documents, certificates of origin and all the other pieces of paper to arrive to submit to the bank.

A month later, with commendable efficiency, all the documents arrived in the office. Beatie performed her usual checking job, I double checked them and we submitted them to the bank.

I assumed then that the money would be released and paid to the specified bank. It would have been nice then to have seen my one percent but I didn't hold my breath. I got on with other things and Beatie believed everything had gone like clockwork and waited for her Christmas bonus.

Not having the heart to tell William what had happened in case he thought I was totally inept and naive, I paid him his agreed amount immediately. Then I went to see Donaldson.

I was perfectly calm as I listened to his explanation. "What can we do, old chap?" he said. "You've done your bit. I understand, the Government wants to keep it under wraps at present. Let them deal with it through normal diplomatic channels. I'll keep you posted."

While Jack stood nervously rubbing his chin by the door, Donaldson went to the window of the Regent Street office and looked out. But I could distinctly see his reflection in the window glass. Donaldson was trying not to laugh.

Oh yes, I thought, case proven but I said nothing, took a deep breath and looked at Jack Woodward to see whether anything had registered with him. But no, there was no expression from the man except one that suggested confusion, uncertainty and a total lack of comprehension. He stood there, rubbing his chin as usual, a man completely under someone else's control or completely out of his depth. Here was an ex-serviceman who had become a yes man and standing there like a dumb waiter too scared for whatever reason even to say boo.

I gave Jack the same smirk I had seen on Donaldson's face in the reflection and then turned and spoke to Donaldson's back. "Ah well," I said, "you win some and you lose some. I'll be on my way, then."

It was then that Jack managed a few words. "See you soon in the Feathers, Ollie."

"Sure," I said and walked out.

On Christmas Eve, I gave Beatie her bonus.

On Christmas Day, William phoned me at home from Nigeria.

"Ollie, I don't underthtand."

"What's the problem, William?"

"About the two million poundth medical equipment. You paid me my commithun but I think thumthing went wrong, Ollie."

"Yes, I know, William," I said. "But don't worry I was expecting it. You did your best and that's why I paid you."

"Did you get paid, Ollie?"

"No. Fortunately, it has only cost me some time."

"But you know what, Ollie? The fucking bathtards sent thirty thix Merthaydeeth Benz cars in the containers inthted of medical equipment."

"Mm," I said, "I was expecting something like that. There's been a spate of theft of brand-new Mercedes around south London."

"You get a Merthaydeeth, as well, Ollie?"

"No, William, still got the Ford."

"All of them are fucking bathtards, Ollie."

"I know, "I said. "Have a good Christmas, William."

"And you Ollie."

GOOD ADVICE

When I'd left the Regent Street office with Donaldson smirking at his own reflection and Jack playing with his own chin, I may have looked and sounded calm but inside I was fuming.

I walked towards Victoria station planning to go home but the anger was not subsiding and I didn't want Sarah to see me like this. So, as I passed the Duke of York pub, I went in, ordered myself a pint and went to sit alone in the corner to think. I had decided to do something about Donaldson some years before. So, why hadn't I?

The answer was simple. I kept going partly because of Donaldson's blackmailing tactics and threats but also in the faint hope that things just might start to ease up and that my link with Donaldson might fade. But it hadn't faded. In fact, it seemed to be entering a new phase of nothing but fraudulent deals involving huge sums of money. But I still didn't understand how Donaldson operated.

I gulped down mouthfuls of my beer.

It was clear to me that he had built a parallel career around his official job and I had become an integral part of it. I was being used as an innocent messenger and a provider of useful information. I was like a salesman for the Mafia and no better than Jack.

Resigning was the problem. I knew too much and that was the reason for the blackmail and threats to myself and my family. They were to keep me from wandering and were likely to continue for ever just to keep me quiet. The more I sat and thought, the more the worry and anger inside me grew.

I went to the bar for another pint and returned to my corner.

Thomas Import Export Limited was my small business that I had started by myself with limited private funds with youthful ambitions to gradually build into something important and international in order to provide Sarah and myself with a good income and, when the time came, an asset to finance our retirement. But it had not grown to match my old vision and I had saved almost nothing. It was just a convenient tool for Donaldson to bounce his fraudulent deals off.

As I drank, I watched two men playing darts with a board that was old, worn and with so many holes that more often than not, darts would bounce off the board and fall to the floor. Thomas Import Export was like that. There were only so many holes it could bear.

I got up to order a third pint but this time, instead of returning to my corner, leaned on the bar and withdrew into my thoughts. I really had no idea how to deal with Donaldson. I'd dismissed ideas of speaking to government officers, a minister, my MP or the police for fear I would not be believed and for fear that Donaldson would take action long before I got anywhere. I drank half of my beer in one swallow and put the half empty glass on the bar ready to depart. Then:

"Need a new TV, mate?"

A young man in open necked shirt and jeans had sidled up and was winking at me. Long black straggly hair hung down to his shoulders.

"TV?" I checked.

"Yeh, mate. Watch TV do ya?"

"Sometimes," I said, "When I'm around."

"Cheap," he said. "Job lot. Me and me mates have a van around the corner. Nice quality. Sony."

"In the TV and radio business, are you?" I asked jokingly.

He took a mouthful of his beer and grinned. "Yeh – today, anyway."

"What about tomorrow?"

"Nah. Got to move on. You know how it is, mate."

"Yes," I said, "You're right. You definitely have to move on."

"In business yourself, mate?"

"Yes," I said.

"Dodging and diving, mate?"

"Plenty of that," I said.

"What's your specialty, mate?"

"International arms trading," I said mainly as a joke

"Fuck," he said. "Really?"

"Yes," I said. "Hence the ducking and diving."

"Fuck," he repeated. "Got anything in stock at present?"

"Only if you order a forty-foot container load."

"Bloody hell," he said, his voice dropping to a conspiratorial whisper.

"Yes," I said. "It is bloody hell; I can tell you. My advice is never get involved. Keep life simple."

"Fuck me. Who are your customers?"

"African despots, Middle East terrorists, IRA."

"Jesus!" he said. "Your own business?"

"Yes," I replied. "Want to buy it?"

"Your business is for sale?"

"Just waiting for the right offer."

"How much, mate?"

"Free," I said.

"Fucking free?"

"Yes." I replied. "But it comes with a liability."

"What's that then mate?"

"You get followed everywhere, your family gets threatened and orders only come from the head of the London Mafia."

"Jesus Christ!" he said.

"Yes," I said, "I asked Jesus Christ, but he's not interested in buying it either."

"Not surprised, mate," the young man said. Then he laughed which suggested he thought I might be pulling his leg. I decided I needed to put him right.

"You think I'm joking?" I said, staring into my now empty glass. "What would you do if you wanted to get out of the business?"

"I'd shoot the bloody head of the London Mafia to stop him destroying me, mate. You gotta get out of this bleeding mess, man, before it's too fucking late. That's what I'd do. Shoot the fucker."

"Thanks," I said. "That's exactly what I thought. Can I buy you another pint?"

"Ta, mate. Don't mind if I do. Now, what about a nice, new TV?"

"No thanks," I replied, beckoning to the barman. "I've got to go home to check to see if my wife is still alright. She's probably sat watching the TV as we speak. But enjoy your drink. And thanks for the advice."

BACK SCRATCHING

It was Farouk who provided a way to solve my problem with Donaldson.

As usual it started with a phone call to the office. "It's Mr Farouk, Mr Thomas," Beaty said.

To me, Farouk was like Smith, Jones or Brown. I knew several and I asked Beatie to ask which company he was from.

"He says it's not business, Mr Thomas. It's private."

As soon as she said it, I knew which Farouk it was. "Alright, Beatie, I'll speak to him."

Beatie handed me the phone but looked at me as though she was being bypassed in some way. The look had become increasingly noticeable over the years. It was as if I should notify her of everything I did, even private matters. I'd thought that perhaps it was because she was always in the office and I wasn't but it was still my business and she was being paid by me. I was becoming increasingly concerned about Beatie's strange manner but dismissed it once again to talk to Farouk.

Farouk and I had known each other for many years.

The first time we met was a day of clear, bright blue sky in the mountains behind Beirut at a hotel on the road to Zahle where the white snow still lay in the shade \amongst the rocks.

This was before the civil war had started and before the city was bombed into concrete rubble. We had met to discuss pharmaceuticals but had ended up talking politics.

I think Farouk called himself Farouk for business and political reasons as he was actually a Christian born in Alexandria into the Coptic Church. He also looked more European than Arabic and my suspicions about his name were confirmed when I once heard him being called Frank and saw a letter from Germany on his desk addressed to Franke. But let us not go into that. We all have our secrets, me especially, and Farouk was a good friend who I trusted.

He ran his business from Amman with a warehouse in Beirut and another office in Damascus and was helped by a small team of Jordanian and Egyptian salesmen selling mostly to pharmacies. Farouk tried hard to keep his religious background quiet but with all the difficulties in the region, his political opinions had matured into a clear set of bottled up principles which he seemed relieved to express to a well-travelled English businessman offering a good ear and some useful information of his own.

Farouk's pent up political frustration had poured out over a meal of humus, lamb cooked in yoghurt and mint, all washed down with too many glasses of arak. And it had soon become apparent that Farouk was not averse to dabbling in other imported items in order to supplement his already substantial income from pharmaceuticals and cosmetics and to satisfy his appetite for small scale subversive politics.

What helped Farouk in this was his network of affluent pharmacists and medical practitioners who were reasonably well-paid professionals and far more inclined to prefer a steady, peaceful co-existence with their neighbours than the angry, unemployed residents of the Palestinian camps.

So, after we had finished the bottle of arak, I agreed to help Farouk by organizing a few deliveries of other items, not in large quantities, but carefully concealed in boxes of codeine tablets, antibiotics and hospital disinfectant.

"Only for defence you understand, Oliver. We do not want to cause trouble. There is already too much of that simmering here."

Indeed, Farouk had no need of guns for they were to be found everywhere in Beirut and most nights were to be heard going off after the restaurants had closed. At the time, hand grenades were less easily available but once bought and imported into the UK in boxes of Tunisian dates ready for the Christmas market were not difficult to re-export. I was well used to this sort of trade, believing that wealth creation through added value was far more important to the British economy than strict compliance to customs requirements. And it was only on a very small scale.

So, a few weeks later, Farouk received his consignment disguised and packed in boxes that were clearly labelled: "Disinfectant – Hazardous Chemicals – This Way Up".

I suppose that admitting to a little arms trading, however small scale, might offend some and be a good excuse to charge me sometime but it was never a particularly profitable exercise although I suppose I could have specialized in it and made a fortune. And I have always disliked things that make a loud noise and kill people. So, it was just a useful service I sometimes provided to oil wheels.

After that first, small, deal our friendship remained low key but we met up in odd places like Paris or Brussels to reminisce or complete another small deal, which in most cases were for less interesting things such as more hospital disinfectant and throat lozenges. But the business was almost secondary. What we shared was friendship, mutual respect and a good understanding and, if he is alive today, I would love to see Farouk again.

Sarah and I were still living in the Victorian terrace in Croydon but, with surprising speed, Farouk seemed able to afford to buy an expensive apartment in Paris, surrounded by other Lebanese. He

Farouk had become one of my sources of ideas and contacts but he always said that he owed me one big favour sometime. It would usually be as we shook hands outside an exotic place called the Byblos Hookah lounge and restaurant near the Champs Elysees.

"Thank you, Ollie," he would say as we emerged from the hot, smoke filled room into the Paris lights. "You scratch my back for me and so I must scratch yours someday, yes? I don't forget your English saying. You just let me know when you have itch."

I waited too long but, eventually, decided that the time for the back scratching to be reciprocated had arrived.

Farouk was unknown to Donaldson or Beatie. Keeping just a few secrets like that was one of the few ways I tolerated the bastard for so long. Sometimes I regret not having spent more time on business of the sort that Farouk and I did. It was a missed opportunity. Perhaps if we had gone into some more formal partnership, I would have opened my offices in Paris and Tokyo and this shabby character sitting here typing on this ancient machine might have become a multi-millionaire. Perhaps I would be sitting in the sun by the pool at my villa overlooking the sea near Cape Town and about to don my suit by Armani, my shoes by some other Italian cobbler and my socks by Debenhams. Whereas, instead, I am sat here looking out at a rainy day in Gloucester wearing a twenty-year-old shirt, some Marks and Spencer's slippers and trousers with the damp and dubious stains around my lap area.

Farouk knew me only as Oliver Thomas who ran an import-export business from south London. He believed I was just rather well connected with people whose identity he had no reason to ask about but whose status might be useful to him if he continued to befriend me and complete the odd deal through me. I saw no harm in that. Neither did Farouk who knew I was a frequent visitor to the Middle East. He saw no reason to ask too many questions and that suited both of us and was the way it had always been. If Farouk had been with me and someone else had referred to me as Mr Reynolds, a wink, a smile and a nod might well have been enough to satisfy Farouk. In fact, it might well have served to increase the trust, such was the nature of our relationship.

So, it was Farouk's constant reminding of a desire to scratch my back sometime that provided a possible solution to my problem with Donaldson.

So, when Beatie took Farouk's phone call and said, "He says it's not business, it's private," it was very timely. The Nigerian case and the Mercedes cars had just passed and was still very fresh on my mind.

Farouk had arrived as a foot passenger on a morning crossing from Calais but didn't like driving on the left so I took my own car and met him at the Red Lion pub outside Dover. It was a cold, wet day, a far cry from the open-air restaurant in Baalbek where we had last met.

It was also a very difficult period in the Middle East, the era of Black September and Wadi Hadad's Popular Front for the Liberation of Palestine and another Leila called Leila Khaled. Bombings and hijacking were almost common place, but it had never stopped me visiting countries like Lebanon.

I thought about all of this as I drove down to Dover. I also thought about Donaldson as I knew from meetings in the Feathers that he was well versed on the politics and clearly maintained a few old contacts of his own there whom I knew. I also knew he was not liked. He was regarded, even then, as untypical of an ex British Army Major working for the British Government and seemed to have formed a reputation amongst the few who knew him as a wide boy.

In the Red Lion Farouk and I ate steak and kidney pie which was a disgrace to the human palate and an utter embarrassment to me who was used to being entertained at Paris's best Lebanese restaurants. Farouk gave me a small order but I think he was, by taking a ferry to Dover to see me, trying to show that he was saving me the bother of going to Paris. Farouk, you see, was already feeling he owed me something.

A few weeks later we met again, this time by accident.

I had taken a Royal Jordanian Airlines flight to Amman with an idea to meet another of my agents and then move on to Damascus. I didn't tell Donaldson where I was going but he seemed to know already.

Donaldson was on my mind for all the usual reasons of threats and insults, but he had recently told me I was being tailed. Putting someone on my tail in Amman would have been very simple for Donaldson. Reynolds had probably been followed before me.

I checked in at the tiny Al Shams Hotel behind the mosque off Sharia Zarqa, dumped my small case of white shirts that Sarah had ironed just a few days before on my bed and decided to take a short walk, because the cooler evening air would be a pleasant way to waste half an hour and to think before I turned in.

I took the mazy route through the souk just in case I was being followed and then walked along the pavement surrounded by the smell of charcoal fires, spicy chicken, lamb kebabs and the night flowering jasmine that hung over the iron railings and stone walls. Then I crossed the road near the mosque.

A dim street light cast a dark shadow beneath the canvas canopy of the grocery shop with its open sacks of dried fruit, rice, herbs and spices and rows of bottles and tins. Black dressed women with round, brown faces, looked at me without turning their heads as they wended their way home from their evening shopping. A fully lit coffee shop was still busy.

And that's where I saw a familiar face.

Farouk was seated amongst some tables set well back from the pavement outside the entrance. He was with a group of much younger men, some of whom were relaxing by pretending to be much older men – sharing pipes, tilting backwards on the back legs of chairs or sitting cross-legged on a red carpet behind. I automatically switched direction in order to give myself time to think because, as usual with Jordan, I had entered as David Reynolds and Farouk only knew Oliver Thomas.

It was far too early to return to the hotel so I put my glasses in my jacket pocket, pushed a hand through my hair to change the styling and tried, in an instant, to become Oliver Thomas.

But the time had been right, the atmosphere conducive, the young men were relaxed and probably a little high on whatever it was they were drinking and smoking and I had, in part, come to see Farouk anyway. So, I turned back, wandered into the café through the clutter of tables and greeted Farouk in Arabic.

"Farouk! Salaam Alekum!"

Farouk stood up, perhaps unsteadily. He grabbed my right hand and then my wrist and held it for a long time, shaking my hand and, in the way he had greeted me when we met at the Red Lion in Dover, planted brotherly kisses on both my cheeks. I was then dragged towards the main table and invited to meet Amin, Farid, Fouad, Talal, Bashir and others and was given coffee and invited to smoke and was soon immersed in their excited conversations. Time stood still.

"Why George Best so crazy? He is so brilliant at football. Why they send him off? You see Beatles? Why they play with crazy Indian man, that Ravi Shankar? They run out of ideas already?

"What about all that oil in the sea? How can they dig in the sea? You go to America, Mr Thomas? You see moon landing on TV? We watch here. Very good. We have no scientist like that in Amman. Maybe we go in fifty years. I want to be first Jordanian to go on moon. No, me. I have better map of solar system. Ha ha. Have you read any Solzhenitsyn books, Mr Thomas?"

Oh yes, this was one of the most enjoyable nights I've ever spent.

After football, George Best, Rolls Royce and North Sea oil and after more smoking and drinking the talk degenerated into more laughter and jokes about girls said to be wearing miniskirts on the streets of London. And then they laughed again as they discussed their doubts about whether such wonderful sights would ever be witnessed in Amman. They were young, intelligent, fresh and well educated.

We talked about Ireland and the IRA and bombs and terrorism, of Catholics versus Christians and of Jews versus Moslems, as though they were still talking about football. We talked about Christians versus Moslems and Moslems versus Moslems and because, by then, they were all drinking something transparent that looked like but wasn't water and breaking up huge blocks of ice with the sharp end of a small, ornate dagger that Amin had pulled from his belt, I soon found out that they were all Christians.

And as the chattering became more subdued, we leaned forward to the centre of the table where Amin had stabbed his dagger. The conversation became more intense and some of it was difficult for me to follow as they were speaking in fast Arabic mixed with English and a little French. Two of Farouk's friends, it turned out, were Lebanese. Farouk told them that his friend, Mr Ollie, was a good man who had helped him out whenever possible and that Mr Ollie had very good connections. And so, as the conversation became more intense, their eyes brightened further and they all started to look around to see who was passing on the pavement and on the road. Fouad and Bashir, particularly, were getting agitated.

This was not just the drink, although that was helping, for I could see something else in their shiny black eyes. They were fired with a passion inflamed by resentment and a determination for some form of justice.

Later, much later, we parted and I went back to my hotel with far more on my mind than I had started out with.

But then, in the spring-like warmth of the following afternoon, on the road out towards Jerusalem, I sat with Farouk again and built on the achievements of the previous night. The restaurant we stopped at was beneath tall palms next to a herd of camels that urinated in gallons and dribbled and spat green froth.

I started by giving Farouk just a few snippets of information that I'd picked up over the years from recent visits to Beirut, Damascus, Amman and Tripoli. It wasn't much but enough to prove yet again that there was more to my work than just running a small trading company. I showed my knowledge of Middle East politics and then dropped names of people whom anyone who regularly read Middle East newspapers would have heard of as string-pullers on opposing sides.

I mentioned casual meetings in hotels where I often picked up snippets of intelligence and I used the word "intelligence" deliberately and frequently. I showed him how good I was at dangling a carrot or two before the faces of hungry individuals who would then look upon me as a good source of more carrots.

Farouk, himself, had been one of these individuals. He soon spotted the similarity.

"I like your English words, Ollie. I now see the man sitting on the donkey holding a stick with a carrot is you. I think maybe I am the donkey."

"Oh, no Farouk," I said. "You're not a donkey. And I do not ride on your back. It is me who has become a stupid ass."

We were sipping ice cold arak and dipping pieces of flat bread into plates of humus. Farouk looked at me, puzzled.

"You? A stupid ass, Ollie? I don't think so."

"Oh, yes my friend. I have decided I am a very stupid one and a very naïve one."

"No, I can't believe. Why so?" Farouk asked and I could see he thought it was the start of yet another English joke. He was holding a small pile of oily, green olives in one hand, a glass of arak in the other and his mouth was stuffed with bread and humus. He couldn't speak so I talked.

"Because I started out in life by believing that all people were innocent, you see," I told him. "Even when I was nine years old my mother warned me about it. But I took no notice. As a young man, I would go along with the wishes of others in the firm belief that they must know far more than me just because they were older or held a higher rank. But later, too late, I discover that they are not so innocent but guilty of serious crimes. But they continue to use me to do all their dirty work."

Farouk stopped his chewing, his eyes wide and curious.

"I am the stupid ass, Farouk. Others have been riding on my back for too long. And the one who holds the whip and smacks my legs to keep me walking is becoming very heavy. You see, the more you feed people, the greedier, fatter and heavier they become. And, what's more, this stupid ass is becoming older and weaker and his back is now bending. But he still stumbles on thinking he can see a big sack of carrots ahead that will feed him forever. But each time it is like a mirage in the desert sand."

I stopped to watch the camels but could sense that Farouk was puzzled. "So, does your wife, Sarah, know, Ollie?" he asked, immediately hitting my sensitive spot. "If what you say is true then you must share it with her."

"I cannot tell her because I feel it may hurt her too much," I said.

"So, do you want to tell me, Ollie?"

I suddenly felt very vulnerable. It crossed my mind that I had just behaved like some sort of smooth salesman, pouring out a syrupy story aimed at attracting sympathy and an order to meet my sales target. But I hadn't started out with that plan. What I had just told Farouk was honest and truthful. I felt a load had been lifted from my heart because, for the first time, I had shared something of my inner self with another man. But I had said nothing specific. No names had been mentioned although Donaldson was clearly the villain in my mind. And I had said nothing about what I did for the bastard.

"It's complicated," I said defeatedly and that might well have been the end of it.

"Nothing is too complicated," Farouk said almost tenderly. Then he helped me further. "You once told me that if nothing is ventured then nothing is gained."

"Yes," I admitted. "Shall I give you some examples?"

He replied merely by opening his hand as if ready to receive a gift and I took up where I'd left off. I don't remember what I said but I know I dropped in words like "official secrets", "information gathering" and "military intelligence" and I might have talked for twenty minutes as Farouk listened.

"It's not just Thomas Import Export," I concluded, "Too much of my time is spent on all these other jobs and too much time is spent away from my wife and family. Too much of my energy is spent on doing the dirty work of others and too little time on my business."

And as we started on the main course of our lunch, I went even further and fed Farouk a banquet of insights into political and military intelligence. I didn't say I was a spy because I hated the word and I was, after all, only self-trained in that job. But I added spice to the meal by sprinkling it with words like "fraud" and "money laundering" and then dropped names into the conversation just as Farouk dropped ice into the bucket containing our bottle of arak. And, when we were sitting back in our chairs at a time when, in England, one might order coffee and brandy, I felt it was time to go even further.

I felt no guilt and no fear. Perhaps I had been emboldened by the arak but I was, indeed, at a stage of nothing ventured nothing gained. And to support everything I said I offered examples of gross hypocrisy, of levels of distrust and of how people hid their real agendas. I may have embellished bits here and there but it was only to ensure I'd made my point.

"It is everywhere, Farouk," I said. "Corruption, and greed, is universal. But do you know people who are so well connected that they can divert charity money donated by innocent, well-meaning people for the poor of Africa into the pockets of the already rich and take a lump for themselves while they're at it?

"Do you know a senior Government official who enriches himself by diverting arms shipments to terrorist groups who then blow up the very people the Government is there to protect? Do you know a Government official who uses blackmail to protect himself? And do you believe any British Government civil servant would organise the assassination of one of foreign diplomats unless there was money to be made?"

Farouk listened intently, his head nodding or shaking at the appropriate times but I still wasn't finished.

I then dangled more unanswered questions that I knew would long hang in Farouk's nostrils like the pungent smell from the camel piss next to us.

"Why, for example, do you think the British Government's stance on the Middle East sometimes appears ambiguous, Farouk? Is it because they are fed lop-sided stories? Might someone be giving out false intelligence or giving accurate intelligence to the wrong side? Who's telling fairy stories? Do we have a traitor in our midst? A man who'd willingly and frequently change his allegiances to feed his appetite for personal wealth? Could there be someone working to counter the good work of others just to line his own pocket?"

And as I finished my story, Farouk's black eyes were as wide as the eyes of students from the night before. A spark had ignited inside him.

"So, who is it, Ollie? Who is the fat man riding on the back of the donkey?"

And so, I named him. "So, that's him, Farouk. Major Alex Donaldson. There's a subject for some target practice. When you're ready just give me a nod and a wink and I'll tell you where to find him."

Farouk was driving us back towards Amman and, although his driving was showing the effects of the arak, I knew I hadn't lost a friend when he said: "I think the time has come, Ollie, for me to scratch your back."

"Well," I said, "I've got a really bad itch in the middle of my back that I just can't reach with my own hand. It's been there for thirty years and I'm far too old to be a donkey."

Farouk laughed and swung the steering wheel just in time to avoid another man on another donkey. "OK, Ollie, I have some very good back scratchers with long arms."

SET UP

It was only a week after my meeting with Farouk and I was in the Feathers again.

Beatie had left a message that I picked up after five one evening. "Mr Thomas. Please meet Major Donaldson this evening at seven at the usual place. Beatrice."

The usual sinking feeling appeared in the pit of my stomach but this time it was accompanied by another. Since the Nigerian scandal and my meeting with Farouk all thoughts about Donaldson brought out a different feeling. It was still anger, but an anger tinged with a growing confidence that I was becoming more in control.

It was seven thirty though by the time I made it back to London and walked into the thick blue haze in the Feathers. Betty the barmaid had, by then, long moved on somewhere to be replaced by two new barmaids, Polly and Nancy.

I must have been abroad when Betty left but, induced by yet another of Donaldson's threatening comments about my family, I had said something about Betty going. "Got tired of the local lecher, did she?"

Jack had looked the other way. Donaldson stared me straight in the eye. "You're so unbelievably naïve, Ollie. Why don't you just fuck off abroad again?"

Looking back perhaps I was naïve but, as I've said, we never discussed private matters except in terms of threats to family.

I squeezed myself between Jack and the back of another man leaning on the bar. Donaldson, on the other side of Jack, knew I was there but was deliberately looking away from me as he always did. The arrogance was something I was well used to.

"Ah, yes," Jack said, trying his best to be counter the rudeness. "Something urgent cropped up apparently. D knows. Pint?"

"Half," I said, "I don't want to be late."

It was Polly who pulled me a half pint of Bass.

"Shrimp?" asked Jack holding something pink and glistening on a tiny stick

"No, thanks," I said. "Well? What is it?"

Jack nodded at Donaldson who was still looking the other way.

"Yes, I saw him," I said. "Has he got a tongue?"

Jack dug his stick into another shrimp and I took a mouthful of my beer. Then I took another mouthful and another. Then I took a spare stick and prodded a shrimp, examined it, licked it, smelled it. Then I put it back in its dish.

"You can't do that," said Jack.

"Do what?" I said.

"Lick it and put it back."

"The vinegar will kill any germs," I said and took another, longer drink from my glass. It was already almost empty. Then I stared into space. My anger was at tipping point but I'd had an idea earlier on the train up from Croydon.

"Right, I'm off," I said as loudly as I could. "Thanks for inviting me but I've got a business to run." I put my half pint glass down with a thump. Polly looked at me and the stranger on my right moved away. It had happened before and was guaranteed to start Donaldson off on the wrong foot and I knew it. "Cheerio, Jack," I said and turned.

Donaldson moved. As I turned, he was right behind me. "Business first, Ollie," he hissed. He blocked my way. "Corner," he said nodding towards a spare table in the far corner.

I winked at Jack. "Business. It must be urgent. Are you joining us or do you want to finish your shrimps?"

"Yes," Jack said.

"Yes, you're joining us or yes you're staying to finish your supper?"

"Yes," said Jack.

It soon became clear that Donaldson had a job for me that meant flying to Athens and then to Cairo. It was nothing unusual. "Pick up from Dimitri at the usual place and time. Transfer to Tahir, who is coming up from Khartoum."

"When?" I asked.

"It needs to be there by Saturday, next week."

"Then use a carrier pigeon."

"That's you, you fucking asshole."

By those later years, Donaldson's language had gradually changed. He seemed far less comfortable using expressions like old chap and dear fellow. In fact, his language had become very coarse and more like the characters from Northern Ireland I'd met in Malta. Maybe it was the company he was keeping.

He went on. "And before you ask what it is, it's confidential. Don't lose it. It's sealed and someone will be watching the transfer so no fucking about. Got it? If it doesn't arrive in the state it started off, then all hell will break loose this end. Do you fucking understand?"

"Naturally," I shrugged.

I'd been here before and it was pointless arguing. Nowadays such jobs might not need a courier and can be sent on the Internet. In those days, and it's not so long ago, it was different. I could actually see the changes coming even then, but time was not on my side. I am, for what it is worth, a form of life that, along with other veterans, may well be nearing extinction.

I got up, ready to go and Jack pushed his chair back as Donaldson sat staring into his beer, clearly not a happy man for whatever reason. I decided to liven up his evening and so sat down again.

"By the way," I said, "I was in Amman last week – as you probably know anyway because I twice saw someone watching me from the shadows. I think it was Kamal this time. He needs better training. That aside, I got wind of a demand for some nice fresh Dollar bills in exchange for suitcases full of unfashionable Dinars. All cash, of course. Sounds like trouble brewing again in Beirut and someone needs to top up their ammunition. Extremely attractive exchange rate terms being offered, I understand. It might be something the US or British authorities should take an interest in. It all sounds very dodgy to me."

I knew Donaldson would like the sound of that. It was his comfort zone. "If you need any more, call me," I added and stood up again.

"How much?" growled Donaldson without looking up from his beer.

"Excuse me? What do you mean by how much?" I replied in pure innocence.

"How many dollars?"

"I've no idea," I said, "I was only given the Dinar amount and that runs into several millions, but the exchange rate means it won't be anything like the same number of dollars. But I understand they are willing to pay twenty percent more than you'd get in a bank."

I could see Donaldson doing mental arithmetic. Jack seemed to be counting something on the same fingers that were also rubbing his chin.

"I can't say more, here," I said looking around. "But I have a name in Beirut."

"Who?" asked Donaldson looking up, clearly concerned I was about to leave and go back to Croydon.

"Sorry. Need to know basis," I said touching my nose and knowing that this would madden Donaldson beyond even his normal boundaries. He stared up at me, his eyes furious, but I knew he wouldn't explode in the pub. Explosions were reserved for the Regent Street office. "But I'm not going," I said, "so don't even ask me. This is one for someone who isn't known so well in those parts. It needs someone fresh. Someone willing to operate incognito but with some understanding of the way these things happen. I don't want my cover blown. It wouldn't do any of us any good if you understood."

I was now deliberately tempting Donaldson to fall into a trap but I still kept going.

"And I wouldn't want many other people knowing about it either," I added, deliberately lowering my voice.

"Sit down," Donaldson said. "We'd need more," Donaldson said, "Far more."

I stayed standing. "Of course, but don't expect me to talk to anyone else. It's far too dangerous for me and for the Department."

"I'll deal with the bloody Department," Donaldson said, falling further into the trap. "Who needs the fucking money?"

"Look," I said, trying hard to retain the initiative, "I've got to go. I need to pack. I'm so busy at present and I'm supposed to be in Paris tomorrow afternoon and you also seem to want me to go to Athens. There are only twenty-four hours in a day. So, if you'll excuse me . . ."

"Sit the fuck down," hissed Donaldson. Jack jumped. "Who needs the money?"

"Someone linked to Assad in Syria," I said still standing.

"So, it's Moslem?" Donaldson asked.

"Of course. They think they're losing."

"Would someone need to go out there?"

I blew a jet of air through my mouth. "Go out there? Of course, we'd need someone out there. Bloody desk bound bureaucrats aren't any good. This needs a pro. Don't you have anyone in place in Beirut?"

I watched Donaldson doing more mental contortions. His face was turning puce which meant that either he was about to explode or that he was slightly drunk. I knew it was both. "No," he said and he looked at Jack who was sat looking worried with a finger now stuck in his mouth. "Nobody. You'll need to fucking go. You've got the local contacts. You could round up some third party to do some listening-in or something. No need to get directly involved."

I sat down. "And still blow everything?" I said. "No, I'm just too well known."

"So, who the fuck is the guy on the ground you'd use?"

"Probably Talal Abdullah," I said.

"Who the fuck's that?"

"Talal Abdullah," I said. "Talal at the AUB."

"AUB?"

"American University of Beirut."

"Ah yes," Donaldson said. "But how the fuck can the AUB help over these few million Dinars?"

"Politics, man," I said knowing I was pushing my luck. "Talal will know. But it's an ideal time to get in there during this lull. I've crept in and out during occasional lulls in the past and it's usually OK if you keep your head down. I doubt it'll last long though. Now is as good a time as any."

Donaldson looked at Jack. Jack looked away. If Donaldson was even thinking of sending Jack it would have been an act of total irresponsibility. But clearly Jack saw the possibility and his face went a strange shape. But Donaldson was no fool in decisions like this.

"Look, I've got to go," I said standing up once more. "If you decide what to do, call me after Friday when I'm back from Paris. Frankly, though, I couldn't care less. And I really don't think it's anything to do with the British Government. It's gross interference in another country's affairs. I'm just passing on the news."

With that I left, leaving Donaldson and Jack still sat around the corner table.

For once I'd felt in control and Donaldson was clearly unsure what to do or say. But, at last, I'd dangled my own carrot. The test was whether he'd reach out to take it.

I wasn't really planning to go to Paris but spent the next two days in and around my office. On the second day, the phone rang. Beatie answered it and I knew from her expression it was Donaldson. I could hear his voice, even from where I was sitting. He clearly thought I was away and in Paris.

"Ah, yes, good morning . . ." Beatie said politely. But she got no further.

"Fucking Thomas back yet? You know where he is?" I heard his loud voice so clearly.

"Ah, yes . . . ah, no. I mean yes, but he . . ."

"Come on, you stupid bitch, when's he back?"

"Back? He's not......"

"Look here, listen. When he gets back tell him to call me pronto, OK?"

I heard the phone being slammed down. I was facing away from Beatie and my head was deliberately buried in a trade catalogue but Beatie was still trying to play a game. She continued to hold the phone for a moment. Then, as if the person was still there, she said, "Thank you for calling. Good bye."

I heard her start her typing again and so I turned to face her. Her face was red and her neck was as pink as her twin set. She coughed.

"Major Donaldson?" I asked.

"Ah, yes, Mr Thomas. He'd like you to call him sometime," she said and coughed again. Then, as I continued to watch her, she bent down to her handbag which she always kept at her feet, withdrew a white handkerchief with some pink embroidery on it and blew her nose.

"Got a cold coming on, Beatie?"

"Uh no Mr Thomas, it's just a tickle."

"Donaldson's a very rude man," I said.

"Yes, Mr Thomas."

"Are you afraid of him, Beatie?"

"A little, Mr Thomas."

"Why's that, Beat?"

"He's . . . uh, not very polite and . . ." she spluttered and blew her nose again.

"Bastards are always rude, Beatie. It's the only thing they're good at. What did he want?"

"As I said, he would like you to phone him."

"All in good time, Beatie. Anything else?"

"Uh, no Mr Thomas, thank you," and she sniffed before starting her typing again.

As I watched her, though, I started to recall some other things she had recently said to me. Beatie was hiding something.

"I have been trying to bring myself to tell you something, Mr Thomas, but it's all very difficult, you see."

Beatie often looked and sounded embarrassed but she had recently been showing signs of genuine concern about something. But I, because of my own problems and not wishing to bother her more than necessary, would tell her not to worry. I would dismiss her obvious concerns as though they had been nothing worth bothering about, as though it was just typical of her to fuss about nothing in particular. "Don't worry, Beat. Nothing to worry yourself about. Don't fret. Got to catch the train." And I had gone again without giving it a second thought.

Then again, some months before, after I'd just got back from somewhere when perhaps I was tired. Maybe I had been a little harsh on her but I could now remember what she said. "I'm very sorry, Mr Thomas. But it can be quite stressful here when you are abroad. We really need to talk privately sometime, Mr Thomas."

I could remember her eyes almost pleading with me to pry into her concerns. But again, I would lose the chance, believing she was feeling overworked. "Never mind, Beat. Don't let the system get you down. Take it easy."

But what was making her so stressed? Now, as I watched her sniffing and wiping her nose, her voice kept echoing back.

"There was a phone call for you, Mr Thomas. Beirut again. You . . . you need to be so careful, Mr Thomas. It's such a...such a dangerous place, these days."

And another time. "Does Mrs Thomas know about this, Mr Thomas?" Or had she said, "Mrs Thomas needs to know, Mr Thomas,"?

Again, some weeks later. "Mrs Thomas must know, Mr Thomas...where you are . . .always . . . just in case. I can always inform her . . . if . . . if something goes wrong."

As I watched her now, tapping away on her typewriter I suddenly felt sorry for her. Her eyes looked up from her typing and peered at me from behind her spectacles. They looked damp, worried, caring and perhaps guilty. Stupidly, I turned to study my catalogue again. Later, I would deeply regret that lost opportunity.

I phoned Donaldson later that same day.

Phoning Donaldson was a mysterious process in itself. The number I used was answered, if at all, by a man who always said he'd get a message to Donaldson. Usually Donaldson would phone the next day or even later. Sometimes Frank would call me as if he'd got the message instead. This time, Donaldson was on the phone in twenty minutes. Beatie took the call again.

"It's Major Donaldson for you, Mr Thomas."

There was no friendly enquiry into how my Paris visit had gone and the call took less than half a minute: a summons to attend the Regent Street office urgently.

I arrived during the London rush hour. As usual, Jack was also there but Donaldson seemed unusually eager to open the conversation. "Beirut," he said.

"I'm not going," I replied.

"Not asking you to. I'll deal with this one myself. Got a gap in my diary and there's a bit of a lull out there at present. Need to refresh myself. Get my head around the situation. Meet one or two people. We need someone with some understanding of the way things work. Been doing some digging. That man Talal. Any good?"

"Talal Abdullah?" I replied. "I've known him for several years. He's an Iraqi doctor. Christian. Works for the Americans and French, I think. Good starting point."

"Just as I thought,"

Under different circumstances it might have been amusing. Donaldson had donned his old Army Major style. I jumped on the opportunity.

"It was Talal who told me about the funds," I said. "He could set a few things up. Get things moving."

"His motivation?" Donaldson had now donned his Senior Intelligence Officer style and I couldn't help but glance at Frank to see his reaction. He was nodding and smiling.

"Talal wouldn't like to see money heading the wrong way," I said. "He'd prefer to screw things up for the Palestinians."

"Exactly what I thought."

Donaldson paused. "Who's the guy on the Syrian side? The one you see with your other hat on?"

"Ashur Mohammed?"

"That's him. Do you have his contact details?"

I shook my head. "He moves around too much. Talal would help."

Of course, I could then have asked questions about the relevance to British interests, but I was not in the mood to put Donaldson off. Quite the opposite. I needed to encourage him. He asked a few more questions which I answered and that was my day finished. I went home because Sarah had said she'd do roast beef and Yorkshire pudding.

A few days later Donaldson boarded a plane for Beirut for his first overseas jaunt in several years and I phoned Farouk in Amman. Then everything went quiet for a week until Farouk called and invited me to meet him in Paris.

I flew next day and we met in the late afternoon in his smart new apartment off the Champs Elysees for a glass of French wine. We talked generalities – politics, the new agency he'd signed with a Japanese pharmaceutical company, that sort of thing. Then he invited me out to eat. "We must celebrate, Oliver. You need to enjoy yourself more. Life is too short. Why did you not bring Sarah?"

"She hates flying," I said. "Anyway, where's your wife, Farouk?" It was a poor attempt at diverting the subject from my private life because I knew Farouk's wife was still in Amman.

"She will join me in Paris soon. My two sons are growing up and we will bring them to Paris to go to the University."

"You're doing well, Farouk. I'm pleased for you," I said, looking around his apartment and sipping my wine from one of his crystal glasses.

"Yes, Oliver, but you are not. I can see it in your eyes. The donkey needs to shed its heavy load and find a fresh field of green grass. Why do you not move away from London? You can run your type of business from anywhere. You are a clever man, Ollie. You could be such a brilliant and successful businessman with all your connections. You are such a passionate man and the most skilful in your trade. You have plenty of time. Your wife, Sarah – I think you cherish her beyond everything. I can see it in the way your eyes move when I mention her. You are like a teenage boy in love with a secret girlfriend. But things are still eating into your soul. You look like a tethered lamb trying to break free before he is sacrificed."

I was standing with my back to the window overlooking the street and, touched by Farouk's words, I turned to look outside. It was getting dark and lamps were shining onto the wet street below. Perhaps I was hoping to study my own reflection but it was Farouk I saw approaching me from behind. He tapped me on the shoulder. "Maybe we have just cut the lamb free, Oliver. Can we hope so?"

I didn't know what to say but Farouk smiled. "Come," he said, "let's go and eat." So, we walked, sharing a large black umbrella, to a packed Lebanese restaurant called Noura.

I knew Farouk was well known but I was surprised at the number of his friends I met that night. We ate mezza and drank arak and, around ten o'clock, all the tables were cleared and a space made for a small group of musicians and an Egyptian belly dancer. Up to that point Farouk and I had said nothing about Donaldson.

But then, as the music and singing grew louder and the temperature inside the restaurant grew hotter, someone came to him to say there was a phone call. Farouk left for a moment and then returned. For a moment he said nothing but continued to clap to the music. Then he leaned over towards me and beckoned me to come closer. "Have you heard the news about your friend, Ollie?" he whispered in my ear.

I tried to appear unsure who he was referring to. "I have many friends, Farouk. Which one?"

"Your friend, the British Major."

"He's not a friend, Farouk. But what news?"

"He is no more," Farouk said. "I think you have an English expression. Pushing up the daisies, yes? Well Major Donaldson is doing just that. It seems he was caught in some crossfire. It was very unfortunate."

"Mmm," I said, "You mean he's dead?"

"His death was announced today."

"I see. When did he meet with this terrible accident?"

"Two days ago," whispered Farouk as the music suddenly got louder, the clapping started again and the dancer swirled around and thrust her hips in our direction.

"The lamb has been freed, Oliver," Farouk said and we both joined in the clapping.

A PREDICAMENT

It was some two weeks after I met Farouk in Paris that the Daily Telegraph ran a small paragraph on an inside page with the headline: 'British Army Major Shot in Beirut.'

I bought a copy of The Times to double check and found an identical paragraph as though based on the same official press release. 'The Ministry of Defence has confirmed that Christian militia were behind the shooting of a British Army officer in Beirut. The officer, thought to be Major Alexander Donaldson is believed to have been working for British Intelligence. The Ministry was unwilling to comment further until more information became available.'

After that, nothing more ever appeared in any newspaper or any other source of news. It was as if more information was restricted by security needs. I gave it a few days and thought I ought to call Jack out of respect.

But Jack sounded unaffected which was odd because the pair had worked together for years. "I can't comment, Ollie. Bit of a shock, I know. But, as you well know, mum's the word and all that. It's a dangerous sport, but there it is. Had a good innings and then got bowled out."

Jack certainly didn't appear to be in deep mourning but it seemed to me that Jack was also secretly grateful for whatever had happened. In my case it took a week or so to grow accustomed to the sudden freedom I felt. Beatie seemed to smile more and Sarah noticed a sudden spring in my step.

Those first few weeks also coincided with my overseas trips dropping off and with no meeting at The Feathers, I was able to be home for dinner more often. "I'll make us a nice ham salad," Sarah would say. "They had some lovely fresh radishes and cucumbers at the Co-Op."

We were sat together eating a Sunday roast lamb and mint sauce lunch on what I recall was a bright spring day. At least it seemed bright for Croydon. But perhaps that was because Sarah had placed a bunch of yellow daffodils in a vase on the table. She was smiling.

"It's so nice to have you home at dinner time, dear. And you're looking so much better recently. You don't have that troubled look on your face."

I saw an opportunity. "So, how about us moving abroad," I ventured. "I could run the business from anywhere – South Africa, Malta, the Far East, Australia? It could be quite a shrewd move in the present economic climate."

"Oh, no dear, let's not rush into things. Let's see how things go for a while. You never know."

"You never know what?" I pursued.

I watched Sarah slicing through a piece of meat on her plate and saw the usual look of uncertainty in her eyes. Her smile had also gone and I thought perhaps I had gone at it like a bull in a china shop instead of tiptoeing around it. "Let's wait a while, dear. We don't want to jump from the frying pan into the fire," she said.

"What frying pan? What fire?"

"Oh, you know dear. We need to be sure that things are safe and right. We mustn't be too rash."

"It's not rash, my love," I said. "It's a very good time to go. We're not too old and not too young. Robert has gone his own way. It would be a fresh start. You'd like it in South Africa. Why not come with me and see what it's like?"

"Well, let's just wait and see, dear. I hate the thought of flying. Just you enjoy your lunch for now. The vegetables are so fresh and I always like a leg of lamb in springtime."

That was it. Decision delayed once more.

Whatever we were to do in future, I still needed to make some bigger money. What I needed was one or two big, profitable orders.

I was, by then, in my late fifties and other things had already moved on. People had moved on. Many of my older contacts were as old as me and already retired or had sold their businesses to other, bigger companies with whom I had no useful relationship. Beatie would now sit there without enough to do and what little regular business we did was only enough to pay increasingly high overheads and an inadequate salary for myself.

With Donaldson gone, the business looking jaded after too many years with too many distractions I therefore began an urgent search for more sales.

But I was to be interrupted once again. And, as ever, it started with the telephone ringing. "Call for you, Mr Thomas. It's a Mr Creighton." I had no idea who it was.

"Mr Thomas? Oliver Thomas?"

"Yes, that's me," I said.

"Bill Creighton, Ministry. Don't think we've had the pleasure before."

"Oh!" I said, still reading something or other on my desk.

"Like to pop in, Mr Thomas? Catch up? Talk? Quick cup of tea?"

"What about?" I asked.

"Catch up. Cup of tea."

"Where?"

"Usual office. You know. Thursday afternoon? Three pm?"

"Which usual office is that?" I asked.

"HQ, of course."

"You mean the Ministry?" I was shocked. Normally my only direct contact with a Government Department was the tax office. There wasn't any more information I could extract but two days later I went up.

I arrived on time and was directed by the reception desk to the fourth floor where I'd met Donaldson once or perhaps twice. I barely remembered the place.

I waited for what seemed an eternity but was eventually escorted by a young woman to an office. The man called Bill Creighton was sat in what might have been Donaldson's old chair. He may have re-shuffled the furniture slightly but still exhibited a key qualification for the job. Like Donaldson, he then stood with his back to the window, a black shape just slightly shorter than his predecessor, with a perfect egg shape outlining his bald, head.

When his hands were not in his pockets, he used them to twist the ends of a pointed moustache that extended beyond his cheeks and looked, to anyone with any imagination, like the head of a black cat.

I have never understood what they all did in that concrete office block. This room was along a long corridor and the whole edifice seemed occupied by men in dark suits with middle aged secretaries fussing around, coming and going through stained, wooden doors, along dark corridors carrying pieces of paper, grey folders and cups of tea. It was deadly quiet except for the hum of photocopiers in recesses in the corridors.

Telephones never seemed to ring either but quiet meetings went on behind those closed doors followed by quiet exits, more shuffling down corridors and all accompanied by the rattling of now empty teacups in saucers.

I had been forced to wait nearly an hour by a photocopier before I was eventually called in. Then I felt like a schoolboy reporting to the headmaster.

"Now then, Oliver – may I call you Oliver – sorry for the wait and all that. Ha! Sorry we've not had the chance to meet before – get to know one another. Things changing around here – change of government and all that – different politicians, different ideas and all that – cuts and axes – you name it. I'm sure you've heard about it, read about it and all that. Essential changes of staff ensue. Ha! Restructuring, reorganising – you know the deal – been around a bit by all accounts – I've seen your file."

There was a slim, buff folder on the desk before him which looked as though it contained about three sheets of A4.

"Is that it, there?" I asked.

"That's it. Nothing much to worry about. But it's budgets and all that now. D's not around the place either, any more – poor bloody blighter – never mind – got to get on with it. All getting on a bit anyway – probably my last stand as well, ha!"

Creighton flipped open my almost empty file and closed it again. Then he sat down. "Cup of tea?"

"No thanks," I said, "I'm too busy."

"Of course. Sorry for the wait."

"Yes," I said, "You already apologised for that."

"So, I did."

"I've only been here once or twice before," I said.

"Yes, the file's not big," he replied, flipping it open once more.

"I did a hell of a lot more than will fit in that," I said pointing at the folder. "But I used to meet Donaldson at the Regent Street office, not here," I added.

"Regent Street office you say?"

"The building next to Hamley's."

"Hamley's you say? What office is that?"

"Donaldson's other office," I said. "There was also his other office in Edinburgh."

"Edinburgh, you say?"

"Yes, the one in Morningside."

"Morningside?" There was a pause. "Mmm," Creighton scratched his bald head.

I knew immediately he had no idea about Donaldson's other offices. Case proven yet again, I thought. The Ministry knew nothing and I hardly registered on their books. For a chap who thought he had worked his socks off for the Queen and country for a quarter of a century I was as about as important as the two-millimetre thickness of my personnel file.

I stared at Creighton and wanted to wring his neck.

"Mm," he said once again, "Ah well. Anyway, here's the gist. You know the score – signed the forms to keep mum and all that. Got to get on with life or what's left – Ha! Retire, old chap. Buy that country cottage at last. You've done your bit – getting too complicated now. You know the way it is – IRA – Middle East – clearing up Callaghan's bloody mess – Jimmy Carter – general state of the economy and all that. Ha! Still got your own business by all accounts – going well is it? Good. Got a pension? Good."

Creighton never stopped to wait for answers to his string of questions but that is about all I can remember of the short time I sat there. There were no thanks, no gold watch and no speeches over drinks with old friends and work colleagues. I had been dismissed and told to retire.

I walked out in a daze and in the street, I asked myself why he hadn't mentioned expenses. Did I not have some sort of remuneration or expense account somewhere? Might there have been a few pounds due to me for twenty-five years of subsidising a Government department from the profits of my own business? A few thousands would have been a gross underestimate.

I had only walked a few yards when I saw the reflection of myself in a shop window. It was then that my predicament became obvious.

An old man, resembling myself but looking older, more worried, and more depressed than I had imagined, stared back at me. That pathetic image of a shabby-looking man with his hands in his pockets will live with me for ever.

Thirty years in business and I had nothing like enough in the bank and, whilst the problem of Donaldson was now gone, tensions were starting at home because Sarah wanted to move to Gloucester to be closer to Robert who had moved there with his job.

My plans, of course, were to move much further away than Gloucester but I was on very weak ground without money. I needed an urgent solution.

A MISTAKE

A **possible solution to my financial predicament** came through a strange encounter in Trafalgar Square.

I was taking a short cut, dodging pigeons and waiting to cross the road when someone came from behind and tapped me on the shoulder. "Mr Thomas ain't it?"

"Yes," I replied. "Good Lord! Ron, isn't it? What brings you here? We met recently in the office down there, when I was left sitting around for hours."

"That's it, Mr Thomas."

"We shared a cup of coffee from a machine that, when kicked, churned out tepid brown water."

"That's me, Mr Thomas. Fucking awful place ain't it, mate."

"Not as exciting as some places I've been, I have to agree," I said.

"Time on me 'ands now, Mr Thomas. Got the push. Like you 'ave I 'eard. Not that I ever knew what you did, like. But times are changing ain't it?"

Looking back, I now know that taking a tip from such a source had been a mistake. But Ron, who now held a position of authority seemingly little better than the one I was about to move to – he had just started work in the rates office at Wandsworth Council – had been happy with the twenty pound note I gave him for his tip. He had engaged me in a long, meandering conversation whilst scattering small pieces of sliced, white bread from a plastic bag. Wings, feathers and pigeon shit flew around our heads.

"Still running your own show, Mr Thomas?"

"Yes."

"Young Forsyth's going out your way, Mr Thomas."

"Forsyth? Who's Forsyth?"

"Yeh – you know, mate – military bloke – the Embassy in Lisbon. You know him. Sure, you do, mate. Going to the Gold Coast or Ghana or whatever they call it these days. It's to do with supplies for the army or something. Big stuff I understand although it's only rumour like. But surprised you didn't know, Mr Thomas. In fact, your name cropped up. I thought they were gonna call you. Your sort of business ain't it?"

If he had worked in Cyprus or Lebanon, I might have known someone called Brigadier Royston Forsyth but Portugal was off my patch and so it was no surprise that our paths had not crossed. But with no Donaldson and having been officially retired from whatever unofficial position I had held for thirty years I decided to find out what was going on and, with my imagination running at an unnaturally riotous pace, started thinking about retirement.

Looking back, I am embarrassed by my dream of a bungalow on a breezy slope facing the sea near Cape Town, of spending happy hours gardening with Sarah, visiting the vineyards at Stellenbosch and inviting Robert and Anne to fly out to join us from time to time. I was a different man; one whose domestic considerations were at the centre of all things. Without a decent pot of money, though, I could do nothing so I took the bull by the horns and phoned Forsyth on the London number Ron had given me. He didn't say much in return but I gave him a good summary of my background, that I was a man with experience in the sort of business he was interested in, that I would be visiting Accra shortly and would appreciate an opportunity to meet.

"We've done a fair bit of trading with West Africa," I said. "It's mostly been in Nigeria but we've got plenty of experience of North Africa and the Middle East and have been operating for some twenty-five years. We're well established."

Forsyth, it appeared, was in London for a briefing session but was moving to Ghana within days. He agreed to meet in a week's time in Accra and as it all sounded positive, I tried calling my Ghana agent, George Owusu to warn him I might need his help. Unfortunately, all phone lines were down and so, not wanting to waste time, I decided to fly out unannounced, hoping George would be there when I arrived. Unfortunately, he wasn't.

Luck can play a big part in this business. Bad luck and mistakes were to play a big part in what happened next but if you've ever popped out to visit someone expecting to find them in and then found them out, it's frustrating. But if you've flown all the way to Africa, believe me the frustration is much worse.

I arrived in George's office to find his secretary, Mary, lying across her empty desk in front of the Mitsubishi fan by her typewriter cracking chicken bones with her teeth and spitting the fragments into her waste paper basket. Mary broke the news of George's long-term absence on private matters up north without once stopping the crunching and spitting of her bones. She really had no idea where he had gone or how long he was likely to be away.

That was the first setback. Without George it was going to be difficult, but time was short so I returned to my hotel to test the local telephone network. Surprisingly, it worked and Forsyth agreed to meet the next day at a local hotel.

Perhaps I was tired. Perhaps I was feeling old and long in the tooth and perhaps my mind wasn't entirely focussed. Certainly, I hadn't done enough checks on Forsyth, distracted as I was by my retirement plans and what I thought would be a straightforward deal. There is no doubt at all that I didn't perform well.

Such meetings need preparation, tact and professionalism which, for thirty years, I had possessed in abundance but if positive results are required it follows that both parties should, at least, remain sober.

Brigadier Forsyth seemed to like whisky as well.

It was he who asked the waiter what types they had, although I could have told him that the choice was likely to be restricted to only one – Johnny Walker Black Label. But within minutes of meeting, I saw evidence of someone who had not travelled far. His accent was faintly Scottish – Edinburgh – as though he had been born there, or educated at somewhere like Fettes.

We sat beneath a flimsy thatch shelter in the open-air bar surrounded by grass and a pleasant urban jungle of banana trees, coconuts and butterflies and the conversation started constructively enough with worldly affairs and international politics, subjects that came easily to myself. Then it roamed over everything else – except business.

He ordered not glasses of whisky but a bottle and had a silver bucket filled with chunks of ice and how clearly, I remember the black clouds that were gathering on the skyline over the sea and the flashes of lightning that could be seen from our table by the wooden steps leading onto the grass.

Now and again I could hear a rumble of distant thunder. A storm was brewing and I watched it approaching. The horizon was turning black and I remember glancing at it from my wicker chair as the carpet of grass surrounding us lay iridescent in what remained of the late afternoon sunshine. The sun itself was slowly sinking behind a row of coconut palms silhouetted against the darkening sky. A cool wind began to blow and the palms waved and hissed faintly in the air. And, gradually, the wind coming in from the sea picked up and green coconuts started to fall with a thud. And I watched it all through increasingly unfocused eyes, as black clouds bubbled upwards into the pink and orange sky, flashing dire warnings.

If I had seen it as an omen then perhaps, I would have ensured that the business side of the discussion was left for another, more sober time and that the drinking session was merely to lubricate the wheels of friendship and confidence building for the future. That would have been far more in line with my usual tactics. Patience, and a slow build up leading to a successful deal, was my normal style.

I specialized in setting the scene, building a foundation, establishing the feasibility and leaving the fine architectural details of the structure to be built as yet undecided. In other words, I preferred keeping my options open at the beginning and judging the time to make a move when it suited me. Oh yes, it was not that I was inexperienced. I had been a master of the art.

But, for some reason, during that afternoon in Accra, I felt different. I was impatient. My private life had become more important than anything else. George's absence had not helped my patience and I was also on my way to Cape Town via Nairobi and Johannesburg and managing as best I could without my suitcase and fresh, clean clothes that Sarah had prepared for my trip. Losing luggage was not unusual but, this time, the airline had lost my case somewhere between Frankfurt and Accra and I was not sure if it would turn up before my scheduled flight out. My mind was on clean shirts and bungalows.

Lost luggage had become a regular and annoying occurrence. It had happened a few months before. I had been flying from Jeddah to Addis Ababa on an Ethiopian Airline flight, crammed amongst Haj pilgrims with their carpetbags and their antisocial habits of trying to cook curry on Butane stoves in the passenger aisle of the aircraft whilst flying at thirty-five thousand feet somewhere over Djibouti.

On that occasion, by chance, I spotted my case amongst a million others stacked in a warehouse at Addis Ababa airport. I had had to bribe a customs man but it still failed to reach me before I left so I had flown to Athens, then to Cyprus with the suitcase following behind from place to place until I was finally reunited with it in Cairo. I related the story to Brigadier Forsyth and the Brigadier had laughed and tried, but failed, to outdo me with a similar tale.

I could tell the man disliked being thought of as a domesticated family man. His own tale about a piece of hand luggage lost between Paris and Lisbon was clearly embellished. In other words, had I been my usual self, I would have marked him down as a bullshitting amateur and factored it into my decision making.

But what had also been puzzling me all along but, again, insufficiently as it turned out, was that the name Forsyth was a new one. As well as the contents of the ABC flight timetable I kept a mental list of the names of military and commercial attachés. My thoroughness had rarely let me down – until then.

The tickets for my onward flight to South Africa were safe in my briefcase but it contained far more brochures on retirement property than technical fact sheets on products of interest to a military attaché. You see unlike the younger Brigadier, I was at an age where

I wanted to give up the jet setting and the bullshitting and become, at long last, a family man. So, my motivation was misdirected, my objectives, just like the horizon, were cloudy and my plans badly thought through.

Instead, we laughed and joked about flying and travelling in Africa and the Middle East. We played verbal table tennis with bottles of Johnny Walker Black Label and an ice bucket as a net and stories as the ball.

And I thought I was winning it all, games, sets and match, as Forsyth poured whisky and threw more blocks of ice into my glass and as I remembered still more stories worth telling.

"How do you travel on Nigerian Airlines without an airline ticket, Roy?" By then, you see, we were on first name terms and shortened versions at that. Roy, the Brigadier had looked deliberately puzzled.

"I've no idea, but I'm sure you're going to tell me, ha ha."

"Well, first you need a good local agent."

"Yes, go on, ha ha."

"Well now. Answer me this, Roy. What do you need to board a plane?"

"Uh, uh, ah yes, a boarding pass."

"That's it. So, you use your agent to give the fellow at the check-in desk a new, shiny ball pen with a promise that there's a good chance of the matching fountain pen and the fancy box it all goes in, if he can get you a couple of boarding passes."

"That's a good one."

"The only problem is getting on the plane when it's now totally overbooked with fifty people having already bribed the same check-in clerk whose desk is already piled high with free gifts."

"Ha ha. So, what next?"

"Well, when the rumour spreads – and rumour is all you get because, as you know, Roy, there is no PA system – that the plane that's sitting shimmering in the heat on the tarmac about half a mile away is yours, you run. Oh yes. You run like bloody hell. After all there's no bus and you wouldn't want to wait for it even if there was. The temperature is in the upper nineties and the humidity the same but you run. You sprint, you push and you shove and you deliberately trip up as many of your would-be fellow passengers as you can. The half-mile is done in less than two minutes. It's Olympic standard running I can tell you and you're carrying your bags as well. Then the first to arrive at the steps is the first to get a seat."

"That's a good one. You want a top up?"

"Thanks. Don't mind if I do."

That's how it had been until the first huge drops of tropical rain started to fall. Then, with the pretentious chandeliers in the hotel flickering warnings of an imminent power failure, I looked at my watch, decided I needed to relieve myself and went to the gent's toilet. And now, oh yes – memories of another reflection. But, leaning, because I could hardly stand, at the grubby wash basin, I stared at the image of myself in the mirror. It was not a pretty sight. I tried desperately to clear the numbness from my brain and to remember my role as a professional businessman. I splashed water onto my face in a forlorn attempt to re-direct my thoughts from Sarah and my trip to Cape Town back to the here and now and towards a complex deal on army supplies. I knew I was making a big mistake.

Even in that state of mind, I knew there was a good chance I was going to make a rare error of judgment. But what could I have done? Time was of the essence and I had already decided I needed to get out of the mess I'd been embroiled in for too long. So, I returned to the bar where the Brigadier was still sitting, legs crossed with the whisky glasses and ice bucket on the table.

In fact, I didn't go directly back to the bar but watched him for a few seconds from the corner of the room. I watched the small, Ghanaian bartender in his red waistcoat, wiping his bar and putting glasses away and I looked at the few other white, hotel guests sitting around, chatting. Then I looked at my watch and tried in vain to see the position of the hands. And then the lights went out.

An intense flash of lightning outside coincided with a huge crash of thunder and the rain fell in torrents. There were a few cheers and some laughter from the other corner. The barman lit a few candles before the dim light of dusk outside had a chance to meet up with the deepening blackness of the clouds overhead and I groped my way towards my seat and fell into my chair.

But I was met with a surprisingly straight and sober look from the Brigadier and I knew immediately that I had totally misjudged the amount the other man had drunk.

But it seemed that the Brigadier, on his own initiative, now wanted to talk business. It was not supposed to be like that. I was the one who needed to retain the initiative. I felt a sudden horror that spread like a hot flush through my body. The heat that flooded through my blood and spilled over into my brain told me that Brigadier Royston Forsyth had done far more homework on me than I had done on him.

Indeed, perhaps, he'd not had to do any homework at all but just read a file given to him by someone else. It was as though my trip to the lavatory had suddenly relieved me not only of the contents of my bladder but my ability to entertain a client. Not only that but I could hardly see.

The room was so dark and my eyes so unfocused that I could barely see the man's face. But I could hear him well enough and knew that the joking was over. His light, Scottish accent was as clear as the crystal chandelier had been before the power went off.

"So, Ollie. You'll find it quite straightforward to arrange the shipment of certain items which, in principle, are already approved for export."

The words were not those of someone trying to communicate under the influence of alcohol. I delayed my reply for far too long but my condition was not granting me much in the way of common sense. And yet I knew I needed to retain some control or there might be unforeseen circumstances. I struggled to reply.

"Naturally it depends on the specification, the quantity, the value, how we are to be paid – that sort of thing."

There was a mental list of other requirements but my brain fizzled out after raising just four of them.

"Naturally," Forsyth replied. "When is your scheduled departure?"

I was unnerved. His style had changed radically since the lights went out and I found it hard to remember what I was supposed to be doing next or when. "Uh, tomorrow afternoon. Nairobi."

Forsyth leaned forward. "Here's the list."

The list had apparently been in the buff folder that had lain, unopened but in full view, on the table since we met. I opened it with fumbling, uncoordinated fingers to reveal a single sheet of paper, clipped to another, which apparently showed the British Embassy, Accra address. Watching me fumble, Forsyth detached the top sheet and pushed the bottom one towards me across the table.

"Not a huge amount as you can see. Tents, camouflage, a few civilian earth-moving vehicles, military camping supplies. The problem is its destination. The shipping is critical."

I understood these types of situations. I was not that naïve. I also knew that every situation was different and had its own peculiarities but my mind was not up to its usual clear and instant analysis. "So where do you want it shipped?" I asked.

"Chad. N'Djamena for transhipment north."

This was not Ghana, Sierra Leone, Liberia or any of the other places I had assumed it might be. And my geography was good despite my condition. That the Libyan border stretched for five hundred miles or so across the north of Chad was not lost on me. Neither was the fact that I was probably not expected to ask many more questions or the deal would be off. A knowing, perhaps quizzical, look was what I would normally have given in situations like that. I gave it the best I could.

And then, while my brain went around in circles, I leaned forward to take the paper, trying desperately to focus on its contents. There was no possibility of seeing it for my glasses were back at my hotel, the type was small and all I could see was a blur that extended about half way down the page. The flickering candles didn't help. There were, what appeared to be, figures on the right-hand side although it was hardly possible to decipher them. But I knew I had to try.

Forsyth was looking at me, perhaps trying to make out what sort of trader he was dealing with. I sat back in the chair, holding the paper to my face to hide it and try, at the very least, to read some of the figures.

There were three columns which suggested a list of items required, some brief specifications, quantities and, probably, estimates of their cost. So, on that assumption, I glanced at the final figure that lay beneath the small line at the bottom. I saw a pound sign and six as yet indecipherable figures that ended in three zeros. So, with at least that much knowledge, I decided to place the sheet back on the table to appear to have finished my first superficial glance.

The Brigadier though was the first to speak again. "Two hundred and forty thousand pounds FOB."

"Yes, I see," I lied. A quick mental sum was still possible, though. At twenty percent or so I could net perhaps forty-eight thousand pounds' profit or commission, depending how I handled it. But it was enough to top up the savings and buy the house in Cape Town.

"We need it delivered before the end of January. Letter of Credit, payable to your company in the UK. Can you do it?" Forsyth was now pushing hard and didn't wait for an answer. "We'll need a Pro-Forma Invoice of course to arrange for the credit. Under its terms, you will have to use a specified shipping company. Understood?"

"Yes."

"So, when can I get the Pro Forma?"

"As soon I return to UK."

I was given the address of a shipping company in East London that I had only vaguely heard of and we swapped a few other details. But within half an hour I was back at my hotel, drenched from walking through the tropical downpour but slightly more sober.

The next day my lost suitcase finally caught up with me, but, with still no sign of George and not needing him now anyway as the deal clearly didn't involve Ghana, I left for the airport. I took the night-time Ethiopian airline flight across Africa to Nairobi, connected with a flight to Johannesburg and on to Cape Town.

In Cape Town, in the October sun of southern-hemisphere spring I made some phone calls to a dealer friend in Turkey and one in Hungary to set the ball in motion for when I returned home. It was not going to be easy and I knew I was going to have to speak to the bank to borrow some money to pay the two main suppliers in advance. I had faced this sort of thing before, though, so whilst it was not ideal, I felt fairly comfortable with it.

I spent the next few days looking at property along roads towards the Cape. By the end of the fourth day, I had collected an armful of brochures, pictures of the local scenery and property details to take home to Sarah to start on my plan of gentle persuasion.

But that was when my well-intentioned domestic plans clashed with the difficulties with Brigadier Forsyth's arms shipment.

CONNED

It's such a pity. I was making such good progress.

Writing about Forsyth brought on a horrendous bout of Thomas's Disease made worse by sorting through the contents of the box that has lain upstairs, unopened for many years.

Everything in that box brings back memories and amongst it's ageing contents are the fading papers to do with the Forsyth shipment.

It is when reading such old office papers that I hear the clatter and ring of Beatie's typewriter as she typed them and see my old desk, my pens and pencil sharpener. The smell of each piece of paper still carries with it the scent of where it had been and what it had done.

On one, I could clearly smell a hotel room in Beirut. It was that room where I had sat and mended my broken suitcase with string pulled inch by inch from the top of the curtains and then threaded through the shattered corners of the case with a toothpick. The curtain survived though without the high-quality pleats it had started with but I had had plenty of time to do the laborious sewing job. A bomb had blown out most of the front of the hotel after I'd finished my dinner in the restaurant and there was no easy way through the rubble to the road outside until it was cleared next morning.

Many of the papers in that box had grown brown spots, as though they were damp when I put them away. Some had been folded because they had been posted. Some were still in envelopes that carried old postage stamps and some were bound with paper clips or staples that had started to rust and left brown marks when I removed them. And inside one brown envelope were the documents related to the Forsyth shipment.

Two nights ago, I removed them for the first time for a quarter of a century and on the top was the original shopping list from Forsyth. Forsyth had not left me the other sheet of paper that showed the Embassy address. Perhaps it had been used merely to flash before my eyes to give the impression of some sort of official sanction. So, I only had the shopping list, the quantities and the estimated costs but the typing is now very much easier to read than it had been when I first saw it.

But, behind this, held together by a large rusty paper clip, were copies of all the other documents to do with that shipment.

There was a copy of my Pro-Forma invoice to the Shipping Company in East India Dock Road, whose name I had been given by Forsyth. Behind that, copies of quotations and invoices from my two, main suppliers and copies of my confirmation orders and dispatch instructions to each of them. It was neat and tidy and professional. Then there was a faded copy of the Letter of Credit and copies of all the other documents and certificates that I had had to present to the bank in order to get paid. Then, last of all, came the letter from the bank, itself, after I had presented the documents.

This was not a copy but the original bearing the signature of a bank official and I read it for the first time for more than twenty-five years. Despite the lapse of time, the letter's contents are still imprinted on my mind.

Even for a professional, dealing with Letters of Credit can be a reason why, even seasoned exporters die prematurely. You live on your nerves at the behest of some bank clerk seated in a darkened office and equipped only with a pair of spectacles and a quill pen of the sort used by Scrooge as he sat at his desk on Christmas Eve.

His job is to find just the smallest error in your own handiwork.

It can be a simple error of a comma being out of place, the failure to dot an I or cross a T. And it's not just your handiwork they judge. It can be a misspelt name or any other problem with the bank draft, the shipping documents or certificate of origin which fail to read in quite the way that Scrooge believes it should.

In places like Fairyland, these bespectacled clerks retain their mean images and add to their private wealth by a willingness to be bribed to overlook such tiny errors. Others are paid to find errors and, in the case of Brigadier Forsyth's shipment, it was clear that I had come across one of the latter - a Scrooge being paid to find errors.

Last night, I had to refill my glass several times to give myself enough courage to re-read that letter. And there it was: "Payment cannot be made due to the following discrepancies . . ." it started.

I had stared at it in disbelief when I first saw it twenty-five years ago, and it had the same effect last night.

Even for a healthy man, this sort of letter is sufficient to trigger nightmares that cause heart failure. That letter contained a long list of irreparable problems. I had omitted this and not complied with that. My invoice was wrongly worded and the certificates of origin unacceptable. The list went on and on and I knew that no amount of bribing would make any difference.

In effect, all hopes of a decent profit to go towards my pension were gone.

But that was not all. My suppliers, of course, had expected their payments up front and I had honoured these. I had paid in advance from a short-term bank loan secured on the house. Oh yes, I lost my deposit good and proper.

And there is no Government Ombudsman to come to the aid of a one-man band small business. Tough, they say. Oh dear, what terribly bad luck.

I was out of pocket by a huge amount. After repaying the bank, my loss was over one hundred thousand pounds of hard-earned funds and my savings were virtually gone. It is, I suppose, fortunate that I had some to lose. Others have been known to put their houses up as security and lose everything. As I re-read that bank letter my stomach churned just as it had the first time. It was like looking at a signed copy of a death sentence.

Beneath that letter were copies of all the documents that I had meticulously prepared and then sent to the bank expecting payment. My real anguish was in knowing that what I had submitted had been perfectly good. I was no start-up amateur. My invoice was perfect, the certificates of origin were good, I was a professional. I had been expert at my job and had also taught Beatie to be as good as me so there were always two pairs of eyes checking and double-checking everything. The important thing is that I knew, even at the time, that something had happened to those documents between leaving my office and arriving at the bank.

But then, along came another problem to compound everything else.

Two days before the letter came from the bank, Beatie had failed to turn up for work. A man, whose voice I did not recognize, called to say she was sick. But Beatie had never gone sick in twenty-five years.

BEATIE

B eatie was just one other problem I was facing. Family issues were also giving me a headache.

Robert had moved with his job to Gloucester and Sarah had already visited Robert and his wife, Anne, at their new home. She was buzzing with excitement about moving closer to them and away from Croydon. "We need to look at some houses, dear. We both need a change now. It's time to pack up our bags."

To Sarah, Gloucester seemed like El Dorado. To me it seemed like Croydon beside a river but as I was too preoccupied with banks and Beatie to argue. I went with the flow.

Sarah sensed something was bothering me but to mention serious financial problems seemed inappropriate. I know I should have been more open but domestic bills were always paid and, just before Forsyth, I'd bought the new Jaguar, the one that is still in the garage now. To Sarah, everything looked fine.

Finally, I decided it was time to break the habit of a lifetime and talk about financial problems. I fretted on the problem for days before going home one night with a set of well thought through sentences to begin a long and constructive conversation.

My plan was to start by explaining why I had gone to Ghana and that the order I hoped to win would have been profitable enough to retire on. But it had been slightly more complicated than I anticipated and that this had happened and that had happened and there was a problem here and a last-minute hitch here and then the bloody banks this and the bloody banks that and some people were not to be trusted and that I was still trying to resolve this and that and soon I'd be ...

But I needn't have worried.

I had hardly got to the sentence about Ghana when: "Never mind, dear, that's life. Win some, lose some. We've got to keep on going. It'll be fine you see. Being close to Robert and Anne will be good. We'll be grandparents, yes? You'll be able to take them to school and pick them up. And it's so much nearer the countryside. The Cotswolds are right on our doorstep. It's not like here in Brick Terrace."

I didn't have the heart to remind her that Gloucester wasn't exactly what I had in mind. Neither did I actually get to admit that the losses were actually over one hundred thousand pounds. But I still don't think it would have mattered to Sarah.

I got as far as, "but I've lost more than expected and, having had to repay the short-term bank loan, it's not looking as good as I . . ."

"Oh, never mind, dear. Beggars can't be choosers. Waste not want not. What you haven't had you never miss." Sarah's reasons for everything being ship-shape and Bristol fashion, as she also used to say, were endless.

But that, in a nutshell, is why twenty-five years later I am still here in Gloucester and looking at the reflection of a wrinkled, eighty-six-year-old man in the window. I had only ever argued with Sarah once and had no desire to argue with her again.

Living in Gloucester was what she wanted and I felt I now owed her something. The fact that Robert and Anne packed their bags and moved to Plymouth and then to America almost as soon as we moved to Gloucester made no difference. Sarah took that in her stride as well. "Ah well dear, we can visit them in Plymouth."

God knows, I had left her alone for far too long over the years. In effect, I felt I no longer had a leg to stand on – as she would have said.

I'm grateful to Sarah, though, because she never ever complained. She made our home life together easy and good, and that is why I then did as much as I could for her.

The other woman in my life was, of course, Beatie.

I had never imagined Beatie with a man who cared about her health and wellbeing as much as I did Sarah's. But then, Miss Beatrice Collins, spinster of Brixton, had never taken a day's sick leave in her entire life as far as I knew. She would usually sit sniffing and coughing through any cold she ever caught leaving sodden handkerchiefs everywhere. The only other hindrance when Beatie was sick was the strong smell of menthol throat lozenges. So, her sudden absence in the middle of all of this added another strain.

But what does an employer who has just lost most of his personal wealth overnight do when his only staff member goes sick at the same time? Well, he does what any good employer does.

He forgets his enormous personal difficulties for a moment and decides to send his loyal employee a bunch of flowers by Interflora with a "Get Well Soon" card attached to the address that he has on file. But still I heard nothing and Beatie still failed to turn up for work after more than a fortnight.

Even the strange man who had called on her behalf never called again. By the third week I was deeply worried and so, on my way back from London one day, I called at the address in Brixton to check. The house, itself, was exactly where and how I had imagined it but the person who opened the door of number 82 was definitely not Beatie.

The lady who came to the door was a dark, nutty brown with long black hair and a red spot on her forehead and clearly not of Beatie's pallid texture or even her ethnic origin. Beatie was as white as freshly fallen snow, a cheese and pickle sandwich and meat and two veg person and very clearly of South London ethnic origin. This resident was of Indian descent and the waft of curry that followed her to the door was not something I would have associated with Beatie's kitchen.

"Excuse me," I said, "I'm sorry to trouble you, but I am looking for Miss Beatie Collins. I understood she lived here."

'But I am Mrs Riaz, sir. My husband is Doctor Riaz. He is a doctor at St George's Hospital, sir. Very sorry, sir,' she said in her polite Indian way.

"So, do you know Miss Beatie Collins?" I asked, because I thought she lived here.

"Sorry, sir," she said. "But perhaps she is the lady who used to live here with her mother."

"That might be her," I said.

"If that is so, sir, she left several years ago, because we purchased this house about five years ago."

I was very surprised. Beatie had never mentioned anything about moving house. So, I thanked her and was just about to leave when Mrs Riaz said, "But we have a forwarding address here, somewhere. Would you like me to find it?"

"Thank you, "I said, and she disappeared along the passage. Then she turned and came back.

"Please to step inside, sir. I won't be a minute. By the way, sir, are you the person who recently sent flowers here?"

"Yes," I replied. "Miss Collins was my employee. I thought she was sick because she hadn't come to work. She worked for me for more than twenty years."

"Goodness," said Mrs Riaz, "that is a long time. I'm sorry, but naturally we couldn't take delivery of the flowers."

"I fully understand," I said.

A few minutes later she returned with a torn off slip of paper. "This is the forwarding address, sir."

I thanked her and left with an address that turned out to be just a twenty-minute walk from our own house in Croydon. So, as the situation was becoming more and more mysterious, I decided to stop off at this other address.

Number 36 turned out to be yet another Victorian brick terraced house with a gate and a handkerchief sized patch of weeds and buddleia for a garden and faded net curtains. I rang the bell but and knocked several times but as no-one answered I turned to go. It was then that I saw the face of a woman in the next house peering from the downstairs window. I waved and beckoned her to come out. With that, a door scraped open and the woman appeared, wiping her hands on a cloth.

"Police?" she asked before I could say anything.

"No," I said, "Not at all. I was given this address as belonging to someone called Beatie Collins. I'm her boss. Is something wrong?"

"Don't you know?"

"No. Why? What happened?"

"They found her body."

"What body?"

"The woman's body."

"Where, when?" I asked, wondering what had been going on.

"Near the bus stop, late one night."

I didn't stand around much longer but phoned the police and was asked to call in. I then phoned Sarah to say I'd be late and why. Sarah was shocked and surprisingly upset about Beatie. I left her in tears on the phone promising to be home soon. Then I called into the police station where I asked some questions and made a brief statement.

But what could I say?

Loyal employee of mine for twenty-something years – very good worker – she was single – no family I knew of after her old mother died – suddenly went off sick – very unusual. I'd had a phone call from a man who didn't give his name. I'd then tried the Interflora idea – got redirected by the new home owner to the house in Croydon – found out she'd died – phoned police.

Finally, the desk sergeant explained that Beatie's body had been found early one morning in an alley way close to the bus stop at the end of her road. Ambulance was called but pronounced dead at scene. Middle-aged lady, dressed in a pink cardigan, grey skirt and a coat and a purse in the handbag identified her as one Beatrice Collins of the Croydon address. Police had found nothing in the said house except personal things, a drawer full of electricity bills and such like, which confirmed her name, but little else. No bank statements, not even any pay slips or other evidence of what she did or where she worked. Complete mystery. Police thought there were signs of a break-in at the rear because the door handle was broken which was why they came twice. But no signs of anything having been taken so assumed the lock had been broken for some time. Not pursued. TV, clothes, neat piles of women's magazines, a bookshelf laden with romantic novels, a single bed with clothes neatly hung in a wardrobe, a bathroom with a medicine cabinet full of cough mixture and menthol throat lozenges and a black cat, wandering around looking lost with its food dish empty. No evidence of any family except a letter found from someone in Brentwood in Essex who turned out to be a cousin and only known living relative. Cousin identified body but confirmed they hadn't seen each other for several years. Cousin claimed she was a lonely widow who was often depressed. Work for a small export business was her only interest in life. Post mortem, death certificate. No known cause of death so went down as natural causes. Cremation had taken place just two weeks ago.

"No pay slips, officer?" I asked.

"Sorry, sir. Nothing. You paid her regularly?"

"Of course, properly, by cheque, national insurance everything."

"Sorry sir, there was nothing. Not even a working telephone in the house. Otherwise we might have contacted you."

"So, who do you think it was who called me, Sergeant? Whoever it was said she was sick, not that she'd died."

"No idea sir. Sorry."

And that was that. "Thank you for calling in Mr Thomas and I'm sorry you weren't notified but we had no way of knowing you were her employer. There was just nothing in the house."

I was about to leave when I thought of something else. "Could you give me the address of Beatie's cousin in Brentwood?" I asked. "It's just that she has a few personal belongings in my office which I could return to her."

I left the police station with a piece of paper with the address and telephone number of a Mrs Dorothy Fletcher. Something wasn't quite right here, but I couldn't put my finger on it.

Beatie had sat opposite me in my office for a quarter of a century and had kept it running with undisputed efficiency through all my prolonged and frequent absences. But her private life had been, and still was, a complete mystery. But I had never intruded, you see.

When I got home, I updated Sarah on the news and she burst into tears yet again. "Poor Beatie," she sobbed. "She was always such a worried woman, dear. She was as worried for you as much as for herself. You should have talked to her, you know. She never said much when she phoned here – mostly just to ask if I'd heard from you."

"She phoned? Did she phone often?" I asked, surprised.

"Only sometimes," Sarah replied. "She was just checking if I was alright. I think she worried about me when you were away. It's all very sad."

And as Sarah spoke the last few words, she had a look in her eyes that I was to see more and more as we grew older. Sarah knew far more about everything than I thought.

"What else did she say, my love?" I asked with my arm wrapped around her and wiping tears with my hand.

"Not much. Just that she was worried."

"Worried for whom?"

"Me, you, herself."

"Herself?"

"She hated the job you know."

"Hated me?"

"No not you. She hated the job. In fact, she was always very concerned about you. She was under pressure from somewhere."

"Pressure?"

"Her family, I think."

"What family? She only had her old mother."

"Maybe not her family, but something else or somebody else." With that Sarah started to cry again and we never discussed it again but I now wish we had.

The following day I telephoned Beatie's cousin, Dorothy Fletcher.

"Oh, yes," she said when I introduced myself, "Beatie mentioned you and her job. Export business, wasn't it? We rarely saw her but it was the only thing she seemed to do. She didn't seem to have much else. She was very lonely. We invited her here for Christmas once but she declined."

We talked for a while about how good Beatie had been. Then I asked my lingering question.

"Did she ever mention a Major Donaldson?"

"Oh yes," Mrs Fletcher said without any hesitation. "Only once but I will never forget it. It was after my aunt's, Beatie's mum's, funeral. My husband and I went back to Beatie's house in Brixton because she wanted to give me some things that had belonged to my aunt. She was, of course, already dreadfully upset about her mother but, while we were at the house, she had a phone call. It was that Major. She was even more upset afterwards. We had a terrible time trying to console her."

"What happened?" I asked.

"I don't know what he said but she was telling him to leave her alone. She was terribly upset and trying to say she had just buried her mother. It went on for ten minutes or so. She even screamed at one point. Beatie never screamed. I've never forgotten it."

"Do you know why he phoned?"

"She didn't want to talk about it. But she did mention his name and that is why I know it. It sounded to me like he was her boss. In fact, I always thought he was until you just telephoned. That Major Donaldson was not a nice man but she seemed completely under his control."

"Why do you think Beatie died?" I asked.

"I don't know. The post mortem was inconclusive. But she was only fifty-five, Mr Thomas. I think she died of loneliness and a broken heart. I think she had just had enough but I don't think we'll ever know, for certain."

It was three weeks after that and two months after the Forsyth problem that I learned more.

I felt increasingly concerned about Beatie's death and Beatie's cousin's words about Donaldson did nothing to ease my suspicions. Something was wrong. In particular, who was the person who'd phoned me? Whoever it was had phoned about two days before she was found dead. So, because I was still feeling genuinely upset about it, I decided to check through the drawers of her desk.

She had left very little behind. It was as though she knew she was leaving and had cleared everything - pens, paper and spare typewriter ribbons. The copies of the documents for the disastrous Forsyth shipment were still in a folder on her desk. I was tired of reading and re-reading them since the bank refused payment and decided to put them in an empty drawer. But, as usual, I couldn't resist one last look.

I had gone through them over and over again to check for accuracy before I submitted them because they were so vital. They were in such perfectly good order that they should never have been rejected. I knew I'd had been stitched up and my suspicions about Beatie's involvement started to grow.

I had checked several times with the shipping company who said they knew nothing. They said the documents they had given me to present to the bank had been perfectly correct and I agreed with them. They pleaded ignorance, threw their hands up in regret and shrugged. Naturally, each of my suppliers including the shipping company had been paid so they weren't too bothered. The shipment had gone and presumably arrived at its final destination. They confirmed all that, which was as far as their responsibilities went.

But, somewhere along the route something had happened. Somewhere between my office and the bank, the documents had been changed.

But not only did Beatie disappear.

Forsyth disappeared as well.

I telephoned the British Embassy in Accra and was told they had no record of a Brigadier Forsyth ever being based there. I really had made one very serious mistake.

I sat in Beatie's chair trying to fathom out what might have happened. I picked up one of her hair clips off the floor and stuck it in the drawer as though she might be coming back to reclaim it. And then I heard her voice, inside my head. "I'll leave it there, Mr Thomas, for safe keeping. Just in case. You never know."

We didn't keep a safe in the office as I didn't deal in cash, but Beatie would, on occasion put an order, a letter, a cable or, later, a telex message inside my ABC Flight Timetable. I went to my own desk and took it out of the drawer for the first time since I'd used it to work out flights and times to fly to Accra, Nairobi and on to Cape Town. And out fell a piece of paper. Printed at the top was the address of the military hospital in Cyprus with its telephone and telex address in Larnaca.

It was a strange piece of paper to be in there.

But, beneath the printed name and address, someone had scribbled the name Credit Suisse, Zurich and what looked like a bank account number. Then there was a name as though it was the account holder. The name was clear – R. B. Forsyth.

I stared at it. It hadn't been there before I went to Ghana. Someone had put it there during the last two months. I then turned it over and found something written in Beatie's own handwriting.

"Dear Mr Thomas. I am so sorry. You did not deserve all this. Forgive me but I cannot live this lie any more. I hope you find this and hope it will be enough for you to understand things. I have been living under increasing pressure. I have tried to tell you but it is very hard. I have now been told I must leave my employment. Yours, Beatrice Collins."

My mind tumbled over itself trying to understand what she was saying. Told to leave? Then it dawned on me. It had been Donaldson who, twenty-five-years before, suggested I needed some help in my office.

"Need to get a good secretary, old chap. Can't be distracted by doing everything yourself. You need to concentrate on managing the business."

"Not yet," I'd said. "Plenty of time. I can't afford it yet anyway. Perhaps in a year or so."

A week later, Beatie had written to me as a complete stranger looking for a job. Two weeks later I'd appointed her and twenty-five years later she was still there. But it was now very clear. Beatie had been planted by Donaldson and it looked to me as though somehow, probably through this man Forsyth, Donaldson had had the last laugh from beyond the grave.

SARAH

I will now skip twenty-five years for there is little to write about
since Beatie died and I closed the business. It is time for me to
write about Sarah.

I have spent much of the last few years taking care of her whilst
spending the rest of the time coping with Thomas's Disease and
nightmares.

In one of those recurring nightmares Donaldson, in a fit of
red-faced rage and with spittle flying everywhere, pulls out a gun
and shoots me. One night, sitting by the gas fire and in the middle
of a repeat of this scene, just as Donaldson fired the gun, I heard a
loud noise from somewhere. I awoke with such a jolt that the whisky
bottle emptied itself all down my front.

I checked for blood but there was none so, deciding the noise
had come from the bedroom, I staggered up the stairs with a growing
sense of panic.

It was not as bad as I thought. Sarah had moved in the bed and
the arm that had, perhaps, tried in vain to pull herself into a sitting
position had, instead, caught a metal tray of tea and toast that I
thought I had put out of reach. Cold tea had soaked into the carpet.
The cold toast, on the other hand, lay upside down beneath the bed
at the head of a messy trail of butter and crumbs. But my immediate
concern was not the mess on the carpet.

Sarah was still half-asleep. Her arm was hanging outside the
bedclothes and the sound coming from her throat was a faint,
irregular gasping for air, like sobs, behind closed eyes as though she,
too, was having a bad dream.

Trying not to breathe whisky fumes I tucked her arm under the blanket and whispered to her to wake up from whatever awfulness was going on in her mind. It was as though she, too, had witnessed an assassination or heard a gun being fired. She mumbled something, incoherently, and I asked her what she was saying but, instead, she gasped for air again as though unable to wake. I smoothed her cold cheek and stroked her forehead trying to bring her back into the land of consciousness. I took her other hand, pressing it as hard as I could without hurting her and then parted the strands of grey hair that covered her ear and I called her name, more loudly this time.

It seemed to work.

The mumbling stopped and her eyes moved behind her closed lids. Her mouth opened, slightly, as though she wanted to speak, but nothing came except another sound like a gurgled, drawing of air. It had been like that just two nights before. It was as though she was awake but did not have the strength to break through a barrier of unconsciousness. I felt utterly helpless but understood how she might be feeling. Fighting nightmares is a similar experience.

After the first occasion, I had mentioned it to Dr Stephenson, during his routine visit. He had merely listened, nodded his head gravely and continued to concentrate on measuring her blood pressure and holding her wrist.

In case you're interested, I have opinions about doctors as well as opticians, dentists and barbers. They seem to think that as long as they lay a cold stethoscope on your chest, stick a thermometer beneath your tongue and wrap a sphygmomanometer around your arm you'll be impressed, their vast skill and knowledge bound up in a few antique instruments that have been in use for hundreds of years.

I also mentioned the situation to the nurse and will never forget how she had looked away. It was as though she hadn't heard me.

I sat there, watching Sarah and listening to her although my heart still pounded in my chest. After a while, her breathing became more regular and the closed eyes stopped their desperate searching. So, I let go of her hand gently and bent down to deal with the mess on the floor.

Then, when my head had cleared, I sat on the edge of the bed and watched her, wondering how she could sleep so much when, for the first time in sixty years of marriage, all I needed was to talk. I needed a very long conversation but an answer to one simple question would have sufficed. "What can I do, my love?"

But all I ever got back was silence.

Her skin looked grey and pale and her mouth was always slightly open. Her breathing was shallow with just a gentle noise from her throat. I brushed away the wisps of hair from her forehead and kissed her cheek. But Sarah had started to look different in a way I cannot describe and it worried me constantly. Her cheeks, too, felt cold as if they were reflecting the cooling of her personality. She had never been like that before. She was slow in turning over in bed and constantly complained of pains in her back and side and even her elbows. I knew she was becoming weak and had painful sores.

I knew Dr Stephenson was concerned about her but she refused to go into hospital.

"She's stubborn, Doctor," I said although I knew I was excusing myself to the one person who would have been aware of how serious the situation was becoming. But I had no wish for her to go into hospital. I had made a pact with myself never to leave her at the mercy of others. Sarah was my responsibility.

I pulled the sheet a little higher and, after a last look, went downstairs.

I would sometimes join her in, or on, the bed but this was becoming more and more unusual because I rarely felt tired enough to go to bed. Despite the greater intimacy, I had no wish to lie there with my eyes wide open staring at the ceiling. Tedious though it was I preferred the chair downstairs.

I'd sometimes switch the television on but I never watched it. A late-night film might be flickering away with the sound turned down so that I could listen for any sound from upstairs. They were occasional visual distractions that I glanced at but I never followed any of them.

More often, I listened to the radio at night – the BBC World Service, switching on in time to hear a few bars of "Sailing By".

Radio is so much better for the imagination. But, often, the radio is mere background talk – conversation, like the babbling of friends. Sometimes I feel I am actively taking part but at other times I leave them to talk amongst themselves whilst I wander off, aimlessly amongst my own thoughts, memories and dreams.

Sometimes I annoy myself by listening to tripe. Music doesn't interest me as much as it did Sarah. She liked all sorts of music – light music, classical music and church music, especially Christmas Carols. Sarah loved Christmas and it upsets me deeply now that on more than one occasion I was away. But when we were younger, she would always go out carolling with groups of friends and neighbours armed with candles and song sheets and dressed in coats and scarves.

"Come on," she used to say. "Come and join us. We need a good baritone. There will be mince pies for everyone at the end of it all."

Smiling, laughing as she sang Good King Wenceslas, Away in a Manger, Once in Royal David's City. Those were her favourites and I always envied the simplicity. Bless her.

I never went of course, but I have been known to venture to the door to look out for her if I thought she was a little late. But it would have needed more than mince pies to persuade me to go. I like some church music, but Sarah thought my particular choice far too depressing.

Faure's Requiem would be the record I'd take with me on the Desert Island. I'd take it to cheer me up and to remind me of life's fragility. I like the words of the English translation and the deep emotion the music stirs in me. The Libera Me is the best part and I always remember the words.

"Music for real men and for those not afraid to die, my love," I would tell Sarah. And she would look at me and walk away disgusted. I would chase after her.

"Don't run away. Faure's Requiem is not music for the faint hearted, my love," And I would quote from it when I caught her and thought she was in the mood. Perhaps, she had ticked me off for some petty domestic offence.

"Oh! Full of terror am I, and I fear the trial to come. That day shall be a day of wrath, of calamity and misery. That day shall be a mighty one, and exceeding bitter."

Then we would both laugh and laugh until the tears came.

"Oh, get away with you! You are a dreadful tease!" That was my Sarah talking as she used to.

I once awoke at five thirty in a panic because I hadn't checked Sarah for hours. My whisky glass fell to the floor and toppled over, but knowing that my head was not up to bending down and my bladder was at bursting point, I left it lying there, the last dregs of whisky soaking into the carpet. But I made it to the toilet.

I then went to the kitchen where I filled the kettle and, while it boiled, went upstairs. Sarah asleep as usual. She was lying on her back, her head turned slightly towards the window and her mouth slightly open. Being unable to bend too far I leaned on the bedside table with one hand, the other holding my throbbing head and looked down at her. In the light from the bedside lamp she looked so pale.

She had begun to look so much smaller towards the end and I knew she had become anaemic. Part of Dr Stephenson's daily cocktail of medicine was for this.

She moved slightly and her breathing faltered as though she might have heard me, but her eyes stayed shut.

For several years, I slept poorly beside her. If she moved or made even the faintest sound I would wake up – instantly. I could never manage seven or eight hours at a stretch. Two is often all I need. But lying by her side was the closest to bliss sometimes. The best times of my life have been spent like that. Just lying, wide awake, watching her, listening to her breathing. I would wake at five thirty or earlier having only slept for an hour or so but it was enough and often, after just a few minutes of lying, watching and listening I would get up.

To lie there any longer would cause me to panic as though I had an appointment or a job to do. This was nonsense of course, but it is impossible to destroy a lifetime of habit. Sometimes, though, I would fight the urge to get up. Sometimes I would continue to lie there, looking at her, touching her face, pushing the hair from her forehead or stroking her cheek. Sometimes I would feel I wanted more than that because my body felt her closeness. When we were young, we would make love in the early morning.

My gentle touching of her cheek and hair would be just the start. I would move my hand along her neck, around her ears, caressing and brushing her hair, perhaps moving closer to touch her ear with my lips. Then I would run my fingers around her neck and down between her breasts. That was when she would move towards me. Her eyes would open then. Or perhaps she would smile, giggle or murmur with her eyes still closed. I always knew when she was ready. We always preferred mornings.

Mornings are fresh, new and unspoiled. Mornings feel uncluttered like fresh beginnings whereas night times are invariably spoiled by a mind that's full of trouble, tension and guilt from the day just passed.

Towards the end, Sarah would still stir if I touched her. Her eyes would open as though she was responding as she used to. But, at other times, she seemed totally unaware of what I was doing. She would lie, perfectly still, her eyes firmly closed as though she had also lost her sense of touch.

The sense of intimacy that simple caressing gives was something I missed, dreadfully. I missed her responding, her quiet murmuring, her smile, with her eyes still closed. I missed the look of contentment on her face and I missed her touching and holding me. I missed the sharing and the togetherness and I missed her voice. More than anything, I missed her company.

The days had become long and monotonous and the nights dominated by headaches and nightmares.

I still possessed enough energy to walk or even to take the car out. But I had no-one to walk with or join me in the car. Perhaps, at eighty-six, I am too old to be driving on modern, congested roads but the desire is still there. I wanted to see long and winding roads from behind a leather steering wheel. I wanted to watch green fields flash by and I wanted Sarah to be with me as we drove over hump backed bridges, along country lanes and picnicked in woods. I wanted to have a ferry ticket in the glove compartment and to park with a view to a distant horizon. I wanted to share that view and know that when we arrived, there would be yet another view to share over the next horizon or around the next bend.

Desires still lurked somewhere, deep in my body and soul.

I wanted to abandon my walking stick. I wanted to explore on foot, even if it was just undiscovered back streets of Gloucester. But more than anything I wanted Sarah to be with me on those walks and drives. I had no desire to walk alone anymore. I have spent too many years doing that. I wanted to take Sarah on holiday, to the sea, to listen together to the rolling waves and the screaming gulls, to breathe the windy, salty air, to sit on a stone wall eating fish and chips and to poke sticks into slimy, rock pools. I wanted to walk with her through woods kicking dry leaves that smelt of autumn.

I wanted her beside me at the supermarket because she was far better at shopping than I was. And I wanted to hold her hand and to make love again when the dawn was still breaking.

"I want our life to start again, my love." I whispered to her one morning. I was tired of the daydreaming and the nightmares and fed up with the repeats and the mental videos of my past life. I wanted my life to start again, to make amends, to put right whatever it was I might have done wrong and to spend time with the most important person in my life. In the cold light of dawn, I wanted my life back not because it had been wasted but because most of it had been good. It was just that there were a few things I still did not fully understand and there were some big corrections I needed to make. I wasn't finished yet.

I was thinking all of that one morning as I knelt beside the bed, leaning on the blanket that covered Sarah so I reached beneath it to hold her hand. I held it and squeezed it, willing her to wake up and talk to me. But still her eyes stayed closed. And then, my own eyes closed and still kneeling, but with my head now resting on the pillow next to hers, I drifted off to sleep.

It was the best sleep I had had for many a long week. I would have been quite happy to die there and then. But death is not allowed to arrive so blissfully at a selected point in time.

And this sleep didn't last long because at seven o'clock, on schedule, the radio switched itself on and I was already dreaming when it came on. It wasn't a nightmare this time but, in my sleep, I had been watching a radar signal. A thin line of rotating light picking up brighter, slowly moving spots of lights. There was a sense of nervous excitement and someone talking. "Come on Ollie, jump to it old chap. Bandits, three o'clock."

Then I was hearing the radar blipping with short, sharp pips as the seven o'clock news began on the radio. Consciousness dawned and, slowly, I opened my eyes. And there before me – how wonderful! I will never forget that sight.

Next to mine, was a pair of light blue eyes topped by eyelashes and grey eyebrows. The eyes blinked at me, slowly, and the corners creased just a little. I could feel my hand beneath the blanket. It was warm and it was holding another and I felt mine being squeezed very gently.

My eyes filled with tears but I stayed there, unmoving, unembarrassed as a trickle of salty fluid ran down my cheek to the pillow because Sarah's eyes were so close to mine. They were inches away, but too close for me to see clearly as my glasses had fallen off somewhere. The eyes watched me as I sniffed back the water that was running inside my nose. They watched and took on a much softer look. No tears formed in those other eyes but, instead, the hand inside my own moved and squeezed it just a little harder. And then the creases near the blue eyes next to mine grew deeper.

This was enough. I had no wish for anything else now. I would have happily stayed like that forever. For us both to die at that moment would have been perfectly acceptable. To have died, perhaps, at that moment would have been best for everyone. But Sarah spoilt the moment.

"Hello dear," she whispered.

I was unsure if she could see the wetness on my cheeks but her words seemed to stop the hard ache that was growing in my throat. I sniffed again, my wet nose just inches from hers. "What are you doing?" she said.

I had no answer ready. All I knew was that my head felt light, my eyes were sore and my back, arm, and now my knees, ached. So, I said the only thing that came to me. Nothing else seemed appropriate. I said it because I felt slightly absurd kneeling and half lying there. My knee joints were crumpled, my back bent double and my hand was inside hers. Whether, too, it was a symptom of the hangover, I am not sure, either. Perhaps it was the seven o'clock news headlines that had just started on the radio but, more than anything it was because, in my mind, I was still hearing the pips and watching the radar screen. It was the only reply that came to me. "Bandits my love. Need to scramble," I said.

Sarah's eyes were looking at me, unsure, and the look on her face changed. And then she spoke the three words I had wanted to hear her say for weeks. "Well I never," she whispered. And her strength was still enough for her to continue. "Dreaming," she said.

I raised my aching head. "Oh no, I saw them on the radar," I said.

The greyish blue blur of her eyes stared blankly at me. It was clear she did not understand, so I just looked deep into them as best I could.

I love Sarah's eyes. I love the questions they ask. I love their scepticism, their doubt and their playful mocking. I love their sincerity, their innocence and their uncertainty. But, most of all I loved their familiarity so I smiled at her and kissed her cool cheek and wiped my own wet one with my hand.

"But," I said, "you know the real problem?" I paused. "I can't get up."

And then I wanted to laugh and to cry all at the same time and for Sarah to join in and laugh as well. I looked down at her, willing her to join me, but as so often, her sense of humour, like her sense of touch, seemed to have gone. I waited a moment and tried again. "I think I've broken both my legs and probably my back."

Still she didn't laugh so I struggled to stand up, holding my back. That was when she spoke, but it was no longer a whisper. "Whisky," she said.

How, in God's name, I wondered, did she know that? Could she smell it on my breath? I breathed into my hand and smelt it but, to me, there was nothing except a sour dryness and, anyway, it was several hours since the last glassful.

Had she heard me downstairs? Perhaps I had talked in my sleep. Perhaps I had laughed or even cried, or perhaps she'd heard the chinking of the bottle against the glass. Perhaps she merely saw me lose my balance as I tried to stand. I even wondered if she had crept downstairs and watched me draining the bottle me but the notion was absurd. "Nonsense," I said, "Just a tipple before I came to bed."

"Did you come to bed, dear?" she said, and I was shocked at that, too. The blue eyes that I could barely see were probably mocking me now as I tried to straighten my back, arching it, checking the functioning and trying to bend it back into shape. I couldn't resist it. I knelt down again and whispered with my lips pressed directly to her ear.

"How, on earth, do you know what I do, Mrs Thomas?"

"Oh, I know everything Mr Thomas," she replied. "Anyway, you didn't kiss me."

So, I kissed her again and sat down on the bed, felt for her hand in the warmth of the sheet and held it. But her hand moved as though she wanted to disentangle it and the moment, that I wanted to last for ever, was over. So, I went to the window and peered out from behind the curtain.

Daylight was still failing to make any impact on night.

I wiped the condensation from the glass and looked out to where the street light continued to do its dismal best. The road looked wet and our small, overgrown lawn with its scattering of decaying, wet leaves that had fallen a month ago, looked muddy. But the cherry tree was bathed in an unnatural orange glow from the street light. It was swaying in a cold wind that swept down the street. A car drove slowly past, its tyres hissing in the wetness and its headlights reflecting off the road. Then I turned around again to look back at Sarah.

She was looking the other way, to the side where I had been kneeling. Then I watched her move, quite sharply as though something was digging into her back. She made a sound like a short cry and her head turned to face me. Her eyes opened and I moved quickly over to the bed. Her face had crumpled as though she was in pain. "What is it?" I asked her but she only groaned. "What is it, my love?"

Tiny beads of sweat were forming on her forehead but it was still cold to touch. I had seen it before and thought it might be pain but I was certain the spasm would disappear as soon as it appeared. Sarah felt the pain but I felt the powerlessness to help.

But I knew there were other problems. She wasn't eating properly. That was why she looked so small and thin. But still she refused to go to hospital. "What can they do?" she would say. "How will you manage?"

Those were her reasons and I did not argue.

But, now, in the dim light, I could see she looked frightened and that frightened me. I sat on the bed, my hand resting on her cold, damp forehead. The spasm had gone but her eyes were shut and she was still frowning. I held her hand and squeezed it but she remained with her eyes closed.

I didn't know what to say. I wanted to say and to do so much – but what?

"Robert and Anne are coming," I said, but as soon as I had said it, I realized it sounded as if I was admitting that time was running out. "I phoned him," I said, but her eyes still remained shut and I was not sure if she had heard or was even listening. It was as though she was again cutting herself off from me.

That was one of the worst things. It was as though she was not interested in seeing or hearing. Sometimes she was still quite sharp. Her accusation of just minutes before that I might have been drinking was shrewd. I found it all so depressing. It had been like that for months now although I felt the trend seemed to be towards losing interest in what was going on.

I tried again. "Robert said they'd fly over for Christmas." There was still no reply and her eyes stayed shut. "Sarah, my love?" I spoke loudly and then again, even more loudly out of frustration. "Sarah, my love." I squeezed her hand and moved my face close to hers. "You want to see Robert – and Anne?" I asked.

I then tried to whisper, but still she did not respond. I was desperate to find things to keep her interested.

And then, something happened that I will never forget. Another spasm came and she groaned loudly. "Help me," she said but still her eyes were shut. I held her hand, firmly, unsure now of what to do or say. I felt totally helpless. "Help me," she said again, her voice fainter and coming through almost closed lips.

I was so close that I was touching her lips with my own. I was desperate to kiss her, talk to her, help her. I was racked with anguish, uncertainty and panic about what to do. "Sarah, my love. I'm here. Everything's alright."

She took a deep breath, coughed weakly and then relaxed into the pillow again and all I could do was wait and watch as her head sank onto the pillow and fell to one side. Then her breathing stopped.

It was only for a few seconds but, just as I was beginning to panic, it started again with a sudden gasp and a fluid sound from her chest. I clung to her hand, desperately looking at her, my other hand gently pushing cold, damp strands of hair from her forehead.

I sat there for what seemed like an eternity, unable to move as I watched the blanket across her chest rise and fall, irregularly and just perceptibly. Occasionally I moved my position just to counter the numbness in my own legs. My mouth was now seriously dry, my head still throbbed and I was desperately in need of a cup of tea but I just could not leave her even to go down to the kitchen. I thought about telephoning the clinic but was concerned that, if I did, decisions about what to do would be taken out of my hands and Sarah had been saying for months that she did not want to leave home – ever. "It's safer here," she would say.

She had made me promise not to leave her or allow her to be moved to hospital and I had agreed. I agreed because I wanted to do what she wanted but neither did I want her to go into hospital with its lack of privacy and even more depressing undertones. If there was to be some quality of life, better that it should meet both our wishes. Then, at other times, I doubted that wisdom.

Finally, as her breathing became deeper and more regular and she seemed more comfortable, I took my hand away and crept downstairs for my tea.

But she had, once more, said the words that constantly went around and around in my head. "I know everything, Mr Thomas."

How much did she know? Did she know everything about the life I had always tried to keep secret?

By midday both the nurse and doctor had called and Sarah had been awake while they were there. To me she seemed better though very tired. After they went, I made her another cup of tea.

The nurse had washed her and also took an advanced order for a 'Meals on Wheels Christmas Lunch Special'. "It's very good, Mr Thomas. Nice big dinner of turkey, stuffing, all the trimmings and you get a pudding as well with custard."

I said to her, "For God's sake, it's still November."

"Better early than never, Mr Thomas."

"So how often will they be serving the Special between now and Christmas?" I asked.

"Now don't start on me, Mr Thomas. After a week, I'm beginning to know you only too well. Try looking forward to it."

I was surely tempted to remind whatever her name was that Marmite on toast with a few glasses of Bell's as pudding was also nice. I also felt like telling her that after eighty-six Christmas lunches could they perhaps try using some imagination and invent something different. Instead, I said: "Thanks. I'll look forward to it. If I don't finish it, you can have what's left."

Three days later, things changed.

Sarah seemed to be asleep, her mouth, as ever, just slightly open and the wisps of grey hair just falling across her forehead. As usual, I brushed them to one side and kissed her cheek. It was even cooler than normal, but the bedroom, too felt cold as though I might have left the window open. I checked, pulled the curtain and briefly looked outside.

The wind had dropped and the cherry tree hung motionless. The road glistened with wetness as usual but whether it was rain or frost, I couldn't tell. But, as expected, the window was shut so I drew the curtains again and returned to the bedside, kneeled down, brushed Sarah's cool cheek with my fingers again and gently pulled back the blanket to search for her hand to wake her.

This was also nothing unusual.

I had been doing exactly that for weeks and always it was the same routine. I would leave the landing light on, creep in, check if she was awake, brush her cheek with my hand, then with my lips, then go to the window. Sometimes I would gently brush her hair back and comb it gently. Sometimes she would stir a little, perhaps murmur something. Then I would kneel, then feel for her hand beneath the blanket, hold it and squeeze it a little and then stay for as long as my knees and back held out.

Tonight, was different. What I felt beneath the blanket shocked me.

I felt the blood drain from my veins because her arm was as cool as her face. My own, warm, hand felt its way down her arm to her hand. Her hand, too, was cold and it had bent inwards in an odd way. My own hand stopped for a moment near her wrist and I moved my left hand to touch her face that was so close to mine.

I reached for her fingers. They, too, were cold. They felt hard and seemed to open again involuntarily. In a sudden rush of horror, I released my own hand and held her face again, this time with both hands. Then I cupped it in my hands but more firmly than usual. I pressed my hand onto her cold forehead and all around her face, around her ears, across her head, around her neck and then across her cheeks again. I moved her hair back and tugged at it very slightly and then bent to kiss her fully on her cold lips. But she did not move or respond.

I kissed her again and held her cheeks, trembling, feeling reluctantly but desperately for a pulse in her neck. But the trembling turned to shaking and I found I was holding all of her small head in my hands. I was shaking it, trembling all the time, pulling, caressing, pulling again and then tried desperately to pull her up from where she lay. I then collapsed and I fell onto the pillow beside her, tears pouring from my eyes.

Twenty-four hours later, I was alone again for the first time since I had discovered Sarah. I had spent the whole time barely knowing where I was or what I was doing. After a full two hours lying in the bedroom alongside Sarah, I had finally managed to telephone the doctor and then sank into a trancelike state of utter devastation, not knowing what I was thinking or doing.

Drained by a grief that I never fully understood was possible, I know I cried like a baby for what must have been hours. A doctor, a nurse, an ambulance and some other people whom I cannot remember ever having met before arrived at various times between midnight and the late morning. The doctor called again in the afternoon offering what help he could, but my body and mind were too numb and weakened by fatigue and utter desolation to understand what was being said to me.

All I remembered was the doctor offering to help if I wanted to go anywhere or if there was anyone else who needed to know urgently. Robert had been the only name I could think of, and the doctor had made the telephone call to Los Angeles for me, handing the phone over for me to speak to Robert for just a few moments.

All I can remember saying to Robert was how desperately sorry I was that I had been downstairs and not with her at the time she passed away and that this would stay with me for the rest of my life. I didn't tell him that words would also stay with me for the rest of my life. "I know everything, Mr Thomas."

ROBERT

Robert and Anne arrived from Los Angeles.
While Robert and I sat in chairs by the table opposite one another, Anne busied herself tidying the sitting room and preparing the first proper meal that had been cooked there for months. Robert and I mostly sat in silence, passing clutter towards Anne and moving our feet to allow her to clear underneath but that day and the evening that followed is only a vague memory and I must have eventually fallen asleep in the chair.

I woke up before daylight next morning, crying and sobbing like a baby but trying desperately to control myself in case Robert and Anne heard. My cheeks were wet but my mouth was dry and my bladder felt ready to burst. But I sat, unable to move as reality kept washing over me.

I slowly recovered some sense of order and, as all seemed quiet upstairs where Robert and Anne were, I assumed, still asleep I went to the bathroom and then to sit in the kitchen for a while. I drank a glass of cold water as I waited for the kettle to boil. Then, before it had boiled, I got up, washed in the kitchen sink, shaved as best as I could manage with a blunt razor on three days of growth and made myself a pot of tea. The shave wasn't good as my hands were shaking, so I stuck patches of tissue on to absorb the blood. As I carried the tray to the sitting room, the stairs creaked.

It was the sound of someone stepping on the top step but I had not heard it for a long time. That was how it used to be when Sarah came down in the morning but it was Robert's cough that stopped the tears from running too far down my sore face. I wiped them away just before he appeared and we sat at the table and talked.

"Why didn't you tell us, Dad? Anne and I could have come over long ago to help."

"No need, Rob. Your mother didn't want it. No need to fuss was one of her favourite sayings. What will be will be and I don't want to be a burden were others. You must remember what she was like."

"But was she up to making a decision, Dad?"

"It was what she wanted, Rob. I tried. I suggested we invite you for Christmas but she didn't seem bothered and she hasn't made it anyway. Fact is she barely knew what day, week or month it was for a long time."

"But that's terrible, Dad. Why didn't you tell me?"

"Because we agreed to stick it out here, just the two of us, depending on one another and not reliant on others for as long as possible, that's why."

Robert fell silent, sipping tea, as though admonished.

"And you know what, Rob? It was the right thing to do. I have no regrets. What could you have done? Worried? What good is that? Remember her as she was, Rob. It has not been a good year but at least we've been together and I would not have wanted it any other way. It was our decision, your mother's and mine. But it's not been easy I can tell you. I just wish I had been with her when she passed away."

I stopped, pulled off one of the bloody paper patches on my chin and dropped it on the floor. Tears were not far away and I swallowed hard, forcing myself to keep going. "But I have other regrets. I've sat here for too many hours over the last year or so pondering on the past. I've even been drinking a bit as well."

Robert interrupted me. "We noticed. Anne found dozens of empty glasses and bottles. You're OK just now though aren't you Dad? There's nothing wrong with you, is there?"

I stared into my empty cup. "I'm OK I suppose. I dream too much. I think too much. I sit around too much. I go over the past too much. I don't sleep much. I don't eat much. I read the foreign sections of the paper too thoroughly. I go to the shop once a day. The nurse comes. I look out of the window. I scribble a lot in a notebook. I watch TV with the sound turned off because it's absolute shit. I listen to similar shit on the radio."

I looked up at my son and our eyes met for perhaps the first time in years. "Thanks for coming, Robert." With that, I have to admit I choked on what felt like a hard lump and tears formed once more. They welled up, overflowed and ran down my cheeks.

And then Robert stood with bulging eyes and his face in a strangely contorted face and put an arm around my neck and his head on my shoulder. Seconds later, though, the top stair creaked again. We both heard it so Robert sat down, wiped his nose with his hand and had just picked up the two empty cups ready to go to the kitchen when Anne walked in wearing a dressing gown.

We both looked at her knowing our eyes were red. It was Anne who spoke. "So, did sleep do you some good?"

I had forgotten Anne's American accent. Somehow, I hadn't noticed it the night before. "Thank you," I said.

"Could you take a little breakfast? Need to eat you know. You've not been taking care of yourself."

For some reason, I felt hungry and it surprised me. "Yes," I said.

"So, what do we normally have?"

I wanted to say I normally have a hangover but thought better of it. Instead, I said, "Normally we have nothing."

Anne looked at me over the top of her glasses just like my mother used to. "You see, Rob, your father needs looking after."

Anne was trying to be kind but Robert sensed something out of order with what she said and the way she said it. "Dad's OK, Anne. He's doing fantastic. Why don't you go to the store – buy some eggs or something."

Robert's American way with words, too, suddenly became apparent and I realised how sensitive I still was to intonation and accent. It produced a sudden flashback to another accent that I had recently heard in a nightmare. "Jordanian," I said aloud, completely forgetting I had company.

"Pardon me?" Anne said, pouring herself a cup of tea.

"Jordanian," I repeated. "Leila was Jordanian. Fried egg on toast would be nice."

The rest of the day passed.

We talked about funeral arrangements, the house, the garden and what I might do with myself when they returned to California. The doctor and nurse called and sat talking with Anne and Robert while I excused myself in the bathroom. The evening passed, another large dinner of steak and mashed potatoes was prepared and eaten, leaving me with an uncomfortable reminder of what indigestion felt like. I asked Robert if he'd like to share a glass of whisky after the meal but, seeing Anne's look, withdrew the suggestion by admitting I felt unusually bloated.

The following morning, Robert came downstairs to find me again drinking tea at the table. It was six thirty. "So, what's with all the paper and notes, Dad?"

He was looking at the back of the table by the window where Anne had neatly piled the clutter spread across the table.

"I was sorting a few things out," I said. "Old papers. There's another box upstairs that I've not looked at for thirty years."

Robert leaned over and picked up a bundle. "Old newspaper cuttings. Nineteen seventy-two. IRA. Hijacks. London bombings. What's all this, Dad?"

"Old records, cuttings, that sort of thing."

"You were out there, weren't you, Dad? Middle East and other places."

"Yes."

"Mum never talked about what you did, you know. And you never said anything, either."

"No."

"Business wasn't it, Dad? Export or something."

"Yes."

Robert was flipping through another small bundle. "What's this all about, Dad?"

"It was a long time ago."

"And this? An old invoice. Thomas Import Export Limited." He stopped to turn something over in his hand. "Rifles, ammunition?"

"Put it back, Robert, it gives me nightmares."

"Is this what you did?"

"Only sometimes."

Robert put the pile down and looked towards me. "You always were a bit of a mystery, Dad," and he leaned over to pick up another pile.

"Leave it, son."

Robert looked at me sharply but then held up another bundle of papers, his eyes gleaming. "But what did you do, Dad? Mum said something once. I asked her where you were because I hadn't seen you for weeks. It was years ago. I may have been about twelve."

"What did your mother say?"

"She said you were up to your old tricks again. I thought it sounded funny. You know Mum and her sayings, Dad. She was well known for them, wasn't she? She had lots of others like that. He's out, playing with fire again. That was a common expression. We always joked about her way with words, didn't we? So, I asked her what she meant. She said you'd probably been – what was it? – operating incognito again – that was it.

"I always remembered those words exactly. I'd never heard the word incognito before. I asked her what it meant. 'Ssh,' she said, 'Your father's work is secret. Mustn't talk about it. He doesn't like that.' Then she said you were probably running around doing dirty work for others. She seemed cross if I remember. An off day I suppose. I ignored it. But she went on a bit that night."

Robert was absentmindedly trying to read a small square cut from an old newspaper but I found myself staring at him. "What do you mean, she went on a bit?"

"It was many years ago. But it wasn't the first time. She often grumbled about what you were up to. For God's sake, Dad, you even missed Christmas once or twice. Mum was really upset. She used to sit by the fire. You remember the one in the house in Croydon? Mum used to read a lot in those days. She took books from the public library. Sometimes she would put her book down and look at the clock. I remember. I might have been doing homework. She worried a lot, Dad. She didn't always show it. When you were home, she was fine. But she worried about where you were, when you were coming home, what you were doing. The office would phone sometimes."

"The office?"

"Yes – sometimes."

"What office?" It was a ridiculous comment but I was imagining Donaldson's Regent Street office.

"The Croydon office of course. The old woman who ran your office. Miss Collins, was it?"

"You knew about Beatie? She wasn't that old."

"We knew her as Miss Collins. She sometimes phoned when you were away. Except once."

"Except once?"

"Yes, I remember quite clearly. It was one evening when I was doing my homework. A man called. It was a funny conversation. He asked to speak to Mum – Mrs Thomas he called her. I said Mum was out and could I help. He asked me to give her a message. I said OK, no problem. Then he said, 'Tell her that Mr Reynolds is in Libya.' I told him to hang on while I wrote it down just like Mum had told me to if someone called. 'Tell her Mr Reynolds is in Libya,' he said."

I was sitting bolt upright, listening intently, my eyes unable to blink. "Mr Reynolds? What else did he say?"

"It was a long time ago, Dad. But it was as though Mum would understand because she knew Mr Reynolds as a friend or a business colleague of yours. Is that right, Dad? Was he? And, oh yes, something else. He also said to tell her that Libya was a red line. That's it – a red line."

Hitherto unconnected chunks of the jigsaw suddenly, clicked together. Even as Robert sat there talking idly and picking up odd pieces of old newspaper from the pile on the table, I could hear Sarah's voice: "I know everything, Mr Thomas."

What was also clear was that Sarah was expected to know what a red line was. And there was only one person who used that expression – Donaldson. Donaldson used it to describe a place where I was likely to be followed or somehow tracked. God, himself, would need to intervene if I ever stepped over the red line. The red line was like the one on a pressure gage. Cross it and there would be an almighty explosion. The red line was Donaldson's boiling point.

"Don't fuck up, old chap. You know it's not in anyone's interest. Think family, old chap, think pension, think security, think common sense and think bloody straight for once. Let's not mess up. I know, let's give this one red line status, shall we? There, that'll show you why you can't fuck this one up."

My mind was in overdrive again. I already knew that Sarah had known Beatie, at least via the occasional phone call. But Donaldson? And Sarah, it seemed, had also known something about Reynolds and that I travelled abroad as Reynolds as well as Thomas, which was why she had used the expression incognito to Robert.

"I know everything, Mr Thomas."

I pushed myself up from the chair, walked to the cupboard, brought out a fresh bottle of whisky and two glasses and sat down beside Robert again. "Dad, it's not yet seven thirty."

"I know."

I broke the bottle seal and unscrewed the cap as Robert watched. The process was performed quickly and efficiently. It was followed by a quick inversion of both glasses, first holding them against the ceiling light to check for dregs from previous use and within seconds both glasses were full of neat whisky. A moment later mine was empty.

"My God, Dad. I've never seen that before. I can't do that. Not at seven thirty in the morning, anyway. I hope Anne isn't coming down." Robert took a small sip, swallowed, then coughed as his throat burned and his eyes ran. "Bit early for me, Dad."

I, though, was already pouring myself another.

"Life's a bloody sod, Robert, I said. "I wish I'd talked to your mother more now. God knows we've had enough time over the years but I'd been trying to forget everything you see. Once I realized your mother had no interest in moving away from here, I went into a type of mental limbo. I tried to persuade her to pack our bags and go abroad but it was pointless. God knows why we stayed in this house, in this place, for so long. But your mother liked it here. She liked the familiarity and the domesticity. She liked having me around. I know I'd spent too much time away from home – far too much – but we could have been together, somewhere else – anywhere other than here."

"Perhaps she was frightened of strange places, Dad."

"No," I said, reality dawning, "I think she was frightened of strange people."

"You're depressed, Dad. Why don't you come over to the States after the funeral? See a bit of the world again if you miss it so much?"

"Perhaps. We'll see."

"But what else is eating you, Dad? There's something else besides Mum isn't there? What's all the stuff lying around here," Robert waved a hand at the boxes and piles of paper.

"Another mistake, I suppose," I said. "Old and dusty boxes should be left to gather more dust not opened up, peered into and sorted through. It has not exactly been a therapeutic pastime. It's what gives me the nightmares, Rob. Then there is the growing feeling, gnawing away at me, that your mother knew far more about the past than she ever let on. You've just proved it.

"But I've never been one to chat endlessly about this and that. I always felt some things were best kept to oneself.

"I've also been wondering about my old sense of patriotism and wondering whether it has now worn off. Some things were so complicated and I didn't ask enough questions. With your mother I struggled to know where to start. I was always waiting for the right time but the right time never came.

"I've also struggled with my conscience. How can you explain willing complicity in doing things that, under different circumstances or on reflection many years later, you consider wrong? I have, you see, done things which I can barely believe I had in me to do. Feelings of duty and responsibility do strange things to a man. Ask a soldier. Ask a politician.

"Then, just as I started to think I might be coming to terms with it all and that it was time to explain, your mother got ill and seemed to disappear into a sort of shell from which she never emerged."

I paused to take another drink. "Am I unique, Robert? Or are other men the same? Why is it that you can live with a woman for more than sixty years, be lost without her and yet be lost for words with her?

"You know something? A pint of beer with a friend always seemed to taste better if we sat saying nothing. And I don't think I am alone in that. Men are not emotionally deficient merely because we don't reveal ourselves to those, we are close to. I can see how pouring your heart out to a friend like women do is therapeutic but I've never been like that.

"I can talk. I can talk and discuss for hours. Talking is what I have done all my life. I can talk about things that I know and understand because hours of thought and consideration have preceded it. But I can't chat. Chat is what comes out of your mouth in an instant and for me that is too risky. I would reflect and analyse chat afterwards and because I often found it embarrassing and self-revealing I stopped.

"It is particularly true if I'm required to chat about my inner thoughts and feelings. I clam up. I have to think where to start and how much detail to provide.

"I actually think men are far more emotionally charged than women, although it is never recognized and especially not by women. Women sometimes try to trigger a debate by saying something trite like 'we need to talk about this'. Sarah tried that approach many years ago but it would be the trigger for me to clam up completely. I would go into a sort of panic and shut down completely.

"I preferred to deal with facts not with trying to unravel or explain a feeling or a mood. Is it any wonder your mother used to bury her head in a romantic novel whilst I buried mine in newspaper editorials?

"I wasn't deliberately trying to avoid discussing feelings. But because feelings and emotion are so impossible for anyone, man or woman, to fully fathom out I would fall silent. I would go into one of my panics and probably end up wandering to the garage to tinker with the car. I may have been tinkering but all the time, unbeknown to your mother, I was trying to find the right words to come back in to talk. By that time, your mother had, of course, completely forgotten about it all. And, of course, the right words never came to me, anyway. After three hours of tinkering I would return although, by that time, mainly driven by hunger or thirst.

"I suppose it has taken me eighty-six years to realise some of this and it might explain why I have spent the last year talking to myself and to anyone who happened to wander into my dreams.

"Do you understand any of that, Rob?"

"Yes," said Rob.

JIM

The funeral came and went although I can barely remember
it.

Then Robert and Anne went home and I decided not to
accept the invitation to go with them to Los Angeles. I still had
things on my mind.

But let me now tell you about Jim.

I have known Jim longer than I knew Sarah but Jim threw
spanners in the works that gave me even more to think about. It was
well past New Year when I finally opened an envelope with a Teesside
postmark on it so I knew it was from Jim. Inside I found a Christmas
card with a robin on it.

This card with its pathetic depiction of a bird renowned for its
association with happiness and the festive spirit of Christmas had sat
amongst the clutter on the table for weeks waiting a moment when
I felt excited enough to want to open it. I was about to toss it in the
bin when I thought that, out of common courtesy, I should at least
open it and read it.

I took another look at the sad robin on its sprig of holly
on the front and found, inside, a printed message proving that
the art of poetic inspiration is also a thing of the past. "Season's
Greetings", it said.

This drab card was enhanced by a spidery signature beneath. In
years gone by it would have been neater and extended to at least ten
words. The spending of just a little time would have been detected in
that it would have included the words "To Ollie and Sarah" followed
by a friendly wish with both senders' names, "Jim and Flo".

The only thing scrawled in blue ballpoint pen on this occasion was "Jim". Normally, Flo would write cards and Jim would add a few, scribbled attempts at humour on the back, words supposedly to remind us of our Air Force days. "I scrambled to get this off in time" or "Sorry for being late. Haven't been in a Mess like this for years!"

Then there were the occasional postcards from holidays with Jim's brother, Eddie, and his sister-in-law Hilda. "Ed and Flo are watching the ebb and flow in Skegness."

It was humour of the bar variety which Sarah and Flo found utterly childish but there was no humour this year and neither was there any sign of Flo's backward-slanting signature. It struck me then that Flo had also passed away and I had a vision of Jim slumped in a chair, wrapped in a tartan blanket covered in dribble and the remains of his breakfast, in his conservatory in Sunderland. Nevertheless, a small lump of sadness came to my throat. Poor old Jim, I thought.

On the other hand, I thought, poor old Ollie. But at least I wasn't wrapped in a tartan blanket and could still hobble to the off license and back.

I tried phoning Jim but only got his daughter, Mary, who had moved into the house to take care of her one remaining parent. And, yes, she confirmed that Flo had passed away a few weeks earlier, co-incidentally almost the same week as Sarah. I told her to tell Jim that Sarah had also died and she did her courteous bit of offering condolences etcetera and said that Jim was asleep but that she was sure he would like to speak to me some time.

Finally, I said to her: "Would you give Jim another message for me? Tell him it was me who nailed Major Donaldson."

Mary asked me to repeat it. I did so.

"Will he understand what that's about, Uncle Ollie?"

"I'm not sure," I said, which was true.

After I put the phone down, I asked myself what earthly reason had there been for mentioning Donaldson and asking Mary to pass on such a message. But I had consumed a few glassfuls just before speaking to Mary and so I put my mind to rest by thinking I could attribute my slurred and strange words to my own geriatric affliction: Thomas's Disease.

I had also had a recent nightmare in which Donaldson had been shot in exactly the same way as that poor man David Reynolds. In the nightmare, though, it had been me who pulled the trigger and all the while I was surrounded by hundreds of old acquaintances: William, Farouk, Farid, George Owusu, Moatassim and Beatie. Even Betty from the Feathers was there, all of them standing around watching without saying a word until the gun went off. At that point they all covered their ears and stood with their mouths open as though shocked by the violence. And Jim had also been there amongst the crowds, his face covered in blood stained bandages from his fresh burns. He was shaking his head as though in disbelief, and it was he who broke the long silence that followed the shooting. In his Geordie accent I heard him say, "Aye, man – that's something that is," and I woke up shouting. "Sorry, Jim, but the bastard had it coming."

Such is Thomas's Disease.

Two days after I spoke to Mary, the phone rang. I picked it up and waited for a squeaking and rustling sound to stop before I heard a voice that sounded as if its owner might be suffering from bronchitis. "Ollie? Is that you man?"

"Jim?" I asked.

"Aye," Jim replied amongst a rustling sound as if the receiver was being moved from one hand to another and the speaker was still getting comfortable.

The accent brought with it a flood of memories and for just a fleeting moment my mind filled with a vision of Jim's scarred face. For no apparent reason, I suddenly recalled an old Jim joke about lady's underwear made from utility fabric and being with him at the cinema during the black out. We were watching The First of the Few and Jim had already started courting Flo. "Aye," he'd said. "I suppose Flo might well be the last of the many." How right he had been.

Only a second or so passed in time, but snippets of Jim's companionship of fifty years flashed through my mind. One minute I was in the bar at the Hen and Chicken with more of Jim's jokes and then it was the clearest vision of sitting in Jim's conservatory surrounded by Flo's indoor garden and Jim's banana tree.

The phone squeaked once more. "Long time, Ollie."

I then expressed my sorrow about Flo and he did likewise about Sarah. "Aye, it all comes to an end," Jim said.

Jim was eighty-nine going on ninety but, with his slow speech and gurgling cough, he sounded more like a hundred and ninety. I was shocked but the shock was about to increase.

"I got your message," he said.

"Message?" I asked.

"Aye, about Donaldson," Jim said. "You said it was you who nailed Donaldson, Ollie."

"Yes," I said somewhat embarrassed. "It's not important."

Jim muttered something incoherent but then said something that threw me completely. "Donaldson's still alive, Ollie."

For a second, I thought I had misheard. "Say that again, Jim."

"Donaldson's still alive."

I could still hardly believe what I was hearing. For more than twenty-five years I'd assumed he was dead. Shot in Beirut and pushing up the daises, as Farouk had said. I said something just as incoherent as Jim had just been but this was quite understandable. Everything I had believed for so long was unravelling. What's more the person unravelling it was my best friend.

I slowly recovered my senses as Jim creaked, groaned and coughed. "What? Donaldson's still alive, Jim? What're you talking about? I thought the man had his chips years ago."

"Aye. There you are man. Life's a bugger."

"So, what . . . how . . . where? Where, the hell, is he? And how the hell do you know?"

"I met an old friend at a Remembrance Day service," Jim said. "Flo and I got taken down to the Cenotaph."

"An old friend? Who the hell was that, Jim?"

"Jack Woodward."

"Jack Woodward?" I shouted.

"Aye, in a wheelchair. Ninety-two. But he's dead now. He died a month later I heard."

"Jack Woodward?" I shouted again. "I thought he was also long gone."

"Well, he's gone now, Ollie."

I sat there, holding the phone, my head in a whirl. "But what about Donaldson?" I said. I still couldn't believe what Jim had just told me.

"Aye, still alive."

"So where does the bastard live?"

"Och! Somewhere near Oxford I heard."

Jim's vagueness and slow speaking slowly got to me and I said: "For God's sake, Jim. I've spent twenty-five years thinking the bastard was lying, pushing up the daisies in a graveyard in Lebanon or somewhere. Now you're telling me he's still alive. Where? For heaven's sake, why don't I know?"

I waited for what seemed an eternity. "Aye. He sold the place in Edinburgh I understand and moved south. It was many years ago."

"Oxford, you say. Where in Oxford, Jim?"

"Aye, not in Oxford," said Jim.

I remember taking a deep breath, summoning as much patience as my increasing headache and beating chest allowed. "So where, Jim? If not in Oxford, where?"

"Aye, near Oxford. He had some big mansion in a village I heard."

"A mansion?" I heard my voice pick up an octave.

"Aye, as I say he sold up. His kids were grown up."

"Kids, Jim? What kids?"

"Och man. His kids."

"I didn't know he had kids!"

"Aye, they were in public school in Repton or somewhere. Half way between London and Edinburgh."

"Repton? It must have cost a fortune!"

"Aye."

I was dumfounded. "How could he afford that then, Jim?" The question was, of course, ridiculous.

"Not my business, Ollie. His wife was a lot younger."

It suddenly struck me that to have kids then there must have been a mother or two around somewhere. But the idea of Donaldson having a wife had also never occurred to me. "His wife?"

"Aye."

"What bloody wife?"

"The one he divorced."

This was getting complicated but it was as though I was the only person who didn't know. But family life had never cropped up in my conversations with Donaldson. Donaldson's private life was his own business. I could not stand the man, so why should I have bothered to ask? I couldn't have cared less about his domestic circumstances. They were totally irrelevant and, in fact, had I raised the subject in a conversation, it would have suggested that I was both interested and concerned for the man. But it explained his trips to Edinburgh and the odd mention of Burton-on-Trent and Derby train stations. I asked Jim a few more questions but it was clear that Jim was the one now starting to get annoyed.

"God's sake, Ollie. What's wrong with you? I haven't got a damned clue about his ex-wife or the one before. He was divorced twice. One was called Betty that's all I know."

"Two wives, Jim? What happened to the first one?"

"Who cares, Ollie?"

"I care, Jim."

"Why? What's the problem, Ollie?"

Jim was asking me what the matter was but I was in the middle of a vision of another Betty – the one behind the bar in the Feathers, the one with the big assets and cockney accent. No, it couldn't be. There were lots of Bettys in those days and she must have been at least twenty years younger than Donaldson. If she was alive now, she'd be seventy. I dismissed it. "I need to know," I said.

There was another pause. "I don't know what happened to his first wife – or the second, Ollie." Jim's voice was breaking up again. It was getting rough and I could hear more gurgling coming from deep down inside. It seemed I may not get any more information before it packed up altogether.

"Then who does, for Christ's sake?" I asked. "You seem to have old cronies scattered around. Do any of them know?"

Jim coughed, productively, and seemed to swallow the accumulated debris. "Och! Cronies? Not many left Ollie. Might still be one or two around but beats me why you need to know Ollie. Let sleeping dogs lie and all that. You seem very agitated."

Jim's observation was very accurate. "I need to know, Jim. Something cropped up and I need to know."

"Aye. I'll check. Someone might know. Did you have a good Christmas, Ollie?"

Suddenly I felt I was going to explode. "Christmas, Jim? What the bloody hell is getting into you? Are you getting senile or something? Christmas! Sorry, Jim, but Christmas was weeks ago. It's not exactly on my mind."

"Then what is, Ollie?"

I felt lost for an explanation. "I've just been thinking too much, Jim – thinking and writing notes and looking at old files. And I've now started typing it all up – for the record so to speak. But if you can, please check on Donaldson's whereabouts, there's a pal."

We said cheerio after that but Jim was as good as his word.

I didn't ask who his remaining cronies were but when I phoned a week later, he named a village near Oxford and a house called Chalford Hall that sounded large. "Happy now then, Ollie? Got what you want?"

"Thanks," I said feeling calmer. "But I thought Donaldson had been killed, you see, Jim."

"You keep saying that. Ollie. But it was all hushed up."

"By who?"

"Aye man – tha' knows – upstairs."

"Upstairs, Jim? What upstairs?"

"Ollie, man – don't play games. Don't tell me you didn't know he was in Intelligence."

"Well . . .," I said but a thousand questions were running through my brain. Not least were what Donaldson's own thoughts might still be on the matter, assuming his brain could still think. My own was working overtime.

What exactly had happened? Why had the authorities, whoever they were, not followed up the incident? Or had they done just that and decided to leave the matter alone? If so why? With Jim still hanging on the other end of the phone, I had been rummaging in the clutter on the table to find the Times and Daily Telegraph newspaper cuttings. "But . . ." I said, at last, "I kept the reports, Jim. I have it here. 'British Army Major Shot' it says and......"

Jim interrupted me. "Aye I remember it. But how long afterwards did the press release come out? It only said he'd been shot. It didn't say he'd died. Neither did it confirm a name. 'Thought to be' it said, a scandalous use of words that a solicitor could not have got away with. But you've forgotten what sort of people run Intelligence. They are all codes and secrets. Even I knew him as D. Perhaps he became another letter. J – Just alive, perhaps. Or R – R for Resurrected."

Twenty years ago, it would have been cause for a laugh, another swig of beer and perhaps another joke or two tagged on to extend the humour. Now, neither of us seemed to see it as amusing or have the strength to laugh. "My God," was all I could think to say.

"Aye, bloody sod," said Jim with almost another touch of humour.

But instead of a joke, Jim then threw yet another spanner into the works. This was a real shock. It was a spanner guaranteed to jam up my mental machinery altogether. Pistons, valves, timing chains, prop shafts and bearings flew in all directions as though my engine had received a direct hit. I felt as though I should be trying to bail out while there was time. In fact, my hand jumped as though trying to open the roof of the cockpit. It often did when I was suddenly frightened. But I had no parachute this time.

"But you're right in some respects, Ollie," Jim croaked. "Apparently, the man who was shot in Beirut did die, though – officially that is."

The confusion was now starting to dull my senses. I had no idea what Jim was talking about and there was silence as I tried to fathom it out. In between Jim said "Aye," once again, contemplatively or just for good measure.

"What do you mean, he died – officially."

Jim didn't now sound like an old man with either chronic pneumonia or senile dementia. "Och, man," he said, "Officially he died but officially he was not Donaldson. Donaldson is still living. O for official, like."

"For God's sake, Jim. Talk sense man. Stop trying to joke. What are you saying?"

Jim coughed again, perhaps to prove that his pneumonia still persisted, but the delay while I waited was almost unbearable. "Well," he gurgled, "It's like this – as far as I heard, you understand. The man who got shot in Beirut was, in fact, Donaldson – definitely sure it was. But he survived. Then, for some reason the powers that be decided they needed to say that someone had been shot and had died. But Donaldson actually survived. Got it now, man?"

My mind was now in such a state that there was no chance of me getting it so I decided to admit it. "No," I said.

Jim wheezed some more, took a deep breath as if he was speaking to a dimwit and went on. "The man in Beirut who got shot was definitely Donaldson but he did not die. He survived. Do you understand? Then they decided it was in the interests of security or officialdom or bureaucracy or whatever, to report the event by suggesting that he had died."

Jim waited a moment but then repeated, "Suggested that he had died. Understand, now?" It must have been obvious from my silence that I still did not understand. Thankfully, Jim seemed to have the patience to try again.

"Och! Man. Someone, somewhere, probably Intelligence, decided to issue a press statement that said an army Major working for British Intelligence had been shot. For reasons best known to themselves they then needed to give the impression that he had died. They stated publicly that the man was thought to be Donaldson. Thought to be. Got that? But Donaldson did, in fact, survive.

"But for the official records, the paperwork and the death certificates and such like it was decided that the man was to be named as someone else – someone called Reynolds, if I remember. Reynolds had also, apparently, been working undercover for British Intelligence. Who Reynolds is or was I don't know, Ollie. I assume it was Reynolds' name that was used for death certificates and to keep the books straight. But the press reports were to give an impression that it was Donaldson."

Jim ground to a final halt but seemed unable to resist a final attempt at humour. "R for Reynolds, I suppose. Not R for resurrected."

Jim had just spoken for far longer than seemed good for him. He sounded completely out of breath but what he'd just said had done nothing for my own health. "Reynolds?" I shouted, "Are you sure, Jim?"

"Aye," said Jim, "Jack told me that when we met at the Cenotaph two years ago. By the way, he asked about you. He said I should pass on his best wishes. Sorry, I forgot. But Flo got sick."

It was as though I was having one of my worst nightmares, except I knew full well I was wide awake. "But I was Reynolds, Jim," I said.

It was Jim's turn to go quiet. The phone creaked and I let it creak for a while. "You still there, Jim? "I asked.

"You, Ollie? You were Reynolds? You worked for Intelligence?"

"Yes," I said. "I did years of assignments for Donaldson as Reynolds. I was there when the real Reynolds was shot in Amman years before. The man was assassinated in front of me. For years, I carried his passport. I was David Reynolds. It's still here – the passport. It's upstairs in my box, it's . . ."

I stopped talking suddenly feeling as though I had been trapped by clever interrogation. I checked myself, remembering other events that might now start to click into place. I began to compare my life since the war to Jim's as a solicitor. Mine was definitely the more complicated. It was true that assignments in the name of Reynolds stopped after Donaldson had been shot but that was what I had wanted to happen.

But it had been my decision to continue to use the Reynolds name for a short while afterwards for my business. Reynolds was the only name that some customers knew.

Memories of other events then rose before my eyes like ghosts from the past.

I'd once spent a night in Larnaca in Cyprus on my way to Beirut with the Reynolds passport in its usual place in the lining of my case when I had heard a single gunshot very close by. A group of people not six yards from me panicked and ran as a puff of stone dust erupted from the side of a building not ten yards away. Gunfire was not uncommon to me and I had been the last one to move. I did not hang around to investigate but I'd never understood who the shot was aimed at and subsequently forgot about it. I now had a possible explanation that horrified me.

Two days later in Beirut I'd had another strange experience. I was coming home and already at the airport check-in when I was stopped by a Lebanese messenger apparently from the British Embassy and asked to return to the Embassy because a business opportunity had cropped up. When I refused the man had become agitated and grabbed my arm. Fortunately for me there had been other people around so I shook him off and he walked away. That was also, perhaps fortunately, the last time I ever set foot in Beirut and I stopped using the Reynolds passport soon after.

But Jim's comments now suggested they'd needed a body of a person with a passport in the name of David Reynolds to bury. How simple it would have been for them. I was finally expendable and of no further use. My blood ran cold. Had I been that close?

Jim's rough voice came down the phone line. "Aye, Ollie, man," he said. "That's news that is. I gave up trying to understand it all many years ago. Pity you didn't tell me before. A few stories there over a pint."

"I suppose so," I said. "But Donaldson was a crook, Jim. A big-time crook into arms trading and money laundering and . . ."

Perhaps fortunately, Jim seemed to be losing the will to carry on because I don't think he heard me. "Aye, a few stories there over a pint, Ollie," I heard him say again before the phone clicked.

I stood there holding the dead phone line for a moment before replacing it and shuffling though the pile of old notes and newspaper cuttings still lying on the table. When I found the note that Beatie had slipped inside the ABC Flight Timetable more of the jigsaw fell into place.

At the time of the Forsyth deal I believed Donaldson was dead so had blamed others, and mostly Forsyth, for what had happened. But if Donaldson had not died but was recuperating somewhere or had already fully recovered, then it seemed more than likely that it had been he who was behind Forsyth. So, who was Forsyth?

I re-read Beatie's note: "Dear Mr Thomas. I am so sorry. You did not deserve all this. Forgive me but I cannot live this lie any more. I hope you find this and hope it will be enough for you to understand things. I have been living under increasing pressure. I have tried to tell you but it is very hard. I have now been told I must leave my employment. Yours, Beatrice Collins."

Then I turned it over to the side showing the address of the military hospital in Cyprus. Then I looked once more at the handwriting beneath - the bank address, the account number and the name R. Forsyth and I stared at it with eyes that now knew

Donaldson was still alive at the time. The handwriting was faint but unmistakable. Donaldson's handwriting had always been terrible.

Beneath the printed address of the Cyprus Military Hospital were the telex address and the POB number in Larnaca and the bank details and the name of Forsyth. Was Beatie trying to tell me that Donaldson was alive and in hospital in Cyprus and that he and Forsyth were working together to destroy me financially? Or kill me? Was Beatie also aware she was at the end of her usefulness to Donaldson? Was Donaldson afraid Beatie might spill some beans? If so, how had Beatie really died? Natural causes had always seemed unlikely.

"I have tried to tell you everything but it is very hard. I have now been told I must leave my employment. Yours, Beatrice Collins."

A few days later, poor Beatie was dead.

Why had I not noticed? The signs had been there for years. Was I so blind to the feelings and fears of others? Beatie's? Sarah's even?

"I hope this is enough for you to understand, Mr Thomas. I have tried to make it quite clear."

"I have been trying to bring myself to tell you something, Mr Thomas but it's all very difficult, you see."

"I'm so sorry, Mr Thomas. It can be quite stressful here when you are abroad. We really need to talk sometime, Mr Thomas, privately."

I could now remember her eyes looking at me almost pleading with me to pry into her concerns. But again, I would lose the chance, believing she was feeling overworked.

"There was a phone call for you, Mr Thomas. Beirut again. You . . . you need to be so careful, Mr Thomas. It's such a – such a dangerous place, these days."

And another time. "Does Mrs Thomas know about this, Mr Thomas?"

Beatie's eyes often peered at me from behind her spectacles. The eyes had looked worried, caring, guilty, perhaps wet even. And I knew now from Robert that Beatie had spoken to Sarah more often than I ever thought.

"Oh, I know everything, Mr Thomas."

The familiar cold sweat broke out again because I had told Sarah nothing – ever. In fact, I had kept everything a total secret because I had decided that it was unnecessary for her to know. Rightly or wrongly, I had been trying to protect her.

I took a deep breath and leaned back. But then I got up and went to get a fresh bottle and poured myself a large glassful because part of me wanted to disappear into an alcoholic fog.

Another side wanted me to remain cool and calm because I knew my thoughts would become confused. I could see a mental abyss before me and knew that if I wasn't careful it would fill with a terrifying tangle of unfathomable intrigue into which my mind would spiral, uncontrollably. That was Thomas's Disease.

It was at that moment that I changed.

I began to hate the introverted depression that had dominated me since I retired. I put the untouched full glass of whisky and the bottle onto the floor and sat there, alone, feeling colder by the minute. So, I turned up the gas fire, pulled my chair closer and held my hands towards it. For the first time, ever Sarah's log effect gas fire seemed comforting.

Then I got up, went to the kitchen and then came back and then I looked at myself in the mirror over the shelf by Sarah's crockery cabinet. I moved the little wicker basket which still contained her comb, brush and hair clips and I smelled them. Tears came to my eyes, overflowed and rolled down my cheeks.

I tried to look at myself in the mirror and felt sure I heard Sarah come up behind me. "What a sight for sore eyes," I heard her say. "You need to pull yourself together, Mr Thomas."

I sat down again, held my hands towards the fire and it was then that I made a decision. I owed it to Sarah. I owed it to Beatie. And I owed it to myself. If Donaldson really was still alive, then I needed to act.

PART THREE: INTERVIEW

MARMITE

Andy Wilson met me in the hotel lobby at 9am.

In the light of day and with my eyes feeling less tired I put his age at about thirty-five, which meant he'd be far more adept with modern technology, phones and so on than me.

He guided me outside to a plain-looking car, not the blue and yellow one like the day before and after I'd thrown my stick and black bag onto the back seat, invited me to sit next to him in the front passenger seat. It was high up and had a big wide head rest which made me smile. If this was an abduction or a bullet was to be fired through the windscreen then I needed a good view.

He saw me smiling. "Sleep well, Mr Thomas?"

"Excellent, thank you," I replied. "It's been a hectic, few days."

He then drove off not in the direction of the airport but onto the main road.

"Taking me home, Andy?" I asked hopefully but wondering where my car was.

"To the police station," he said.

"To be formally charged?"

"More questions," he said.

The journey didn't take long. I was then escorted inside this office block with police everywhere. He signed something at a desk and I was then escorted to an office with a desk behind which sat another young man in jeans and tee shirt. I assumed this was their idea of plain clothes but I didn't ask. The tee shirt stood up. "This him, Andy?"

Andy nodded. "This is him, Clive. Mr Oliver Thomas."

"Old spy and fiction writer," the tee shirt said as if trying to be amusing. I winced. The word spy still grates with me.

He didn't shake my hand. He didn't even come around the desk but sat down again which I assumed was the way all suspected murderers were treated.

"Clive Peterson," he said from behind the desk. "I'm not stopping. I'm leaving you in the capable hands of Andy here because he was up all-night reading this." He poked at my typewritten notes with a finger as if I'd ruined their bureaucracy by not typing it on their official forms so I glanced at Andy to see if I could detect similar signs of disdain.

"I read it," he confirmed though I detected a stifled yawn. Had it bored him I wondered? Had it kept him up late?

Clive Peterson stood up. "Right then. I'm off." He pushed past me and said to Andy, "Call me when you're done." Then I heard him whisper, "He looks like my grandad." Then he left.

I didn't see Andy's reaction. Instead, he pointed to a chair for me and took over Clive's behind the desk. He picked up my notes, flipped through them and then pushed them aside. "So, Mr Thomas, as you're looking better than yesterday, can we pick up where we left off?"

Andy was right. I felt good. The chair was comfortable, I'd had a good shave without cutting myself and I'd carried the stick rather than actually using it. It was now on the floor by my bag. "Did you finish read my notes?"

"It was an interesting read. Is there any truth in it?"

I wiped my glasses on the hem of my jumper. "How far did you get?"

"To the end."

"Congratulations."

"Trouble is it ends with you merely saying you decided to act which doesn't, of course, answer the big question." He turned to the last page of my notes and prodded it with his finger just like his colleague. "Can we start here? Where it ends?"

I still remembered my last few typed words about owing it to Sarah and Beatie and myself to act. But just before I left Gloucester, I'd also scribbled a few more words in pencil about "working on an audacious plan." He hadn't mentioned that yet. "Can I ask you a question first?" I said.

"One," he replied.

"Is the bastard dead?"

"If you mean Major Alex Donaldson, I can confirm he's still in intensive care. You don't seem to like him, Mr Thomas."

"I thought you said you'd read my notes," I replied.

"But you can't go around shooting people, Mr Thomas."

"Who says I shot him? And, anyway, why not? Donaldson killed people, although he usually subcontracted killings and assassinations."

Andy Wilson got up and walked around the room. "Mr Thomas. Would you be so kind as to fill in the big gap that exists between when the notes finish and you arrived back here?"

I was feeling very relaxed. "I haven't touched a drop of whisky since the moment I made that decision." I told him.

"I'm so pleased. Now can you please start from the bit scribbled at the bottom that says, and I quote, 'I am working on an audacious plan.' What audacious plan? Did it involve a gun? And did you fulfil it?"

"I'll tell you what I did next," I said. "But it's important we put things into context and I provide the evidence. Then we can move onto my trip to Nice and Malaga. How long have we got?"

He sighed. Perhaps he was getting used to me. "I'm easy," he said. "But just be aware I'll not hesitate to jump and cut out the slightest bit of crap that you might feel inclined to offer. Is that good enough for you?"

"That seems very fair," I said. "By the way, you can call me Ollie."

"I'm Andy. Proceed."

"Well," I said, "I blame the audacious plan on Marmite."

"Marmite?"

"Did you read about Thomas's Disease?"

"I hope I never catch it."

"Marmite is the cure."

"I hate the darned stuff."

"Well, pray you never suffer from TD because within Marmite's dark and sticky heart there are ingredients that include a cure for TD. It's also a brain stimulant."

"I'm waiting for the audacious plan."

"I'm getting to it. But it involves Marmite. Having decided the need for a plan I resolved never to touch another drop of whisky. Instead, I made myself some tea, toast and Marmite. Then I took the car for a spin as I've always found driving conducive to constructive thought."

"Was it taxed and insured, Mr Thomas? Ollie?"

It was a good question. "Probably not on reflection," I admitted.

"Where did you head for? The south of France?"

"The Forest of Dean."

"When will we get to the Malaga part, Ollie?"

"Soon. The Forest wasn't where I'd planned to go but it's where I ended up. I just needed to drive and think. I took some Marmite on toast with me."

Andy seemed surprised. "You took a picnic?"

I remember that night so clearly. It was a dark night, cold and damp but, by two o'clock, and having got as far as Coleford and with no traffic on the road except a few large trucks and one police car I turned around and came back.

"When I returned around 3am, Andy, my mind was as clear as a bell and the plan was crystallizing."

"Can we discuss the plan, Ollie?"

"I finished off the cold toast and Marmite, slept for an hour in the chair and set off before daylight."

"Where did you go?"

"Oxfordshire."

LITTLE OLLIE

During the night it had turned frosty and the road outside was quite slippery when I checked but I tossed the stick onto the back seat of the car and set off. Fred Carrington would normally watch me coming and going but it was still dark and there wasn't even a light on at number 26. I quietly closed the garage door and was soon out on the road to Oxford.

I didn't rush but after a while, as the traffic became busy, I pulled in at a fuel station and bought a map of Oxfordshire. By eight o'clock and by navigating along country lanes I found the village mentioned by Jim as Donaldson's last known address. On the narrow road it was marked by a sign that said, "Little Avening Welcomes Careful Drivers".

By then it was a clear, spring-like morning with the low sun already clearing the early frost. It was a neat and tiny village of old houses and cottages hidden behind high hedges and wooden gates but almost as soon as I arrived, I found I was back in open countryside again so I stopped, reversed and drove back again. In what seemed to be the centre of the village there was a red mail box beside an almost invisible junction leading into an even smaller country lane. So, I parked the car and studied my map again. Little Avening was just a dot.

But as I sat there, a knock on his windscreen made me jump. A middle-aged woman with an annoyed look on her face glared at me through the glass so I put the map on the passenger seat and wound the window down.

"You can't park here, you know. No one can walk by," she said in a most angry tone and then stuck her head through the window to within six inches of my face. A surprisingly strong smell resembling smoked fish wafted in with the cold air. "We can't walk past, do you hear? I'm trying to walk my dog. Can't you see?"

She withdrew her head, bent down and lifted a tiny animal resembling a large white rat on a string apparently to give the creature a better view of the interior of my car. The creature yapped and bared a pink tongue and a set of teeth so small and perfect that I felt I was looking at an advert for private dentistry. A puff of doggy steam came out with the yap.

"Quiet, Ollie," she said.

I hadn't, of course, uttered a word so far and certainly not introduced myself. I was about to say something when she bent down to place the dog back on the ground and for a few minutes I lost sight of them so I leaned out of the window only to see a large, rotund rear covered in tweed. The other end was patting the dog, which was staring up at her and still panting little puffs of steam.

"There, Ollie, it's only an old man. There's a good boy."

She suddenly stood upright and so I quickly withdrew my own head and looked for my glasses. "I do apologise, madam," I said. "But I was trying to locate a house."

"I see. Along as you don't sit there for too long, I suppose."

"May I introduce myself, madam?" I asked.

She sniffed. "Well, yes. I suppose so."

"It seems I may share my name with your dog, Madam. You see, my name is Oliver Thomas. Friends call me Ollie."

The woman stared and then burst out laughing in a way I have always associated with late middle-aged ladies from Oxfordshire who wear tweed. "Oh, I say, how amusing. Ollie meet Ollie. Ha, ha, ha!"

"Yes," I said, "It's rather a coincidence. But do you, by any chance, know Chalford Hall?"

"Chalford Hall?" she said. "Of course. I live there."

I was shocked, not least because I had half expected to meet one of Donaldson's wives at Chalford Hall. This woman didn't, in the least, fit the picture in my mind.

"It's up the lane," she said, pointing to the smaller lane opposite the mail box. "Are you delivering something? You don't look like a courier to me and the car is a bit fancy. Things usually arrive in white vans, these days. Also, you don't quite look the sort, if I may say so. How old are you?"

I was, I admit, taken slightly aback at her impertinence. "I'm eighty-six madam," I said. My age was, of course, of no relevance at all and I was sorely tempted to ask how old she was.

"What is it you require?" she asked somewhat formally.

"I am looking for someone I used to know and I understood he lives there."

"Well it might be my husband I suppose but he's abroad at present."

This looked promising but I still couldn't imagine her with a ninety years old husband of Donaldson's type. I decided to probe a little as she peered at me through the side window. "My friend is getting on in years. He would be about ninety now. His name is Donaldson."

"Ah," she said as if light was dawning. "We bought the property from someone called Donaldson, not that we ever met him."

This made more sense. "Do you know where he lives now?"

"Oh, I've really no idea. Is he still alive? He wasn't living in England when we bought the place twenty-five years ago."

Jim's information about where Donaldson was living was clearly many years out of date and for a moment I felt let down as though my mission to track him down was already hitting the buffers.

The woman bent down to the other Ollie and picked the creature up again. It bared its teeth at me again but stayed silent and almost seemed to be smiling. "So how far have you come?" she asked.

"From Gloucester," he replied.

"That's a jolly, nice car," she said. "My husband had a Jaguar once. He now keeps a Maserati in the garage for weekends but usually runs around in the Bentley. I use the Porsche for shopping. Would you like a cup of tea?"

I was taken aback but the sudden show of a friendly side, but was in dire need of a drink of some description. "That's very kind," I said.

"Then would you mind awfully given Ollie and me a lift up the lane. He's getting a bit old now and gets very tired paws." She patted his tiny head. "Don't you, Ollie, my little precious."

With that I opened the passenger door and she and Ollie got in, the dog wiping its muddy feet all over her tweed skirt. "I don't normally get into cars with strange gentlemen," she said and gave her Oxfordshire laugh, "But you look harmless enough and I like the car."

A few minutes later we passed through an impressive gateway with stone pillars and up a tree-lined drive to a large Cotswold stone house worthy of the title of Chalford Hall. She'd gossiped most of the way.

"It's far too big, actually," she said as we drove onto a semi-circular gravel driveway with wide stone steps leading up to a large front door, "But my husband likes it. He says it's a wonderful place to get away from the City."

"What does your husband do?" I asked, surprising myelf by the rapid way our relationship was developing after only fifteen minutes. I didn't get an immediate answer because she was struggling to clamber out whilst still holding little Ollie. She led me up the steps and turned the large door knob. It clearly wasn't locked.

"Come in, come in," she said as little Ollie bounded away, slipping and sliding on a shiny tiled floor. She closed the door behind us. "Oh, George," she said remembering my earlier question. "George is the founding partner of Griffith-Pace Securities. Worth a fortune even before I married him. Mother was so pleased. Come in, do. Wipe your feet, Ollie. Sorry, Mr Thomas, I mean my little Ollie here."

PRISCILLA

"That's how I came to meet Priscilla Griffith-Pace," I told Andy Wilson.

"I only hope it's relevant, Ollie," Andy replied. "Fancy a coffee?" He got up, walked away and returned with some plastic cups, put them on the desk and slid one towards me. "Where were we, Ollie?"

"Chalford Hall."

"Ah yes. Proceed."

"We sat in a room with a huge log fire and large bay windows hung with red velvet curtains that overlooked acres of rolling fields with mature horse chestnut trees just coming into leaf and a shimmering lake. It was all very pleasant compared to what I had left behind in Gloucester."

"Sounds lovely but what light was she able to throw on Donaldson, Ollie?"

"Not a great deal as it turned out."

"Ollie, for Christ's sake........"

"But her gardener, Nigel, turned out to be very useful," I told Andy.

Cilla said that when they'd bought Chalford Hall from Donaldson it was empty. Locals in the village told her Donaldson was rarely ever seen and they didn't like him. Neither did they like the woman who they assumed was his wife. She was an alcoholic and alcoholics were not the sort of person the residents of Little

Avening were used to. Neither were they keen on people called Betty with strong London accents. There were also two teenage boys who boarded at Repton had but were rarely seen.

"Everything started to fit," I told Andy.

But Cilla, thinking Donaldson was an old friend, apologised. I soon put her right. I told her that his reputation was far worse than petty local gossip. Whilst working for British Intelligence, I said, he made a vast fortune by running a Mafia-like organisation that was second to none at the time.

Cilla was shocked but then suggested I meet Milly the cook and Nigel, the gardener because Nigel had known Donaldson.

I met Nigel in a greenhouse out the back. He'd been at Chalford Hall for forty years when the house had been in the Jarman family but when Sir Walter Jarman died the family couldn't afford to keep it going so, they put it up for sale and Nigel had temporarily lost his job.

Then the Donaldson's arrived, he told me. Betty and two boys. The boys were at school and Betty was left by herself. Luckily, he'd got the job of gardener back again. Donaldson used to stay there for a few days then return to Scotland or London.

Nigel confirmed everything about Betty being an alcoholic who spent most of her time in the kitchen drinking gin and red wine. He'd felt sorry for her. She and Donaldson would argue a lot and there was evidence of so much physical abuse that the cleaner left. The house became dirty and untidy.

"But then, Andy, Nigel mentioned another man, a friend of Donaldson from Edinburgh who arrived and stayed at Chalford Hall. The new cleaner, Cheryl, claimed that this man and Betty were having an affair. Donaldson though had seemed unconcerned as if it was part of an arrangement between the three of them."

"And what was this guy's name, Ollie?" Andy asked me.

"Royston Forsyth," I said with a raised eyebrow. At last, Andy sat up.

"Forsyth himself? The Brigadier?" he said.

I nodded.

I asked Nigel if Mr Forsyth was, by any chance, a Brigadier but Nigel shook his head. "Very unlikely," he said. "He and Donaldson would sit around drinking and talking business most of the time."

Forsyth, Nigel said, worked for a Swiss bank in London. Discussions were all about money. Nigel knew that because in the summer they would sit outside the greenhouse drinking beer and he could hear them.

I asked him why he thought Donaldson decided to sell the house. He said he didn't know but Betty disappeared. Suddenly she wasn't there. Around the same time he'd also heard that the two boys were expelled from school for some reason.

"Then came more crucial pieces of evidence," I told Andy. "I asked Nigel if he knew where Donaldson had gone after Chalford Hall was sold."

Oh yes, he said, he went to live in Cannes in the south of France but he also had a place in Malaga. Nigel grinned at me. "I know that because I found some papers in a sack that I used to start a bonfire," he said. "I kept them because Major Donaldson left owing staff wages going back several weeks. I always thought that one day I'd go out there and track him down."

Nigel then went to a drawer beneath his neat bookshelf, pulled out a heavy pile of old Gardeners World diaries and laid them on the table. "Here we are," he said. "The 1986 version. The last year we ever saw him or Forsyth."

From the inside back cover, he took out two folded pieces of paper. "There," he said.

I looked at them. They were abbreviated statements from Credit Suisse in Zurich, pieces of paper I'd not seen since my days in Libya. Donaldson had made a big mistake in not destroying them but Nigel was right. They showed account numbers and also two addresses – one in Cannes and one in Malaga.

"Cilla then invited me for lunch, Andy. We had smoked haddock and white parsley sauce."

BETTY

My talk of food seemed to awaken Andy because he suggested lunch. "I'll order something," he said.

As he left, the desk phone so I picked it up. "Andy," the voice said. "Malaga phoned. The old guy is still in intensive care but things are not looking good. The Spanish police are now searching the property but they confirm your man was seen leaving and pointing the gun at staff."

"Thanks," I said thinking there was both good and bad news there but also some matters which I'd need to explain.

I pressed the red button and returned to thinking about lunch with Cilla and the drive home afterwards. Fred Carrington had been standing by his gate when I arrived. "Evening, Mr Thomas," he called. "Been out today?"

Whilst looking for my front door key I told the nosy fellow that I'd popped over to Oxfordshire for lunch. "The wife of a friend of mine who runs a Merchant bank in the City," I said to shut him up.

"I'm off to Nice at the weekend," I added. "Then I'll probably head down to Malaga. I might be away for a while. I'm far too busy to stand and chat. I've got papers to work on this evening. By the way, you need to get someone in to chop that monkey-puzzle down. It's looking increasingly sad and it might be kinder to put it out of its misery."

Andy returned. "I've ordered fish and chips," he said. "Where were we, Ollie? Please proceed. "

I proceeded by describing what Nigel had saved from the 1981 bonfire.

Both letters were from Credit Suisse, Zurich, one of them to Mr R Forsyth and the other to Major A. Donaldson, both showing the Chalford Hall, Little Avening address. The letter to Forsyth confirmed the transfer of the sum of 750,000 US dollars to a Santander Bank account in Barcelona. The letter to Donaldson stated that the balance of his account with Credit Suisse stood at 4,535,868 US dollars as at 4th October 1981 and that an amount of another 1.500,000 dollars had been transferred on 3rd September 1981 to a Santander Bank account in Malaga.

"Sums of money any honest, nine to five, civil servant was unlikely to accumulate and how many other accounts did they have?" I told Andy before adding, "How's your own police pension growing, Andy?"

The letters also showed addresses – an address in Cannes for Forsyth and one in Malaga for Donaldson so, as soon as the local travel agent opened for business next day I booked an air ticket to Nice, made an appointment to call in later on another matter, made some other arrangements and sat back, feeling like a new man with a reason to live.

"With an air ticket and a plan of action I felt as if I'd picked up where I left off thirty years ago, Andy."

The door opened and in came our lunch – plastic boxes of fish and chips - and at Andy's request continued with my story as we ate.

"I gathered up my type-written report, tidied all the old papers and newspaper cuttings I'd been working on and, apart from one item which I placed in an old shoe box, took the bus into the city, collected my air ticket, dealt with the shoe box, returned home and slept like a log," I told Andy.

By ten next morning I was ready to go with the black case on the back seat of the car when I spotted Fred Carrington. "I'm just off to France and Spain on business, Fred," I said and then watched him trudge home with his shopping basket.

Andy interrupted. "Can we please leave out the neighbours and focus on your trip, Ollie?"

"Certainly," I said as I finished off the battered fish and the last chip.

It was late afternoon when I arrived in Nice.

I took a taxi to the Negresco Hotel on the Promenade des Anglais only because it is fairly central and because I'd once eaten lunch there with Farouk. The Negresco is not my sort of hotel. It's more like a stately home complete with antiques, museum and art gallery and I had no intention of staying there but I got talking to the doorman, Charles, who, in keeping with the rest of the hotel, wears a strange hat, red and blue fancy dress, white gloves and Wellington boots. But he seemed to like my reminiscences and my tale of eating langoustines and Chablis with Farouk (who paid). Apparently feeling sorry for me and my old, black bag, he then told me he could arrange a sizeable discount so I got a room the size of a football pitch with an antique bed and fell asleep watching a pornographic French film on a TV the size of a cinema screen.

By nine o'clock next morning, Charles found me a nice Mercedes taxi and I set off for Cannes.

It was a delightful spring morning which brought back more memories of my travelling days, especially when we passed the sign for Grasse. I had known an export agent once who specialized in Francophone Africa and dealt in canned, tropical fruit. Michel lived in Grasse but we never met there but by accident in hotels in places like Accra, Freetown and Douala.

The taxi passed on, into Cannes and eventually dropped me outside a big, iron, gate by a high stone wall overhung with trees covered in white flowers. I asked the driver to wait saying I had no idea how long I would be but that I'd pay him for his time. Neither did I know what to expect when I pressed the large black bell on the gate. I put my ear to the metal grill and heard the rough voice of an elderly woman.

In rather poor French I announced my name as Christopher Stanton from England and that I was trying to make contact with an old friend of mine, Royston Forsyth. I then apologized for my French in English.

The voice said, "Christ almighty" in an accent that rang of east London. "What did you say your name was?"

"Christopher Stanton," I said, "I'm sorry to call without an appointment."

I heard her sniff but then say, "OK, wait. The gate will open. Come in." And with that, the gates clicked, slowly opened inwards and I walked inside.

The driveway was longer and steeper than I expected but the lawns and gardens made the walk a pleasant enough one. I eventually arrived at the house, an ornate brick and stone villa with orange roof tiles, a high chimney and a thick covering of ivy. I walked up five wide steps towards a shiny black door feeling for the first time that my stick, which I'd left in the taxi, would have been useful. I rang another bell and the door opened immediately as if I'd been watched all the way up the drive.

An elderly lady stood there wearing baggy trousers and a half-zipped up jacket. The entire outfit was in powder blue and, despite her age, which looked seventy, she wore a pair of white plimsolls. Her hair was not grey but a pale shade of yellow with streaks of auburn. Her face was full, red and freckled as if she spent lengthy periods sitting in a deck chair somewhere sunny. In her ears were two large earrings that dangled almost to her shoulders. I took all this in as I stood there gathering my breath.

"Yeh?" she said. "What's going on then?" It was spoken in perfect Whitechapel English and, even though she'd only spoken a few words I instantly recognized the voice. This was Betty from the Feathers and we were face to face for the first time for almost fifty years.

"Good morning," I said, touching my forelock. "I'm sorry for disturbing you. My name is Christopher Stanton and I was hoping to catch up with an old friend of mine, Roy Forsyth, as I heard he was living here."

"'I see," she said, looking at me suspiciously "And why would you want to see him?'

"Old time's sake, I suppose," I said.

She exploded. "Well you're too bleedin' late, mate. The fucking bastard pegged out fifteen years ago."

She might have sprayed me with something because I felt sure I could smell gin. "Oh dear," I said, 'That's sad."

"No, it fucking well ain't. Fucking bastards, all of them. Friends of them, are you?"

"Oh dear," I repeated, "I didn't know him too well you understand, in fact I think I only ever met him once.'

"So how is he a bleedin' friend, then?"

It was a good question. I backtracked. "Perhaps I should call myself an acquaintance," I said.

"So, what the bloody 'ell do you want?" she said, putting both hands on her hips.

"Just to catch up with him, I suppose," I said, "I was visiting Nice. But it looks like I'm fifteen years too late. What happened to him? How old was he when he died?"

I was asking too many questions and she wisely ignored them but part of my mind was hearing the bawdy banter in the Feathers where she used to pull pints of Bass bitter and empty little jars of whelks and cockles into small white dishes before sprinkling vinegar over them. I could even remember some of her words. 'Bloody jars. Can't ever friggin' open them without breaking my bloody nails. Wanna go, Ollie? Your hands are so much bigger. Big hands, big cock, eh? You open my little jar and I'll warm your cockles, eh? Want another pint while you're trying?'

She interrupted my thoughts. "How did you know where to come?"

"Another old acquaintance," I said. "Roy still owes him money."

That did the trick.

"Fucking bastard. How bleedin' much? And who's your other acquaintance?"

"The gardener at a place where Roy used to live."

"You mean Nigel?' she asked lowering her hands from her hips.

"Yes, that's him,' I said, "Nigel. He's still working at the old place. Chalford Hall. Do you know him? I bumped into him in a pub in Oxford and he told me he was still waiting to be paid. We laughed about it. He said Roy had moved to Cannes. It wasn't really worth bothering about after so long but he clearly hadn't forgotten. So, I said to him that as I was visiting Nice, shortly, I'd see if I could sort it out for him. Debts are debts I always say. You must never give up trying to get money that you are legitimately owed. It's only fair and just."

"Fucking bastard," Betty said.

"Nigel or Roy?" I asked trying to appear impartial.

"Fucking Roy Forsyth, that's who."

"You don't seem to like him, madam."

"Like? Like? He and his fucking partner, Donaldson, should have been shot years ago. I tried strangling both of them. Police were called several times."

"Were they up to no good?" I asked with my head to one side as if finding it difficult to understand how bad anyone could be.

"Scottish Mafia, that's what I used to call them. I married that sod Major fucking Alex Donaldson so I got to knew a few things that would make your bloody hair curl."

I very much doubted that but said, "Oh dear.'

"Oh yes," she said, "But if I dared to say anything.…..." She stopped and drew a flat hand across her neck. 'Kkkuk!' she said, apparently imitating the sound of a throat being cut.

It was then that I saw her infamous cleavage. It was the very same one that entertained customers at the Feathers fifty years ago and that featured in recent nightmares. It sagged with wrinkles but it was definitely the same cleavage that always reminded me of a large and speckled peach. But the real give-away was the gold chain with the cross that hung down and mostly disappeared inside her powder blue top. Her voice was hoarse and had dropped an octave as if she'd spent the past fifty years smoking and drinking. But this was, without question, Betty from the Feathers and I felt sorry for her. The proof was there for all to see. Betty, too, had been drawn into Donaldson's life and suffered.

"I threatened to report everything I knew to the police," she went on. "I even said I'd speak to the local MP. It was all tied up with Government stuff and politics, you know. Fucking bastard worked in the Government or somewhere or other though I never really understood what it was all about or how he got away with it. Fucking criminal more like."

"How dreadful," I said, "Why didn't you do something?"

"Ha!' She laughed falsely. "Do something? Kkkuk! Say something? Kkkuk! Run away? Kkkuk! But threaten to kill myself? OK, no problem. Feel free. Go ahead. Here's the knife. Nice man."

"Oh, dear,' I said again.

"I was stupid," she continued. "I then got involved with his bloody mate, fucking Roy Forsyth. Thought he might be better and it would eventually turn out OK, but like hell it did. He was tarred with the same brush. I found out later they were in cahoots and up to their necks in the same shit. I find out later that Roy Forsyth had done time for embezzlement. Ex banker. Nice way with words. Smart suit and tie. Smooth as a rattlesnake. He was even a local Councillor once but got caught taking a bribe. Educated bloody criminals I called 'em. They were partners in crime and both from some public school in Edinburgh. They made a bloody fortune, but search me how. I never understood.

"The only saving grace was that my twin boys got paid to board at Repton. But then they got expelled for bringing drugs in. Hah! But I know exactly where they came from – their own fucking father, that's who. He thought it was funny. He'd planted heroin in their suitcase when they went back to school after Easter. The poor lads were frightened to death of him. But it was to get at me, to have something else to hold over me like a noose. That was how he operated. He always found something to hang over you like a threat. "

"What happened to the boys?" I asked.

"They got taken to Spain to help their father's business. I never saw them again. God knows what they're up to. They're probably tarred with the same bloody brush by now but they were too young to know any better."

"Don't you ever see your sons?" I asked.

"No," she said and I detected some genuine sadness eroded though it may have been over time. "They probably think I'm dead." She sniffed and wiped her nose.

"When did you last see them?"

"Twenty-five years this month. They'll be forty-five in August."

"Why don't you go to see them?" I asked.

"And bump into fucking Alex Donaldson? No thank you. Anyway, if I as much as put a foot in Spain, I am likely to find myself upside down in a ditch somewhere. Nice fucking bloke is Alex Donaldson."

"Is Mr Donaldson still alive?" I asked.

"Oh yes. The bastard bought a fancy, place, the size of a Texan ranch, near Malaga. Like bloody Dallas it was. He moved there with another floozy. He'd be too bloody old to service the wench nowadays but I guarantee he's found a way to keep her quiet."

I stood there feeling desperately sorry for her. She was getting more and more agitated but perhaps she just wanted to talk to someone who listened. Her face became quite flushed and her mouth with its smear of lipstick twisted sideways. Then she paused and looked at her watch so perhaps it was time for another gin.

Of course, I could have started on my own list of grievances to show she wasn't the only one with grievances but that would have taken months. So, I said, "Well, I'm sorry to hear all that. I'd better be on my way," and took a step backwards.

She sniffed again. "How much did they owe Nigel?" she said.

"Six hundred pounds," I said.

"Wait," she said and disappeared. A minute later I heard the plimsolls squeaking on the wooden floor and she handed me an envelope with a large bundle of notes hanging out. "Here," she said. "It's five thousand euros. That should cover what Nigel was owed, with some interest. I don't need it. Wish him well for me. He was a good gardener. You can't get them for love nor money around here."

Betty, despite her bad experiences, did not seem short of cash. Perhaps, though, this was a portion of Donaldson's silence money. I thanked her, apologized for arriving out of the blue without an appointment.

I started down the steps but sensed she was watching me. At the bottom I couldn't resist one last look at her and so I stopped and turned.

"Are you sure we haven't met before?" she said, clearly puzzled.

"I don't think so,' I said and continued down the driveway. At the gate I turned around yet again. Betty was still standing in the doorway so I waved. And she waved back. I knew then that she'd remembered me.

Andy Wilson had listened to me without a single interruption. Neither had he told me to speed things up. So that explains the cash you found in my bag, I said. Am I now cleared of any suspicions of theft?

"I think we can strike that one off," Andy said. "What happened next?"

RAFAEL

I spent a further two days and nights at the Negresco.

The place was too ornate for my liking but I became very friendly with Charles on the front door and he pointed me towards a café where I ate croissants and coffee for breakfast and boeuf bourguignon for lunch. In the evening, he pointed me towards another one where I ate dinner. By the third morning, I no longer needed any breakfast.

"The change of scenery certainly improved your appetite, Ollie. More coffee?"

I accepted and he left returning with two more plastic cups. "I've added extra sugar this time and stirred it," he said. "Can you continue where you left off, Ollie?"

I apologised for the time it was taking but reminded him of my warning the day before. He sighed. "So, next stop Malaga. Am I right, Ollie?"

On the third morning, Charles organised my taxi for the airport.

"You seem to make friends very easily, Ollie." Andy said.

I told him I always had, that it came naturally but that I'd not had much practice recently.

"So how did you put up with life in Gloucester for so long?" he asked. "I mean, I thought you said the drinking and the so-called Thomas's Disease was a reaction to boredom."

I needed a moment to reflect on that but then said I thought I may have gone a little over the top in saying I was bored and depressed.

In fact, it was only when Sarah became ill, that I found life depressing. She slowly disappeared into her illness and left me with no one to talk to. It was as if she had left me. I missed her company. For most of the time in Gloucester, life was good. We would go on short holidays to Wales and to Cornwall and spend hours in the back garden. Sarah loved her flowers and her vegetable patch. It is a fact I find hard to admit, but so did I.

I found that a quiet life of living within our means, as Sarah used to say, was perfectly satisfying. She had a whole list of sayings about that. Waste not, want not. Make ends meet. Make do and mend. That was her philosophy. And I know she liked having me around the house. We were making up for lost time, you see, and I liked being there. It was the best time of my life.

I miss my Sarah, I told Andy. And he coughed and drank his coffee.

So, I said goodbye to Charles. I joked with him in poor French. I told him he should smarten himself up a little, polish his ridiculous boots and straighten his hat. Charles told me to buy a new pair of shoes. Then he shook my hand, opened the taxi door and I got in. When I looked back, he was waving at me.

"So, you went to the airport, Ollie?" Andy said.

Air France, I replied and then asked him if he'd ever been to Malaga. He said he hadn't so I told him not to go there. Avoid it, I said. I have never liked Malaga. It has a certain tone about it, which does not appeal to my sense of order. Perhaps it's Picasso's influence.

Before I left Gloucester, I had wondered whether to stay in the city or outside but decided to stay in the city centre near the Cathedral in case I needed to lose myself among crowds. I even pre-booked the hotel it as it was important for my plan.

It was a small hotel in a busy street called Ataranzanas, close to the Picasso Museum and port, an area I'd known before. It hadn't changed much. I checked in and enquired if a small parcel had been delivered to await my arrival.

It had. It was waiting for me and it, and my bag, was carried up to the first floor where I found myself in a rather dim but adequate room overlooking a small courtyard.

Andy interrupted. "Sounds cosy, Ollie. What was in the parcel?"

I told him to be patient, that I'd come to that, Andy.

The hotel was much more to my liking and I decided to go immediately out into the street, have a look around to get my bearings, buy a local map and a small backpack and find a café. Later, with the evening drawing on I returned to my room and opened my parcel. Inside, wrapped in several layers of foil to confuse the x-ray machines, was an item that had sat in an oily cloth at the bottom of the old box in the bedroom at home for twenty years.

Andy interrupted once more. "You sent something by courier in advance, Ollie? Why not take it with you?"

Because it was my gun, I replied.

Andy jumped. "Your what?"

My gun, I repeated. The one you referred to yesterday when I was arrested."

I took the gun out, checked it, placed it on the bed, wrapped it up in its old cloth again, put it into my new haversack along with an envelope containing some other papers I'd brought with me and I turned in for the night.

"I imagine you slept soundly with your gun lying next to you, Ollie," Andy said trying to be amusing.

I told him I'd slept very well but felt hungry when I awoke next morning.

After a quick look at the breakfast room I decided it was not for me and wandered outside into the street again. By nine thirty I was back having drunk a nice cup of coffee with a couple of churros. Nourished enough to last a full day I gathered everything from my room and went to find a taxi.

The address on the paper Nigel had given me was, like Little Avening, a dot on my new, detailed map of the Malaga area. San Licata was marked as near Antequera but I decided it could only be a tiny hamlet, if that.

My Spanish is not as good as my Arabic or French but I soon found a taxi driver who spoke reasonable English and was willing to sit around and wait for me, paid by the hour. Then, under a clear blue sky, we drove out of Malaga through rocky terrain strewn with conifer trees and a carpet of yellow wild flowers.

We drove through Antequera, headed for Cordoba and, after passing through another village turned right off the main road and followed a dried-up riverbed until we reached a small lake surrounded by conifers. Rafael, my driver, then stopped, looked around and scratched his head.

"I never go this way before, señor," he said. "But I think this is the place." He pointed to a rough track between more trees and rocks. "But no cars ever come this way."

I suggested we try another route and, fortunately, Rafel was clearly enjoying the drive.

"OK, señor, you pay," he laughed. He and I were getting on very well.

We bumped our way through potholes for another mile or so, the track getting steep and higher until we reached a summit where the stony track suddenly dropped steeply down again onto the other side.

"I think this road only good for donkeys, señor," Rafael said.

Before us was a panoramic view of a valley and way down, shimmering in the heat of late morning, a large house or villa with a red roof and outbuildings, all surrounded by a white wall in an, almost, perfect oval shape. A narrow but tarmacked road led away from what looked like a pillared gate in one side of the wall and disappeared behind another hillside.

Rafael pointed. "I think that is the place, señor. But we come on wrong road, I think. Much better if we come from Cordoba side."

I agreed so we turned and went back. Rafael and I were already on first name terms. "How you know about this place, Ollie?"

I told him it was probably the headquarters of the Spanish Mafia and that I needed to speak to them about some unfinished business.

"No! I think you joke, señor. You don't look like the Mafia to me, Ollie."

I asked him why I didn't look like a Mafia sort.

"Mafia, they are rich and wear the gold rings and smoke the cigarra," Rafael said. "You look more like the man who ride on Spanish donkey, if you don't mind me saying, Ollie."

I told him I didn't mind that at all, that I was more like the donkey than the man riding it. Rafael thought that was very funny and laughed and laughed until tears ran down his face. When he'd recovered, he said, "I think you are a very funny man, Ollie. You are a good one for the joking."

I told him I was out of practice but that I needed to start practicing everything again.

"You mean the joking?" Rafael said.

No, I replied. I need to practice living again.

"But joking is good for the living, Ollie," Rafael told me. "You know any Spanish jokes?"

As he drove, I tried to think of a suitable joke. English jokes must always include an Irish man, I told him and he began to laugh already. "Tell me one, Ollie."

So, I told him a joke about Julio Iglesias, the Spanish singer. An Irishman had once asked him why the Spanish used the word manyana so much. Julio Iglesias said that it was because the Spanish were very relaxed people. Maybe a job will be done tomorrow, maybe the next day or maybe next week, next month or next year.

"Yes, that is Spain, Ollie."

Then Julio Iglesias asked the Irishman if the Irish had a word similar to manyana. No, said the Irishman. We don't have a word to describe that amount of urgency.

Rafael laughed. "That is a good one, Ollie. Do you know any more?"

I have one more, I said. Do you want to hear it?"

"Of course," Rafael said.

I asked him again. Do you want to hear it, Rafael? He glanced at me, puzzled so I said again, do you want to hear my joke?

"Of course. I already say."

Are your ears good? Can hear OK, Rafael, I asked.

"Of course, my ear is very good."

Do you know about the Spanish man, Fabio, who was very deaf?

"No," said Rafael.

Fabio told his friend, 'Hey, Felipe, I have just bought myself an aid for deafness that is a wonderful. When I put it in my ear nobody knows I am wearing it.' And Felipe, his friend, says, 'That is fantastic. What will they invent next? It must be very expensive. How much did it cost, Fabio' And you know what Fabio says, Rafael?

"No, Ollie. What did he say?"

"Eh? The time? It's a quarter past two."

And Rafael laughed so much he had to stop the car for a moment to wipe his eyes. Then, as we got moving once again, he became more serious. "So, you have business with these Mafia, Ollie?"

Unfinished business, I said. My real business was export.

"Ah, export," Rafael said. "My sister, she has a very good business. She is making fine table cloths You want me to speak to her about business, Ollie?"

I told him I was always on the lookout for opportunities and handed him my business card – an old Thomas Import Export card that I'd found in my old box.

Rafael stuck it into the top pocket of his shirt. "But how old you are, señor? Excuse me for my asking."

Eighty-six, I said. But today I feel like thirty-six.

"It's the good life, Ollie," he replied. "You must keep active, not stop. Keep the joking. Keep going until drop dead like donkey. Best way to die I think."

I agreed. You never know if death is just around the corner, I said. And with that, we rounded a corner in the road and I told Rafael to stop.

"You ready to die so soon, Ollie?" Rafael laughed.

Perhaps, I said and Rafael stopped laughing.

I also stopped the true story I was relating to Andy Wilson.

I asked Andy what he thought of Rafael from my description.

"Rafael? I like him," Andy said.

I agreed and said he was just the sort of man I had always got on with. Not only friendly but with business contacts as well. An opportunist that I'd like a longer chat with sometime.

Andy nodded. "You want to carry on, Ollie?"

SAN LICATA

We were approaching the white wall we had seen from the other side of the mountain when I told Rafael to stop. The pillared gateway hadn't looked big from the other side but from this side it was big and impressive. It was a timber arch in U.S. cattle ranch style with 'San Licata' painted in large, black letters across the top.

It was then that I remembered the name. Licata was the small town in Sicily and memories of Libya, Farid, the IRA, arms shipments and a mugging in Malta flashed through my mind. Licata was also the name of the boat used to carry the IRA shipment.

The gates were wide open. A driveway led through a bright green lawn bordered with short conifer trees and a man was spraying water onto the grass with a hose.

"We go in?" Rafael asked.

I told him to wait, that I needed to think.

"This place looks like Spanish Mafia," Rafael said. "How long you want to think, Ollie?"

I told Rafael to drive up to the gate and wait for me outside. I checked the contents of my backpack and then, taking my stick this time because I wanted to appear old and infirm, I got out telling Rafael to wait.

I walked through the archway and the main villa came into view. It was deceptively large and built on a split-level, the land to the rear lower than the front. The surrounding wall disappeared down the steep hillside behind the villa, reappearing further along near smaller houses and outbuildings. The view beyond the villa looked out across miles of open Spanish countryside. The garden itself was mostly grass and white concrete but for the few trees that bordered the driveway.

The driveway led towards the red-tiled villa and some wide, semi-circular steps leading to a high, wide doorway that opened into a darker interior. The driveway itself then forked and led away to the other houses and buildings on my right.

Several cars – new BMWs and a Mercedes – were parked along the driveway with a pick-up truck and other, smaller cars parked in dark shadow under a corrugated shelter beyond the main house. It had all the characteristics of a big home-based family business and reminded me of one I had once known that perched on the side of Mount Vesuvius in Italy.

I asked Andy if he'd like to know about that place at Somme Vesuviano near Naples. "Another time," he said. "Just keep going."

For me that Spanish place was so similar. That Naples business was run by a family called Perillo so I asked Andy if he remembered the Perillo name.

"The lawyer in Malta?" he said which proved he'd been listening.

I walked along the driveway using my stick as an unnecessary prop until the man watering the grass spotted me. He dropped his hose with the water still running from it and ran over, shouting in Spanish so I waved my stick in what I thought might be interpreted as a friendly manner. The man stopped some distance away but continued to shout something in poor Spanish. I asked him if he spoke English.

He looked at my stick and then at me. "OK, watta ya want? Watta your name?"

I told him I didn't have long, that my taxi was waiting and that I just wanted to speak to Mr Donaldson.

"Which Mr Donaldson?" he said. "We have a many here."

It was an interesting reply but I said I only wanted to speak to Major Donaldson.

"Major Donaldson, he very olda man now, no see visitatori."

That proved he was still alive so I then asked about any other Donaldsons.

"Which wunna you want? We have a many here."

I suggested a son, but "He havva two son. Which wunna you wanna?"

I didn't really mind, I said. I just wanted to leave a message.

"We donna do that 'ere. We dunna see visitatori 'ere."

I asked if it was possible to leave a message.

"Watta your message?"

I was well prepared. I delved in my backpack, pulled out some paper and gave it to him.

"OK. I givva to Peter."

Peter? I checked.

"Yah. He wunna olda brother."

I asked if that would be Major Donaldson's son?"

"Yah. Peter, he twinna brother Simon."

I bullshitted, telling him I remembered Peter and Simon, that I'd lost touch with the family some years ago and then commented on what a nice family they all were. I also enquired about Donaldson saying he must be quite old by now.

"Yah. He very olda now. Have sedia a rotelli. He not do so mucha now. How you knowa family?"

I first tried to work out what a sedia a rotelli might be and concluded it was a wheelchair. Then confirmed it was all a long time ago, a long story and that we worked together for many years. Partners in crime as you might say, I said.

I asked Andy if my acting out of an accent was good. Did he recognise it?

"Is it Spanish?" Andy said.

I admonished him. It was Italian. In fact, it was Naples Italian. The man still holding the hose pipe was from Naples or very close by.

Andy apologised. "Sorry, Ollie. Carry on."

Partners in crime, I'd said. It almost made me laugh but I had a job to do. I winked at the man with his hose pipe and tried some equivalent Italian. Same camorra, I said.

"Camorra?" he repeated and his Naples pronunciation of the Italian word for gang was spot on.

Yes, I said. Donaldson was my boss. The big capo. My big boss.

"OK," the Italian said. He was loosening up nicely. "He still the big capo. Watta your message?"

I replied by saying I was sure that Major Donaldson would love to see me. That we'd known each other for many years, that he was my amico. E impresa familiare,

I knew my Italian was rusty but hoped a few words about Donaldson being a friend and it being a family business might oil the wheels. But:

"We donna have visitatori here. Only visitatori importanti."

I told him I was a visitatori important and held out my arms and hands, palms upwards, like a true Italian seeking help.

"Watta your name?"

Mi chiamo, David, I said, holding back the surname Reynolds but hoping that the hosepipe Italian might think David was my family name.

"Watta your message?"

But I want to meet him to give it to him with my own hand I pleaded.

"Ees not possible."

I gave up, temporarily. Never mind, I said. Can you give this to either Peter or Simon? He dropped his hose pipe, came closer and I handed him my sheet of paper.

"Ees Arabic?"

I agreed. Some of the words were in Arabic but the rest was in English. I'm sure the Major will understand, I said.

"OK, I givva to Peter. Maybe the capo he wanna see you, I dunna know."

I said grazie mille and told him I'd be back the next day at the same time and hoped to meet him.

With that, I raised my stick as a sort of salute, turned and started to walk back to the gate, But I'd already seen someone watching from the shadow of the villa and I had only gone a few steps when I heard a voice behind me.

When I turned, shading my eyes from the scorching sun, another man in jeans and tee shirt was walking towards the hosepipe man. I heard him say, "Che cos'e, Umberto?" and hosepipe man, said, "I dunno, boss. He come inna 'ere and wanna speak to Maggiore."

I saw the tee shirted one grab my piece of paper from Umberto, the hosepipe so I turned once more heading for the gate and Rafael's taxi.

Rafael clambered out and came towards me as if to help someone old enough to be his grandfather struggling in the heat with only a stick to help him. But before he had reached me, I heard the English voice again. "Hey, old man. What do you want?"

"You must have felt insulted, Ollie?" Andy Wilson said.

Not at all, I replied. I wanted to appear old and frail, pretended not to hear and continued plodding towards the taxi. Rafael then grabbed my arm. I leaned on him, looked straight into his face and said I was OK and was going back in there but if I didn't come out again in one hour, to phone the police;

Rafael was shocked. "La policia?"

Yes, I said. And if they ask what's going on tell them you think an old man has just died.

"Madre de Dios. You wanna die like the donkey now, Ollie? So soon?"

I told Rafael that I had no wish to die but that there was another old man in there who was older than me.

The English man who I assumed was either Peter or Simon, was already through the archway. "What's going on?" he called out. I could see he was holding the paperwork in his hand.

Give me half an hour before calling the police I said to Rafael.

"One minute you say one hour, Ollie, then you say half an hour."

I turned to look at the English man. "What do you want?" he said.

I told him I just wanted to catch up with Alex Donaldson.

"What about?"

Licata, I said.

"What do you mean?"

The paper, I said, pointing at what he was holding in his hand. It's a Bill of Lading for a shipment that went out of Libya many years ago, on an Italian vessel called Licata. That's what I want to speak to Alex Donaldson about.

"Who are you?"

I told him my name was David Reynolds and handed him my passport.

"Pffff," he said. "It's expired."

I know, I told him. I've just not got around to renewing it.

"How do you know my father?"

I didn't answer that but said I assumed he was one of his twin sons. Which one, I asked.

"Never mind," he said. "How do you know my father?"

I told him we went back sixty years – back to the war. He was my boss once, I said.

"So, what's this Licata shit?"

Alex would know, I said. How is he? Must be getting on a bit now. I'm eighty-six. He must be ninety. But, oh yes, your father and I go back many, many years. It's such a long time. I just wanted to catch up, that's all.

"How did you know he was here?"

I remembered laughing at the point. Alex always said he would know where to find me, I said. I found him, instead. So how is the old bugger? Still smoking Craven A or has he given up because they don't make them any longer? We used to meet in the Feathers in Mayfair. We had some real laughs together. I worked for him for nearly forty years. Is he in? I'm sorry to call unannounced but we always had that sort of arrangement. Your father would call me when I was busy and I was expected to drop everything and run.

I dropped my useless stick onto the ground but held my back as if it was about to break. Then I bent down to the haversack again. Phew, I said. It's hot. It feels nearly as hot as Kufra and I'm not as used to it as I once was. But I've got something else here that Alex might like to see – for old time's sake.

I handed him an envelope though whether I was giving it to Peter or Simon I still wasn't sure at that stage. Whichever twin it was, tore the envelope open and withdrew two sheets of paper I'd typed back in Gloucester.

"What the fuck is this?" the twin said. He turned it over to read the second page.

It's an invoice, I said. The total amount is just over six million pounds.

"Are you fucking crazy?"

Oh, no, I said. It's an invoice from my business, Thomas Import Export Limited. It's neatly broken down into various items.

I waited a moment for him to read it. As you see, I said, the items on the front page include back pay, unpaid travel expenses and consultancy work. On the second page, you will see a further, much longer list.

I watched him scan the pages.

You will note, I said, that it includes items such as losses I incurred on a shipment of military supplies destined for Chad, which, by the way, will be the subject of a criminal investigation unless my invoice is paid in full. I'm sorry to put it so bluntly. There is also a breakdown of costs I incurred in trying to stop the shipment of several forty-foot containers containing stolen Mercedes cars instead of medical equipment. These, incidentally, were paid for partly by charitable donations that included a sum of £535 raised at a garden party I once attended in Walton-on-Thames.

There is a small, separate item, number 37, which are my company's charges, previously unclaimed, for train fares to visit the Scottish office of your dear father.

Item number 46 is a much bigger sum and covers danger money for having helped organize a meeting for a Member of the House of Lords in the West African bush who was then assassinated, My charges in this case are for not saying anything about this to anyone unless asked by a Judge in the High Court, in which case I will reduce the amount shown.

At last the Donaldson twin looked up. "You're bloody crazy."

Not in the least, I said. But unless I get paid for it, I will go straight to the Police, the Inland Revenue and Her Majesty's Customs and Excise once I get back to England with a file a foot thick about Alex Donaldson's business activities over the last sixty years."

"You are fucking mad."

I told him to stop repeating himself. What's more, I went on, a copy of the invoice and its accompanying files is lodged with a solicitor back in England and, if I fail to return to England for any reason, he is under strict instructions to release the contents to the powers that be.

I stared at him wondering if it was starting to sink in.

In case it wasn't, I added: And as I'm so old now and couldn't care a fuck whether I get away from here dead, alive or embedded in a block of concrete ready to be shipped to Naples or Sicily to be dropped with a splash into the Mediterranean it's entirely up to you. I'd always fancied being fed to the fishes somewhere near Amalfi if that's convenient. But the question is, do you want the whole of your Scottish, Italian and Spanish arms dealing, drugs smuggling and money laundering operation cracked wide open?

He was now standing with his mouth open and an unexpected twitch in his cheek.

So, can I see him or not, I asked.

"Fucking hell," he said as Umberto the hosepipe Italian sidled up and peered over his shoulder. He then said "Fuck," again and as he said it, I noticed one of his father's features. A bubble of white spittle appeared on his lower lip. "Umberto," he said, "Go tell padre, he has a visitor."

Umberto scurried away along the driveway towards a large puddle of water that had formed from his hosepipe. Donaldson's son then returned to the paperwork in his hand. He'd not yet looked at the Bill of Lading with the Arabic lettering. "And what the fuck is this?"

Your father knows, I replied.

"Tell me."

It covers a shipment of arms that was sent from Libya to Northern Ireland during the IRA troubles. The boat was called the Licata and the file on that is particularly thick.

"I know nothing."

Why would you, I said. You were probably still at school in Repton.

I pointed to the pretentious archway over the entrance. As far as I know there is no Saint Licata, I said. Licata is just a small place in southern Sicily. But maybe your father held ambitions of sainthood for himself, although I would venture to suggest that any sainthood is more likely to be granted by the chap living beneath our feet rather than the one living in the clouds above.

He growled and walked off with my expired passport and the papers.

Umberto hadn't gone far. He'd stopped just past the puddle with a look of uncertainty on his face. As we passed him, he followed like a nervous dog.

When I arrived at the bottom step, Umberto and the son had already disappeared into the cooler, darker interior so I stood for a moment for a different view of San Licata. At the end of the driveway was a warehouse with its doors wide open. Two men were loading pallets into the back of a small truck with a forklift so I waved and they carried on.

Umberto then appeared once more looking flushed and worried. I told him he'd left his water on. The driveway was flooded. He seemed not to care. "Si, signore," he said, "I know issa wet. Please to follow."

I followed him up the marble steps onto more marble – a wide, brown marble-tiled hallway with doors off to the right and left and another wide, semi-circular stairway with a thick red carpet that led downwards.

Umberto headed down and waited for me at the bottom as I deliberately hobbled down, holding onto the brass banister with my left hand, my stick in the other and my backpack across my shoulder. It was all show Andy, because I actually felt quite sprightly.

At the bottom I followed Umberto along another darker, cooler corridor with an enormous crystal chandelier hanging from a carved wood ceiling. Umberto knocked on the door at the far end and waited until the door opened.

The son, whichever one it was, stood there. "OK 'berto. Wait outside the house."

Umberto bowed and scuttled back along the corridor and up the stairs.

DONALDSON

I have to admit, **Andy, my stomach**, which had only seen two churros and two small cups of coffee all day, was churning, though it was not with hunger. It is not every day one gets a chance to renew your acquaintance with a murderous, international, crook especially one who you once thought was dead.

"I've never been in the position myself, Ollie. So, I wouldn't know. I don't suppose you even got a cup of coffee."

Patience, Andy, I'm coming to it.

"You were offered a cup, Ollie?"

No.

Once inside this vast room there was a lot to take in. This was not the Negresco in Nice but just as ornate. The floor was the same marble as elsewhere, but a vast, Chinese carpet started from near the door and extended into the far distance. A large, four-poster bed with cream drapes and gold sashes stood on one side heavily polished wooden tables and chairs on both sides.

A large and probably antique desk covered in marquetry and a green leather writing area stood on my right. A telephone in shiny brass and a table lamp with a green shade were the only items on it.

At the far end was a wide, open patio door leading onto a white, tiled, veranda with a wall of short pillars and a red awning over a white table and chairs. Two wide windows on either side of the patio door were open giving a view over an expanse of open Spanish countryside beyond. A faint breeze moved a red velvet curtain that hung from close to the ceiling.

For a moment, the bright sunlight from the patio made everything inside except the green lamp on the desk look dark but I saw the son walk across the carpet towards one of the windows and then sit on a sofa made of shiny, gold fabric with gilt arms.

It was then that I saw the silhouette.

The dark figure was sat in what looked like a wheelchair set against one of the open windows. Its head was bent slightly to one side and something small, like a ring, flashed on a hand resting on the arm of the wheelchair. The shape coughed and gurgled and, for a second, I could only think of Jim.

Then it spoke. "Fucking Ollie Thomas."

It was only three, slowly spoken words but the voice was rough and deep. It trembled slightly with the faintest hint of a Scottish accent.

"Mr fucking Reynolds, back from the dead."

I tried moving closer in the hope of seeing some detail but was stopped by my stick which had embedded itself in the deep pile of the Chinese carpet. I almost toppled forward but quickly regained my position and my dignity and stood with the stick still stuck in the carpet, my hands clenched over the handle.

I stared at the black figure in the wheelchair.

"Oliver, fucking, Thomas."

I was determined not to look directly towards the windows. I had not come all this way to see a silhouette again. My eyes needed to grow accustomed to the light and I wanted a detailed look of the ninety-year old Donaldson to see what living in this style for forty years had done to his features.

"Bless my fucking soul. I hoped you were dead," Donaldson growled.

No such luck, I said.

"But I heard your dear wife is gone."

The fact that Donaldson knew about Sarah shocked me but I held my ground and didn't flinch. We all have to go sometime I said and was proud of the quality of my voice. It sounded thirty years younger than Donaldson's.

"Enjoying your retirement, Ollie?"

"The time passes."

"Didn't get to retire anywhere nice then?"

"Gloucester is fine."

"Matter of opinion I suppose."

I chose not to respond to that.

"Did she tell you that if you moved a fucking inch, we'd get you?"

"Not in as many words. But I guessed."

"Good as gold she was. Just like Beatie Collins."

Yes, I said. The two most important women in my life.

The silhouette manoeuvred itself up in the chair and coughed like Jim again. I could see him clearer now. "Going globetrotting again then, Ollie."

Only recently I said.

"Been anywhere beside Spain?"

Only as far as Little Avening I replied.

"A bloody detective as well as a fucking salesman, is it?"

I heard the spittle emerge and settle somewhere. He was already stressed.

Just catching up on my invoices, I replied.

"So, I see. It's a big bill, Ollie. Six million quid is a lot."

I left off a lot because I wasn't sure if you could afford it, I said. Out of the corner of my eye I saw the son stir on his golden sofa.

"You're a joke, Ollie. A stupid, fucking sucker. "

Perhaps, I said, but I tried to run an honest business. And being blackmailed isn't nice.

"But you worked for the Government, Ollie. Governments aren't nice."

I was patriotic, I said.

"An admirable quality, Ollie, but very naïve."

I didn't do it for the money.

"I can see that, Ollie. It shows."

You, on the other hand, worked only for yourself, I said.

"But look what I've got, Ollie." Donaldson raised his hands to the surrounding opulence. "What have you got?"

A clear conscience, I replied.

Donaldson clearly tried to laugh at that but choked on something slimy instead. "What the fuck do you want, Ollie? Money? What for? To go abroad at last? What have you got left, Ollie? Your good looks?"

The son settled into his sofa again and I scratched my nose. My confidence was rising from somewhere. There was no fear just a sense that we were nearing the closure I'd wanted for years.

Any chance I can see your own handsome features, I asked. Why don't you stand up and get away from the window and let me check? All you've ever been in your life is a black shadow. You've cast it far and wide. At least I can stand. For all I know I could be speaking to an impostor.

"Why don't you just fuck off back to the suburbs where you came from, dear boy."

I aim to, I said, but I thought I'd pay one last visit to your office. It's a nicer view than Regents Street. Nice carpet too and a nice golden bed to match. Got a golden piss pot underneath it, have you?

I was now deliberately winding him up because I'd waited to do that for far too long. I'd even dreamed of suitable phrases to use. Donaldson's reaction, though, was to cough productively and swallow whatever came up.

The climate doesn't suit you, I said. You should move somewhere more temperate. Somewhere like Alaska. The cold would match your sensitive nature.

Donaldson was starting to growl like a dog but whether it was temper or more thick mucus gathering in his throat it was impossible to tell.

"You always had a nice turn of phrase, Ollie. But what the fuck do you want?"

Andy then interrupted me just as I was reaching a critical part of my explanation.

"What did you want, Ollie?" he asked. "Why did you go there? Get to the point, Ollie. Bastard though he was, why go to all that trouble if it wasn't to shoot him?"

I know Andy was trying to establish a motive for what had happened but he still didn't fully understand me or what happened next.

I wanted to see the bastard, I told him. I wanted to ask questions. I wanted to put him right on things and to correct any misconceptions he had. I wanted to see what he'd done with his accumulated and ill-gotten gains, to prove to myself that money doesn't bring happiness. I wanted to add the final chapter.

Andy yawned, stood up and walked around. "Mmm," he said. It was a disbelieving sort of sound but it didn't bother me.

I smiled at him as he returned to the desk and leaned over it with his face just a few inches from mine. For all his patience, Andy was now trying to act the tough cop. "So why take a gun?" he said.

Just in case, I said. And I haven't finished yet.

At that moment, the phone on the table rang. Andy picked it up and took it to the corner of the room away from me. It was pointless because I heard every word.

"Yes?... I see…. What time? Do they know what happened? I'm still trying to get to the bottom of it…. Yes, he's still here. Oh yes, he's very co-operative, it's just the time it's taking to get anywhere. Sixty years crammed into less than twenty-four hours. OK. Thanks."

I waited.

"That was Clive," Andy said. "Major Donaldson died about an hour ago." He returned to the desk and sat down. "You'd better hurry up and tell me what happened, Ollie," he said, gravely.

The bastard wasn't well before I arrived, I said.

"But that's no excuse for what happened. You can't go around shooting people just for the sake of settling old scores."

Who said I was settling old scores? But neither was I paying homage to the bastard. I was there to close the book and to see for myself how it all turned out. I've already documented the past. Now it's up to you.

"Yeh, nice statement, Ollie. The longest in history. We'll put it up for the Guinness Book of Records. Come on, man, tell me what happened."

I looked at him. He wasn't a bad young man and he had a job to do. know I took a breath. I'm not completely innocent, I said. I've done some questionable things over the years, but who hasn't and what you've read are abstracts, a flavour. And I've admitted to certain things in writing, including a few days of being unfaithful to my wife. How many do that these days?

Go ahead and arrest me, I went on. But for what? For being complicit? For being an innocent victim? For being naïve? For being threatened and black-mailed?

I admit to all that, Andy. Stick the handcuffs on. Feel free. What you still don't seem to understand is that when you live a certain style of life and put every ounce of energy into it, sometimes life itself comes up behind and bites you in the bloody arse.

And anyway, I went on, I told you it would take a while. And sixty years crammed into twenty-four hours takes twenty-four hours not twenty-three. Can't you wait?

That outburst seemed to quieten him. He sank back into his chair. "So, it wasn't revenge, Ollie?" he said.

No, I said. I admit I insulted him but I've done that many times before and it was always tit for tat. And insults aren't a crime.

Andy sat forward again. "Did you expect Donaldson to write out a cheque for several million pounds while you pointed your gun at his head?"

I shook my head.

"If not that, then what the hell did you want?" Andy pursued.

It was a well-planned confrontation, I said.

Andy got up and then clapped his hand to his forehead. "A well-planned confrontation? What the bloody hell is a well-planned confrontation, Ollie? From this side of the table it looks like you went in there carrying a gun to kill Donaldson. That's premeditated murder for Christ's sake."

I sighed again. What have I just said, Andy?

"That it was a well-planned bloody confrontation, whatever that is."

I also told you to wait because I haven't finished yet!

"OK, Ollie," Andy sat down again. "Please carry on. Where were we?"

Donaldson also asked me what I wanted, Andy, though he didn't ask quite as politely as you. Donaldson said, "What the fuck do you want?"

It was, nevertheless, a good question but I had worked out what I wanted on the drive back from Chalford Hall.

I shifted the bag on my shoulder, checked my foothold and took a few steps towards Donaldson.

Forty years ago, Donaldson would have sprung at my throat or reminded me of my family's vulnerability but he was now looking frail and vulnerable himself, even with his middle-aged son sitting next to him.

The son, presumably Peter, also looked increasingly uncomfortable on his gilt sofa. He kept looking nervously towards his father as though he had been brought up to know his place and that his place was to listen, keep quiet and await instructions. This was Donaldson's style, honed over ninety years. Donaldson needed to get his own way – always.

If Donaldson felt remotely undermined, he threatened.

If he felt remotely at risk from others, he blackmailed.

If he felt afraid of losing something he wanted, he bribed.

If a scrap of paper was finished with, he screwed it up and threw it into the bin or the flames of the nearest coal fire and if a scrap of human life was finished with he was willing to do the same thing.

If it meant keeping people apart from one another in case they learned too much, he kept them apart.

Donaldson would not have sought help from his son because that would have been a sign of weakness. He would try something else first.

I took a deep breath. What do I want? I said. I wanted to pay you a visit. I wanted to see how you were living. I wanted to judge for myself whether being naïve by trusting people and having a sense of duty and patriotism was best in the long run.

Donaldson stirred in his wheelchair but seemed to have very little energy. He'd even lost his growl.

I pulled my stick out of the carpet and prodded it into another spot. With my eyesight improving all the time I could see Donaldson clenching and unclenching his fist. I was also starting to make out more of his features.

This was Donaldson all right but looking thinner and smaller and more wrinkled than when I last saw him. His skull showed through hair that was now much greyer and sparser and his hands were covered in deep veins and mottled with brown spots.

"Why don't you just fuck off back to Gloucester?" he managed to say.

I intend to, I replied. You, too, should try a cooler climate, Major. I've got a lovely Cherry tree in my garden you could sunbathe under.

"Fuck off. Why are you here?"

Hasn't your son told you? I said. I've already given him my invoice and one copy of the whole file on you is in this bag. There's another copy back in England with my solicitor so, you can shoot me now if you want because frankly, Major, I just don't care anymore.

I stared at him but, out of the corner of my eye, I was watching Peter, the son, put his hands on the arms of the sofa as if to stand up.

Do you want to pay up? I asked. If so, I'll open a Santander Bank account in the same branch as you in Malaga and you can transfer it later today. Then I'll give all the proceeds to charity. How about that?

"Fuck you."

You sound tired, Major. You used to argue your side a lot better than that. Losing your powers? Running out of fresh ideas for blackmail? Is there something wrong with you? Perhaps you should go back to bed.

Peter stood and went to the back of the wheelchair and whispered something in his father's ear but I was in no mood for distractions yet.

If your son thinks money might get rid of me, let me say this, I aid. I pointed my stick at the invoice that lay on the floor next to Donaldson's wheelchair. That invoice is a rough calculation of how much you and your Scottish friend Forsyth cost me over the years but, frankly, I don't need money. If there's one thing I learned from Sarah over the years and especially during the time I took care of her when she was sick, it's that money is totally irrelevant. Whatever threats you made against Sarah, were like water off a duck's back to her. Sarah took it in her stride. She stuck by me without saying a word. And I stuck by her without saying a word either. You had no effect on us, Major. Yes, I might have liked living somewhere else, but what the hell. I have no more regrets and it looks as though I'll far outlive you.

Donaldson was emitting a sound like, "Fff . . ." as he blew air. His hands were moving as if he was desperate to stand up. In years gone by that is exactly what he'd have done – pointed his gun or threatened me. This time he merely coughed and the effort made his face redden and his eyes stare.

And another thing Major. The thought of taking money from you fills me with a sense of utter disgust. I wouldn't even give it to charity. They'd probably want to know where it came from and as I wouldn't be able to give them assurances that it was not the proceeds of crime, I'm sure they'd hand it back.

So, what do I want? Nothing other than to see with my own eyes what all this has got you and perhaps write a final chapter to the report I'm filing.

But I'm not too bothered about the final chapter. I've already told your son I couldn't care a damn whether I get away from here dead, alive or embedded in a block of concrete. So perhaps your son would like to march me off the premises and you can give the orders to others to pour the cement. That would be your usual method, Major. Subcontracting dirty jobs was always your preferred method.

I paused.

Alternatively, I said, I'd be perfectly happy to be found lying dead by a bus shelter.

Peter moved from behind the wheelchair. "What do you mean?" he asked and looked surprisingly shocked.

Oh, come on, I said. Surely you know what happens to innocent people like Beatrice Collins and others. Your father uses people for as long as they are useful and then issues a disposal contract? Am I right Major?

Donaldson gurgled incoherently.

Disposal was, of course, the last resort but your father had all sorts of other ways to exert pressure. He's tried them all – threats, blackmail, bribery.......

"Get out of here," Donaldson's gurgling became understandable. He waved a weak hand.

Please, I said. What's happened to your powers of persuasion? Have they run out? It's too late to threaten my family now, Major.

I then looked at, and spoke to Peter standing alongside his father. Are you surprised? I said. How much more has he kept from you over the years?

"I don't know what the fuck you're talking about, he replied. "I suggest you just get out. Can't you see my father isn't well?"

Donaldson's face was turning puce. In the past, it would have been the precursor to an explosion but he now seemed barely able to breathe.

I pointed my stick at Peter. Do you know your mother is still alive? I said.

Donaldson trembled and Peter's mouth opened.

Betty lives in a nice house, paid for by your father, I said flicking my stick towards the window. Donaldson's face reddened even more deeply. She's living in the south of France, I said. But she can't come here because she's too scared.

"My mother?" Peter asked and he looked at his father.

"Are you Peter?"

"Yes."

"Then go and see her before it's too late. She's OK. But she's far too scared to come here."

Donaldson moved. "Fuck off," he growled. "Get out." He coughed, almost choked on something in his throat and his right hand disappeared behind his back as if something was making him uncomfortable.

Peter stared at me. He moved to the back of the wheelchair and I saw that his lips were trembling. "You're lying. How do you know about my mother? Where is she?"

She lives in Cannes, I said. I met her.

"Christ!" said Peter. "And what happened to Beatie?"

My instincts were proving reliable. Suffering from Thomas's Disease was, for the first time, showing it had advantages.

One day, I said, someone phoned me to say she was sick and wouldn't be coming to work. A few days later she was dead. But then I found a note from her which proved she had been living in fear of your father for twenty-five years. I've still got the note. What's more it has your father's handwriting on it.

"Christ!" said Peter again.

Were you the one who was told to phone me, Peter? I ask because it's the way you said Beatie. I only mentioned Beatrice. What was wrong with her? Why did she die?

"Fucking hell!" Peter said in reply and looked at his father who was trying to turn his head around to see where his son was standing. To me it looked as though I had just thrown a few hand grenades into the room. Peter's eyes were all over the place as if scanning the room looking for more skeletons hiding in the ornate cupboards.

Fucking hell is a very good description, I said. I eased the haversack off my shoulder and put it on the carpet. Do you really know what you're involved in here, Peter? Do you realise the amount of evidence I've got of fraud and corruption and links with organisations like the old IRA? By the way, is Umberto's family name Perillo by any chance? Because I'm sure I met him once in Naples. How much control have you got here? Are you just another yes man? An errand boy? A wheelchair pusher? Are you actually afraid of your own father? Do you want to appear in a court with your father in handcuffs as well as a wheelchair?"

Donaldson's red cheeks were extended as he blew air. The knuckles of one hand were white as he gripped the arm of the wheelchair. The other hand was still behind his back. He began to hiss and spit saliva and Peter moved to the side of the wheelchair.

I think I'd better be on my way, I said. You don't look at all well, Major. I then bent down to my bag and opened it. Here, I said. Do you want the whole file Peter, or shall I give it to your father?

"Fuck you. Get out of here." Donaldson was leaning too far forward in the wheelchair as he tried to get out. His face was puce. His eyes were round and staring at me.

I'll leave it here, I said, and placed the brown envelope on the carpet next to my stick. I picked up my stick and lifted my bag over my shoulder. I'll be on my way, then, I said. I turned and walked two steps.

Behind me I heard the wheelchair move. It squeaked and something rattled. Then I heard Donaldson's growl and Peter's voice. "No, Dad."

I turned to see Donaldson trying to get out of the wheelchair and Peter trying desperately to pull him back by his shoulders. Donaldson was almost purple. His eyes never blinked as he stared at me with of spit dribbling from his lips. He raised a feeble arm in my direction. "Fuck you, Ollie, you bastard."

It was then that the other hand that had been behind Donaldson's back forced its way out. He was holding a gun. "No, Dad, no," I heard as Donaldson pointed the gun directly at my head. But then the wheelchair toppled forward with Donaldson in it and the gun pointed downwards. Donaldson fell in a clumsy heap on the floor with the wheelchair on top of him and Peter lost his grip.

It was then that the gun went off.

There was a loud crack and Donaldson fell completely out of the wheelchair like a bundle of rags and settled on the edge of the Chinese carpet with the wheelchair partly on top of him.

I stood for a second with the gunshot still ringing in my ears but then turned. My stick caught in carpet again and I stumbled. My backpack slipped off my shoulder and the only remaining item inside fell out. I picked it up, still wrapped in its oily cloth and, without bothering to return it to the bag, carried it, stumbling towards the door.

Behind me, Peter was kneeling over his father and, at the same time, kicking the wheelchair out of the way. I walked as fast as I could along the corridor to the stairs where Umberto was standing with a horrified look on his face.

Berto. Quick. Correre. Ammalarsi. Padre sick, I said pointing towards the door behind which Donaldson lay in a pool of blood that was already spoiling the Chinese carpet.

I paused. That's what happened, I said to Andy Wilson.

"You didn't shoot him?"

He tried to shoot me but accidentally shot himself.

"That's your story?"

Go check the bullet inside his vest.

"So, where's your gun?"

In Spain.

"Where?"

Hidden, I said, and watched Andy sit back in his chair and stare at me.

I adjusted my glasses and looked at my watch. Got any more questions, Andy? I said. The twenty-four hours are up in five minutes."

Andy sat forward. "Yes," he said. "Do you want a cup of tea and a sandwich?"

Thanks, I replied. Tuna mayonnaise.

"Stay there. Don't go away."

When he'd gone, I looked at my old, black bag, rummaged through my dirty clothes, pulled out the envelope containing five thousand Euros and put it on the table. I was still staring at it when Andy returned.

"They don't have tuna so I've ordered you smoked salmon," he said and then pointed at the envelope. "Betty's money?"

I nodded. I took a flyer about Betty, I said.

"What do you mean – a flyer?"

I just guessed that Peter thought his mother was dead. I didn't really know. But I think that's what finally tipped Donaldson. One of his many secrets was out.

"OK," said Andy, "Tell me what happened after you practiced your Italian on Umberto and walked out of the villa because we have reports that you pointed the gun at staff."

I didn't point it but I may have waved it, I said.

"How do you mean?"

I came out into bright sun. I could hardly see a thing. People were running towards the house shouting and I nearly fell down the main steps. I dropped the gun. It fell out of the cloth and bounced down the steps. The running people stopped running so I picked it up, waved it and kept on walking as fast as I could to the main gate.

"That's it? You waved it?"

Of course, I said. I couldn't have used it anyway. It's broken. I removed the trigger mechanism many years ago. I hate guns. I hate the noise they make and they make me nervous.

"So why did you take it?"

Just in case, I said.

"And where is it now?"

In Spain.

"But where? The Spanish police may need to recover it for evidence etcetera."

It's outside the main gate of the villa, I said.

"On the ground?"

I deliberately dropped my bag over a large stone, I bent down to pick it up and, at the same time, pushed the gun under the stone. It's a well-known practice in my business, Andy. It's on the right-hand side of the roadway, under the fifth stone back from the big round boulder.

"And your taxi?"

Rafael was waiting for me. He hadn't phoned the police but he'd remembered a Spanish joke.

"You want to tell me, Ollie?"

I laughed. For some inexplicable reason, tears started before I could even begin.

"Come on, Ollie. Share it," Andy said.

It is very funny, I replied. It is, I suppose, a joke of the boyish sort but Rafael had had that effect on me. He'd made me feel thirty years younger. It's about a man called Pedro, I said, and immediately began to laugh.

"Come on Ollie. You're making me laugh and I've not heard it yet," Andy said.

Pedro was picking olives in the field when he suddenly felt the need for a shit. He tells his boss he's desperate and boss says it's OK but don't take too long. So, Pedro goes off to the shed. Twenty minutes later he still hasn't come back so the boss goes to check and knocks on the shed door.

He calls out, 'Hey Pedro, Que pasa? Why you take so long?' Pedro opens the door and says, 'Sorry boss,' but then goes back inside to the hole in the ground and stirs it with a stick.

The boss watches for a minute and then says, 'Hey Pedro, Que haces? What are you doing?' And Pedro says, 'Señor, it's my coat. He has fallen down the hole.' His boss says, 'Pedro. Your coat, he will be no good when you find him.'

And Pedro says, 'Si Señor, I know, but he has my lunch in the pocket!'

When I stopped, both Andy and I were laughing so much that tears were running down our cheeks. But then someone knocked on the door. "I think that's your lunch," Andy said.

FRED CARRINGTON

Fred Carrington was in his garden snipping dead heads off his few daffodils when my taxi pulled up outside the house. I tried desperately to avoid him but Fred called across the road. "You're back then Mr Thomas."

"Yes," I said, fumbling for the front door key in my black bag.

I put the bag down to see if it had dropped to the bottom but deliberately kept my back to Fred in the hope he'd go away. But he came over. "Where's the car?" he asked.

"I left it at the airport," I said. "It needs tax and insurance."

"Oh, dear," Fred said with a smirk. "The police were looking for you. I happened to see them when I returned from shopping. They rang your doorbell. They then returned to their car and I saw them on their phones."

I nodded because I was still searching for the key.

"It was three days ago," Fred said. "I spoke to them and told them you were abroad."

"That's kind of you, Fred," I said.

"I told them you had said you were going away on business."

He smirked again as if he really hadn't believed a word I'd said before I left.

"That would have been useful, Fred," I said.

"Yes, they seemed interested. They asked me how old you were because they seemed to know you were well past retirement."

"It's positive age discrimination, Fred. They need to ensure they meet their equality targets."

"They asked me if I knew where you were. Of course, I told them you had said you were going to France and Spain. They then got back into their car and I watched them make some more phone calls."

"Was it a big, blue and yellow car with flashing lights and sirens, Fred?"

"It was a Ford Focus."

"It must have been important to send the top brass around, then Fred," I replied.

"Yes," Fred said, "But then they got out again and asked me if I knew when you were expected back. I said you hadn't told me but that you had once said you had spent many years travelling in foreign parts and often mixed with some pretty seedy individuals."

"That was even more helpful, Fred."

"They then asked me if I knew whether you possessed a fire arms certificate but, naturally, I said I didn't expect so but that I couldn't be certain."

"Sorry, Fred, I should have told you I was taking the gun with me."

"Oh dear, is there a problem?" Fred enquired.

"None at all, Fred, I've found it now," I said, and I held up my front door key and let myself in.

About The Author:

Terry Morgan lives in Petchabun, Thailand. Having travelled extensively with his own export business his novels cover international politics, commercial crime, corruption, fraud, science, environmental issues and occasional satire.

Website: www.tjmbooks.com

Other books by Terry Morgan

Whistleblower

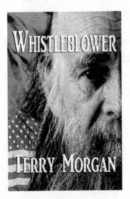

Vast amounts of international aid money are being stolen by those at the heart of the political establishment. Ex politician, Jim Smith, threatened and harassed into fleeing abroad for accusations of fraud secretly returns to renew his campaign. A realistic thriller covering events in the USA, Europe, Africa, the Middle East and Asia and a sensitive study of a stubborn and talented man who steadfastly refuses to fit into the stereotype of a successful businessman and a modern politician.

"Highly convincing....... This could all be happening right now. Another realistic and highly entertaining story...."

"This book has the sort of political intrigue that captivates viewers of shows like "House of Cards," but the main man is actually a decent person in "Whistle blower." As someone who prefers protagonists on the correct moral side of the spectrum, it made the book that much more enjoyable. (AMAZON)

"Whistleblower", by Terry Morgan, is an international thriller that stretches from England to Thailand with many stops in between.

"The plot centers around the timely topic of international aid money and the criminals who feed on it. The hero, the story's whistleblower, is British ex-politician Jim Smith, and the story follows him around the globe as he seeks to put a stop to the corruption.

"Morgan, a world traveller who now resides in Thailand, knows his locations well. Cities in Italy and Africa come alive, and Jim Smith's home in off-the-beaten-path Thailand is wonderfully described, allowing readers to feel like they're there--this is no easy thing to do, and the authenticity of the various settings is a real strength of the book.

"Another strength includes the protagonist. Smith is not a typical hero. He's older and lacks the suaveness and action-hero credentials of a James Bond or Jason Bourne, but he more than makes up for it with his intelligence and depth--a big pleasure in the book is being invited into this man's life as he tries to pick up the pieces after an underhanded campaign aimed at ruining him.

"The plot moves along briskly, and the technology, players (politicians, intelligence agencies, criminals), and small details about the finance industry all add up to a novel that's rich in credibility and intrigue. Anyone interested in seeing the world from the comfort of a good armchair should read Morgan's book." (AMAZON)

An Honourable Fake

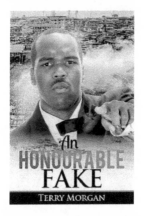

At age fourteen Femi Akindele, an orphaned street-boy from the Makoko slum in Lagos decided to call himself Pastor Gabriel Joshua. Unqualified and self-taught and now in his mid-forties Gabriel has become a popular and highly acclaimed international speaker on African affairs, economics, terrorism, corruption, fraud and the widespread poverty and economic migration that results.

An Honourable Fake is a mix of African & international politics, terrorism and corruption with a big cast of characters - US politicians, corrupt businessmen, fake pastors, Lagos gangs, terrorists, the head of the Nigerian State Security Service, a young girl, Halima, from northern Nigeria who escapes abduction and Mark Dobson from London-based international criminal investigators, Asher & Asher.

The settings move between crowded Lagos, Abuja and Kano and the hot and dusty borders with Chad and Niger to Washington, Los Angeles, London and Cairo.

"A rare sort of political thriller – a black African hero."

"Accomplished and knowledgeable – a class follow up to Whistleblower."

Vendetta

Eccentric, untidy Oxford University Professor of Biology "Eddie" Higgins has become the 'scientific adviser' to a local cosmetics company run by its new and vivacious chief executive, Isobel Johnson. It doesn't begin well. *"Yours is an industry dogged by exaggerated claims, impossible claims and false claims,"* he tells her. With locations moving between the UK, Thailand and Malaysia this third book in the Asher & Asher series exposes the role of Russian and Chinese gangs exploiting cosmetics and energy drinks companies in counterfeiting, money-laundering and drug smuggling.

The Malthus Pandemic

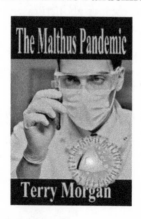

The first book in the Asher & Asher series of international criminal investigations. A virologist with extreme views on the need for human population control has engineered a virus, Malthus A, with no known cure or vaccine but now needs help to spread it worldwide. With tests and sporadic outbreaks of the disease already in Thailand, Nigeria and Kenya, a criminal pharmaceutical company ready to sell ineffective treatments and the WHO and sceptical Western governments reluctant to act can Asher & Asher stop it being released?

Prisoners of Conscience & Circumstance

Set around the year 2050 when overpopulation is causing food and energy shortages, mass unemployment, social tension and civil conflict. An ex-politician and professor of biology talks to a grandson no longer able to cope with life in an overcrowded city. A follow-up to the author's previous thriller, 'The Malthus Pandemic', this hard-hitting, illustrated novel contains facts and forecasts supported by original papers.

"Not for the faint hearted."

Short Stories:

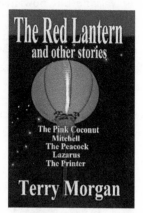

The Red Lantern is a selection of six short stories about international crime, corruption and terrorism taken from five of the author's full-length novels – An Old Spy Story, Whistleblower, Vendetta, An Honourable Fake and a currently unpublished novel, Park Road.

God's Factory & Four Men

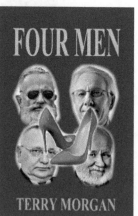

Terry Morgan writes mainly serious novels with a strong international background but intersperses it with less serious satire and humour like 'God's Factory' and 'Four Men',

CPSIA information can be obtained
at www.ICGtesting.com
Printed in the USA
LVHW091506070121
675993LV00013B/169